Wolf's Blood

L.Q. Hebb

Full Moon Publishing, LLC
Glade Spring, VA 24340
Fullmoonpublishingllc.com

Edited by CP Bialois
Cover Design by Danielle Stamper

ISBN-10: 1946232009
ISBN-13: 978-1946232007

CONTENTS

ACKNOWLEDGMENTS

There are so many people who I would like to acknowledge and I cannot even begin to express how thankful I am to the people who have helped me through writing, editing and publishing my book. These people have been my pillars thought life, supporting me and helping me reach the stars.

Firstly, there is my mother, Gai, who has sat by me and spent hours upon hours helping me edit and finalise my book.
Then there is my father, Noel, and sister, Mika, who have supported me and encouraged me to peruse my dreams.
And of course there are my wonderful friends, Caleb and Cory, who have inflated my ego and are the reasons I continue to write and create stories.
Finally, I would like to thank Ronda for taking a chance and helping me achieve my dreams and I would also like to acknowledge "Brenny Boo", who has done nothing to contribute to this book but has been a great friend and he asked for a mention so I have obliged him.

WOLF'S BLOOD

-Prologue-

The wolf lets out a final howl as Tyler plunges his stake into its heart. It snaps its jaws and tries to pull away, whining and stumbling. Tyler pushes the wolf with his boot and the it changes to its human form, coughing as blood splutters out of its mouth. He groans one last time before falling to the pavement dead.

"Well done!" Tyler's father congratulates him with a slap on the shoulder. Tyler fakes a smile and wipes his stake on a blood-stained rag. His father pours gasoline onto the man's body and Tyler pulls out his matchbook and lights a match. He then drops the burning stick onto the man's body and it ignites immediately.

Tyler and his father are hunters; they travel from town to town slaying werewolves.

"Next stop, Mercy Lake," Tyler's father informs him.

Tyler rolls his eyes. For years now, his father has been saying that they were going to Mercy Lake, the place where his mother was violently slaughtered by werewolves. But they have never returned. Instead, his father drags him all over America, chasing down other werewolves, and following leads that the Hunter's Society provides.

"Come on son," his father says as he starts walking out of the ally. "The missus and El will be waiting."

His father remarried a year after Tyler's mother died. The marriage came with a stepsister, Elisa, who she preferred to be called El.

Tyler sighs and follows his father as they walk back to their apartment where his step mum had made dinner. She greets the two with a warm smile, but Tyler ignores her and goes down the hall into his room. Tyler is sick of this life: always on the move, killing werewolves

1

every night. He wishes he could get out of it, but he wants to please his father. Tyler doesn't like werewolves, but he doesn't hate them either.

There is a knock on the door and El enters the room. "How did you go tonight?" she asks. She wants to hunt werewolves more than anything, but both her mother and Tyler's father disagree.

"We got a few," he says, hanging up his stake on one of the hooks in the closet.

"That's good." She nods, then clicks to something, "Oh! Renee came over and said that she wants to talk to you at the park on Monday."

Renee was just a fling Tyler was in the middle of, and though he had slept with her a few times, he knew he had to end it soon because they would be leaving town. Tyler pulls off his black leather hunting jacket and then his shirt over his head.

"Hey, there's a girl in the room," El laughs and Tyler rolls his eyes. His stepsister likes having a big brother, even if they were only several months apart. Tyler however does not like having a stepsister.

"Then get out," he says, and she groans and leaves, shutting the door behind her. Tyler flops onto the bed and falls asleep on the covers. Tyler is woken by violent shaking; his eyes snap open and he sees his father standing over him.

"We have to go, boy," he says, and Tyler rubs his eyes and gets up. This isn't unusual. When Tyler is woken with a rough shake from his father, it usually means it's time to leave town. Tyler puts on the shirt and jacket he wore last night and grabs his stake and ties it to his jeans. He then grabs his already packed duffel bag. Tyler rarely unpacks, knowing far too well that they never stay in the same place for long. He takes his duffel bag to the car and throws it in, then helps load the rest of their minimal belongings into the car. After everything is packed, they get into the car to leave the town.

"So where are we going, dad?" Tyler asks, yawning.

"Mercy Lake," his father replies, looking in the rear-view mirror. Tyler's eyes widen—finally, they are going.

El and Tyler's Father talk about werewolves and ways to kill them without getting your hands bloody. Tyler already knows this information, so he falls asleep. He wakes up just as they enter the town of Mercy Lake. They dive past the friendly welcome sign with a picture of the lake the town was named after. He stares out of the window as they travel the streets, seeing a girl that looks miserable as she kicks a rock off the pavement. The two lock eyes and the girl smiles and waves.

Tyler ignores the girl. His father continues to drive until they reach the street that they used to live on, and pulls into the driveway. Tyler can't help staring at the familiar house they used to live in— the house his father never put it up for sale after his mother was killed. It still looked exactly the same, and he assumes his father has someone looking after it. There are no neighbours behind the house, but one on either side of it. Tyler opens the car door, holding the stake in his hand. The stake is made of silver with the engraved head of a wolf embedded in the outer casing. It's the same symbol found on the Native American totem poles. Tyler presses the button on the side and the stake extends to a deadly point. On the extension is engraved a Native American axe. The symbols represent the werewolf hunters, as the first hunter used a silver tipped axe to slay a wolf.

Tyler walks to the front door and opens it with his stake at the ready. He then proceeds to check the whole house for any signs of a werewolf while his father and his stepmother and sister unpack the car. He always checks the houses they use for signs of werewolves. He checks his old room last. Slowly, he grasps the handle and pushes it open. The door slowly opens and Tyler enters the room. His old room looks exactly as he left it: wooden post bed, wooden chest of drawers, a wooden wardrobe, and a window. He looks at the walls that are filled with his childhood drawings of his mother father and little sister, who was also killed by wolves. Tyler presses the button to deactivate his stake and walks around his room, allowing old memories to fill his mind. After a few minutes, he heads back outside to grab his duffel, takes it to his room, and unpacks for the first time. He checks his phone and sees that there are ten unread messages from Renee, asking where he was and why he didn't call back. He sends a quick message.

Sorry, had to leave town. It never would have worked out between us. Never going to see you again. Move on. -T

Tyler throws his phone on the bed and walks out of his room and into the backyard. "Old town," he whispers, taking in a deep breath before jumping the fence. "New wolves to kill."

The backyard backs onto the protected woods of Mercy Lake. Tyler begins to walk, checking his surroundings. His boots make a crunching noise as he walks, his eyes alert and stake at the ready. A lonely owl hoots above and other animals scurry around the woodland floor. He wishes there was some way out of hunting. He doesn't want to hunt werewolves. He should hate them for what they did to his family, but he doesn't. They are, after all, part human, aren't they? Tyler thinks about it and he realizes he has aided in the killing of over a hundred wolves and the murder of over a hundred people. Something snaps up ahead and Tyler automatically looks up. A lonely buck freezes in place and looks at Tyler. Tyler lunges forward to scare the buck and it runs off. As he does, he notices a house in the distance with what looks like a barn next to it.

Suddenly, he hears a bloodcurdling howl behind him. He turns to see a grey werewolf. With some werewolves standing five feet in height, with a tall frame, and giant muscle mass, they could definitely over power him. The thought terrifies him.

Tyler holds his breath. The wolf has not yet spotted him, as its eyes were on the buck that Tyler spooked. Werewolves don't look like normal wolves, and this one is no exception. With its dark-grey back and light-grey belly fur, it also has a distinctive black marking on its head. This one is only about four-foot-five in height; not the biggest one Tyler has ever seen, but it was up there. The wolf moves in a blur and pounces on the deer, biting into its neck. Tyler was going to attack, but he heard his name called and he trekked back home. He needed to come up with a plan and befriend a wolf. He only had a couple of months untill his curse took hold.

"Dad enrolled us at Mercy Lake High," El says as Tyler jumps the fence. "We start tomorrow."

"Great," he groans, rolling his eyes. Tyler has been to many schools, and all of them have been a challenge. Don't get attached, don't make friends, and, most of all, look out for werewolves had become his motto.

"It is the start of the new school year today, and that means we won't have missed anything," El says. Tyler ignores her as he goes back into the house. Both she and Tyler were sent to a special school not long after their parents married. It was a school that taught young minds how to hunt werewolves. El only got to learn the theory side of hunting and how to wield a stake in an emergency, while Tyler learned both the theory and the practical sides. Always the top of his class.

El always gleans every bit of information from every Hunter she met.

Tyler sighs as he opens the door to his room and begins to arrange it to his liking.

WOLF'S BLOOD

1. NEW YEAR

-Rose-

A thick evil laugh sounds ahead of me and a yellow ball of dust is thrown at me. I scream and duck as the laughter fades. A low-tuned growl replaces the sound of laughter, and then I hear my father's voice shouting. It makes my blood turn cold. Then I hear the sound of his body hitting the ground. I run into the ally where the growl comes from. I see a white wolf standing over my father's body. It lifts its head and growls at me and I see its full size. It is almost taller than me. It runs towards me, and I'm glued to the spot. It pounces on me, then bites down hard on my neck. I scream and wake up. The dream begins to fade out.

I awake and I'm still in my bed; my heart racing and sweat clinging to my body.

My name is Rose Salamander. I live in a small town called Mercy Lake, and the dream is only one of many that I have been tortured by in the month since my father died. Over and over again I see my father die— each night a different scenario. My father died two days before Christmas. I lie in my bed, staring at the ceiling as my heart slows to its regular beat. I roll over and look at the clock on my nightstand. Two o'clock in the morning.

I sigh and give up. I rarely sleep anymore because of the nightmares lying behind my eyes, waiting until I fall asleep to play out and torture me.

I remember my father, his smile, his laugh, his kind touch, and the way he said he loved me. I remember how his casket looked at the front of the church. I remember the feeling of sadness that rested in my chest.

I loved my father with all my heart; he was taken from me by a pack of animals— savage wolves. His body was mutilated. He was out

1

with his friends hunting deer and other game. Then his friends came back covered in blood, and my father was nowhere to be seen.

I remember that Christmas day, unwrapping presents. One was labelled with 'love from dad'. It was a new phone, one I had been asking for for months. My father was my best friend. Closing my eyes, I hug the covers to my chest.

When the sun comes up, I crawl out of bed and run a hand through my hair. It's a new day and a new year. I get up and put on a casual tee and jeans, then a pair of sneakers and brush my hair into a ponytail. I then grab my bag and head downstairs to eat breakfast with a fake smile, knowing that my mother, Dixie Salamander, will be down there with an empty bottle of wine and her new boyfriend, Garth Benson. But I am wrong. Instead, mum is in the kitchen making breakfast and dancing with Garth, just like she did with dad. The way they are smiling makes me sick, it has only been just over a month since we buried dad and here she is dancing with Garth like she used to with dad. I try to make it out the door without being noticed but mum sees me.

"Come, have some burned pancakes," she says, laughing as Garth spins her around.

"I'm good," I say, grabbing a piece of fruit from the bowl on the bench and heading out the door. As soon as I'm out, I look at my prize to find a bruised apple. I groan and throw it in the trash and make my way to school. As I walk, I kick a stone off the pavement. An approaching car makes me look as it drives past. Inside the car they look like the perfect family: a mother, a father, and two kids. Everyone seems happy except the boy. He seems down and looks how I feel: alone. I fake a smile and wave, he ignores me. As soon as I step one foot in the school grounds my friends are on me smuggling me with hugs and comforting words. I step back and look at my attackers.

"Welcome back!" Samantha beams. Her blond hair glows in the sun as she smiles at me

"Back to hell," Cleo snorts. She has dark brown hair and is also short in height and a little chubby in weight.

Caleb nods at me and I nod back at him. His light, ash-brown hair has darkened over the holidays, which makes the freckles on his face stand out more.

"First day of senior year," Caleb, my best friend, sighs over-dramatically. "This is going to be so much fun."

I agree with him and we walk into the main building as the bell rings, signalling the official start of the school year.

-Zero-

I hear her squeals and laugh from across the schoolyard— I have been going to school with Rose since I can remember, but I don't think she has ever noticed me. She is beautiful with gorgeous, flowing dark-brown hair and sapphire eyes. My name is Zero Dunn, and I am a werewolf. I live in a pack with other werewolves.

Our pack leader, the alpha, is Aamon. He was turned in his twenties about fifty years ago and left his own pack to start his own rogue pack after being a wolf for ten years. The second in command, the beta, is James. He was turned around the same age as Aamon. However, he has only been a werewolf for thirty years. Then there is me, a sentinel. I have been trained by Aamon and James to take their place if anything should happen to them. Next is Shea. She was turned under the same full moon as me, and is a sentinel like me. Lastly, there is Dante at a tender age of fifteen. He is the scout of the pack and holds the lowest rank despite being turned a month after me and Shea, but I don't think he minds. He makes sure that the pack is safe when hunting. While the rest of us hunt, he keeps a look out for humans.

We werewolves are nothing like ordinary wolves. We are much bigger with sleeker bodies. We are all rather large— the smallest wolf I've ever met was only three feet. He was only a pup, but some of us can stand at five feet or taller. We never age, heal quickly, and have superior strength and speed. We can change in and out of wolf form whenever we please, and there are limited things that can kill us: a silver stake or bullet to the heart will result in death as long as a human is the one doing the killing; otherwise we only go into a deep sleep until the stake or bullet is removed. Decapitation is another way for us to die, and venom from a vampire will cause us a lot of pain before killing us.

I'm still staring at Rose and her laughing gang when Shea places a hand on my shoulder and whispers,   "Aamon is allowing us to stay in school, because we need an education, not because he wants us to have a relationship."

"I know," I mumble, shaking her hand off. Shea will never admit it, but she has had a major crush on me ever since Aamon turned her. The bell rings and everyone heads into the assembly. Rose and her friends sit together one row behind Shea and I. The headmaster welcomes us and then he sends one of the assistances to hand out the class time schedule. This allows us to talk among ourselves while we check out the schedules. Rose and her gang laugh at the teachers they have and whoop at the classes they have together.

Shea leans into me and takes my schedule and laughs. "All our classes are together," she says. "I wonder how Aamon did that?"

"What?" I exclaim as I snatch the schedules out of her hands and look at them. She is right, all of our classes are together. It's like our schedules are the exact same copy. I let out a groan and wonder how I will survive.

-Rose-

The headmaster brings our attention back to the front of the room to divide us into our homerooms. Everyone divides into their classes and then we walk to our homerooms to get acquainted with the teachers. After homeroom is dismissed period one begins. My first is Spanish with Mr J. Alan, or the A man. He is one of my favourite teachers.

"*Holá* class, welcome back to school," Mr. Alan, says taking a seat on his desk. "This year we will be doing history." The room falls into a groan and boos. "Now hold on, this could be fun."

"Yeah, as fun as a theme park with no power," Sam says from the back with a laugh.

"Welcome back, Sam. I forgot about the endless insults you throw at me before getting shutdown with my witty come backs," Mr. Alan says, causing a rupture of laughs. Then he pins his eyes on me. "And if it isn't my favourite student, Miss Salamander. I did not expect to see you so soon."

"Morning, Sir," I say, nodding my head and ignoring the hint of my father's death.

"And what do you think about the history of Spain?" he asks me.

"I think it's boring." I shrug, sitting back in my chair and folding my arms over my chest

"Really?"

"*Sí*," I say with a fake half-smile.

"Well, I guess then I should cancel our field trip to Spain then?" he asks. His response is followed by a wave of nos. "Well, pay attention, but first, the attendance."

He goes to the desk and pulls out a sheet of paper with all our names on it. When he calls out to a Zero Dunn, a voice sounds from the right hand corner of the room, confirming he is here. That's when I notice him, really notice him. His sandy blond hair and dark intense eyes are looking right at me. Our eyes are locked on each other and I can't help wondering what he is thinking; only the call of my name brings my attention back to the front of the room.

After Spanish I head to my Art class, but my mind is on Zero again. You can imagine my surprise when I walk into the room to find him sitting at the far corner of the room. His eyes are on me again and mine on his. I walk to my seat and break the contact. We sit and the teacher, Miss B. Ryan, rushes into the room. She is also a really good teacher with awesome skills in the art world.

"Okay class," she says as she finishes the roll. "Let's do something easy: get out your drawing books and draw whatever comes to your mind,"

"This will be good," Cleo says sarcastically from next to me. "It's the same thing we do every year."

"I think it's good. We can relax for a whole class," I reply as I start to draw.

After half an hour of drawing, I zone out, staring at the page and thinking about my father. I look up and suddenly am staring right at Zero. His eyes pierce through mine. My chest tightens and my heart hammers.

Suddenly, something hits my arm hard, making me look away from Zero.

"What was that for?" I ask, bringing my attention back to Cleo.

"You zoned out on me," she says and I shrug. "I was asking how your holidays were. I was trapped away and haven't heard much."

"Oh," I sigh, not expecting that question. "My holidays were..."

I zone out again and the image of my father's face flashes before my eyes. I stand up in a rush as I feel the tears well in my eyes. I leave the room and run down the halls into the bathroom. I go into a toilet stall as the tears spill over. I told myself I was okay. I told myself that I could do this. But I can't. I can't pretend like I don't care. I miss my father. I leave the bathroom once the tears stop, but I don't go back to the classroom. I walk out onto the school grounds and sit in the sun, breathing deeply and feeling the wind brush against my skin. Soon the bell rings and lunch is in session. My friends find me and sit down with me.

"You left your bag," Cleo says, handing me my bag and I nod in appreciation, but stay silent.

"What's wrong?" she asks.

"Nothing," I mumble, picking at a blade of grass.

Cleo looks to our other friends and Samantha whispers into her ear.

"Oh my god," Cleo breaths, looking at me sympathetically.

"How are you doing, honey?" Samantha asks. Her eyes are enormous and everyone is waiting for me to fall apart.

"I'm fine. It's been a month since he died and I'm coping," I lie with a fake smile, but I'm not coping at all. I miss him. My father was the only one who listened to me; he made me feel safe and secure.

"If you ever need to talk, we are here for you," Caleb says with a smile.

They all pity me. After all, they still have their parents. My life has been filled with death—my twin sister disappeared years ago and is presumed dead. Her disappearance is also blamed on the animals.

"Where is Sam?" I ask, noticing him missing.

"He said that he was going off grounds for lunch," Caleb informs me as he shrugs his shoulders like it's no big deal.

After school, I walk home by myself. My house has its back to the woods where my father was attacked. It is a two story house and my room is the only room upstairs. It used to be an attic until dad allowed me to move out of my old small room and into the bigger one with a balcony on one side and a window on the other. As soon as I'm in the door, the smell of potato bake and steamed vegetables overwhelm me. It's my favourite dish that my father used to cook. I walk into the kitchen to see Garth cooking.

"Your mother told me that you like this, so I decided to try and cook it," he says with his back to me. "I hope it's to your liking."

I roll my eyes and ignore him and dump my bag in the living room before going out the back door to our stables where my horse is waiting to be ridden. Indi is a dapple-grey mare, and she hasn't been ridden since my dad died. So today I decide to saddle her up and take her for a ride in the woods. The wind gently blows in my face as I walk Indi out of the stables. Despite everything that has happened, I do not fear the woods like my mother does. It is peaceful to me, but that doesn't mean I am not cautious. I mount Indi and then ride her deep into the woods. I stop under an apple tree and tie her to a low hanging branch. This tree is so out of place, it's the only one in the whole woods. I feel a connection to it as I feel like I am an apple tree in the woods filled with large trees looking down on me. My father told me that the tree must have come here by accident, from a dropped core or animal droppings. He was always making up stories for things.

I pick two apples off the tree and hold one out to Indi, but she isn't paying attention. She snorts and stomps her feet, her ears are flattened back and her eyes are forward. I hear a twig snap and my heart races. Out of the corner of my eye I see a grey blur. A wolf is now just standing in the clearing right in front of me. I almost mistake him for a bear. The wolf is large, and I mean really large; bigger than the average sized wolf. The wolf is dark grey with hints of light grey streaked through his fur, and a black, circular marking on his head. It just stands there watching me with intense eyes. He does not look like any wolf that I have ever seen, but it is definitely a wolf. It's unmistakable, with giant muscle mass and giant teeth and claws. I know that if I turn to run it will probably chase me, so I stay frozen, glued to the spot. This is how I am going to die, like my father. My heart races as it takes a giant step forward.

-Zero-

She stands there frozen. Her face is pale and her heart beats rapidly, and it kicks up a notch when I take a step forward. She is expecting me to attack, and I should. But I can't do it. I take another step forward and press my nose to her hand.

"What are you doing?" Shea growls in my mind, appearing behind me.

"I could ask you the same question," I reply, turning to her and growling.

"She is a human, she saw us, and we must kill her. Let me kill her for the safety of the pack."

"No," I growl. As she steps forward, I snap and lunge towards Shea. She flattens her ears and snaps back, trying to get past me and to Rose. I bite her hindquarter and she whimpers and runs home. I turn to Rose and she gets on her horse and gallops away. I hear my name howled on the wind. Aamon wants me home; probably to lecture me about biting Shea. I howl back in a response and run home. When I get there I'm in my human form. James is tending to Shea who is whining like a baby; her clothes are torn and bloody.

"What the hell were you thinking?" Aamon says, coming into the room with a bowl of hot water and some towels. "You attacked one of you own."

"She was almost about to attack a human," I say in rage.

"That is because the humans cannot know what we are!" Aamon shouts. "If they reveal our secret, we will have hunters crawling all over the place."

"It doesn't mean she will tell anyone!" I growl, glaring at him.
Killing humans isn't right and that's what I stood for.
However, the rest of the pack feels differently except for the omega,
Dante.

"It isn't right," I say, keeping my temper under control. "We are not
wild animals. She hasn't done anything to the pack."

"She might. Maybe I'll go back to her house tonight and have a
little nibble," Shea says with a small giggle. I lose it and turn wolf and
attack Shea again, but Aamon and James pull me outside.

"Listen up, pup," Aamon shouts, turning wolf and barking at me. I
bark back and we size each other up until I remember that Aamon is
older and stronger than me, but I am a wolf, my instincts take over as I
lunge forward. Aamon barks an alphas bark as he stands tall. I know I
am not going to win this, so I tilt my head to the floor and turn my ears
back. Aamon pulls his lips back and growls at me. I lay my wolf body
onto the ground, pressing my stomach into the dirt. I do and say
nothing until I transform back into my human form. Then I say, "You
changed me into a wolf because I was dying and had no family. I didn't
agree to it."

"We know, mate, we know," Aamon says, changing and stepping
forward. "None of us ever do."

I go back inside. Once I am sure they are gone I take off running
into the woods again, changing into a wolf as I go. I am looking for Rose,
but when I find her she isn't at the tree. I go to her home where I see
her through her window. I stay hidden in the shade of the trees.

-Rose-

I return home quickly with my heart pounding and my pulse racing.
I put Indi away and go inside, ignoring Garth and my mother. I go
straight to my room and lock the door behind me. I remember the wolf
didn't try to kill me. It could have and yet it protected me against the
other wolf. I head to my computer and search images of different
breeds of wolves. Alaskan Tundra, Eastern Timber, Interior Alaskan,
Mexican, Texas Grey, common Grey; none of them looks like the beast I
saw this afternoon, so I decide to go back further in time. I research the
dire wolf and as I scroll on it seems the wolf I saw was a dire wolf.
However, they became extinct ten thousand years ago. I close my
laptop and move away.

"I was hallucinating," I say to myself. "I am in shock after my
father's death. I am going mad."

I take a long, hot shower and then fall asleep in my bed where the nightmares continue to torture   me— my father dies in front of me again, and again, and again.

Only the sound of my alarm going off, telling me that it is six o'clock wakes me from the nightmare. I sit up covered in sweat and my throat's dry and itchy from screaming. I get out of bed and hobble over to my dresser. My phone then goes off saying I have a text.

"Meet group @ coffee house 4 hot Choco's?" Caleb texts.

"Sure, meet @ end of street @ about 7ish?" I reply.

"Cool, cu then," he says.

I get dressed and grab my bag for school and head down stairs to fill my lunch box. I open the downstairs fridge and find a brown paper bag with my name on it. I open it to find it stuffed with wonderful food; I transfer the continence of the bag into my lunch box and place both my bag and box on the counter. I go out the back and give Indi some grain and lay down new hay. I leave the house before anyone is awake and meet Caleb down the road and we walk to the coffee shop next to the school where we order hot chocolate for the whole group and go to a booth that fits all of us. As soon as we sit, the rest of the group bounces through the door and piles into the booth and starts gossiping. The hot chocolates are placed on the counter and the waiter walks off. We make small talk and once we finish our hot chocolates, we walk to school. My first class is history. My teacher, Mrs. Corl, comes into the room with a frustrated look on her face. She is an old cow with a bad temper and she doesn't like me at all. She thinks I'm useless and a bad influence on everyone. This term we're doing wars and propaganda during World War One.

"What are you doing tonight?" Cleo asks, tapping my shoulder.

I turn around. "I don't know. Why?" I ask back in a whisper, and the boy beside me shushes me. I glare at him and give him the finger before turning back to Cleo.

"Full moon party tonight," she whispers with a silent squeal.

"I can't go, mum will kill me," I say, subconsciously writing notes. "Besides, I was going riding tonight. The moon will be bright enough to ride in."

"Fine, sounds good to me," Cleo says and the door to the class opens and a new guy walks in. He hands a slip of paper to the teacher and takes a seat in front of where I am sitting. My heart skips a beat. It's the kid from the car that I saw a day ago. He looks hot, but he seems like bad news. I want to hit him for some reason and a part of me cringes in his presence. A shiver runs down my spine as I stare at his back. He turns around, like he knows I was looking at him. I quickly look down and pretend to write notes. He turns back around and begins to get out his books.

-Zero-

Don't go riding tonight, Rose, I think as I hear the words leave her mouth. She will be bitten and I won't be able to stop it because I will want to bite her, too. The full moon does something to a wolf's conscience: shuts them off from humanity and makes them want to turn the first person they see.

"Maybe I will see if Samantha and Caleb would like to come, too," Rose says, turning around to face her friend after the new boy turned back around. All I can think of is her getting bitten. I can't believe she would do this to me. The rest of the day is torture. I have two more classes with Rose, and I don't know if I can take my eyes off of her. I begin to wonder what she would look like as a wolf.

As the school day ends, I begin to get twitchy. I think of what it would be like to have her blood in my mouth, to run alongside her, and if her and I became partners. I suddenly shake the thoughts out of my head. No one deserves to be turned.

"Don't go ridding tonight," I mumble.

2. THE NIGHTMARE BEGINS

-Rose-

After school I walk home and go into my father's hunting room. I find his bow and quiver and then sneak them up to my room. He always preferred hunting with a bow— he told me that guns were too quick and loud. I stay in my room until my mother goes to bed, then I sneak back downstairs and go out to the stables and I mount Indi bareback and ride into the woods.

The night feels eerie, like the air is thick and energised. I look up to the moon and it is round and full. Something stirs under my skin. It's the same feeling I get every month. I push Indi forward and she snorts and her ears flick back—something is wrong. I hear the sound of footsteps ahead and pull an arrow from the quiver, I pull the arrow back with the bow and take a deep breath and look around. Then Caleb and Samantha step into view. I almost fire and my heart thumps in my ears.

"What are you doing out here?" I hiss, putting the arrow back into the quiver. "I could've shot you!"

"Cleo told us you were out here. We thought it would be best that you weren't alone,"
Samantha says and I roll my eyes.

"What are you doing out here anyway?"

"Hunting for the beast that killed my father," I say, dismounting Indi and walking over to my friends.

"Are you crazy?" Caleb exclaims. "Do you know how many wolves are actually out here? How do you know which one is the one that killed your father?"

"I'll know it when I see it," I grumble, trekking forward. I find that Caleb and Samantha came on the backs of horses. I tie Indi with the others and continue to hunt down the wolf.

"Look," I sigh, turning towards them as they follow me. "You don't have to come with me. I can do this on my own."

"You are going to get yourself killed," Caleb argues. "We aren't leaving you out here alone."

The moon rises higher in the sky as we continue forward, and then the air becomes thicker as the sound of screams fill the air.

"What the hell was that?" Samantha says and Caleb pulls out a gun.

"Relax," I say. "We are just passing near the full moon party."

We continue forward, and the woods grow silent, an eerie quiet falls over us and goose bumps cover my body.

Then a burst of wolves howling fills the woods. By the sound of it there are a lot of them. The howls are thick and throaty; my heart races as fear spreads over me.

"Maybe we should head back," Caleb says, and then it starts. Wolves surround us, all are the same size and body features as the dark grey one I saw yesterday. The difference is the markings. I see the grey she-wolf from yesterday, and then my eyes rest on the dark grey wolf and he is looking only at me, growling like the others. I notice something strange. Some of the wolves seem to have tattoos on their right shoulders. But they are all growling, their lips pulled back and white teeth shining.

"What should we do?" Caleb whispers to me, snapping me out of my thoughts. All of our backs are together and facing the wolves.

"Don't shoot. There are too many," I whisper back. "They will be on us in a heartbeat."

"Guys," Samantha says with a nervous pitch in her tone. "Look!"

We look at where she is motioning and see a black wolf bigger than all the others steps into the light.

"Is it meant to be that big?" Samantha asks, pressing her back to mine.

"No, none of them are meant to look like that. They look surreal," I whisper. The wolves are just looking at us and growling.

The black wolf lunges at me, and I accidentally fire my arrow, it hits the wolf straight in the centre of its head. It growls at me and doesn't die. My heart races as the wolves begin to close in on us. Time seems to slow. I see their muscles contracting, ready for the attack. I lose sight of the black wolf in the movement, but then I hear a bark and all the wolves attack with snarling fangs. I grab Caleb by the arm as Samantha gets tackled. I pull him along and we run. We manage to dodge the wolves, but my heart is hammering. Caleb keeps up with me, but my lungs are beginning to heave and I am slowing down.

"Come on!" Caleb shouts, and I try to push myself further.

Caleb runs in front of me and I watch him fall as a wolf comes out of nowhere and tackles him to the ground. His gun is knocked out of his hand and my heart races as the wolf bites down onto his shoulder. He screams and I see his blood spurt out.

I fire an arrow into the wolf's hide and the wolf growls and looks up at me.

"Come over here!" I shout and the wolf stalks towards me. "Yeah, come this way." I fire another arrow into the wolf's shoulder. He yelps and then deepens his growl. The wolf doesn't stop.

The wolf looks over my shoulder and then goes back to Caleb. I freeze. Slowly, I turn around to see the dark grey wolf from yesterday. It growls at me and I prepare to run, but too quickly the wolf is on me and dragging me away, it has me by the shirt and pulls me away from Caleb, who is now deserted by the other wolf. I scream in fear and manage to grab Caleb's gun and fire at the wolf. The bullet misses by a few millimetres and my heart races as the wolf bites down on my wrist, causing me to scream and drop the gun. Pain races through my arm and tears well in my eyes, blurring my vision.

I punch the wolf in the nose with my uninjured arm and it drops me. It growls at me and flattens its ears— its teeth shine in the moonlight, slick and red with my blood that also stains his mouth. The wolf lunges at me as I reach for the gun again. It pins me to the ground and places a giant paw on my arm.

I scream out and try to keep my face away from its sharp teeth snarling and snapping inches from my face. Its growl is thick and powerful, causing my stomach to lurch and threatening to bring up tonight's dinner.

My hands search the dirt, trying to find anything that could be used for my defense. I find nothing. The wolf presses down on my body and its claws break my skin. I cry out and tears prickle my eyes. The wolf matches my cry with a howl before its jaws clasp around my shoulder and it bites down, hard. Burning pain rockets across my body as I scream out and dig my nails into the dirt.

It releases my shoulder and then licks the wound attentively. He then looks at me, his eyes set hard and fierce. He bites my shoulder again and I scream, the pain burning in my body. I wonder how long it will be before I die, and if my father died the same way.

-Zero-

Her blood is in my mouth, and God, does it feel good. The blood is rich and it smells amazing.

"Oh, Rose, be my flower forever," I think as I bite down on her flesh again.

The rule is that you have to bite the victim, lick the wound, then leave them, but for me that was too hard to do. How could I turn my back on her when she is just lying there? We must lick the wound to administrate the venom for them to turn into a werewolf. She is now screaming more than all of the others and she is struggling to get away, but I didn't want her to go. I want her to be with me forever. I lower my mouth to bite her again and then I am thrown sideways as Aamon comes out of nowhere and tackles me to the ground.

"You have taken it too far," he growls as I stumble to regain my balance.

"Stay out of it," I growl back, flattening my ears and opening my mouth. *"She is mine!"*

I try to get around him, but I am dealing with a wolf that has twice as much experience than I will ever have. I back off and go home, and as the sun comes up I turn human. Within the hour Aamon comes home, human.

"What the hell was that?" he yells, slamming the door. It almost comes off its hinges. "You could have killed her!"

"What? Like you guys tried to do last night?" I say, crossing my arms and rolling my eyes.

"You were the one who said that you don't want to kill anyone, mate," James says, coming into the house in a cooler manor. He stands just behind Aamon. "No human should be bitten more than once. That is the rule."

"What did you do with her?" I ask, getting concerned that they might of killed her.

"I turned human and carried her to where her friends were, they didn't know what I was," he says, turning to Aamon. "I had Dante follow her to the house. Lucky we had gotten a bite, otherwise, I wouldn't have been able to change and she would have died." After wolves make a bite on the full moon, they can change back and their humanity is restored.

"She still might," Dante says with a sad note as he comes through the door and closes it behind him. "Rose's mum took them to the hospital. Rose started having seizures in the car."

"They are all part of our pack now," Aamon says, walking away.

"What? How do you know?" I ask, glancing at him.

"Because, I bit the Blondie and Dante got the tall brown hair, and of course you hitting Rose," he says, running a hand through his hair.

"This is good," Dante says perking up. "We will be stronger."

"Agreed. Tomorrow night they will come to us, it is in their blood," Aamon says. "But for now we sleep and regain our strength because the first thing they will do is attack the pack." Everyone goes upstairs to sleep and I can't help but think of what I have done. How could I take Rose's life away from her?

-Rose-

I wake in the hospital with my heart racing. How am I still alive? I remember the wolf that bit me and how it would not stop biting me. My wrist is bandaged with a white cloth and my shoulder is aching, throbbing from where the wolf bit me.

"Honey, are you okay?" My mother asks, jumping from her seat and coming to my side once she sees that I have woken up.

"I'm fine," I say flatly, looking away and moving my hand as she reaches for it. For some reason I felt abnormally angry and frustrated.

"What were you and your friends thinking?" Garth asks from the corner, he stands there with his hands in his pockets and leans against the wall.

"We were hunting, like we used to with *my* dad," I say, avoiding his gaze.

"You sure scared both your mother and I," he grunts.

"Why would I scare you?" I scowl at him "I'm not your daughter, and you're not my father."

"Honey, not now, not here," mum pleads in a quiet voice.

"Why not? I'm moving out tonight any way," I say and I am not even sure where that came from.

"What!" mum exclaims, jumping back.

"I'm going to live with one of my friends." A lie—might as well keep going.

"Why?" she gasps.

"Because I hate you," I say, scowling at her. I don't really but hey, I am angry and hyped up on painkillers. "Dad has been dead for a month and you jump into bed with the first guy you see."

This makes mum run out of the room crying, and Garth sighs before chasing after her. As soon as they are gone Cleo and Sam bust through the door, placing chocolates, flowers, and balloons on the table next to me.

"Sorry we took so long to get to you," Cleo says. "We stopped at Samantha's room, then we went to Caleb's."

"It's Okay," I say, sitting up and gasping.

"You needed stitches," Cleo says softly, taking my hand. "Are you okay?"

"So what is it we hear that you are moving out?" Sam says before I could answer. I glance at him. How did he hear that? He must have been more than a room away.

"Yeah, moving in with a friend," I lie again, looking out the window.

"That is exactly what the other two said," Cleo says, gasping. "Mum would let you live with us, but not all of you."

"No, no not with you. Somewhere else," I say.

"Where?" Sam asks, raising an eyebrow and crossing his arms, it's a look that you would give to a child if they said they were moving out. I am not a child.

"I don't know, but I am leaving tonight." Sam and I lock eyes and I swear I could see his skin ripple like water.

"Right, that is exactly what the others said!" Cleo yells. "Maybe they were abducted by aliens and told to go to the corn field to be abducted, and then told not to tell anyone."

"Right, cause they abducted us then they put us back to say goodbye." I laugh and roll my eyes. "Does Mercy Lake even have a corn field?"

"Hey, I'm no alien, but that could be the way they think." She shrugs. "Chocolate?"

"Sure," I say as they get the chocolate out and we all sit cross-legged on the bed talking about aliens. Then the other two come into the room saying that they were discharged. We all sit on the bed taking about Cleo's idea and eating chocolates.

"Visiting hours are over," a nurse says, coming into the room holding a clip board.

"Is she staying overnight?" Samantha asks, sliding off the bed.

"Yes, she had a seizure when she came in, so we have put her under observation."

Everyone says their goodbyes and head home. I quickly fall asleep. When I wake, it's about eight o'clock and I have the feeling that I need to go somewhere. It's like my body knows and it takes control. I tear the tubes and wires from my body and the machines start to beep and cause all sorts of panic. I smash the window in my room with my fist just as a nurse comes into the room calling for someone. I'm lucky to only be one story away from the ground. I jump and land on all fours, literally—I'm a wolf like the ones in the woods. I don't take much notice, though. Instead, I run and don't stop until I reach a house. It's two stories and I feel it has a basement, I notice that I am back in human form. From behind me Samantha and Caleb come.

"What are we doing here?" Samantha asks.

"One moment I was asleep, then I woke as a wolf," Caleb says, rubbing his forehead. "The next thing I know I am here as a human."

"Something about this place makes my hair stand on end," I growl, now a wolf again.

Samantha is a blond wolf and the smallest of us all and Caleb is a dark brown and I am a white wolf. All of us have crazy markings and sleek body features. We all charge into the door and knock it down. We seem to be in the kitchen and there are other wolves, the dark grey one, the brown one, and the grey one I know. Then two more grey wolves appear and they are all growling.

"*Don't fight us we are not going to hurt you,*" the brown wolf says, walking over to us—too close, so I attack him. My wolf instincts take over and I lunge for the neck. Caleb and Samantha attack as well, fighting off the others as the brown wolf and I fight. I am able to pin him to the ground, but the grey female tackles me from the side.

I'm quickly on my feet and back up, growling at her. I attack first, catching her by surprise and she fights back, but she is not strong enough. In no time I have her pinned. The dark grey wolf is on me now. I fight back but he is stronger. He keeps me occupied while the rest of the pack pins my friends. The brown wolf turns to his human form, binds their legs and tapes their mouths shut, then he shouts something at Caleb and Samantha before moving to me.

They are all on me now, pinning me down. They turn human to bind me and I keep growling and struggling to get free. The dark grey wolf turns human and holds my head down. I look at him and see who he is for the first time—Zero. I let out a small whimper and go limp.

"I am the alpha in this pack," the brown wolf/human says. "This is my pack and you are just a part of it."

I let out another whimper and close my eyes as they drag my friends and me down into the basement. There they remove the tape and loosen our binds before leaving and locking the door behind them.

-Zero-

"Zero, you have first watch," Aamon says, walking off with the others. I sit at the door remembering the fight and her whimper as she saw my face. How could I make her a wolf when the day before I was complaining how we don't have free will and then just take hers? Downstairs I can hear them snapping the ropes and whimpering about what they should do. After a few minutes they turn human.

"What the hell?" The male voice says.

"Caleb, shut up!" a female says to Caleb. "They could be listening."

"Samantha, calm down," Rose says, sighing.

"What the hell are we? I thought werewolves only existed in fairy tales and stupid books," The one called Caleb asks.

"What the hell does this mean?" Rose asks, her voice filled with sadness.

I can picture her leaning on the wall with her arms crossed.

"It means that we need to get out of here," Caleb declares.

"Good plan, but you are missing some important things. A, we are down here and they are up there," The other female, Samantha, says. "B, the door is locked."

I can hear her walking toward the door. There is a loud rap at the door and I jump.

Samantha continues, "...plus, reinforced with steel."

"And C, they out number us," Rose sighs.

I imagine her sad face.

"Let's call the police," Caleb says and my heart pounds.

"Caleb, you idiot, they could be listening," Samantha hisses.

"How about we text Cleo to call the police and get us out of here," Caleb says again.

I run to Aamon. "They have phones," I stammer.

Aamon, James, Dante, Shea, and I go and take the phones and we leave, locking the door again. I take my place once again against the door.

I hear Rose sigh and then I hear all three of them begin to pace. I walk away from the door for a moment and suddenly the basement erupts in noise—the new pack members are trying to get our attention. The howls turn to barks and back again, before I know it Aamon has busted through the door and is in wolf form, snapping and growling at them. The noise stops, but Rose is growling back at him while the others are backed in a corner in their human form. Rose has her hackles raised and her ears flat. I walk next to Aamon and stand next to him in wolf form. Rose's attention fixes on me and her growl deepens. She stands like an alpha and it seems like she is in a natural state.

"*What the hell do you want with us?*" she barks in an alpha voice.

"*We need new pack members,*" Aamon responds calmly, but still with his alpha tone.

"*Well, we decline,*" she says, pulling her lips back and producing a deep growl that makes my blood turn cold.

"I don't," Caleb says with a meek mouse voice. "As long as I can get out of here,"

"Me either," the girl says, "I know when I am beaten."

Rose growls at Aamon and he growls back.

"*Fuck you,*" she growls deeply.

"*Fine then,*" Aamon says turning to the other two. "*You two come with me.*"

We walk out of the room and I take my stand at the door.

"My turn," Shea says taking my place with a flirtatious wink. "Go rest up."

"Fine," I sigh and go upstairs.

"Excuse me? Shea you and Zero have school tomorrow," Aamon says. "James will take watch."

-Rose-

They left me, they tucked tailed and left me behind. I pace along the floor and realize that I am still in my wolf form. Somehow it seems natural to me. I shift back to my human state and look around the basement. The walls are concrete, probably reinforced, and then I notice the moonlight flooding through the small window above me. I find a heavy brick and smash the window glass, wasting no time I climb up and wiggle through the hole. As soon as I am out of the house I run fast and hard. I hear a wolf howl and hear the other wolves give chase. My two feet pounding on the ground turn to four as I shift my form. I pick up speed and run to my house, hoping that the wolves won't risk attacking me so close to humans. I decide to run into the stables and climb up into the rafters. I hide as my smaller human self and hope that the wolves don't find me.

But they do, two wolves walk into the stables, their claws scraping against the concrete. I notice one as the wolf that turned Caleb. Anger rises up in me and I growl subconsciously.

One of the wolves shifts and looks up at me.

"Why don't you come down here?" the man asks. "My name is

James, I won't hurt you. You are a part of the pack now."

I glare at him. "No, I'm not," I argue. "Just because one of you bit me, that doesn't mean that I am a part of your pack."

"It is in your blood now," James says. "You cannot deny it. We can teach you how to control what you are, how to fight and how to be a werewolf."

"No thanks," I growl.

"Come down," James pleads.

"Or what?" I question, "You'll kill me?"

The man sighs and the wolf with him huffs and changes form.

"My name is Dante," the wolf says. "I was turned not long ago, I know how you feel. You're angry and confused, but we can help you. You'll find out that we are not as bad as you think."

"You bit my friend," I say. "You turned him into a monster."

"We are not monsters," the alpha wolf says entering the barn with Zero by his side.

I growl at them and they growl back as I grouwl and shift into a wolf.

"Rose, come down," Zero pleads.

Some part of me wants to do as he wishes. So I drop from the rafters and land in my wolf form. I lunge at the others and they all change and attack back. James bites down on my hindquarters and Dante grabs the back of my neck. Aamon pounces on me and holds me down, asserting his dominance. I try to fight back but he bites down on my neck, causing me to change form. I whimper as pain flows through my body. They bind my wrists and my ankles again as Aamon holds my neck in his jaws.

"*I am the alpha,*" he says.

I whimper and my body goes slack.

He lets me go and James picks me up in his arms.

"So much for not hurting me," I mumble and he huffs and carries me back to the house.

-Zero-

She looks terrible and exhausted. I feel sorry for her. Her body is covered in bloody cuts and bites. Her shoulder looks worse since Dante took a massive chunk out of her. My hand freezes over her other shoulder where I bit. I remember that night, and my heart sinks. I snap back to reality and apply ointment to the bite mark and she lets out a sigh as the pain is relieved. Because she is newly turned she doesn't have the full powers a wolf would have like healing. After we have finished we go back upstairs and lock the door.

"Shea, Zero," James says, "You guys still have school tomorrow, go and rest."

"Okay," I sigh. "Can I get Rose something to eat and drink?"

"Sure, kid."

I go to the fridge to get leftovers from dinner: roast lamb and vegetables. I heat it up and head down stairs to Rose's prison; she is awake but curled up in her wolf form and whimpering. The chains are tied to her neck and all feet. I clear my throat and she sits up. As a human she looks so sad. I sit down and hand her the plate with a knife and fork. She looks even more surprised when I hand her a cup of water.

"It's not poisoned," I say, placing the cup and the plate on the ground.

"Why?" she croaks hugging herself, looking so fragile.

"Because we don't want to poison you," I say, confused.

"No," she says, shaking her head then tapping her shoulder. "Why?"

"Why did I bite you?" I ask and she responds with a nod. "It was the full moon. It makes a wolf lose its humanity. I'm so sorry."

"So the food isn't poisoned?"

"No, not poisoned," I laugh.

She breaks a piece of meat off of the bone and crawls over to me, chains rattling with every move she makes. I think about moving back, but it doesn't look like she wants to hurt me so I don't move. She holds the meat up to my mouth, I take it from her hands and she moves back to the plate and takes a small bit of potato, then holds it up to my mouth and I take it. She does this with every piece of food on her plate then she makes me take a drink of water also. When she finishes with me she goes back to her plate and eats the meal while taking small sips of water.

She looks so beautiful, like a fallen angel from heaven. She looks up and notices that I am staring at her.

"My name is Rose," she says, tucking a stray piece of hair behind her ear.

"I know," I say back. "I'm Zero."

"I know," she laughs, finishing her last piece of food and last drop of water.

I pick up her plate and walk over to the stairs.

"Thank you," she says.

"You're welcome," I say, opening the door.

"Wait," she says, sadness returning to her voice. "Can you stay with me?"

"I... I can't," I sigh with difficulty.

"Please?" she says, starting to cry. "I don't know what's happening, I feel numb and sore. What's happening to me?"

"I can't," I say, walking out the door and forcing myself not to run back in and hold her. Instead, I wash her dishes and head to bed.

The next morning when I wake, I go into the kitchen to make toast. Shea is there pouring milk into a bowl of cereal. Dante saunters into the kitchen, running his fingers through his unruly bed hair. He yawns and stretches his shoulders before turning into a werewolf. Ever since Aamon turned him, he has been a devoted were-pup. Dante sees no benefit in furthering his education and refuses to attend school. After breakfast we make our lunches and then head to the bus stop.

Aamon is spending the day explaining to Caleb, Samantha, and Rose what it means to be a werewolf and what changes they can expect to happen to their bodies and, most importantly, what it means to part of the pack.

Shea and I arrive at school and I am surrounded by three of Roses friends.

"Where is she?" Cleo asks.

"Who?" I ask innocently, looking away from their judging eyes.

"Rose," Sam says, glaring at me. "She 'broke' out of the hospital yesterday."

"She texted us all, just saying, 'Zero Knows'. We have seen you looking at her, so where is she?" Cleo demands.

"I don't know," I snap, trying to push past, but Sam blocks me.

"We are worried as hell," Sam says with concern in his eyes that shows he likes Rose more than just a friend.

"So are her parents," Cleo says with softness in her voice.

"I don't know where she is," I say, putting my hands up and pushing past them.

"We will talk to Caleb and Samantha when they get here," says Cleo.

You do that, I think as I head into homeroom to let the day start. It was quite boring without Rose to spy on, but she was on my mind all day. My head is filled with thoughts of her.

In the fifth period, Aamon came to the school to collect Shea and me.

"What is it?" I ask with worry in my voice as I get into the front seat.

"It's Rose. Something is wrong with her. She is having seizures," he says and my heart sinks. "I need the whole pack there for strength and you in case we need to put her down."

"No, I can't kill her," I say almost in a whisper. "Why me?"

"No one is telling you to, not yet," he says, starting the car. "But you are the one who put this on her, and you should be the one to end it."

We get home and as soon as we are in the door I can hear her screaming, and it breaks my heart. The rest of the pack, including the new ones, are in the kitchen waiting for us. James, however is not there. I guessed that he would be with Rose since he has the most medical experience from before he was turned he was a second year nurse at the local hospital and has since completed his training and continues to work part time at the hospital.

"Please, help her," Samantha whines.

"I will try," I say, going down to the basement. To my horror, Rose's body is flopping like a fish out of water and her screams are full of pain. She stops convulsing, and just lies there eyes wide open, staring into space.

"This has been going on since you left," James says.

"What is it?" I ask, trying to keep the pain out of my voice.

"We don't know," Aamon sighs. "It has never happened before. Then again, no other wolf has been bitten multiple times either."

I ignore the comment and lean down next to Rose and stroke her head. During the fits, she has knocked open the wounds on both shoulders.

"Rose, can you hear me?" I ask quietly.

"Yes," she responds, her voice barely audible, "Zero?"

"Yeah, it's me," I say with my heart breaking as she sighs.

"It hurts," she says, as she closes her eyes and tears spill.

"It is going to be okay," I reassure her as I take her hands. "But you need to keep your eyes open."

"Will you stay with me?" she asks, opening them.

I nod. "Of course, I will," I say, stroking her hair.

"Zero, I forgive you," she says squeezing my hand and her eyes begin to close. "For turning me."

"Why?" I ask, trying to keep her eyes open.

"Because you couldn't help it," she says and her body turns into a screaming, convulsing mess.

"I think we need to call an ambulance," I say, standing back, not fully confident in James's ability to help her.

"Can't," James says over her screaming. "She will talk."

"No, she won't," I say, clenching my fists as my temper rises.

"How the hell do you know, mate?" James snaps.

"I... I don't."

"Exactly. So until I can be sure she won't talk, she stays here," he says as the screaming stops.

"I won't talk," she says and coughs. This isn't an ordinary cough as blood sprays from her mouth as she rolls over to her side.

Aamon runs to the top of the stairs and yells for Dante to call an ambulance. We carry her upstairs and lay her on the floor in the dining room so the paramedics don't get suspicious.

"New pups to the basement," Aamon says.

"We are not pups," Caleb says, growling.

"Go!" I yell as Rose starts coughing blood again, they listen and go to the basement.

"Zero, you go in the ambulance with her and I will follow with the car," Aamon commands.

"Okay," I say as Rose goes into another fit.

Within twenty minutes there are two paramedics next to Rose. They place her onto the stretcher and wheel her to the ambulance. I hop in the back next to Rose and hold her hand. When we get to the hospital they wheel her into surgery. Aamon and I wait in silence. Over an hour passes before a doctor walks out, wiping his hands.

"She is going to be okay," he says and I notice blood on his shirt. "We have her on seizure medication and we've stitched her shoulders and now she's resting peacefully."

"Thanks, Doc," Aamon says.

"She might have internal bleeding somewhere, but we couldn't locate it."

"Can we see her?" I ask.

"She is sleeping, but yes you can," he says, leading us to her room. She is hooked up to machines, all making different sounds. I notice a machine is administering morphine and am glad she is receiving pain relief. I take a seat next to her bed and watch her with cautious eyes. Her hand twitches and I brace myself for another seizure, but it doesn't come. Instead, her eyes begin to flutter. She is waking up.

-Rose-

I wake to the sounds of machines, the smell of cleanliness, the metallic taste of blood in my mouth, and the sight of Zero. My body feels sore and my shoulders ache. I try to sit up, but my body is refusing to follow orders, so I lay still and look at Zero.

"You stayed," I say, my voice barely audible.

"I promised I would," he says, looking down to his hands.

"Thank you. I don't know what it would be like waking up alone."

"It's okay."

"Good to see you awake," Aamon says, moving out of the corner and making himself visible.

"Good to be awake," I say flatly. "What happened?"

"You had a seizure," a doctor says, coming into the room. "You also might be suffering from internal bleeding."

"Is she going to be okay?" Aamon asks.

"Yes, she is healing very quickly. She should be discharged in a few days," he says as the rest of the pack come into the room. "It would also be smart to give her some sugary food," he says as he walks out.

I see Caleb and Samantha and I remember how they left me, I glare at them and then look away.

"Visiting hours are over," a nurse says, coming into the room. I am glad that she walked in. I can't deal with them anymore. All but Aamon leave. He walks over to the bed and stands over me.

"You will not say a thing," Aamon says.

"I won't," I promise. He leaves with one final warning glare and then I am left alone. I fall asleep easily, despite the sound of beeping machines. When I wake, Cleo is standing over me making faces. I jump and our heads collide.

"Ouch," she giggles, rubbing her head.

"Your fault," I say, rubbing my head and giggling also.

"Where did you go, anyway?" Sam asks all serious. He's standing in the corner with his arms crossed over his chest with a scowl on his face.

"Around," I say, looking away from their suspicious eyes.

"What was with the text?" Cleo asks.

"The text?" I say, going serious. They all pull out their phones and show me the text that I sent them when I had my phone. "Oh. that text. Um, I don't remember."

"Must have hit your head too hard," Cleo says, going to her bag and pulling out a container of Hokey-Pokey ice cream and four spoons. "Look what I smuggled in."

"You didn't smuggle that in," Sam laughs, relaxing and crossing over to the bed in a blink of an eye. "They let you bring it in."

"Can you at least let me feel the littlest bit rebellious?" she asks, sitting on the bed and laughing. We all take a spoon and eat, gossip, and laugh. It was exactly what I needed. I was happy until Zero, Caleb, and Samantha come into the room carrying a giant basket. Sam tenses at the sight of Zero and it looks like his skin ripples.

"The rest of the school found out of your trip to the hospital and they made this basket," Caleb says, putting it on the bed. Cleo dives into it, naming everything in there: various sweets, cards, flowers, and balloons. The rest of the gang come and sit on the bed except Zero, who just stands in the corner. We eat the sweets, read the cards, laugh, and gossip more. By the end, we are completely sore from laughing, except Zero, who keeps a serious face the whole time. He doesn't eat anything, doesn't laugh, and just sits in the corner of the room. A nurse comes in and ushers them out at four o'clock and I am alone again. A doctor comes in and checks my clipboard.

"How are you feeling?" he asks as his eyes scan the board.

"I'm okay," I say bluntly. I really hate doctors.

"You should be able to be discharged tonight. Your friend said he'd be back then."

"Fantastic," I say, rolling my eyes. "When do the tubes get taken out?"

"When you are discharged," he says, leaving me and I wait. I soon get bored and decide to eat more sweets and read the cards again. Zero and Aamon come in at eight o'clock and the doctor discharges me. We head outside where a black hummer is waiting. We all climb in and Aamon drives us to my place.

"What are we doing?" I ask, tensing and thinking that they are taking me back to my mother.

"Getting you some supplies," Aamon says, hopping out of the car. "You know, clothes and things."

"Awesome," I say, going to the door and it's locked. "Locked, try and keep up."

"Where are you going?" Aamon asks.

"Just keep up," I say, going to the Stables. All the horses are there and they start to whinny as soon as I step inside. I smile. I notice the water and food buckets are empty.

"Can you guys help me?" I ask, getting halters and leads from the tack room.

"With what?" Zero asks as serious as Aamon.

"I need to move them into the field," I say, putting a halter on Indi and leaving the leads on the door of her stable as I halter the rest.

"Sure," Aamon, says taking a two leads and handing one to Zero. We walk the horses into the field. I turn on the electric fence and fill the troughs one with oats and grains and the other with water. We let the horses go and they start to run and kick up playfully. We go back to the stables and put the halters away. I then go up to the loft and stop at the window directly across from my bedroom window. There is a plank that I laid between the windows, so I could get in and out without being noticed. I cross and open my window, then step inside. The others follow as I start to pack.

"Need a hand?" Aamon asks.

"No, I can handle clothes," I say bluntly as I shove my clothes into the bag while keeping a careful eye on the two males in the room.

-Zero-

Her room was quite big and full of drawings and paper. I notice the walls and the drawings—wolves and horses. I scan the drawings and see the ones of her and I before I bit her.

"Did you draw all of these?" I ask, examining the drawings closely.

"Most of them," she says, not missing a beat in packing as she continues, "My father used to help."

I admire her talent.

"Quite an artist," Aamon says.

"Yeah, I have a photographic memory," she says, not even looking at us.

She moves to the laptop on her desk and shoves it in her duffel bag. She then grabs a sketchbook and pencil case and places them into the bag and zips it up. "Ready to go?"

"Yep," I say, heading to the window, but she doesn't follow. "What are you waiting for?"

"Something's wrong," she says, stiffening and dropping her bag. She quickly heads down stairs.

We look around, but we don't find anything. She morphs into her wolf form and begins to sniff around. I am able to fully see her as a wolf, she is white with a black stripe down both her sides starting at her eyes, and a black tip tail. Her eyes are yellow. She looks stunning. In a heartbeat, a wolf appears and tackles Rose to the floor. Rose whimpers as the wolf holds her down and snaps his jaws only inches from her face. The wolf has brown fur with no markings or visible attachments to a pack.

Aamon and I turn wolf and attack the new comer, but Rose is doing fine on her own, she has managed to knock the wolf off of her and pin it down. I help her hold it down while Aamon finds the weak point. The weak point of a wolf is a place on the back of its neck where if pushed with enough pressure will force a wolf to shift to a human and render them unconscious. Aamon eventually finds the spot and the wolf is in human form and out stone cold.

"Garth?" Rose exclaims, moving backwards.

"You know him?" I ask, looking at her and she nods.

"Yeah, he is my mother's new lover," she stammers, running to the window.

Outside a white she-wolf paces. She has no makings or visible ties to a pack.

"Pure Bloods," Aamon glowers as his face hardens in disgust.

"What?" Rose asks turning to Aamon.

"When a wolf is created by a bite, it has unnatural markings, but when a werewolf is born it has no markings," Aamon explains. "Pure bloods seldom live in packs. Most pure bloods will only be with another wolf if the pair are mated. They find us non-pure bloods beneath them."

"So who is the she-wolf?" I ask, leaning on the window.

"How should I know?" Rose answers shrugging.

"Well, let's get out of here before *he* wakes up," Aamon says, heading upstairs and we follow.

Rose grabs her duffel bag and heads to the window, but not the plank. She jumps and my heart pounds. She lands flawlessly, and Aamon and I follow. However, I am not as graceful, I land awkwardly and fall face first into the dirt. Without missing a beat, Aamon hauls me up and we go to the side of the house where Rose is peeking around to the front, checking to see if the she wolf still remains.

"Clear," she says and we make a run to the hummer fleeing without ever being seen.

When we arrive home, everyone welcomes Rose with a smile, but I know that in a couple of minutes all smiles will be gone.

3. The Beach

-Rose-

I start to make my way down to the basement, with my bag in hand and my hopes low. Zero stops me and gestures for me to follow. I follow as he leads me into a decent sized room with metal walls and a metal door, with its own bathroom and a king sized bed. I turn to look at Zero.

"What is this?" I ask, raising an eyebrow.

"Your new room," he shrugs as I drop my bag.

"I see Zero has shown you to your room," Aamon says, coming in. A growl automatically erupts from my throat.

"Yes," I say, sitting on the bed as the rest of the pack enters. "What's going on?"

"We are short of money," Aamon replies, speaking more to the others, than to me. "With three new mouths to feed, money is going to run dry quickly. James and I cannot be the only ones to provide for the pack. Some of you will need to get jobs."

"I can get one at the coffee house," I say, perking up, thinking if I can get a job then I could probably escape.

"No, not necessary," he says shutting me down.

"Why?"

"Because you won't be leaving this room, and you have dropped out of school today."

"What!" I shout, standing up and everyone except Aamon and Zero changes. "This isn't fair! I don't see Samantha locked up."

"Because you ran away," he says calmly. They all leave and I hear the door lock several times. I start banging my fists against the door, and as my anger rises, I change into the wolf and scratch and claw at the doorframe. But the only damage I do is a couple of dints and scratch marks. I soon realize there is no escape and feeling defeated I turn back to my human form.

"You can't do this!" I shout. "Let me out! Please."

With no response, I crawl into the bed. I pull out my sketchbook and begin to draw. I draw until I fall asleep with my face pressed to the page. I am awoken by the slamming of my metal door and sit up quickly looking around. On the floor I find a plate with cold pizza on it. My stomach growls and I realize how hungry I am. Before I can think about it I snatch the pizza off the plate and scoff it down. It tastes horrible.

When the pizza is gone I stare at the white ceramic plate. I pick it up and turn it in my hands as anger surges through me. I shouldn't have eaten the pizza. I scrunch up my nose and then launch the plate at the door; it shatters into pieces and I smile. They are punishing me for running away. What rational person willingly stays in a house full of monsters?

As I crawl back into bed, I wish for this nightmare to be over. But of course, my wish does not come true. I awake the next morning in my metal room. I go into the bathroom and take a shower, washing my hair and scrubbing the filth from my body. I wrap myself in a towel and walk out into the bedroom to find Zero looking at my sketchbook on the bed. I jump back in surprise as he stands and looks at the floor.

"Sorry," he stammers, looking away.

"It's okay," I say, going to my bag on the bed. I take clothes out and duck back into the bathroom. "I'm just going to change."

"Take your time," he calls out. I change into a tank top and dark blue skinny jeans.

"Hi," Zero says nervously as I step back into the room.

"Don't you have school?" I ask, putting my hands on my hips.

"No, mother," Zero laughs, rolling his eyes and crossing his arms over his chest. "You do realize it is Saturday."

"So, what are you doing here?" I ask raising an eyebrow and walking over to my draws.

"It is training day," Zero explains, walking over to the door and opening it. "Aamon takes us all out to train and to sharpen our skills. Most of us are only a few months older than you. Believe it or not, becoming a werewolf takes time to adjust. So I'm here to collect you."

"Why do I need an escort?" I ask and Zero sighs.

"You know the answer to that," he responds.

I roll my eyes as he walks out of my room. I follow him closely and when we reach the kitchen door he turns to me.

"There is one other thing," he says, picking up a chain and collar.

"You have to wear this."

-Zero-

I swear Rose looks as if she might kill me. Her hands are placed on her hips and her eyes glare daggers at my face. However, she does not protest as I buckle the collar around her neck and lead her outside.

"This is so degrading," she hisses. "What if I were to morph right now, would the collar snap?"

"No," I say, as we meet up with the others. "It would simply expand as you do. Aamon brought it from a very shifty man online."

"So, there is a possibility that it might not work?" Rose asks, hopeful.

Aamon approaches us and takes the chain from my hands. "It works," he snarls. "I tested it myself."

"Kinky," she smirks.

Aamon's eyes flare as he yanks the chain, forcing Rose to the ground. Aamon chains Rose to a tree and then walks away. Rose smirks as she sits up with her back against the tree; her hair shines as the sun kisses her body.

Aamon claps his hands turning the attention to him.

"Here is how this is going to work," he says, addressing the newest members of the pack. "I want each of you to fight with the wolf of my choosing. I want to see what I am working with."

He pairs James and Caleb together, and orders them to fight in their werewolf forms. Caleb has speed and agility, but James has strength and age, the fight was close, it almost seemed like Caleb would win. However, he is stunned when James bites down on his leg. Caleb has never fought as a werewolf before. As a werewolf, our pain tolerance is increased. James takes Caleb's brief pause to his advantage. He kicks his back legs up and pushes Caleb to the ground, and then bites down on Caleb's throat. James doesn't bite Caleb hard enough to hurt him, just enough to get the message across. Caleb has lost.

Next, Aamon pairs Shea and Samantha together. The fight gets messy, blood drips from the both of them, but because Shea is cocky. She falters a lot, thus allowing Samantha to win.

Aamon is eager to start the next fight, he orders me to fight Rose.

I don't want to fight her, but if I don't, Shea will. Rose was unchained from the tree, but the collar remains. The pack forms a circle around us. Rose walks to the middle then stands with a bored look on her face. Upon Aamon's demand, Rose morphs into a werewolf and growls at me.

"I'm going to tail you," Aamon whispers and I shift into my wolf form. Tailing is a method in which a werewolf can protect another werewolf in its pack magically. So if Rose's anger forces her to kill me, I will be revived. A werewolf can only tail once.

I circle her and she stays the same. I emit dangerous territorial growls as I walk, but she isn't fazed, her lips are curled and her teeth gleam at me. She follows my every move, watching me with her yellow eyes. I launch myself at her and she flattens her ears and moves aside. I land wrong and my feet slip out from under me. I look back just as she launches at me and she grabs onto the back of my neck and throws me away as if I were trash. I get up quickly and we engage in battle. We run at each other and rear onto our hind legs, scratching and biting each other. Rose yelps as I get a better footing and take her down, but she is smart and doesn't stay down long.

With a bark, she brings up her hind legs and pushes me off before I can make the final blow. We size each other up and begin to circle each other. The pack is silent, watching our every move. Foolishly, I let a twig snap distract me and Rose takes the opportunity. She leaps off the ground and onto my back 'killing' me with a bite to the neck. I fall to the dirt and roll into submissive position, but almost immediately am revived.

Aamon walks over to us and slips his hand under Rose's collar dragging her back to her chain and hooks her back to the tree.

"That was all right," he says, shaking his head. "Rose, you should work on you form."

"What?" she exclaimed turning human. "I beat him!"

"But it was sloppy," he replies.

She looks like she was going to argue, but was cut off by a blood curdling howl. We all turn to see a pack of pure blood wolves twice the size of our pack come into the clearing. They all howl again and our pack morphs into our werewolf form.

"*I've never seen so many together,*" Dante whimpers, stepping back, behind me.

"*State your business,*" Aamon demands, projecting his thoughts to them.

"*We came for her,*" one says, nodding towards Rose, who perks her ears up, but then growls and flattens them against her head.

"*Why?*" I ask, pulling my lips back and opening my mouth with a growl.

"*That is none of your business, pup,*" he growls, saliva drops from his mouth. He and his pack begin to charge after seeing that we won't let her go.

No matter how much Rose annoys Aamon, he would never leave her to fight for herself. She is a part of the pack, after all. The pack and I charge to the intruders, but Rose remains pulling on the chain.

-Rose-

I pull and pull, but to no avail. The tree is strong with a thick trunk. The collar around my neck chokes me. I scratch at the dirt and tense up as two black wolves walk over to me and I snarl at them.

"*Come with us,*" one male says, stepping close to me. "*And we won't tie you up or lock you in a pen.*"

I look at the fight and then back to the wolves.

"*We know where your sister is,*" the other says, and my ears flatten against my head.

"*Lilly is dead,*" I growl. She and I were twins, but she was taken eight years ago.

"*No, she is alive and a werewolf,*" the first male says and, after a brief pause, continues, "*So will you come with us?*"

I stare at the wolves in front of me. If there is a chance that my sister is alive I have to find her. I nod my head. One of the wolves turns into his human form and he unbuckles the collar and lets it fall to the ground.

I run with them and the rest of pack follows behind us. My name is howled on the wind, but I don't stop, I run with the black wolves. There are about twenty wolves that I run with and they all form a circle around me. We arrive at a house and the two wolves who freed me walk me inside, shifting their forms as they walk through the door. I follow them, keeping my wolf form. I snarl at every man or woman I see. My hackles remain raised and my muscles remain tense.

"Sir," the male says, walking me into a large living room. "We have brought her."

"Thank you, Seth," the man says. His voice is so familiar. "You can leave."

"Yes, Sir," he says, and he and the other man leave the room. The man in question stands with his back towards me. I growl deeply and he turns. My growl falters as I see his face—no different from when I last saw him, my *father*. My wolf form fades away and I stand facing the man I thought to be long dead.

"Dad?" I ask, my voice shaking.

"Yes, it's really me," he says.

I run to him he takes me in his arms and holds me tight.

"Why didn't you tell me?" I ask, stepping back with tears running down my face.

"I couldn't. It's our law that a human mustn't know about us," he answers, wiping my tears and kissing my forehead.

"Were you born this way?" I ask pulling back.

"Yes. I faked my death because my pack needed me," he responds, turning away from me.

He takes a dagger from the table besides him.

"What is this all about?" I ask, raising an eyebrow and placing my hands on my hips.

"We need you to go and rescue your sister, who's held captive in a vampire coven," my father says, handing the weapon to me.

"Vampire coven?" I gape.

My father hands me a loaded gun and extra ammunition and says, "Yes, vampires are real."

I strap the gun to my other thigh as he continues, "And they pack a hell of a bite." Next he pulls out a map of Mercy Lake and lays it on the table. Then he hands me an earpiece.

"The house is located here," my father says, pointing to the map. I move closer for a better look.

"Will I have back up?" I ask, putting the earpiece into my ear.

"No," he says and I tense. "But I believe you can do it."

"Why can't you do it?" I ask and my father sighs.

"The vampires have our scents," he explains. "They will smell us coming from a mile away. Once you have your sister, go back to your pack."

"Go back to the pack?" I gape. "Why?"

"Because my pack and I are leaving the country. You and your sister need to stay here." he says. "You don't belong with pure bloods."

I open my mouth to argue with him, but he glares at me, silencing my protests. He then shoves a needle into my arm.

"Ouch!" I shout, stepping back. "What was that for?"

"We will need to track you, to guide you to your sister," he replies.

"Why is she there anyway?" I ask, rubbing my arm.

"Collecting information," is all he says.

"Will I find a ten-year-old her?" I ask, remembering that she disappeared around that age.

"No, she was changed a month before you. "You need to go now," he says as the sun starts to set.

"Be swift, and silent," he cautions, leading me out of the house.

I morph into a wolf and take off running. My father directs me to an old house that is barely holding itself together.

"Rose?" says a voice similar to mine through my earpiece. "Could you hurry up?"

"Lilly?" I gape, changing to my human form.

"Yeah," she whispers, and I hear voices in the background. I walk onto the old, wooden porch. I give an exaggerated sigh and silently pray to the gods for strength before kicking the door. As soon as the door swings open I see a hoard of what I assume to be vampires. I point my gun at them and they growl, they don't look like the stories suggest. They have a round head with no eyes or noses and a mouth full of pointed teeth. Their skin is pale grey and they have four hands and two feet. They attack me as soon as I step inside. I fire my gun at them and they drop quickly. I hear more coming—their growls echo off the walls as they stalk towards me. Some walk on two legs, while others prowl using their hands.

"What are they?" I ask, putting a bullet into the head of the one closest to me.

"How should I know? Just hurry up," Lilly's voice hisses through the communicator.

I bear my teeth at the monsters as they growl at me moving forward slowly. I roll my shoulders and hope for the best as I shift form. I stare at the vampires through my werewolf eyes, and they back away from me ducking their heads. I step forward snarling as I walk past the vampires. I walk into the old broken kitchen. Blood stains the walls and I move quickly as panic rises. I change to my human form as I walk down to the cellar following the only other werewolf scent.

"Rose, I'm in here," Lilly calls from down the end.

"Coming," I call, running to her. She sits in a small cage away from the bars. When I place my hand on the bars my skin burns and blisters.

"It's made of silver," Lilly says.

I scrunch my face and then look around the cellar. I cannot find anything to open the cage. I go back to Lilly and she stares at me, watching my every move. I look at the lock on the cage and then take a pin from my hair. I pick the lock and quickly pull it open, ignoring the burning of my hands. I hand Lilly my gun and dagger as I morph into my wolf form. We race back upstairs where the vampires are waiting. They screech and scream at the sight of us. We have to pass through the kitchen, killing all that stand in our way.

We are almost out the door when a vampire jumps on Lilly; she falls onto her back. I snap at the beast and charge before it has time to bite her. I leap and knock the vampire back and hear its bones crack. It lets out an ear-piercing wail. I slam my paw onto its face, causing it to cave in and blood to burst up onto my leg. It is still screaming and I bite its neck decapitating it.

"I owe you," Lilly says as we burst outside.

"You're welcome," I say, turning human.

The vampires follow us outside.

"Hey, dad, we could really use back up now," I say into the communicator, but there is nothing but static. "Dad?"

"He has left to flee the country, remember?" Lilly shouts. "He won't have signal."

I groan and turn wolf. Lilly follows my lead and she looks exactly like me, but with a blue stripe down her side. We run and I take lead in returning to the pack. We slow to a half run as the sun starts to kiss the earth. I see the house on the horizon and we pick up the pace again.

"Is this the house?" Lilly pants, turning human.

"Yeah," I pant trying the door again. "It's locked."

Lilly rolls her eyes and then bangs her fist on the door.

-Zero-

There was a knock followed by several kicks at the door. I get up from the chair in the kitchen, surprised that no one else has awoken from the noise. I go to the door, unlock it, and open it to find Rose and another Rose. I look at the one on the right.

"Rose?" I ask, raising an eyebrow and looking from one to another.

"No," she says. "Lilly."

"What?" I stammer in confusion.

"I'm Lilly," she responds, and then points to the other one. "That's Rose."

I look at them both and recognize the difference. Lilly has more freckles and lighter hair than Rose. Rose is also slightly taller. Then I realize that there is blood splattered all over their clothes.

"Are you going to let us in?" Rose asks.

"What the hell happened?" I ask, not moving a muscle.

"Details can be reached inside," Lilly says, pushing her way inside.

I let them in and lock the door again. Lilly places a gun and a dagger onto the table as she and Rose takes a seat. They look like they haven't sat down in years.

"What is with the blood?" I ask, crossing my arms.

"Well," Rose began. "The black wolves took me to my father were I got the weapons, then I had to walk into a vampire nest to save my helpless twin here," she says, pointing to Lilly.

"I'm not helpless— you saw me with that gun," she snapped, making Rose laugh.

"You missed like half of them."

"Wait," I say, cutting in. "Slow down. I thought that you said your father was dead and you never said you had a sister."

"I did think that my father was dead," Rose grumbles. "Turns out he is a werewolf— a pure blood. He faked his death because his pack needed him."

"What exactly did you kill out there?" I ask, noticing the black blood oozing down her skin.

"Oh, you know," Lilly starts. "Pale-grey body, mouth full of teeth."

"Four arms, two legs, no eyes, human vessel," Rose continues.

"They are not vampires," Aamon says coming down the stairs. Both girls jump to their feet and turn to face Aamon.

"How long have you been standing there?" Lilly asks.

"Long enough. The things that you faced weren't vampires, they are vampire demons."

"What is the difference?" Rose asks as she and Lilly take their seats again.

"Vampire demons are summoned by warlocks— a vampires best friend," he says, taking a seat at the table. "They look after the vampire's mansions while there are gone away for a certain amount of time."

"What other paranormal monsters are out there?" Rose asks, throwing up her hands. "Wait, don't answer that. I don't want to know."

"Fine, how about we talk about you running with the pure bloods?"

"They told me they knew that my sister was alive!" Rose shouts, jumping to her feet. "Of course, I would go with them!"

"It was irresponsible and stupid!" Aamon shouts back, standing and placing his hands flat on the table with a loud bang.

"I found my sister! I would do anything for her, like you would for you pack!"

"That is different," Aamon says, lowering his voice. "You brought an unmarked wolf here. She is not part of my pack."

"I beg to differ," Lilly says rising from her seat then walking away from the table where she takes her wolf form. She looks exactly like Rose with the exception of having blue marks instead of black. *I am part of your pack.*

"Who made you?" Aamon asks as she takes human form once again.

"Little grey wolf—Dante," she says turning back. "My father helped me fight the urge to come here. Instead, I kept an eye on my sister in keeping with my father's instructions," she says, eyeing me.

Aamon says nothing in return. Instead he sends them upstairs and into the metal room. Aamon follows them upstairs and locks the door behind them before returning back downstairs.

"What are we going to do?" I ask, rubbing my eyes.

"I don't know," he sighs, taking the weapons from the table. "Maybe we should let them go."

"Let them go? What do you mean?"

"Make them into Rogues," he sighs, sitting back down.

"No!" I exclaim. To make a werewolf rogue is dangerous. Most of them lose their minds and lose the ability to transform to a human. "Let me talk to them, please."

"What does it matter? We can make new ones next full moon."

"NO! Please, let me talk to her. Please. I'll make sure she won't run away again," I argue.

Aamon looks at me, pondering my suggestion. "You can try, but first they will remain in solitude for a week to cool down and adjust to this situation."

I head upstairs and unlock the room. I walk in and Lilly is lying on the bed. She looks fresh out of the shower with some of Rose's clothes on. I could hear the shower going.

"Rose shouldn't be long," Lilly says, not looking at me.

"You two really look alike," I say, leaning on a wall.

"Really?" she says sarcastically. "We are only identical twins." She sits and looks at me, her eyes blue like Rose's. "Do you have a girlfriend?"

"Are you offering?" I smile, winking at her in a playful way.

"No," she scoffs, looking over my shoulder. "Rose might be though."

"What!" she exclaims, standing in the doorway of the bathroom. She is wearing a black tank top and blue jeans.

"You should see your face right now," Lilly laughs hysterically as she lay back down. "You look hilarious!"

"Not funny, Lil," Rose laughs, throwing a pillow at her. They look so happy to be together again, but as she turns to me she has a worried look on her face. "What's up, Zero?"

"Aamon is considering stripping your marks and leaving you out with the Rogues. I'm here to convince you to stop running away and fighting us."

"Fine, I won't run," she says, and I am surprised at how easy that was. "Plus, dad told us to stay put, anyway."

"You will have to stay in this room for a week without protest to prove to Aamon your sincerity."

"No problem," says Rose and Lilly in unison.

"I have had more than enough excitement to last me for a long time and besides it will give me plenty of time to catch up with my sister," adds Rose.

"Well, that was easy," I mumble as she takes a seat next to Lilly. I stay and talk about the rules and regulations of the pack and what must be done every day. I tell them how Aamon will let them out of the room and house if they follow the rules and are home by midnight. They agree and I stand to leave, but Rose pulls me up outside the door and closes it behind her.

"Thank you," she says.

"What for?"

"For talking to Aamon. I heard every word."

"Oh," I blush. "It's okay."

"No, I owe you one," she says, standing on tiptoes and kissing my cheek. "Thank you."

"No problem," I say as she opens the door and goes in. I feel like I had the power to do anything now.

-Rose-

"I owe you one," Lilly says mocking me in a high-pitched voice.

"Oh shut up, would you?" I groan, throwing a pillow at her.

"So, you do like him? He is hot!" she says and I sigh.

He is hot yes, but he doesn't feel the same way. I felt him tense when I kissed his cheek and I have seen him and Shea in class. There is something between them and I can't interrupt it for some schoolgirl crush.

"Why did dad leave again?" I ask, changing the subject.

"The vampires had sent the demons after him," she sighs, her mood somber.

"Why?"

"Because I stole something from the nest's queen and they blame him."

"What did you steal?" I ask and she pulls a ring off of her finger. "What is that?"

"I stole this ring. It's highly valuable to her." Lilly smiles. "I just got too cocky."

"Why?"

"Because I wanted to prove to father that I could be a part of his pack," Lilly says, flinging the ring across the room. "But I got caught."

"I thought that you didn't know the difference between vampires and vampire demons," I question.

Lilly shrugs and lies back on the bed.

"I knew what they were," she admits. "I just didn't know which ones were the demon and which were the vampire."

"So what do the vampires look like?" I ask.

"They look like normal people for the most part," she sighs. "And they have four fangs they use to suck blood. They have super strength and speed. A wood stake through the heart would cause them to die straight away. They are deathly afraid of fire and their skin is like lighter fluid— extremely flammable. But they can heal from being burnt alive."

"Well," I say on a lighter note. "At least they don't sparkle."

"Yeah," she laughs.

We spend the next week talking and telling each other about our lives, eating the food that Zero brings to us, but never seeing anyone else and never leaving our room. One morning I turn as the door opens expecting Zero with our breakfast, but to my delight Samantha and Caleb walk in.

"We heard that you were back," Samantha says looking at Lilly. "Didn't know you had a twin, though."

"This is Lilly," I say and notice Caleb staring. "Wipe the drool."

We all laugh except Lilly; she blushes and ducks her head. I look at Lilly and raise my eyebrows. She looks at me and smiles lightly.

"What are you doing here, anyway?" I ask, looking away from her and back to my friends.

"We came to see if you guys wanted to come outside, seeing how you're allowed to now," Samantha says.

I turn them down making an excuse, but Lilly jumps up and walks out with them. There is a quiet knock on the door and Zero walks in with a basket full of clothes. I sit up and look at him. He is wearing a flannelette shirt and jeans. He smiles at me and something ignites in my soul—it spreads through me like wild fire.

"Just getting clothes for James to wash," he says nodding to the basket in his arms.

"Oh, okay," I say, hopping up and going into the bathroom. I grab our pile of dirty clothes and take them out to him.

"Here you go," I say, placing them in the basket in his hands. I go back and sit on the bed. I hear him sigh and leave, closing the door quietly. I sigh, then roll over onto my stomach. My mind always trails back to Zero and his smile, his eyes, and his body. But the feeling I feel for him is weird and completely animalistic, like it is my wolf that is drawn to him.

I growl deep in my chest and then roll onto my back as a hot blush spreads over my cheeks, down my neck, and into my chest. The door opens suddenly and I sit up so quickly that spots dance in my vision. Zero steps into the room and my cheeks deepen in colour.

"I wanted to know if you wanted to go for a walk with me," he asks, smiling at me.

"Everyone is gone and I was wondering if I could show you my favourite place."

"Okay," I say, getting up and putting on a pair of sneakers. We head downstairs and out the door. He takes his wolf form and so do I. We run and I feel like I belong next to him.

-Zero-

I take Rose to the beach. We walk onto the sand as humans, making sure that no one saw our wolf form. The wind is soft and gentle against our skin. Rose looks at me with wide eyes that sparkle in amazement.

"What?" I ask, and she looks up at me.

"This is not what I pictured when you said your favourite place," she says, taking off her shoes and leaving them under a tree.

"Oh, and what did you think my favourite place would be?" I ask, raising an eyebrow.

"Oh, I don't know," she says, reaching the water. "Maybe a boxing ring or something."

"Do I look like the boxing type?" I tease, crossing my arms over my chest.

"No, I suppose not," she laughs and comes up to me, placing her hands on my arms. "You are too soft."

"What makes you say that?" I ask, raising my eyebrow again.

"Well, for one," she says, sweeping me off my feet and into the sand. "You just got beaten by a girl."

I jump up and go to tackle her, but she is too fast and dodged the attack. I chase her down the beach then back up again. She runs into the sea and dives. After a while she comes back up and smiles at me. I take off my shirt and run in after her. She half swims, half runs away, but I catch her and wrap her in my arms, content with the idea of never letting her go. She looks up at me smiling and I smile back. She reaches up and runs her hand through my hair. Our faces are only centimetres away from each other, but it isn't enough. I close the gap and kiss her, wrapping my arms tight around her body. The surprising part is that she is kissing me back! Her arms wrap around me, her lips feel soft on mine. The waves were not too rough and everything feels right. I have kissed a lot of girls but not like this. It feels so right.

The feeling is shattered by the feeling of being watched. I pull away and scan the beach to find a figure walking onto the beach and then to the edge of the water. He looks straight at us as his lips turn into a smile. Rose and I wade onto the beach and the stranger looks at Rose and bows.

"Miss Rose Salamander," he says, smiling.

"Yes, that's me," she says tensely.

"May I speak with you? Privately?" he asks, glaring at me.

She looks terrified of the new stranger, who happens to be a vampire.

"Why do you need to talk to her?" I growl, stepping in front of her.

"That is none of your concern," he says, flashing his fangs. "Don't try and play hero, not to me, boy. I could tear you to pieces in a single moment."

"Um," Rose starts breaking the tension. "Okay."

"Rose," I hiss, looking at her. "He is a vampire, plus he just said that he can tear me apart in a minute."

"And you're a werewolf," he says, rolling his eyes. "I won't hurt her."

"Zero, it's okay," Rose says pushing me. "Go home. I will be back before midnight."

I begin to protest, but with one look from Rose I decide otherwise. I pick up my shirt and leave.

"Good boy," says the vampire and I growl at him.

4. The Confusion

-Rose-

After Zero is out of hearing range the stranger turns to me. "Shall we walk?"

"Yes," I say as we start walking. "Who are you and what do you want?"

"Do you know what you are?" he asks, smiling. He is taller than me with dark hair and dark eyes and he looks to be in his late thirties.

"I am a werewolf," I say and he laughs. He is beginning to irritate me and I clench my fist. "I don't like being laughed at."

"My apologies," he says, taking control of himself. "I just came to tell you that you need to call your father as soon as possible."

"How do you know my father?" I ask, anger in my voice.

"I'm a friend of his and your mother, too," he says as we turn around and head back in the direction we came. "You need to call him as soon as possible." H hands me a card with his number on it. "We will be in touch, Rose."

And he left me there while he makes his way to the dunes. What the hell was that about? Who is he? Why did he say I needed to call dad so soon after he left? Is he in trouble? Questions were filling my head and making me angry, but I forget them as I touch my lips and feel the blood flow to my cheeks.

Zero kissed me and I loved it— he was so soft and gentle to me. But I want something more; rougher and animalistic. I guess he isn't dating Shea after all. I walk up to the dunes, collect my shoes, and head home. Walking was taking longer than I thought it would so I slip on my shoes. I take on my wolf form and set out at a slow run. Half way home I was tackled side on. I'm up on my feet in an instant and see Zero. He is laughing when he turns human.

"Now, we are even," he laughs.

"We will never be even, Zero Dunn," I laugh back, turning human.

"What did that guy want?" he asks as his face turns serious.

"Uh," I say, walking. "He knows my father and mother, and said that I need to call my dad ASAP."

"Is that really all?" he says, taking my hand in his. He's too protective; a definite turn off for me.

"Yes, that's it." I smile and he wraps me in his arms and squeezes me. I pull away and say. "Last one home is a rotten egg."

I turn wolf before he could reply and take off sprinting toward home. He is hot on my heels, but I manage to get home before him.

"First!" I shout, turning human and touching the house and he arrives just a second later.

"You cheated," he panted, turning human with a smile. My stomached tightened and something didn't feel right.

"Whatever you say, rotten egg," I laugh going inside and taking my shoes off as the feeling passes. Zero heads to the fridge and pulls out two bottles of water and throws one at me. I catch it and take a drink. A moment later, the rest of the pack piles through the door, laughing and pushing each other. Shea comes in after them and scowls at me. I give her a smile hoping to kill her with kindness.

I look around and I can't see my sister or Caleb. I groan and ask Zero where Caleb's room is. He gives me directions and I make my way upstairs and walk into the room to find Caleb and Lilly laying on each other playing tonsil tennis. I roll my eyes and clear my throat; they jump in surprise and push away from each other. I start to laugh and they throw a pillow at me. I duck my head and go out, closing the door and, in turning too quickly, I bump right into Zero and stumble. As I do, he catches me and sets me right.

"Better watch out, rotten egg," I say, steadying myself. "I might knock you off your feet again."

"Don't tempt me," he says, handing my phone to me. "Aamon said that you may call your dad and keep the phone."

"Really?" I say, taking the phone and hugging him. "Thank you!" I let go, head to my room and dial the number on the card. After three rings my dad picks up.

"Hello, Rose," he says his voice sounds rough and raspy.

"Hi, dad," I reply with concern. "What's up?"

"Listen, sweet heart, you need to know something."

"What?" I say, my voice turning serious.

"Your mother and I are not human and you weren't born human, either."

"Is mum a paranormal?" I ask taking a guess. "A werewolf?"

"No, your mother is not a werewolf," he says, then, after a while, he adds. "She is a witch."

I almost drop the phone, "A witch?"

"Yes, she is a witch, and so are you."

I drop the phone this time but quickly recover it. "What do you mean?"

"Well, not actually a witch. More a werewitch. You have the gene of a wolf from me and the gene of a witch from your mother. We didn't know about it until your first birthday when you manipulated a knife to get yourself a piece of cake. Your mother knew then. The next night, she summoned a circle of paranormal to bind your werewolf and witch genes to the powers, or commonly known as the elements. This is why I got you to call. You need to be released from the bond—next Wednesday at Mercy Lake. The Circle has been summoned. If you are not released the witch power could kill you. Do you understand, Rose?"

"Yes," I said weakly. "What is The Circle?"

"It is a powerful group of paranormals of the same bloodline as the Circle that bound you. It is made up of a vampire from the nest of Tylorn, a witch from the coven Roy, a warlock from the coven, Webster, a Fey from the charm of Marsh, a ghost from the fraid of Macintosh and a werewolf from the family of Dunn."

"What is a warlock, a fey and a ghost? Are they like the stories say?" I stammer, trying to get things straight.

"I can't talk any longer, honey, I have to go," he says and the line goes dead. I scream and throw my phone at the wall and it shatters into pieces. I sit on the bed and tuck my legs to my chest and cry.

I remember something my dad said, "*A werewolf from the family of Dunn.*"

Zero

Tears flow from my eyes and I hear the door softly open then click shut. I did not dare to look up. Arms wrap around me and I uncurl from the ball and look up at Zero's eyes.

"What happened?" he asks, his voice soft and kind.

"Do you know much about you family history?" I ask, wiping tears from my eyes.

"Yes, quite a lot actually," he says wearily. "It's actually ironic. Father is a werewolf and my mother, a human— I got my mother's genes. They sheltered me from the truth. When I was bitten and turned, my father disowned me, saying that I was a disgrace to the purebloods of the family."

"That's horrible," I gape, staring into his eyes.

He shrugs his shoulders and sighs. "He was killed a few days after I was turned," Zero says. "He attacked Aamon. Aamon took me under his protection and I've never really thought about it since. When my father died my mother gave me all of his things before leaving town. I have a book on his life and my family's history. I'll go and get it."

He leaves and is soon back holding an ancient book with papers and sticky notes poking out of it. He sits next to me and hands me the book. I flip through the pages and find a page with the tenth of July as the date.

I read:

10 July 1995

Today, Dixie came to me carrying a small child no older than my own son. She asked for help. Her baby needs the binding. She said that she has summoned the circle and needs my help as a member of the wolf clan. Of course, I said yes because she was my best friend. She told me to meet her at the edge of Mercy Lake tonight at 11:40. I asked why the child needs binding and she made me swear an oath not to tell anyone but the next generation of Dunn's. She told me of the child curse: werewitch. I could not believe my ears. This has only happened once according to history and the other child is now dead. I refused to let that happen to this child; the child was Dixie's child and I could not let that happen. I met Dixie at 11:40 at Mercy Lake. She was standing in the middle of a circle with the child wrapped in a blanket. I took my place in the circle and looked around. Among us were some of our friends that I had long forgotten. Dixie had torches with the mark of all of the different paranormal. She placed them in front of us, and then she gave us all different objects. Mine was the father's wedding ring; she told us that these objects would help the bond.

The torches lit in a sudden blaze as she started to chant. The fires started to change to different colours and the wind picked up. When she finished, the fire from the torches jumped out and wrapped around our wrists. She said that this was a vow. The fire did not burn our skins but the Vampire, Jace Tylorn, jumped more than all of us. Dixie asked us if we would keep the secret, only passing it onto the next generation. We all vowed to keep the secret and the fire died. She began to chant again, and we joined her as the fire blazed higher and higher until we finished chanting until it died. Dixie told us that the bond would need to be broken in the month of the next Warik. We all agreed to meet on the 20th January 2012 for the child to be unbound. If we were unable to attend, a member of our bloodline would attend in our stead. Every one headed home like nothing had happened.

I stared in disbelief, but it was true. I am a werewitch. I wonder if Zero knows. I start to shake and Zero touches my arm.

"Are you okay?" he asks and I shake my head.

"Next Wednesday," I whisper.

"Yes, that's when I have to go and 'unbind' this child," he says, taking the book and placing it gently on the floor.

"So, you have the ring?" I ask, raising an eyebrow.

"Yes, the child's father's ring is in my possession," he says, pulling out a ring on a necklace. "I've never taken it off since the day my mother gave it to me."

"Why is the gender not noted?" I ask, eyeing the book.

"For the child's protection. Anyone could find the child from the gender and mother's name."

The effort of the day catches up with me and I am totally exhausted. I move closer to Zero, curling up and resting my head on his chest. He wraps his arms around me and kisses me gently on top of my head. I wonder how I am going to tell him that I am the werewitch child and what his reaction will be. In the comfort of his arms I soon drift off to sleep.

-Zero-

She has fallen asleep on me and she looks so peaceful. I start to wonder why she was so interested in the werewitch child. But I forget it when she snuggles in tighter to me. Lilly quietly walks into the room and looks at Rose, then to me.

"Where the hell am I meant to sleep tonight?" she whispers. I look at the clock and see that it is seven o'clock.

"Caleb's room," I suggest and she nods, then turns and leaves. I slowly lie down next to Rose and fall asleep.

When I wake up, Rose is still asleep on my chest and my arms have gone dead with pins and needles. I smell bacon, eggs, and toast cooking downstairs. I think Rose does too because she starts to stir and slowly wakes up. She looks up at me and smiles. She gently kisses my lips then sits up and yawns.

"Morning," I say, sitting up and moving my hands and arms in an effort to circulate blood.

"I am in desperate need of a shower," she laughs. "Go downstairs and I'll meet you there."

I laugh as she runs into the bathroom, then get up and go downstairs. I see Aamon talking to some man at the kitchen table. James is at the stove cooking breakfast and listening to the conversation. The man sees me and smiles.

"This must be Zero Dunn," he says, getting up as I make my way to the table; he shakes my hand. "My name is Luke Salamander." He says and gestures for me to sit. I do.

"You're Rose and Lilly's father?" I ask.

"Yes, and you are the son of Kate and Mark Dunn," he says. "Do you know about the ritual on Wednesday?"

"Yes, but the question is how do you know?" I ask and lean forward.

"Oh, so she hasn't told you," a woman says, coming into the house wearing a long black dress with a black hooded riding cloak and another folded in her hand.

"Who are you?" I ask.

"My name is Dixie Salamander." I freeze. Dixie is the name of the one in the book. "Where is Rose?"

"What's it to you?" I ask. She twitches her hand and the air in my lungs leave me and I fall to the floor gasping for air. I hear a scream from the stairs and see Rose running towards me.

"Mother!" she screams. "What are you doing?"

Her mother smiles and twitches her hand back again and I can breathe. Rose kneels beside me and helps me sit up.

"What the hell was that!" she yells, glaring at her mother.

"We needed to know where you were," she replies, taking a seat.

"Why?"

"The ritual needs to be done tonight. I have summoned the powers and the Circle."

"What ritual?" I ask, getting up confused.

"Why don't you tell him, Rose," her mother asks, putting her hands on her hips. Rose stood up and glares at her mum.

"The werewitch ritual," Rose mumbles, looking away from me and my heart clenches.

"You are the werewitch?" I stutter, my eyes widen.

"I was going to tell you, Zero. I was, but," she says hanging her head. I go to say something but her mother takes her arm and leads her out of the house whispering something to Luke before she leaves. Luke turns to me and gives me a sad smile.

"She always gets her way," he sighs. "Come with me."

I follow silently as he leads me to a house in the woods. He unlocks the door and ushers me into the dining room before walking off down a hall. The dining room is filled with roses and lilies.

The Vampire I met yesterday is seated across the table. "Hey, wolf boy," the vampire says. "Name's Jace Tylorn."

"Zero," I say gruffly.

"I know, I heard you on the beach," he replies. Jace introduces me to the others in the room. "This is Emily Mey, she is fey, and this witch is Tamika Roy." The Fey and Witch are both around my age. They nod their heads as I say hello. Next Jace leads me to the men standing near the door to the kitchen. "These are my closest friends. Peter Webster is a ghost, and this is Paul Macintosh. He is a warlock." We shake hands and nod to each other.

The paranormals are different than what I thought. The ghost looks like an ordinary human, but I have learned that they can pass through walls and can become invisible when they choose. They can also possess any other being that has a soul and can borrow powers from other paranormal beings. Faeries are human-sized with wings resembling leaves coming out of their backs, and they can manipulate some aspects of the elements. Warlocks draw their power from the negative energy that surrounds our world. They have the power to create and destroy any demon they want and can mutate plants and animals. The most powerful of all paranormal beings are the witches. They draw their power from the positive or white energy that surrounds us. Witches can transform themselves into any being, animal, or object they desire and can also change any object, animal, or being into whatever they want. They can disappear and reappear at will and have the greatest power of all the paranormals to manipulate objects.

Luke returns and hands us all black outfits to wear and orders us to change. For the females it is a simple long black dress. The males are given black tee shirts, black pants, and duster coats. We are all left inside the house until nightfall, then Luke returns to collect us and tell us how the ritual will work.

-Rose-

My mother takes me to a house where she make me dress in a long black dress and black heels. She applies black lipstick, mascara, eyeliner,

and paints my nails black. I feel as if I'm dressing for Halloween. When night falls, my mother leads me out of the house by my arm.

"What are we doing?" I ask.

"We are getting you to Mercy Lake to remove the binding," she says stiffly.

"But why?" I ask, almost tripping on a stick. "Why not on Wednesday?"

"Because by then it would be too late," she hisses and I flinch backwards. "No more questions."

We arrive at Mercy Lake and she glances at her silver watch. "It is only nine thirty," she sighs as my father arrives. "We shall prepare now, and, Rose, you can walk along the lake or something."

I glare at her but begin to walk. I look back at Zero but he is talking to the stranger from the beach. I leave them behind and start walking. The wind is prickling my skin and causes my hair to whip past my fase as I think about everything that is happening.

"Please," I whisper, remembering the other child. "I don't want to die."

"Who says you will?" a voice says from behind me. I spin and see four people: two female and two male. They are all covered by tattoos, but they are not normal tattoos. One female has all green tattoos of vines, rocks, and leaves. The other has water drops and waterfalls in blue tattoos. One male has red fireballs and lava tattooed on him while the other has what appears to be a very light ice-blue curvy lines tattooed all over his body that looks like they are moving. I jump back in surprise and almost fall straight into the water, but one of the males is by my side in a heartbeat. He helps me up and we go back to the others.

"Who are you?" I ask, glaring at them and the man with the red tattoos scoffs.

"My dear," says the one with vines that ripple as she talks. "We are the *powers*. My name is Theresa."

"My name is Vulcer," says the one with fire, making a ball of flame in his hands.

"I am Hydra," says a female, making water fly at the ball of flame.

"And my name is Aither," says the last male, bowing as a gust of wind rushes past. "And you are not going to die."

"What about that other child werewitch? He died." I point out with a raised eyebrow.

"He chose to use his powers for evil," Theresa says, shrugging. "I have looked into your heart I see nothing but kindness."

"But, we will watch over you, making sure that you don't change your mind," Vulcer says, making his skin burn bright with a smile.

"You are scaring the poor child," Hydra says, glaring at him.

"I'm not a child," I say almost in a growl.

"Aither, stay with her," Theresa says. "We must check on something."

And in a blink of an eye they leave. Aither sighs and turns around, and the tattoos all vanish. He looks my age and has sandy blond hair and blue eyes.

"How long have you been a power?" I ask, breaking the tension.

"Almost a year. My father just stepped down," he says, putting his hands on his head and letting out a breath.

"Rose!" a voice calls out. I turn around and see Zero walking toward us.

"Who is that?" Aither asks as his breath prickles my skin. "Your boyfriend?"

"That is Zero," I say, pressing my lips together.

"Should I be jealous?" he asks with a slight chuckle.

"No," I scoff, turning around walking away from Zero. I hear Aither laugh as he catches up to me. Zero calls my name again but I ignore him and keep walking. Zero turns wolf and runs to me.

"Rose," he says, touching my arm.

"What!" I shout, yanking my arm away. I look at him and he freezes when he sees Aither.

"What is wrong?" Zero asks, focusing his attention back on me. It feels like the world is crashing down around me.

What is wrong with me?

"I don't know," I whisper, shaking my head and running a hand through my hair. "I just need time to think."

"It's almost midnight," he says roughly, his eyes widening as the other powers came into sight. "What the hell?"

"Rose, we need to talk," Theresa says.

I turn to Zero and sigh. "Whatever you need to say, you can say to both of us," I say turning to the Powers and Aither's tattoos appear again.

"Fine. That woman up there is not your mother," Vulcer says and my heart races.

"Vulcer!" Hydra hisses and looks at me. "She has your mother captive and the only way to get her out is to go forward with the Ritual and then take her power."

I don't say anything, I hang my head and remember the last sentence I said to my mother, *I hate you.*

"I'm sorry," Theresa says, "but you have to go now. We will be with you even if you can't see us. If you need help just call."

Zero and I walk back to the spot where 'my mother' is. She has drawn a circle and placed the torches around it and leads me into the middle of the circle.

"Just say whatever comes to mind," 'my mother' says as soon as she is out of the circle. The paranormals all place an object down at their feet. Zero places his father's ring down, the stranger places down a single clear earring stud, I see the witch place a large claw tied to a string down— I am guessing a tiger or bear claw, the fey places a red rose sealed in a resin at her feet, the ghost sets a vile of crystal blue water down and he smiles at me, and the warlock takes off a ruby necklace and places it on the ground. As soon as the necklace hits the ground the torches spring to life and my mind goes blank. Words fly through my mind and I begin to recite them.

"*Earth, fire, water, and air*
Release me from your hidden lair
By the sight of the flame, the tree, the air and sea
Undo the spell you cast onto me
With the witness of the Werewolf and the Witch
Undo the magical stitch,"
As those words leave my mouth, the torch of the wolf and witch dims.
"*With the witness of the Vampire and Fey*
Undo all you say."

Two more torches dims and I continue,

"*With the witness of the Warlock and Ghost*
Release my soul from its mortal host."

As the last torch dims, the wind picks up and I start to speak in Latin.

"*Dimittere mea anima et fiat eam ire, dimittere mea anima et fiat eam ire, dimittere mea anima et fiat eam ire!*"

The torches spring to life again and the flames latch onto the paranormals' wrists. I close my eyes and continue to chant. The wind gets stronger and my dress flies in the wind. I'm hit with a force like something is entering my body; I stop chanting and embrace the power. It's short lived because I feel a stabbing pain just below my ribs. I collapse, the fires dies, and the wind stops. I look up to find the woman who was acting as my mother standing over me with a bloody knife. I hear Zero yell but the woman puts up a shield between us.

"Finally," she says with a sharp breath. "I can take your powers."

"No," I moan, clutching where she stabbed me as I roll to my side.

"Oh, yes," she says, bringing her foot down onto my leg. I hear a loud crack and I scream, knowing that my leg is broken. "Then I shall kill every single one of your friends." She brings her foot down onto my other leg and I scream louder curling into a ball. "Paranormal or not."

"No," I whimper, thinking of Zero and the other innocents. She drops the shield and look up to Zero and his eyes go wide.

"Should I start with the dog?" she asks. By the looks of it, she has glued them to the spot with her powers. She starts to walk to Zero and grabs his face. "He is handsome. Do you love her?" she asks Zero.

"Yes," he mummers, clenching his teeth.

"You have feelings for this freak of nature?"

"Yes!" he shouts.

Tears sting my eyes and my heart races as she walks back to me.

"How about you? Do you like the dog?" she asks. I don't answer and she stands on my leg and pain races through me, making me scream. "I can't hear you."

I scream, and she walks over to Zero and raises the knife to his neck.

"NO!" I scream, raising my hand and I feel a force flow out of my fingers and a yellow light hit's the woman.

Her eyes widen as she drops the knife; she hisses, turns, and begins to walk to me.

"Help," I murmur and she is stopped in her tracks when a fire surrounds her. I see the powers step into view. Vulcer's tattoos are flaming brighter than all of them. Aither rushes to me and kneels next to me. I groan as energy flows out of me.

"*You have abused your power, I will take them and give them to the child to keep,*" Theresa says in Latin to the woman. Suddenly, I have an intense feeling of being hit with energy again, but this time it hurts like being hit in the stomach. I gasp and Aither is leaning over me. I feel as if I can't breathe and I straighten out and start to gasp like a fish out of water. Aither leans over me and touches his lips to mine, giving his warm breathe to me. I wrap my arms around him and accept his gift, but he is torn away and I'm left gasping again. I look over to see Zero yelling at Aither whose tattoos are glowing just like Vulcer's.

"Leave her alone!" Zero shouts.

"If you want her to die, then I will," Aither says, putting his hands up.

"What do you mean? How can she die from not being kissed?" Zero asks.

"I am the element of air, I wasn't kissing her," Aither says, laughing.

"Guys!" Hydra shouts. "She is going to die. There is no time to explain the situation."

My eyelids start to drop.

"Save her!" Zero shouts at Aither. Aither moves next to me, his lips on mine again, breathing into me. I wrap around him as my lungs start to fill with oxygen once more. After a while he moves off me and I can breathe again, but that does not stop me from passing out. My eyes roll as the pain slams into me. I close my eyes and slump into the dirt.

-Zero-

"I thought that you said you were saving her!" I shout as Rose falls to the ground.

"I did," the air dude says, picking her up. "She fainted because she is in a great deal of pain."

I stand in shock as he starts to walk away with Rose in his arms and another guy by his side.

"What do we do now?" Jace asks as he and the rest of the paranormals gather behind me.

"We all go back to Zero's place," says the woman with the green tattoos as she picks the knife off the ground.

"What about me?" the woman asks, still surrounded by flames. The other just looks at her and throws the knife—too fast for the naked eye. It sinks straight into her heart. She fell into the fire and was engulfed, burning her to ashes in seconds. The knife thrower is joined by another woman who makes water fly from her hands and onto the fire. Water woman and knife chick walk in the direction that fire and air boy went carrying Rose. The rest of the paranormals stand there for a while confused and in shock. Moving like zombies, we pick up our objects and follow the element to Aamon's house. When we get there, the four elements are standing at the door talking with Aamon. Air boy is still holding Rose, although she is now awake. Aamon spots me and the other paranormal.

"I can't fit everybody in this house," Aamon says, nodding towards me.

"Well, you will have to make room," the knife lady says. "They are all Rose's guardians, bound to her and sworn to protect her."

"Who the hell are you again?" James asks appearing at the door.

"I am Theresa, element of earth," she sighs as her tattoos seem to tighten around her.

James gasps and mumbles an apology.

"I'm Hydra, element of water," says the other woman.

"These are our brothers: Vulcer, element of fire, and that is Aither, element of air," Theresa says, pointing to air boy.

Aamon sighs and moves so that we can all pile inside. Aither walks in and places Rose on one of the couches. Rose flinches as she touches the couch, then sighs in pain. Caleb, Samantha, Lilly, Dante, and Shea all walk into the room. They look at Rose and then at rest of us.

"What happened?" Lilly asks, walking to Rose.

"Got in some trouble," Rose says with a small laugh then winces in pain. "But I'm a werewitch now."

"Damn girl, turn my back for one minute and you go and almost get you killed," Lilly says, laughing.

Theresa walks over to Rose and places her hands on her legs. She murmurs something and Rose's legs heal.

"We would love to stay and chat," Theresa says. "But Mother Earth has requested our presence at the great hall."

They all just vanish into thin air. Aamon sighs and takes a seat on a wooden chair.

"I think we all need to sleep. It has been a long day," Aamon says, rubbing his hands over his eyes. "Everyone is going to have to bunk up tonight. Zero and the Vampire, Shea with the Fey, Samantha and the witch, Caleb, Dante, Warlock and the Ghost will all bunk together. Am I missing anyone?" he asks standing.

"Rose and Lilly," Shea says, rolling her eyes and folding her arms over her chest.

"They bunk together," Aamon says, shooing us upstairs. We all sigh and begin to walk upstairs. I let Jace into my room and flop onto the bed; I turn my head to see Jace standing at the door awkwardly. I sigh and slide off of the bed and stand across from him.

"If you think that I am going to sleep on a bed with another man, you are mistaken," Jace says, leaning on the door.

"You have the bed I will have the floor," I say, turning wolf and laying down. He steps over me and crawls into the bed. Before long I fall asleep and dream about Rose; she and I are back at the circle.

I walk over to her and go to take her in my arms, but she turns away.

"What are you doing?" she asks, growling in a territorial wolf growl.

"I thought you liked me," I say confused.

"Did I say that when I was asked?" she snarls and I realize she didn't.

"Why?" I say.

She looks at me and her eyes flash yellow. She turns wolf and growls at me. *"WHY!"* she growls. *"You made me like this!"* She turns away and runs off into the woods.

"Rose!" I shout after her. *"Rose! I'm sorry."*

I am woken with a cold jolt to find Jace standing over me with an empty cup in his hand. He smiles at me and I find that I am human again.

"I'm guessing that you were dreaming about a certain flower?" Jace asks, smiling. I can see his fangs through his smile and it gives me the chills.

"What gives you that idea?" I ask, sitting up and rubbing the back of my neck.

"You were screaming, 'Rose! Rose I'm so sorry'," he laughs, mocking me.

I get up fast and glare at him.

"What time is it?" I ask, changing the subject.

"About eight o'clock," he says, going outside. I follow shaking my hair along the way to dry it. We go downstairs to see Luke and the woman from last night. I turn wolf and tackle her to the ground. I stand over her with my snout just inches from her face. The blurs are too fast and too strong for me to catch, and I'm knocked sideways. I turn to see Rose and Lilly as wolves growling at me with their backs to the woman.

"What the hell!" I shout. "This woman tried to kill us, and yet you guard her like a dog would a bone."

"Theresa killed that woman, this is my actual mother," Rose says, turning human and then helping the woman up and embracing her.

"You've got to be kidding me," I growl. "How do we know that this is not another impostor?"

"I think that I would know my own mother," she snaps.

"Yeah," I scoff turning human. "Like last time."

I didn't even see her move, but one minute she was standing there with her mouth hanging open and the next she was running at me.

I growl and take my wolf form. So does she. I make the first move and lunge at her. She dodges, then runs through the door and I chase her. As soon as I am out of the door she attacks me and I play the role of defense, blocking, then throwing back the attacks. Rose's 'Mum' comes out and rolls her eyes. She holds up her hands and then twists them. I see Rose drop, then I follow.

"It is just a simple paralyze spell," Rose's mum says. "Stop fighting."

Rose's mother walks back inside and I pull Rose aside.

"Rose," I say holding her arm in my hand. "I am concerned about you. We don't know the full story of this werewitch business. There are too many secrets being kept, and I don't know how to protect you."

"I don't need protecting," Rose spits, pulling her arm out of my grip.

"I am just concerned that your mother might be using you for your powers," I say calmly.

Rose growls deep in her chest. "She is my mother!" Rose hisses, walking inside and away from me.

-Rose-

I can't believe that he would say that to me! Insinuating that my mother would use me. When I see my mother inside she looks guilty of something, her head is low and she doesn't look me in the eye.

"Rose," my mother says. "We need to talk."

"Sure," I say, my heart beating loudly. Something is wrong. "What's up?"

"Your Father, sister, and I are leaving. We're going back to my home town, New Salem."

"To get away from me," I ask harshly. "I get it."

"I'm sorry," mum says softly. "It's too dangerous for us."

"What about *me*?" I scream. "Isn't it dangerous for me, too?"

"I don't want to leave Rose!" Lilly shouts, standing from her seat at the table. "And I won't."

"New Salem is paranormal paradise," Dad sighs, rubbing the back of his neck.

"But not for a filthy mix-blood like me," I spit, anger boiling up in my throat.

"I'm sorry, but that is the way it is," my mother says.

"Can I come?" a voice asks from the stairs, Caleb. My mother nods and glances over his shoulder to the others.

"I would like to get out of Mercy Lake," Samantha agrees.

"You got to be kidding?" I say with a growl in my chest. "Caleb only wants to go with Lilly and you're his sheep!"

"Calm down, Rose," Aamon says from the sink.

"Calm Down? You have to be joking!" I shout, going to the door and opening it. "I am losing everyone!"

I slam the door shut and turn wolf, I run. I guess Zero was wrong, my mother doesn't want to use me. She wants to leave me and is scared of me. I run to the only place that I can think of; the only place where I am pretty sure they won't find me: Sam's house. I don't know if he is even home, but I take my chances since his parents work early at the police station.

His parent's house also has its back to the woods, but it has a picket fence guarding it from wild animals. When we were kids, Sam and I loosened some pickets as an emergency exit from the tree house we made in the tree close to the fence. I find the loose pickets and squeeze through and notice that the sun is now shining full in the sky. I hear the front door shut and keys rattle.

"Sam!" I shout running to the front door. I round the corner and almost run into him.

"Rose," he says pulling up short. "What are you doing?"

"Sorry," I say, noticing the motorbike helmet in his hand. "Are you on the way to school?"

"Yeah, but I thinking of taking a sick day. Come in," he says, going back to the door and opening it. I walk in after him and close the door. He removes his jacket and places it on the table with his keys and helmet. I turn and meet his eyes, and when I do, they are not normal. His pupils are dilated and his hands are in fists.

"What is-" I start but I am cut off. Sam has moved like a blur and has a hand around my throat. I gasp and stagger backwards and he pushes me against the wall and slams my head backwards causing my vision to blur.

"Who the hell are you?" he yells.

"Rose," I gasp as his hand tightens on my throat. "I'm Rose."

"No, you don't smell like Rose, witch," he snarls, revealing fangs. He's a vampire. "Rose is a wolf, you're a witch. Now where is she?"

"How did you know that I was a wolf?" I gasp and he tightens his grip and snarls again.

"I know that *Rose* is a wolf, because I smelt it on her at the hospital." I struggle and his grip tightens once more. "You smell like a witch."

"I am a werewitch," I gasp, clawing at his wrist with no affect. "I am still Rose!"

"Prove it. Tell me something only Rose would know."

I rack my brain and try to think of something only I would know. "The tree house," I rasp, my windpipe is being crushed under his hand.

"What about it?" he says, loosening his grip a little.

"It's where we kissed on my fifteenth birthday," his grip lessened more and I see his eyes narrow as he thinks of that day. It was my fifteenth birthday and Sam and I went to the tree house to celebrate. We stayed up late talking and laughing, and then it happened. He leaned across the couch that we were sitting on and kissed me— sweet and passionate. My first kiss.

Sam lets go of my throat and I collapse to the floor and gasp for air.

"You smell of witch, but also of wolf," he says and I look up at him. "Why?"

"I'm a werewitch," I gasp and his eyes widen. He studies me for a moment before he moves with lightning fast speed and knocks me to the floor. He holds my arms down with his hands. He is too heavy to kick off and fear races through me. His eyes narrow as he leans down and his lips brush my neck. My body goes stiff as he pierces my skin with his fangs. I scream out in agony, but Sam clamps his hands over my mouth. When he removes his fangs, he pushes away from me and gasps. My blood stains his mouth, but when I put my hand to my neck I feel nothing, the wounds have healed.

"How?" he asked.

I start to explain everything right in that hallway, from being bitten to running away. I didn't keep anything out.

"Caleb and Samantha, too?" he asks and I nod.

"Your turn," I say, standing up and stretching.

"What?" he says, standing as well and walking into the lounge room where we both sit.

"Your time for a story. How did you get all-" I say, mimicking fangs in my neck. "Vamped out?"

"Last year," he sighs. "Vampire attacked the house, killing mum and dad."

"You've been alone all this time?" I say as sadness fills my heart.

"Yeah," he sighs, getting comfortable. "The vamp turned me and then left. I'm coping."

"What about the whole sun thing?"

"Sun thing?" he asks, raising an eyebrow.

"Doesn't the sun burn you?" I ask, remembering old folk law.

"Nah, that is a lie made by the vamps so the people would be less suspecting," he says, chuckling. "What are you doing here again?"

"I need to get away. I don't like it back at the-," I was cut off as a loud explosion sounds in the hall. We jump to our feet to see the hallway in flames..

"Vampires don't like fire, that is no lie," Sam says, his voice quavering. Demons come out of the hall growling and snapping their jaws. Behind me Sam hisses.

I racked my brain for an answer and a spell comes into my head. I start to see words fly at me and I say them in my mind.

Fire, Fire burning bright

Fire, Fire Douse your light

I repeat the words in my head over and over again, and the fire dies. Sam hisses again showing our other problem, the demons. I turn wolf and growl at them. There has to at least be a dozen of them with more coming in. I lunge towards them and start to fend them off, but they are fast and able to cling to walls. Sam is attacking, biting, and tearing their heads off. I jump and tackle some, biting and tearing their heads off as well. They were coming fast and in numbers.

"We can't hold them off much longer!" Sam shouts. I go to answer, but a cloud of smoke appears and the demons retreat a little. An African American woman wearing a cloak that covers her face steps forwards with a grin.

"Wherever you go, whoever knows the truth, trouble shall come," she says as a window shatters in the other hall. My Guardians run into the living room ready to defend me. The cloaked woman points to every single one from the Circle. "Heed my warning. This girl is trouble; she is a disease."

She snaps her fingers and she disappears, along with her demons.

I stand there. *What just happened?* I think, but I don't stay long enough to find out. I run.

-Zero-

She runs straight out of the house. I take off after her and the Guardians follow. I find her standing on the edge of a cliff looking out at the beach. You can see everything from up here, from the town to the lake. She is crying and my heart clenches. I walk slowly to her and touch her shoulder. She spins around and looks at me with red eyes from crying. Before I can even open my mouth, she wraps her arms around me in a tight hug. I put my arms around her and tell the other Guardians to leave. Once we're alone, we sit away from the ledge, her arms still around me.

"I'm losing everyone," she sighs and looks out on the horizon.

"You will never lose me," I say, holding her hand.

"I'm afraid that I must," she sighs. "In order to protect you."

"What do you mean?" I ask, turning her to look into my eyes. She closes her eyes and shakes her head.

"She was right. Trouble finds me and hurts anyone who knows what I am."

"We will work it out," I say as she opens her eyes. "We will."

She shakes her head again and kisses my cheek. "No," she whispers. "We won't. *I* will."

"How?"

"I have the strength and knowledge of two witches, I will figure it out."

"No, you need us to help," I say, nodding to the direction where the Guardians had stood. She stands up and shakes her head and begins to walk back home. I sigh and walk after her in silence. There is an eerie feeling hanging in the air, but I ignore it as Rose takes my hand and leads me inside. There, she calls everyone –including the Guardians and Sam- into the living room. She begins to talk but is cut off by her mother.

"One moment," she says handing a key to Rose. "The house is yours and there is a car parked in the garage as an early birthday present. Go ahead."

"Stand Still," Rose says with a powerful force.

"What?" I try to say, but the words don't form. I cannot move, and neither can any of the others. Rose looks at me and gives me a sad smile.

"You will remember what I tell you to remember," Rose starts turning to her parents. "Mum, Dad, you believe that Lilly and I are dead. You will move to New Salem and live your life." They both faint as she turns to Lilly. "Lilly, you go to school, but to you I am just a werewolf. You live in the house with me." She drops as well and my mind races trying to find a way out this. "Aamon, Dante, James, Shea, Samantha, and Caleb, your lives will go on as before the whole werewitch thing happened. Aamon, you have let me live in my own house with Lilly." They drop. "Circle, the ritual was a fail and I am just a werewolf," they faint. "Sam, I know what you are, and you know that I am a werewolf." He drops as she then turns to me. "Zero, I am the wolf you turned." Darkness.

5. Starting Over

-Zero-

I wake with a pounding headache in a trashed room. There is something missing though. I feel like I have just woken up from a dream. There are glass bottles and plastic cups and plates everywhere and Rose is at the sink running water over her face.

"What happened?" I ask, getting up and rubbing my head. She turns the water off and turns around with a smile that seems hollow.

"You guys sure know how to throw a party," she says, leaning on the sink. I hear another groan and look around. I notice another girl like Rose get up and make her way to the sink.

"Who is she," I ask, my head is a little foggy.

"I'm Lilly. Dante turned me and I'm her twin, remember?" she asks, filling a cup with water and gulping it down. "Great party by the way, it was crazy."

"I don't remember a thing," I say, taking a seat at the table.

"Of course, you don't. You drank so much. Have fun with that hangover," Rose says, bringing me a cup of water, then sliding her duffel bag over her shoulder. "We need to get going Lilly. Zero, remind the pack that I will be back tonight."

"Where are you going?" I ask.

"Home," she says, jingling a set of keys. "We need to sort out living arrangements."

"Are you driving?" I ask, remembering that Aamon is allowing them to stay at their own place.

"Yes," she says going to the door. "I didn't drink anything,"

They leave and I'm alone with the pack knocked out. I try to remember what happened last night, but it's all blurred and fuzzy around the edges. All I remember is drinking and passing out. I groan and rest my head on the table. The rest of the pack wake up and complain about the mess. I tell them that Rose and Lilly have gone home, and then we start cleaning. It takes about an hour and a half to tidy the house back up. Aamon tells us that we can take the day off of school so we can work off our hangovers.

Everyone runs out the house and heads off in different directions to shop or hunt, but I decide to go over to Rose's place. Something about her makes my heart flutter. On the way, I pass the paddock where Rose is keeping the horses. They whinny at me and run over. I give some of them a pat and head to the house. I look at her window in the attic and see her walk past. I smile at her beauty, then make my way into the stables and climb up into the loft and cross the beam that leads to her room. I softly knock on her window. She comes to the window.

"What are you doing here?" she asks, opening the window and letting me in.

"Aamon said that we could have the day off, so I came to see you," I say, jumping through the window.

"Why?" she laughs a sweet and soft laugh, then walks over to a couch.

"Because I like you," I blurt.

She stops mid step and turns. "I like you, too."

-Rose-

"What?" I gape. This is not good; this is not what I planned.

"I have liked you for ages," he says, ducking his head. "I have never had the courage to say it out loud."

I sigh and shake my head. Why does this have to be so hard? I can't let my guard down around him. This is going to be very difficult to explain. I look at him and my eyes sting from holding back tears, his face loses all expression.

"What about the beach?" he asks, his voice quavering.

"Things are a little difficult now," I say, looking down at my hands. "I do like you, but at the moment-"

In a blink of an eye Zero pushes me up against the wall, holding my hands above my head.

"What are you doing?" I ask just over a whisper.

"Changing your mind," he says, and then his lips are on mine, his body pressed against mine. It is one of those kisses that make my knees weak and my heart race. His lips leave mine, but he stays just as close, still holding my hands up above my head. "How did I do?"

"Zero-" I groan, trying to wriggle out of his grasp.

He smiles at me and comes in for another kiss, this time more powerful, pressing closer and closer. I don't even know where my body ends and his starts. There is a sense of neediness and passion this time. It's a kiss that would make your parents faint and then ground you for life— a mind and life changing kiss. Zero lets my arms go and wraps his arms around my waist. I let my hands fall and then loop them around his neck. After a while he pulls away, then looks at me and smiles. I smile back and my knees feel weak.

"How did I do?" he asks.

"Good," I stammer. "Very good."

His smile widens as he kisses my cheek. I glance at my watch and gasp. I am almost late for my job interview. I push him away and run downstairs yelling at Lilly that I will be back soon. I grab my keys and bag from the table at the door. I jump into my new five door jeep wrangler and start it up. I have had my license for about a year now, but I haven't had a car to drive.

"Wow," Zero whistles jumping in beside me. "Nice."

I laugh and roll my eyes as I back out of the driveway. I drive over to the coffee diner and park the car.

Zero smiles at me and laughs. "You are so cute when you're rushed," he laughs as I jump out and bound through the door. The interview took a little longer than twenty minutes, but I got the job. They told me that I could start tomorrow at seven o'clock in the morning. I found Zero waiting for me in a booth with a coffee and a chocolate mocha with whipped cream and chocolate sauce on top. I slide in next to him and he smiles and slides the mocha to me.

"How did it go?" he asks.

"I start work tomorrow," I say, groaning then taking a mouthful of the sweet beverage.

"So, did I change your mind?" he flirts, slipping an arm around me. "Or do you need more persuading?"

"Very funny," I laugh, then stop to think about the situation. Zero leans in, his breath causing the hair on the back of my neck to rise.

"What do you think?" he breathes, nibbling on my ear, then kissing my neck. Can I do this straight after I took his memory? He continues to kiss my neck and nibble my ear. I let out a passionate hum and he returns it back. Oh god, how can I say no to this?

"You have persuaded me well enough," I mumble, closing my eyes.

He then trails kisses from my neck to my jaw line, and turns my head, causing my eyes to open and look at his. He kisses my lips softly and passionately. The door opens with a couple of high pitched screams. Zero and I pull apart to see the new comers, Cleo, bounds into the booth and is followed by the rest of the gang, except for Caleb. Cleo's boyfriend slides in after Cleo and puts an arm around her. They all fix me with wide eyes and big smiles.

"What?" I ask, getting uncomfortable with the stares.

"We saw you kissing!" Cleo says. "I need details and go slowly."

"It's nothing to talk about." I blush.

"Bull shit!" Samantha squeals. "We are in need of an all-girls gossip slash sleepover, ASAP!"

"I don't know," I say, glancing at Zero. "I have stuff going on at the moment. You are not listening to me."

"Exactly," Cleo says tapping her hands on the table in an excited jitter. "Otherwise, you would have talked us out of it."

"Fine," I sigh, sliding out of the booth. "I have to get home." Zero slides out and follows me.

"Hey, Zero," Sam says, calling Zero's attention back. "The girls will be busy that night, how about hanging with us?"

"Sure," Zero shrugs as I head for the door. "See you then."

I drive back home in complete silence with Zero next to me. When I get home I tell Zero to do the same. He complains for a while but he eventually heads home. I walk inside, lock the door and slide the deadbolts into place. I lean back into the door and sigh. I call out to tell Lilly that I am home and I am answered with a thump and giggles. I groan and tromp upstairs where I fling myself onto my bed. Lilly has gotten to second base with my best friend, fantastic...not! I smell the smell of death and rotting meat. I immediately bolt up into a sitting position and growl deep in my throat.

"That's not very nice," Jace says from the shadows.

"What do you want?" I sigh, rubbing my eyes. "Can't you see that I'm not the werewitch child?"

"I know that you are," he says as the smell leaves the room. I freeze and the hairs on the back of my neck rise. "I can smell your fear and hear your pulse is racing."

"How did you find out?" I ask, almost in a growl.

"For those spells to work you need a connection to the paranormal or person that you are going to use it on," he says, leaning on the wall near the window. "Whether that is an enemy or friend. It didn't work on the circle because we are not connected to you at all. By the way, how did you manage to get all of us out to the woods?"

I shrug my shoulder and sigh as I say, "If it didn't work, how come you guys passed out?"

"When a witch messes or screws up a spell the victim gets stunned, then faints." He shrugs, pushing off the wall, then using vampire speed to sit on the couch. I get uncomfortable with his presence.

"Why are you here?" I ask, eyeing him. "Because I don't remember inviting you to dinner for a long chit chat about the paranormal species."

"We are here to protect you," another voice says from the window. I turn and see the fairy perched on the windowsill.

"Who is we?" I ask, now fixing my icy glare on her.

"The circle, your Guardians," Jace explains and I mentally groan. "Two will be with you at all times. One you can see and the other at a distance."

"What about Zero? I don't want him to know," I ask. Jace seems to think about it for a while, he gets up to pace and rubs his chin.

"Not a hard question," I say after a while. He turns and glares at me, I send it right back.

"Alright," he sighs. "He is too weak anyway. You should find a human to turn on the next full moon."

"What!" I say, bolting to a stand. "Why?"

"Because you need a werewolf in the circle," Jace says. "It will help to stabilize your powers."

"Why do I have to turn a human?" I gasp. "Why can't we just find another wolf?"

"So you can control it. Tamika has put a spell on us so that any memory or compelling spells will not work on us," Jace warns.

"I have no need of anymore," I say giving up. "I would actually like to know about this paranormal business."

I then proceed to tell him everything about myself both past and present. Afterwards, Jace tells me about what is going to happen and how it is going to happen. Every night, starting tonight, a paranormal will come and teach me about themselves and their species. Also, there will be two paranormals guarding me from all who want to take my powers. After a lot of thinking, I start to tell Jace about Zero and me but his body tenses.

"What is it?" I ask and the hairs on my neck rises.

"Vampires, and demons," Jace says and his skin seems to ripple like when you throw a stone into the water. The fairy, now standing inside the window, leans out and gives an animal like call. A call returns and the fairy turns to Jace.

"How far away are they?" he asks and his skin ripples again.

"Not too close, but not too far," she nods and turns back to the window and calls again.

"Can I help?" I ask. Jace turns to me and shakes his head. "Come on, you know I can."

"Every fibre in my body is saying no," he sighs, but reluctantly gives in. "Fine, do you have weapons?"

"Yes, well, some," I say. He stands and shakes his head.

"You're a wolf, you will figure it out," he says as the fairy hands him a belt loaded with weapons.

"Why do you go against your own?" I ask. He sighs and clips his belt on, then turns and shakes his head. Down below we hear the loud crack of a door shattering to pieces. I hear a scream then two sets of growls. I run down the stairs and see Lilly and Caleb fighting off demons and vampires. I turn and growl at an incoming demon. It growls back and opens its mouth to show three rows of sharp pointed teeth and starts to run up the stairs to attack. I morph as I leap and tackle it down the stairs. I bite down on its neck and shake, decapitating it. I turn to see Jace and the fairy rushing down the stairs. Jace is firing two guns, and as the ammunition runs out, he takes out a sword and a dagger and continues to attack the creatures. The fairy unfolds two clear wings that are just visible and shrinks and flies straight into the mouth of a demon. It lets out a howl of pain as the fey emerges out of the beast's mouth. Now, however she is carrying a small dagger covered with blood. I am tackled from the side as a vampire pushes me to the ground. He leans on me with all his weight and his fangs slide down. He put so much pressure on my shoulder that I hear a crack and pain shoots from my shoulder up to my neck, causing me to yelp in pain. A silver slash comes out of nowhere and decapitates the vampire, and then my shoulder heals instantly. I am on my feet in seconds. I nod to Jace and he nods back, slicing another demon in half. I leap on an approaching vampire and bite and tear his head from its shoulders. Dark thick oozing blood covers my mouth as I continue to kill vampires and their demons. We continue to fight until there were none left. The house was covered from top to bottom in the blood of vampires and demons.

"Great," I pant, turning human. "This is going to take forever to get out."

"I can arrange for someone to come and clean it," Jace says, laughing.

"Excuse me!" Lilly shouts. "What the hell just happened?"

"We were attacked," I say, wiping my bloody hands on my jeans.

"Obviously," she scoffs, pointing around the room where all the blood is. There is a loud bang and Zero busts in the door.

-Zero-

I hear screaming from Rose's house and as I come into the house I find it covered in blood and Rose standing in the middle of it with Jace.

"What the hell happened?" I ask, looking at Jace. "What is he doing here?"

"*He* just helped *your* girlfriend fight off a dozen vampires with demons," Jace says, pointing around the room.

"Why is he here?" I ask, looking at Rose and she blushes.

"We were talking," she says in a whisper, and I untangle the words.

"You were sleeping with him," I translate, scowling.

"NO!" she shrieks, looking up in horror.

"Then what were you doing?" I ask, shaking my head in disbelief. "What were you '*talking*' about?"

Rose doesn't answer, confirming my fears. I shake my head and say, "Straight after you agreed on going out with me. That is harsh."

"No, it's not like that," Rose says with a pain in her voice.

"Then what is it?" I ask, folding my arms over my chest.

"I can't tell you, Zero," she says and I raise an eyebrow. "It is for your safety."

"Shouldn't I decide whether I want to be safe or not?" I ask, rolling my eyes.

"We didn't do anything," Jace says, stepping forward and I growl deep in my chest.

"We are over, Rose. I am leaving."

"Zero, wait! You have to believe me," she says, walking towards me as her tears fall.

"No! You have been trouble from the start," I yell, and she stops dead in her tracks and gaps at what I have just said. I turn and leave. Rose calls my name and I hear her start to come after me, but Jace pulls her back saying that I should just walk it off and I will be back later. Yeah, right. My anger boils over and I turn wolf and run into the woods. I run untill I get to a clearing. I pace back and forth growling, then lash out at the surrounding trees, biting and clawing them. I stop mid leap when I hear a giggle from behind me, I turn and growl at the intruder.

"All this for a silly little wolf girl?" a female vampire says, looking at the damage around the clearing. "Pathetic."

"What do you want," I growl, turning human. "I am not in the mood for the undead."

"Clearly," she scoffs, leaning on a tree. "But I can help you with your little dilemma."

"How?" I ask, tilting my head.

"My masters' master Lord Fen's birthday is coming up and he wants the perfect gift," she says, pushing off the tree. "And that little wolf girl is perfect. I have been watching her for a couple of days now. She is everything Lord Fen wants. I sent some of my comrades in to capture her, but it seems that she has company."

"What's in it for me?" I ask.

"Well, your little bitch of a girlfriend will be gone, and her new boyfriend Jace will be gone, too." She shrugs.

I think about the deal and something seems to snap in my head. "What would I have to do?" I ask.

"All you would have to do is deliver her to a certain location where my men will abduct her and take her to the lord's castle. It's that simple."

"When would you have me do it?" I ask, smiling.

"After hunter's season," she says, smiling back. Hunter's season is when a group of paranormal hunters come into town and try to rid the world of paranormals. It happens in Mercy Lake once a year for two months and it is coming up the next full moon.

"That sounds easy enough." I shrug. She walks over to me and places her hand on my chest.

"Great," she says, looking into my eyes. Her eyes narrow and I can't move. "Just one other thing, you can't go back on your promise or I will kill you."

I slowly nod my head and a twisted smile comes to her face.

"Great. I will be checking in on you every now and again," she says, releasing me and crouching down. Then with a powerful push she leaps off the ground and into the air landing in a close tree. She leaps again and again jumping from tree to tree.

I turn around and head back to the house. When I get there, the house is cleaned and four new people are standing in the house with Rose and Jace. My anger comes back when I hear them talking in hushed voices, but I keep it under control. Rose notices me, and everyone turns to look at me. I nod towards Rose and she nods back. She turns back to the group and continues to talk ignoring me and everything else. I shake my head and walk out of the door and head home. Aamon is waiting for me with shaking hands.

"We have bad news," he says, looking at me with blood shot eyes. "Call the pack."

I roll my eyes and walk back outside and turn wolf. I howl for a pack meeting and then go back inside, turning human as I go. Rose and Lilly were the first ones there with Jace trailing behind them. I stop him at the door and growl, "Pack members only."

"That's okay," Rose says over my shoulder to Jace, whose skin ripples and his fangs slide down. "Jace, wait for me outside. I will be there soon."

The rest of the pack arrives shortly after and we take our seats around the table and Aamon begins. "The hunters are coming this week," Aamon says. "They are going to be here on the full moon."

The whole pack stiffens except Rose.

"Who is coming?" she asks, and I snort and roll my eyes.

"Only the most ruthless and toughest paranormal hunters," Dante says. "They normally come later, why have they changed?"

"Because something has happened. Paranormal killings are increasing and Mercy Lake has become a beacon for the hunters," Aamon says. "They're coming in force and we need to prepare for the worst."

The whole pack goes into survival mode and we head down to the basement except for Rose and the new pack members, who have a confused look on their faces. I explain the whole situation of hunters and why they are here again.

"When the hunters are in town, we lock ourselves in the basement during the full moon so we are not tempted to go out and kill," I finish, crossing my arms.

"Why don't you fight for your land and protect the packs that do fight?" Rose asks, raising her eyebrows.

"Because it's not fair on them," I say, leaning on the bench. "They are just humans, and we are faster and stronger than they are."

"Well, count me out. I'm not planning on being locked up with a bunch of dogs," she says, pushing back her chair and walking to the door.

"Don't expect us to open the basement door for you when the hunters are after you," I say, pushing off the bench and walking to the basement with the new wolves. I hear Rose sigh and leave the house. My anger boils, but I keep it under control as we go through the drills and practice of being in the basement.

-Rose-

I meet Jace outside and we head back to the house where the powers are waiting.

"So, what did they want?" Jace asks, ducking under a low branch.

"They want to lock the pack up in the basement when the hunters come," I say, shrugging as we reach the house.

"That is a whole month away," Jace says, opening the door for me.

"Yeah, well, I guess the hunters decided to come early," I say, rubbing my neck and stepping inside and focusing my attention on the Powers. "Sorry," I say, taking a seat at the kitchen island. "Pack meeting and couldn't decline."

"That is okay," Theresa says, nodding towards me. A shiver races down my spine. "We understand."

"So, did you figure out why they attacked her?" Jace says to the powers and the circle. "Because I came up with nothing."

"We are working on it," Vulcer says, his tattoos flaming. "Stop ordering us around, or you will end up as a pile of ash."

"Whoa," I say, stepping between Vulcer and Jace, whose skin is rippling, "There's no need for that, he was just asking."

"I don't need to obey the likes of you either, werewitch," Vulcer says, flaming brighter and the circle tenses.

"Oh, for the love of God," Hydra says, grabbing Vulcer's arm, making her tattoos bright as well. "Chill out."

Vulcer's tattoos dim as Hydra's brightens. After a few seconds, she removes her hand and slaps him across the face.

"Stop being rude," she says as his mouth makes an O in shock.

"What exactly are we going to do about her?" Aither asks, nodding towards me.

"You are going to stay with her and never let her out of your sight," Theresa says.

"What!" everyone says in unison.

"Why me?" Aither says.

"Because you are the youngest and you need training," Teresa says, not phased at all by all of our gaping mouths.

"I'm pretty sure that the circle and I are capable of her safety," Jace says, moving forward.

"I'm sure you are," Theresa says, holding up a hand. "But with the help of a Power, her safety is more secure."

"Doesn't he have the air to control or something," I ask, not liking my situation.

"We still have the old air power. He will be able to work for us until we need Aither back," she says. We all look at her and wait for what she will do next. "Well, this has been fun, but we need to go. Aither, remember what you have to do." She disappears along with the other powers and Aither is left behind. Aither sighs and puts his hands behind his head, his tattoos disappear and he looks around the room. I roll my eyes and walk outside onto the back veranda. I lean over the railing and look over into the paddock to see all the horses prancing around. I push off the railing and walk over to the gate. I hate being treated like a child. I don't need to be looked after, I can hear everyone arguing in the house and I decide to take Indi and go for a ride.

I race into the stables and grab Indi's reigns and head over to the paddock again. Indi trots over and I give her a soft pat. She gives a soft whinny and I put her reigns on and open the gate. She follows me out happily and I mount her bare back and click her into a walk. We walk into the woods, and then go towards the other side into town. I stop Indi on the edge of the woods and dismount to walk along the footpath with the reigns in hand. As I'm walking, I bump into a guy my age.

"Sorry," I say, looking up into his eyes. "Guess I wasn't looking. Hey, you're in my history class."

"That's okay, and yes I am," he says, laughing. "But I haven't seen you since the second day."

"Sure as hell it isn't, missy," the man beside him says before I could say anything. This man was more likely to be his father.

"I said I was sorry," I stammer, taken back by the rudeness.

"Well, you should have been lookin' in the first place," he says. "What in hell is a little thing like you doing out at a time like this? Does your folks know where you are?"

I look around and notice that it's twilight.

"I can take care of myself, Sir, and my parents are gone," I say. From behind me, Indi snorts as she begins to munch on grass growing on the side of the footpath.

"Then who is lookin' out for ya?" he asks, crossing his arms, trying to make himself bigger.

"I am capable of looking after myself. I have lived here all my life," I say, rolling my eyes and placing my hands on my hips to make myself look tougher. "Now, if you don't mind, I need to go home."

"Just watch out, miss, there are plenty of things out there that would love to get them a piece of you," he says, moving aside.

"You're hunters," I gasp, putting two and two together.

"Yes, we are," he says, not even trying to hide it. "Don't worry, miss, we will get anything that shouldn't be."

My wolf form shudders beneath my skin and I continue to walk along with Indi behind me. I walk a couple of meters when I hear someone shout and the son runs up to me.

"Can I walk you home?" he asks when he catches up.

"Sure," I shrug, acting cool, even though the werewolf inside of me wants to turn and rip him apart.

"Thanks," he huffs and continues at my pace. "Sorry about my dad. He can get a little crazy at times."

"That's no problem. He's just looking out for me," I say, tugging on Indies reigns to make her catch up.

"Yeah, he does it too often," he says, then realizing where we are going he stops. "Whoa, where are you going?"

"Home," I say, stopping and turning around on my heels to face him.

"You live in the woods?" he asks, raising an eyebrow, and I can see the curiosity pull at him as he reaches for his belt where a leather tube is hanging.

"No, I live on the other side of the woods. This is the quickest way," I say, forcing a laugh, which helps him relax and he removes his hand from the tube. "What are you scared of? The big bad wolf?"

"No," he scoffs. "I just don't think that you would be able to fight anything if something did happen."

"I think that I would be able to look after myself quite well," I say, and my eyes flash yellow. I look away quickly and blink rapidly till the yellow disappears. I turn to face the stranger again and say, "Listen, I have to go home. Now you can either grow a pair and come or you can sit here shaking in your boots."

"Okay then, didn't expect that," he says, looking in the direction his father left in. "I guess I could come."

"Great," I say, mounting Indi and holding a hand down to him. "Hop on."

"Couldn't we walk?" he asks, stepping back a fraction.

"We could, but this way is quicker," I sigh, rolling my eyes. "Indi is the safest horse out here. She won't let you fall."

He sighs and takes my hand, and I help him climb up onto the horse. His big, lean body sits comfortably behind me.

"Hold on," I say with a smile.

"What?" he asks, but I have already clicked Indi into a steady gallop and he quickly grabs my waist and holds on. I laugh and ease Indi over a fallen log. He squeezes my waist and I gasp as dark and sinister images, as well as bight and happy ones, fill my brain, pushing on my skull. I subconsciously pull back on the reigns and Indi stops. He removes his hands and the images stop with the passing of a baby from one pair of hands to another, the child has my eyes.

My eyes snap open and they are yellow again. I slide off Indi and begin to run home. I hear him shout out to me, but I ignore him and once I know he is out of seeing range I leap and change into a wolf and sprint the rest of the way home. I change just before I hit the door and open it, then I bound into the living room and start to pace mumbling to myself. Aither and the circle rush in and begin asking questions about where I'd been and why I'd left, but I completely ignore them and continue to mumble and pace. Aither grabs me by the shoulders and shakes me.

"What is wrong," he says as I focus on him.

"What happened?" Jace asks, getting nervous.

"Guys give her room," Tamika says. moving towards Aither and me. He removes his hands and moves back. She goes to look into my yellow eyes and I see the images again, flashing in front of me and ending with the baby that has my eyes. I scream and shake my hands in front of me, tearing away the images.

"Take them away, make them stop!" I scream, dropping down to the floor and covering my head. Aither kneels down next to me and places a hand on me. Everyone stands in a circle around me and looks nervously at each other wondering what to do. Tears stream down my face as all the dark and evil memories replay over and over in my head. I feel a hand touch my back and Jace leans down next to me. I move away from him and closer to Aither. I weep more and he places his hands on my back, then slides me closer to him and I wrap around him in a sweet embrace. He returns the hug and rocks me back and forth. There was a knock on the door and my yellow eyes snap open as Jace goes to answer it.

"Hi, a girl left her horse out in the woods, and she told me that she lives on the opposite end of the woods," the stranger says. "The lady down the road said that she lives here."

"Yeah, she lives here," Jace says. "She is not really up to visitors, though."

"Ah, okay, well, I saw the stable outside. I'll just go put the horse in there and head home," I hear the stranger say.

"What's your name, friend?" Jace asks, his tone sharp and cruel.

"Tyler, Tyler Harding," he says, walking off to put Indi away. The dark images float through my mind again and I see an image with the Guardians and Aither fighting and dying, I reach out to try to protect them. Electricity flows out of me and onto the floor in the form of a circle, it grows until it reaches the Guardians' feet. They gasp as it leaps up onto each of their left wrists.

"Jace!" Tamika shouts and Jace runs into the room, the electricity jumps to his left wrist and pulls him closer to the circle. The electricity also takes Aither and my wrists. Our wrists all glow bright, then fade, leaving a metal manacle bracelet, where the light was. I look up at Aither's eyes and weep.

"Make it stop," I sob, turning into his chest and clutching on for life. I smell the sweet scent of spring and honey. Aither places his hand on the back of my head.

"Sleep in a sweet slumber," he whispers and I fall asleep. I dream of the springtime and flowers bursting everywhere, I dream of happiness and cute little animals.

When I wake, I am in my room and still in Aither's arms. He is gently stroking my hair and humming a slow and happy tune. I stir and he stops humming and releases me. I sit up and look around, all the Guardians are in my room whispering and discussing something. When they notice that I'm awake they quiet and turn to me.

"What happened, Rose?" Jace asks, walking closer to the bed. "Do you remember?"

"I..." I start, but I don't remember and stay silent.

"We need to keep a more careful eye on her," Aither says, finally breaking the silence. "She is never to leave any of our sights."

They all nod in response and then we all head down stairs where Lilly and Caleb are making breakfast, Lilly in a light shirt and shorts and Caleb in just shorts. Lilly looks from me to the rest of the gang and smiles.

"Big night was it?" she laughs, taking a sip of coffee.

"I could ask you the same question," I say, raising an eyebrow and she laughs. I sigh and turn to the Guardians, "Raid the fridge for all its worth, but be warned, I need to go shopping," they all look in the fridge for food except, Jace, Aither, and the ghost. I sigh and say, "Well, I am heading out to the shops and it would look really weird if you all came with me."

"I'll come," Aither says stiffly.

"Me too," Jace says, standing. "I need to do a little shopping myself, too."

"Okay then, when we get home we have to talk about certain arrangements," I say, grabbing my keys and wallet and heading out the door with Jace and Aither trailing behind. We drive to the shops in silence. When we get there, I make Jace and Aither push the carts as I walk and dump things into them— one for the paranormals and one for me and Lilly.

"So, what are we doing to do about your 'food'," I ask Jace.

"We can drive over to the blood bank and I can pick up some," he replies, dumping packets of seeds in his cart.

"What are they for?" I ask, noticing herbs and assorted vegetables.

"Tamika, will need them for spells and potions," he says in a hushed voice.

"What about you?" I ask Aither. "What do you need for food?"

"I don't need to eat," he says gruffly.

"Suit yourself," I shrug, taking an orange off the shelf and raising it to my nose.

"So, what are these manacles that you have so thoughtfully bestowed on us?" Jace asks, as I scrunch my face up and put the orange back.

"I don't know yet," I shrug as we reach the check out. We pay and drive to the blood bank where Jace leaves Aither and I alone in the car.

"Well, you're just a bundle of fun," I sigh, leaning back in my seat after about a minute of silence.

"I prefer the silence," Aither sighs, turning his gaze from the window to me.

"Sure," I say, rolling my eyes. "What's wrong?"

Aither ignores me, so I turn the radio on. I smile and tap on the steering wheel as Jace jumps into the back with a large blue cooler.

"Ugh, I am going to pretend that I don't know what's in that," I say, taking the car out of neutral and driving home. I pull up in the driveway and the Guardians rush out to help carry the food inside.

"Oh, how lucky am I to have people helping me at every waking second," I say as I open the back to get grocery bags out. I scrunch my nose and carry my share inside where we place the bags on the floor and Lilly and Caleb come to help us put it away. Afterwards, I tell Lilly that I am going into the hunting room and I don't want to be disturbed. I lead the Guardians and Aither down the hall and into the hunting room.

"Right," I say, settling on one of the couches. "We have a lot of issues to discuss, starting with living arrangements."

"What about them?" Jace asks.

"I can't have all of you guys living here at once," I say. "Aither has been told that he has to stay with me, so that makes one."

"Well, I can also stay in the house at all times," Jace says, taking a seat on another couch. "And the Guardians can be kept at a halfway house that I own."

"Sure," I shrug. "That will work, but I have rules."

"Lay them down," Jace says, folding his arms over his chest.

"Number one," I say, ticking them off on my fingers. "No using your powers unless in an emergency situation like we are under attack. Number two," I say, turning to Jace. "No drinking blood in my presence. And number three, please, please, please don't crowd me, and if I ask to be left alone, I please respect it."

"We can work with that," Jace says, standing up. "Now, we have some things that are in desperate need of discussing."

"What are these things?" the warlock asks, lifting his arm to show off his thick metal bracelet.

"This is the third time I have been asked!" I snap, my eyes turning yellow. "I am still trying to figure it out."

"Amazing," the ghost says, flowing over to me. "I have never seen this in a wolf. Her eyes turn yellow when she is angry."

"What might be the cause, Paul?" Jace asks, coming over to me as well.

"I'm not sure," he says, and my eyes grow more yellow as they continue to aggravate me.

"Enough!" I snap, my eyes growing bright yellow. I stand and make my way to the door. "This meeting is over."

I leave the room and take deep breaths until my eyes fade back to blue. I shake my head and walk out of the hall and into the kitchen. The house phone rings and I immediately pick it up. "Hello?" I say.

"Rose? Hi, it's James. Is Lilly close? I need to talk to both of you," he says.

"Sure," I say as Lilly comes into the room.

"I heard," she says as I turn on the speakerphone.

"You're on speaker," I say, laying it onto the counter.

"We are joining the Alpha pack tonight," he continues. "We will all meet at Aamon's tonight at nine o'clock."

"Wear black," James says and hangs up. We have about two hours to get ready. I sigh and leave Lilly and head up to my room and change into the black outfit my father gave me. I make my way downstairs where Caleb and Lilly are waiting. Caleb is wearing a black shirt and jeans, and Lilly is wearing the similar outfit to me. Aither and the Guardians stand in the middle of the room with their arms folded across their chests. As a precaution, I grab my gun and knife from the draws in the kitchen and place them into my thigh holsters before turning to the Guardians.

"Pack meeting," I say, heading to the door and grabbing my keys along the way. "I will be fine in a large group."

I head out the door and climb into the car. Lilly and Caleb arrive a second after. We drive over to Aamon's with an hour to spare and head inside and see the pack getting ready.

6. Alpha Pack

-Zero-

Rose, Lilly, and Caleb walk inside. I sigh and swipe my black shirt from the basket on the table. As I remove my shirt and notice Rose staring, I smile and wink at her and she blushes and looks away. I tug my black shirt over my head and make my way over to Aamon.

"So, why join the Alpha pack now?" I ask, leaning on the table in the kitchen.

"I think it will be better if we do, for I have a feeling that this pack is falling apart," he replies putting his head in his hands. I leave Aamon alone and make my way over to James.

"He is a mess," I say, nodding towards Aamon, who is still at the table.

"He gets that way when facing the mother of all packs," James says, leaving to get the pack ready for deployment. Rose is pacing back and forth in the living room and fiddles with a thick metal bracelet on her arm, I walk in and lean on the wall, she doesn't notice that I'm here as she continues to pace. I follow her every move. She looks like a worried angel after the fall, wondering how to get back up to heaven. Her boots click at every step she makes. I clear my throat and she stops pacing and looks up at me.

"What are you doing?" I ask.

"Thinking about something," she replies and the light makes her eyes seem yellow for a second. "What's up?"

"Nothing," I say gruffly and leave her to her pacing. James calls the pack into the kitchen and says that we need to leave now and that we will be traveling as wolves. We all head outside and turn. Aamon orders us to run side by side with the one we turned, and Rose makes her way over to me as the rest of the pack 'buddy up'. Aamon lets out a howl and we all take off running following Aamon and James to the valley of wolves. We reach the valley in an hour and we stop at the top, panting.

"Stay in your forms," Aamon says into our minds as we walk down to the valley floor. We see all different wolves with similar wolf markings on their right shoulders. We walk to a raised stone where a giant black wolf with a white tattoo of a wolf howling, waits for us.

"State your business here, outsiders," he speaks into our mind.

"We wish to join the Alpha and gain the protection of the pack," Aamon says nervously as he lowers his head.

"I know you, you are the pack from west of the lake," he says, and Aamon bows followed by the rest of the pack.

"Please, we wish for sanctuary in the pack," Aamon says, standing. The giant wolf leaps towards Aamon and nips him on the shoulder, tearing a fang-shaped hole in his shoulder. Aamon yelps and drops to the ground in a submission.

"You have been granted protection by this pack. From this day on, you shall you be known as the Shadow Pack from the West, and bear the marking of the tooth on your shoulder for all to see," he says, and then turns to the rest of the pack. *"Do you wish to follow in you leader's paw step?"*

One by one we all nod our heads in agreement and Aamon marks us with the marking of the tooth. When he reaches Rose she stands there and doesn't nod.

"Do you not wish to be a part of this pack?" the leader growls.

"I have no wish for it, no," she growls back.

"What's your name?" the older wolf asks.

"Rose Salamander," she says, pulling her head back and sticking out her chest.

"Ah," the wolf laughs. *"So you wish to follow in your father's paw step and continue to be a rogue. Be warned that if any harm is to come to you, we will not have pity for you. You will be the lone wolf from the west."*

"I understand."

"Then do you understand that as a rogue you are not allowed to step a paw in my sanctuary?" he says, crouching down. The whole clan turns to look at her with teeth barred. *"And that you must be chased out and, if caught, killed?"*

Rose's eyes widen as she slowly backs away with her tail between her legs. The old wolf barks and spit flies from his mouth and all the clan begin to bark. Rose turns and leaps onto the nearest ledge and the chase begins. She rushes to climb out of the valley. All the wolves join in the chase, each trying to be the one to catch her. We are almost upon her when we hit an invisible shield. I stop and look up to see a man, covered in white tattoos, with his hands outstretched toward us holding us back with the shield he is somehow creating. Rose turns and the man yells for her to run, she turns and continues her way up and out the valley.

We all bark and growl at the intruder and we slam our bodies against the invisible field. Rose is almost at the top when the man lets go out of exhaustion and disappears. Rose has a head start, but the clan are experts at scaling the walls of the valley, and in no time they are right behind Rose and snapping at her heels. Rose makes it to the top and is out of sight by the time the pack reaches the summit. The clan, however, quickly recovers and is on her heels once more.

-Rose-

I run for my life and don't stop after Aither helped me by slowing the clan down with a force field, but he could not hold them for long. The clan is close. I try to evade them and make a few sharp turns to get them off my trail. The result is coming to a ledge that overlooks the beach. I turn human and look down, from the ledge is about a two hundred foot drop to the ocean below, I turn around to head back into the wood, but the clan has caught up and is starting to surround me, snapping their jaws. Aither appears next to me, and his eyes widen as he sees the wolves creep closer.

"Any ideas?" I ask in a whisper.

"None," he whispers back. "What about you?"

"I have one, but it is very dangerous, very high risk," I say, looking back at the ledge. "I can see well as a wolf at night, but for the jump I will need to be human."

"You want to jump," he gapes. The wolves growl and step forward. "You won't survive!"

"It's the only option," I hiss and turn my back to the wolves. I take a running leap as Aither calls for me to stop. Time slows as I free fall into the water. I can hear the wolves snapping and trying to reach me. Time slams back into me as I hit the cold water. It embraces me in its watery arms. I kick my legs and push up to the surface and take a deep breath. I hear a barking as I see the clan pacing at the top of the cliff. I sigh and smile as I start to swim to the shore, but I am weighed down by my boots so I turn wolf and swim. My eyesight is fantastic and I can see that the shore isn't far. When I reach it I shake the water from my fur. I hear the wolves begin to howl as I begin to walk up the beach. A moment later, Aither appears ahead of me. I change to my human form and walk the rest of the way to him.

"Well, that worked," he says with a huff.

"But for how long?" I say, looking around. "I don't even know the way home. I don't know where I am. I haven't been this far deep into the woods."

"I can jump to your house," Aither says. "But I cannot carry or transport anyone with me."

"Go and get the Guardians," I say. "I will try to find my way home."

Aither goes to speak but my eyes flash yellow and he leaves. I sigh and make my way off the beach and back into the cover of the woods. I walk for over half an hour when I notice the moon being covered by dark heavy clouds. I turn wolf, with wolf eyes I can continue walking in the night. I hear something up ahead and I crouch down, staying low and still with me ears pricked listening in the night.

I slowly creep forward, and as I look into a clearing I see the young hunter sitting on a log with his back to me. I freeze in place.

"Mum, I need you. Dad is out of control and he keeps talking about a collar and all this stuff about the wolves. He said that he is now settling down here," he says. "I need you."

I begin to back up and step on a twig. In a heartbeat he is up and throws a knife towards me. I turn human and catch it, and after some thought, I step into the clearing.

"Hi," I say as I throw the knife back at him, which he catches easily and puts it back in his boot.

"You're in my history class; the one who left me in the woods," he says with a small laugh. "Probably not the first time it has happened to me, though."

"Yeah, sorry about that," I say with a small laugh then turn on my heels and walk away.

"Hey," he says, catching up. "I never caught your name."

"That is because I never threw it at you," I say, stopping and turning around to face him. "It's Rose, by the way."

"Okay, Rose," he says, leaning on a tree. "My name is Tyler."

"I heard," I say. "I need to go. I have somewhere else to be."

"In the middle of the night?" he says, folding his arms over his chest. "What are you doing out here anyway?"

"Sightseeing," I say, rolling my eyes as I keep look out for any sign of werewolves.

"Dressed like that?" he says, looking me over. "You're all wet."

"Yeah, I know. Look, I am in a lot of trouble at the moment, so I need to keep going."

"You are a hunter, aren't you?" he says as his eyes widen and I roll my eyes.

"Yes, but not the kind of hunter you are thinking of." I sigh and keep walking.

"A paranormal hunter," he shouts and runs to me. "A werewolf hunter."

"That is exactly the hunter you were thinking of," I say and keep walking. "Which means I am not."

"Come on," he says again, catching up to me. He is becoming annoying. "The way you are dressed, what you have said, and the way you caught that knife. You are a hunter."

"No, I'm not," I say and my eyes flicker yellow. Off in the distance I hear a wolf howl then another one closer. "Shit." I turn to Tyler and he has the leather tube in his hand. When he presses a button on the side it extends coming to a sharp point, "That won't work, there are too many of them."

"How do you know?" he asks, raising an eyebrow.

"Because they are the *trouble*," I say, turning wolf and I cast a spell that allows me to communicate with him. *"Get on my back,"* I say in his mind.

"You are a werewolf... one of them," he says, backing up and holding the stake with the point towards me.

"Yes, and you are a hunter, but if you don't get on my back you won't be," I growl, my ears flicking in every direction trying to pin point the pack. *"Listen I am not one of them. I don't kill people. You misjudge me."*

"How can I trust you?" he says, taking up a stance of defence.

"You are going to have to, if you want to live," I say urgently. My ears flick backwards as I hear the wolves coming closer.

"Just get on!" I snap. Howls rise through the night sky. I watch as Tyler's eyes widen in fear. He knows how many are coming, and he knows he cannot beat them. Tyler grabs my fur in both hands and swings onto my back. I leap forward and Tyler grips onto my fur, almost pulling it from my skin. I remove the spell that allows Tyler to hear my thoughts as my feet pound against the ground.

Perfect, I thought, *how can this get any worse? I am probably going to get killed after this.*

The sky lets loose with an awful crack of lightning and it begins to pour down rain. Perhaps things aren't as hopeless as they seem. This rain will wash away my scent. I run until I am certain that I have lost the other werewolves. As the storm worsens, I decide to take shelter in an empty cave. As soon as I am in the cave Tyler leaps off of my back and pulls out his stake. I morph into my human form and glare at him as I shake from the rain.

"If you are going to kill me do it," I pant as lightning cracks again, lighting the cave with its brightness. "But don't make me suffer."

Water drips down off my body and onto the stone floor. When he doesn't make a move or attack, I step closer to him and put my chest against the stake right where my heart would be. My skin tingles at the touch of the stake through my clothes. I stare straight into his eyes and water drips down my hair and onto my face.

"Only a human can kill me with a silver stake," I say, and my body starts to ache. I look up into his eyes. "It would be so easy right now. All you'd have to do is push and apply a little pressure..."

He curses under his breath and then turns away taking the stake from my chest. My body starts to mend.

"Why didn't you do it?" he asks, glaring at me.

"Do what?" I ask, raising an eyebrow and letting the exhaustion catch up to me.

"Kill me. Werewolves wouldn't think twice about it," he says, turning back to face me. "And a wolf wouldn't show a human, let alone a hunter, their other side."

"I am not like most wolves," I say, sliding down the cave wall and pulling my knees close, shivering from the cold rain. I break the silence. "Where is your mum?" I ask, remembering the clearing.

"She died," he says, sitting next to me.

"Do you mind telling me?" I ask, changing the subject. "Totally cool if you don't."

"We used to live in Mercy Lake once, I had a sister, too," he sighs, fiddling with the now deactivated leather tube/stake.

"What happened?" I ask, watching him closely.

"One afternoon my family decided to go on a picnic," he starts leaning back on the cave. "I was about five years old and my sister was three. Dad and I packed the whole thing and mum said we were her 'strong men'," he says, laughing to himself. He begins to turn his stake in his hand and my muscles tense out of instinct. "We had our picnic in that clearing. We joked around and ate. Just as we were cleaning up, a giant werewolf came out of nowhere and I heard my mother scream. It attacked and Dad tried to fight it off with a knife as my mum, sister, and I tried to escape. Then another wolf jumped in front of our path. My little sister screamed and it jumped on her and ripped out her throat. Then it attacked me and bit my arm," he says pulling up his long sleeve to show bite scars. "Mum threw a rock at its head and distracted the wolf by running away. I crawled over to my sister and held her close. My father showed up and cried over my sister's body, and then we went looking for my mum and found nothing. My dad eventually gave up and took me to the hospital. After that, my father made me train for weeks on end until we finally learned enough to start hunting wolves. He then enrolled me into a hunters school where they taught me everything. We have killed thousands all over the world, and now dad has said that we will finally settle back down in Mercy Lake. Dad enrolled me at Mercy Lake High and says he is going to settle down and give up killing, but I don't think he will."

"Wow," I say, letting out a sigh. "Pretty big life you live."

"Yeah, what about you? How did you become a werewolf?" he asks, and I sigh as I tell him my life story, except the werewitch part. At the end, I sigh and sleepiness catches up to me. Lightning cracks and lights up the cave and I see all of Tyler's features: his strong jaw line, his dark green eyes, his messy black hair, and his totally gorgeous body. And that's when I fell. I knew that I could never hurt him even if I tried.

"So, what now?" he asks, yawning and snapping me out of my trance.

"Now, I am going to sleep," I say, turning wolf and putting the spell back on so that he could understand me.

"Why in your werewolf form?" he asks, shifting away slowly.

"*Because it is warmer,*" I say stretching and then curling up into a ball, I did not intend to fall asleep but I did.

I woke with a couple of hours to sunrise. I yawned and began to move when I noticed that Tyler was asleep, all curled up and with his head on my side. I relax again and lie still until I hear twigs snap under heavy feet. I gently turn human and lay Tyler down so I don't wake him. I stand up and make my way to the entrance of the cave. Everything smells damp from last night's rain. I hear the feet come closer, they sound like they are moving at a very fast pace. I take out my gun and slow down as I near the entrance. I raise my gun and a familiar face steps around the corner, Jace. I sigh and holster my gun as he smiles and steps inside.

"How did you find me?" I ask, and Tyler groans as he rolls over. I turn and Jace raises an eyebrow.

"Aither figured out how to use the bracelets," he says, focusing back on me. "We all split up and searched for you."

"Well, you found me," I say, looking back at Tyler, then to Jace. "Can we get out of here? I have work today."

"Sure," he says. "Just keep up."

"What do you-," I ask, but he zooms off and stops a hundred meters away. I smile and turn wolf and bound after him—I can run faster than him as a wolf, but I stay beside him the whole time. We reach the house just an hour later and I still feel like I could run for miles. I turn human and jog up the steps and into the house with Jace right behind me.

"I notified the Guardians that I found you and they will be here soon," Jace says, putting a mobile phone back into his pocket.

"I need a shower and then I am going to work," I say, heading up into my room to retrieve my clothes, then back down for a shower. Afterwards, I go into the kitchen now wearing a black tank top and slacks. I grab my keys and feel Jace behind me touching my arm.

"What happened?" he asks, spinning me around and holding my arm up. There is a long, thin slice running up my arm that's now freshly bleeding.

"I don't know," I say as it covers up and heals. "I'm fine."

"Right," he says, releasing me. "Let's go."

"Are you coming with me?" I ask, heading to the door.

"I am your guardian for the day," he says, opening the front door. I roll my eyes and walk out and he closes the door behind me. I drive to the diner and walk into the kitchen while Jace slides into a booth. I sigh and slide an apron over my head and begin my long day. It is quiet and I have little to do, so I just end up cleaning tables and taking meals out to people. After school the diner is swamped with students ordering drinks and sweets. The diner was pretty much empty now and the manager said I could take a twenty minute break. I slide into the booth next to Jace and sigh, exhausted.

The doorbell clangs as a customer walks in. I straighten up and see it's Tyler with Zero following. I groan and see no one at the counter, so I slide back out of the booth and hurry to Tyler's booth first. He looks terrible. He's in the same clothes as yesterday and his hair is a mess. His green eyes seem to shine in the light of the diner. He didn't notice me untill I'm standing next to his booth.

"What can I get you?" I ask Tyler, getting my note pad from my apron pouch.

"Hi," he says, eyes widening. "Uh, just a cup of black coffee."

"Sugar?" I ask, writing it down on the pad.

"Ah, sure," he says, fidgeting. I sigh and make my way over to Zero, who gives me a twisted smile.

"What can I get you?" I say and he looks me up and down.

"How about a piece of the hottest thing I can see?" he says and I roll my eyes. "Enjoy the run last night?"

"What can I get you?" I ask again and he stands up and wraps me in a hug from behind. I see Jace tense and his skin ripples, but he relaxes as I shake my head and mouth, *"It's okay."* Zero tightens his grip and begins to nibble on my ear, then turns me around and kisses my mouth, crushing me closer against my protest. When he's finished, he pulls back and makes a *'mmm'* sound.

"Zero, stop," I hiss and try to move out of his grip, but he holds me tight and smiles.

"But you taste so good," he moans, holding me tighter and kissing my neck. I notice that Zero has the marking on his right shoulder and I feel a shiver run up my spine as I realize the marking stays even when they are human.

"Zero, stop," I say again, squirming. "I need to work."

Zero does not say anything to this except tightening his grip and toughen his kisses. Jace finally has enough and is over in a flash.

"She said stop," Jace says, his skin rippling. Zero lets me go and quickly grabs a knife from the table and slams it into Jace's heart. I scream as Jace goes down onto the floor. I kneel down and shake Jace's shoulders screaming his name.

"Oh relax, baby doll," Zero says, picking me up by the arm with an iron grip. "He's a vamp. He's just paralysed; it's not even wooden."

"What the hell is wrong with you?" I scream and my eyes turn yellow. Tyler has gotten out of his booth and is now running at Zero with his silver stake extended. Zero turns and just hits him out of the way, slamming him into the counter and rendering him unconscious. Rage burns in my chest as I quickly turn around and punch Zero in the jaw.

"I never want to see you again," I say as my eyes glow brighter. "Leave now. I don't want to see you again, ever!"

Zero scowls at me then walks out the door, shoving his hands into his pockets. It was too easy. Still, I wait until he is out of sight before my eyes change back to blue. I lean down next to Jace and quickly pull the knife out of his chest. He gasps as he comes back to life. I sigh in relief then leave him and make my way over to Tyler.

He's slumped in a heap on the floor and I check for a pulse and panic as I can't find it. I call Jace over and tell him that I can't find anything. Jace begins to feel around Tyler's head and neck and sighs as he shakes his head.

"Zero has broken the spine and the spinal cord," he says, slumping back. "If he was a paranormal he would heal, but, he is human."

"He tried to save me," I say, placing my hands on the back of his neck and closing my eyes. I concentrate hard, trying to find a spell to heal Tyler. Finally, I find one that would switch his illness and give it to me. Before Jace could stop me I started reciting the spell.

Powers gather and switch our position.
I open my eyes as they turn deep yellow.
Give me his pain and let him live. Heal him with my health.
The clouds outside blacken and the wind picks up. My eyes glow brighter as I continue.
Break my neck, and then let me heal.
As the words leave my mouth I hear a terrible crack. Darkness engulfs me and I stop breathing.

-Zero-

"How did I do?" I ask the vampire from the woods.

"Perfectly," she giggles, standing up from the bench across the road from the diner. "You are such a good actor. Paralysing the vamp and killing the innocent? So good."

I smile and eye the forming clouds.

"Now, do as your little pathetic wolf girl says and back off," she continues as we start walking down the road. The wind picks up and the vampire looks around. "Well, I have to go, my puppy," she says, turning down an alleyway. "Behave and I will be back soon."

She leaps onto a trashcan, then onto the roof in one slick stride. I grin and make my way back towards the diner. Jace walks out carrying Rose, who is unconscious. The hunter walks out after Jace and I stop dead in my tracks. I killed the hunter, not Rose. I frown, but then turn and walk away, no longer caring. Shea walks up to me and smiles.

"Hey, Zero," she says in a perky voice.

"Hello," I say with a wicked grin. I slip my arms around her shoulders and walk along with her.

"Some weather, huh?" she says, blushing.

"Yeah," I sigh, looking back up at the clouds. "What are you doing tonight?"

"Uh, I'm free all night, I guess," she says, shrugging.

"What do you say to hanging out in my room tonight and watching a movie?" I grin, squeezing her shoulders. "We haven't spoken much lately."

"That's because you are so caught up with the ugly flower Rose," she scoffs, rolling her eyes.

"Yeah, well, I am done with her. My attention is on you." I smile.

"Well," she says, pushing a stray hair behind her ear. "I have some shopping to do, so I guess I will see you tonight."

"Sure," I say, removing my arm from her shoulder. She smiles and walks ahead of me. I roll my eyes and then turn around again. She' was so easy and played right into my hands. I walk right past Rose's house where her car is parked in the drive way and the door is ajar. I know that she said to leave her alone, but curiosity gets the better of me and I decide to find out what is going on. I go around into the stables and then up to the loft to where the plank is. I carefully cross it without being seen and end up at her window. I see her lying on the bed still as death. I open the window carefully and slide in, not making a sound. I can't see the rise or fall of her chest and I panic. What happened? Then I remember the hunter walking out behind Jace at the diner. I hear voices downstairs and rush to the window. I slide out just as the door opens. I fumble and slip off the plank. I fall and land as a wolf, where I run into the cover of the woods and head home. When I reach home, I turn human and head to my room where I start to pace.

"Okay," I think. "So what if she is dead? She was going to die anyway. Did I kill her? I was so caught up in the adrenalin-"

My thoughts are interrupted when Shea softly knocks and enters my room. I turn to her and smile as all my thoughts leave me. She ducks her head and blushes as she closes the door behind her, and I walk over and wrap her in a hug and kiss her cheek.

"So," she says, clearing her throat. "What movie do you want to watch?"

"Movie pile is over there," I say, nodding to the stack of DVD's next to the TV. She searches though the pile as I remove my shirt and chuck it into the dirty pile. Shea picks a DVD and inserts it into the player and turns around. I slump down on the bed and pat beside me. She blushes and slowly makes her way over. I take her hand as she slides in next to me and the movie plays. I get bored about half way through and decide to have a little fun. I wrap around Shea and begin to kiss her.

"Wait," she says, pulling back. "Why now? Is it because Rose dumped you."

"Please, I dumped Rose," I scoff, rolling my eyes and coming up with a lie. "I thought of you the whole time. I just never knew if you liked me back."

Her eyes widen and she presses up against me, kissing me back with a fiery passion. Her body presses against me and I know what she wants. I decide to give it to her. I roll her over and lie on top of her and tear off her clothes. She gasps and I continue as she rubs up my chest and abs. She smiles up at me and finally, when both her and my clothes are lying on the floor, we give in to the animalistic passion. As she grips the sheets and moans in ecstasy, I can't help but to think of Rose.

-Rose-

Air slams into me and my neck cracks back into place. I don't know how long I have been out, but I have a pounding headache and my lungs hurt from the rush of air. I am in my room and I look around and see the Guardians and Aither in the room. I slump back onto the bed and take a deep breath as my breathing returns to normal. Jace helps me sit up to allow the air to come in easier and Aither hands me a cup, warning me to slowly sip the water.

"How are you?" Jace asks, his eyes full of worry.

"My neck hurts," I say, rubbing my neck, Jace softly laughs as I take a sip and immediately spit out the foul-tasting liquid. "What is this?" I ask, wiping my mouth.

"Boiled asclepias tuberosa," Emily says, stepping forward. "It helps with healing. Tamika made it."

"Right," I say, placing the cup on the bed side table. "Well, I can heal by myself, thanks." I get up and walk out of the room with the Guardians following behind me. "How long have I been dead?" I ask at the bottom of the stairs.

"About two days," Aither says, appearing next to me.

"What's happened while I was out?" I ask, walking into the kitchen and grabbing a drink of real water.

"Well, a friend said that she came to collect her horses," Jace says, ticking them off on his fingers. "Your sister has moved out. Oh, and your boss found the blood and said you are fired."

"Fantastic," I groan, finishing my water and heading into the living room where Aither waits. Jace sends the rest of the Guardians home and then joins us in the living room.

"Now that you have no job, all of your free time will be spent training and fighting," Jace says, taking a seat on the couch opposite to me.

"What? Why?" I ask. "I am a wolf. I can just snap my prey in half."

"What if you were in public?" he says and I shrug. "And there were hunters everywhere. You can't use your witchy powers or you will die. What would you do?"

"Run," I scoff. "Aren't you guys meant to be stopping those situations by guarding me?"

"But what if you can't run?" he asks, raising an eyebrow. "We won't be around forever, you know."

"Wait, isn't that the whole point of being a paranormal? Living forever?"

"But paranormals can be killed," Aither points out. "And not all paranormals live forever."

"Fine," I sigh, leaning back into the chair and rubbing my neck. "But I am not starting today."

Jace nods and stands and leaves. I sigh and continue rubbing my neck. Aither sits next to me and sighs.

"You are doing it wrong," he says and I glare at him.

"What?" I ask, looking at him. He turns me in the seat and takes my neck.

"If you want to unknot the neck, use circles," he says as he begins to work circles around my neck in a light massage. The knots are gone in seconds, but he keeps massaging, working his way down to my shoulders and upper back. I lean back against him and sigh as exhaustion and pain catches up to me. He wraps his arms around me and a sweet scent of honey suckle and watermelon flows around me.

"How do you do that?" I ask, closing my eyes.

"I am the power of air," he says. "I can make the air smell nice just by thinking of the smell."

"That's cool," I say, opening my eyes. "Where did it all go wrong?"

"What?" he asks.

"I was happy as a human. I had plans to do something important; get a degree, marry a man, and have kids." I say as tears brim my eyes. "Then I get turned into a werewolf and find out I was always destined to be paranormal. Is my life just going to be one big mess forever?"

"No, it will get better with time," Aither says.

"I just don't feel safe anymore," I say. Aither shifts me forward. I turn around and sit back on the chair, as Aither removes a necklace that was tucked under his shirt. On the necklace is a ring that has blue swirls that look like they are moving.

"Take it," he says, placing it into my hand. "Whenever you are in trouble or unsafe, squeeze it and think of me."

"Where did you get this?" I ask, turning the ring in my hand and watching the swirls move.

"My father made it," he says and my eyes widen. "He used his powers to make the swirls move like our markings."

"No," I say, handing it back to him open-palmed. "I can't take it."

"Yes, you can," he says, closing my hand. "My father once said that this ring has some sort of connection to the wearer and it may protect them. I want you to have it."

"Thank you," I say, sliding it over my head. "I will look after it."

Aither nods his head, but his words are interrupted by a fist banging on the door. I get up and rush to the door, where Cleo is waiting with one of Samantha's arms around her shoulders and the other wrapped in a thick towel.

"What happened?" I ask, moving aside and letting them inside. I help Cleo drag Samantha inside and help her onto the couch, Aither raises an eyebrow as he moves out of the way and stands next to the couch.

"I don't know," Cleo says. "This morning Samantha appears on my door step, bleeding heavily from her shoulder. Rose, what is happening? These past days have become really freaky. First Caleb and your twin Lilly have barricaded themselves away from Sam and I. Second, Sam has been disappearing at all times of the day, and no matter where we look we can't find him. Third, Zero is going out with this slutty little home wrecker. Fourth, you are living under a rock, and finally, Samantha appears on my doorstep drenched in blood with a bite the size of a tiger's. I tried to take her to the hospital, but she says that she had to go here. What is happening?"

"I don't know," I say, unwrapping Samantha's shoulder and gasping at the large bite mark. Aither sucks in a deep breath as he stands next to me.

"Cleo get out," I say, Cleo starts to protest but I shoot a glare at her and she slowly backs out of the room. I lean down next to Samantha and take her hand. "Samantha," I say and she opens her eyes.

"What happened?"

"I stood up to the wolves," she says in a weak and small voice. "And they kicked me out and took my mark. I didn't want to be one of them, Rose."

"It's okay, you are going to be okay," I say, focusing on the wound. I turn to Aither. "Why isn't it healing?"

"Because the alpha wolf said that it will heal like a human's wound, causing me more pain," Samantha answers.

I look back at her, then to Aither. I grab his arm and drag him out of the room and into the kitchen where Cleo is talking to Jace. I tell her to go and keep an eye on Samantha as I needed to talk to the boys.

"What would happen if I was to use my 'witchy' powers to heal Samantha?" I ask Jace with worry in my voice.

"The forgetting spell that you put on her will disappear and she will remember everything," Jace says, leaning on the kitchen island and taking a sip out of his water bottle I assume is filled with blood. "Because that is technically healing."

"Well, that's not so bad," I shrug and go to leave.

"Well, it is, because it will also rub off on all that have forgotten," he says, placing the bottle down and walking over to me, standing really close so that I can smell the blood on his breath. "Is that something you can risk?"

"Watch it," Aither says, stepping between Jace and I. His tattoos burn bright on his skin, giving off a warning signal. Jace grumbles but backs off.

"What if I were to use a spell that would only work on her and Sam?" I ask, searching my brain for a spell. "What if I took off theirs and replaced it with a healing spell?"

"That could work," Jace says, turning around and going back to the kitchen island. I quickly turn and rush back into the lounge room and tell Aither and Cleo to leave as I need concentration. Samantha has fallen asleep on the lounge, which makes it easier for me to perform the spell.

I call upon the powers, help me.
I have made a mistake, forgive me.
I call for strength, power me.
Remove the spell from Samantha and Sam, wake them.
Heal Samantha.

The spell finishes and I see Samantha's skin start to knit back together and close the wound. My head pounds but I ignore it as Samantha wakes up with a gasp. Her eyes widen as she looks at me. I see her register all that has happened as she slides off the couch and wrap me in a tight embrace.

"Good to see you, too," I say, hugging her back and forcing back tears.

"Don't you ever do anything like that again," she says, pulling back. "We are in this together. Don't forget that, ever."

"I won't," I say, as she hugs me again.

"Does this mean that everyone remembers?" Samantha asks, sitting back up onto the couch.

"No," I sigh, leaning on the couch. "I made the spell only so you and Sam would remember. I need friends that I can trust, and he is the only other one I can trust at this time."

I hear Samantha sigh.

"Here," I say, standing up and taking her hand. "You can borrow some of my clothes and take a shower."

"Thanks," she says, standing up as I lead her to my room. She picks out an outfit and then we head back downstairs, parting ways at the kitchen as she goes to take a shower. I grab a bottled water out of the fridge and take a large mouthful. Then, out of nowhere, Sam busts through the door and wraps me in a tight hug.

"Sam," I say, gasping as he tightens his grip. "I need to breathe. I like breathing."

"I remember," he says, letting me go and taking my hands. "I remember everything."

"I know," I say as Aither and Jace rush into the kitchen, followed by Cleo. "I took the spell off."

"Holy cow, Sam," Cleo says, coming into the kitchen and resting on the stool next to the island. "Are you taking steroids? Cause you moved like lightning."

"You know him?" Jace asks with a raised eyebrow. Sam turns around and stands in front of me.

"Yes," I say, moving in front of Sam and eyeing Jace. "He is one of my friends. Are you okay?"

"He is a vampire," Jace says, twisting a smile and making his skin ripple. My head spins as Sam also ripples his skin and steps in front of me again.

"A what?" Cleo asks, looking at me. All the colour drains from her face. This is so not good.

"A vampire," Jace says, turning his attention to her. "A blood sucking, immortal, vampire. Just. Like. Me."

All the colour drains from my face as Jace slids his fangs down. Cleo screams as Jace lunges for her, but Sam is quick to react and jumps in his way and the two collide in a hissing mess on the floor. Cleo screams and backs up and into Samantha, who stands in her werewolf form. Cleo screams again and bolts out of the front door. I sigh and freeze the vampires in place. This is going swell.

"Aither, Samantha, go after her. I will take care of these two," I say as my head pounds again. They stare at me for a second then they run out the door in hot pursuit of Cleo. I unfreeze Sam and a second later Jace. Sam is able to pin Jace down and I rush to his side. Sam's eyes widen as Jace hisses at him.

"What is it?" I ask, seeing his face. "What's the matter?"

"He is compelled," Sam says as Jace struggles.

"How do you know?" I say, looking into Jace's eyes.

"See right in the corner?" Sam says nodding his head in the general direction, and I notice a black dot in the furthest corner of Jace's eye. "That's how you can tell."

"Okay, we now know he is compelled. How do we un-compel him?" I ask and Jace hisses and struggles to get away. Sam hisses back and bites down on Jace's neck, spreading blood all over the kitchen floor. Slowly but surely, the black starts to fade and in time leaves, and Jace begins to blink rapidly. Sam releases him and then helps him up.

"That's how," Sam says, turning to me and wiping blood from his mouth.

"Can my house stay clean for one day without getting blood everywhere? That would be nice," I say, rolling my eyes and raising my hand, using a simple spell to clean the blood up.

Aither walks in carrying Cleo over his shoulder. "What happened?" I ask rushing over.

"She wouldn't stop screaming so I used a little bit of pressure in the air to knock her unconscious," he says, answering my question as Samantha steps into the kitchen. Aither turns to Jace as he walks into the living room to place Cleo on the couch.

"I'm so sorry," Jace says, almost as if he was fumbling for words. "I didn't know what was happening. That isn't supposed to happen to me."

"You were compelled," Sam says with a shrug and Jace gapes.

"That shouldn't happen to me," he snarls. "There are only two vampires in the world who can compel me."

The voices blur and mumble as my head starts to spin. I collapse to the ground gasping for air. I hear Jace yell for Aither, and soon he, Samantha, Sam, and Jace are all clouding my vision. Aither's body tenses and I am surrounded by sweet air, but that only suffocates me more so he cuts it off. I feel an electric power build up in me and a powerful urge to release it. My veins seem to appear closer to the surface and I scream in pain. The scream comes out more as a squeak as I roll over and images burst through my vision. They are the same visions that corrupted my mind when I was with Tyler. I finally had enough of all the pain and danger, and my eyes glow bright yellow and outside thunder rumbles overhead. I scream again and it comes out full and strong as yellow electricity flies from my fingers and dance around the room and absorbs energy from the electric appliances. The energy flows into me and I am hit with a large shock and the lights flicker and all the electrical appliances seem to activate. The toaster keeps popping, the fridge opens and closes, and the kettle boils as the microwave whirs to life. Soon the energy overwhelms me and I collapse, letting the darkness consume me.

7. Rose Moon

-Zero-

It has been three weeks since the incident at the diner and the full moon is coming up which means that there will be plenty of hunters trying to get their hands on us. Shea skips up to me and gives me a big kiss from out of nowhere.

"Hey, handsome," she says, taking my hand and walking along with me. "Don't look now, but a certain flower is coming."

I turn and look in the direction she's looking and see Rose walking across the road. I thought she was dead this whole time, but she is alive. I don't know why, but I feel happy about this. Rose looks in my direction and I smile at her; she scowls at me and takes the arm of the stranger next to her, Aither. He looks across at me and ushers Rose away.

"What a loser," Shea says, turning up her nose. "He could do so much better."

I sigh as she leads me into a deserted dress shop.

"What are we doing?" I ask as she hurries around the shop.

"The seasons' dance is on tomorrow," she says, going over to the dress rack.

"Yes, but so is the full moon," I say, leaning on the counter. "That means no humanity."

"We lose our humanity at midnight," she says, taking a dress and rushing over to the change room. "There is always time for a dance."

She closes the curtain and I decide to look around. From out of the shop's window I see Rose walk past and enter the shop. I catch her eye and she tenses as she hurries along to a rack of dresses. Shea comes out if the changing room wearing a dark blue skin-tight dress that shows way too much skin. I try to make Rose jealous and rush over to Shea and wrap her in a hug and kiss.

"You look amazing," I say with a flirtatious smile. "You should totally wear that to the dance."

Shea squeals and we are hushed by the owner. She blushes and I hear Rose laugh. Shea and I turn around as Aither takes a frilly dress from the rack.

"Does this make my butt look big?" he asks in a high pitched voice making Rose laugh.

"Stop it," she laughs as he laughs, too. "Come on, let's get you a suit."

She drags him to the back of the store. Shea scoffs and continues to show off her dress, pulling at it here and there.

Rose and Aither both go into different changing rooms and then come out. Rose is wearing a long light blue dress that hugs her skin at the top and loosens at the bottom. Aither comes out after wearing a suite with a light blue undershirt with a blue tie.

"Blue is so not my colour," Shea scoffs, going back to the rack and choosing a different dress. She kisses me as she goes by, saying, "I want you to find a suit that matches this." She holds up a red dress, then disappears into one of three of the dressing rooms. I stuff my hands into my pockets and head to the back of the shop where I find a suit. I take it off the rack and head to the front where I find that Rose has left. I sigh and the rest of the shopping trip is a blur and before I know it, we are home with an arm full of shopping bags.

I drop the bags on the kitchen and then head upstairs and throw myself onto the bed. After about a minute, Shea slowly walks in, wearing sexy lingerie. I sit up and raise an eyebrow at her and her face turns bright red.

"I picked this up yesterday," she says, tucking a loose strand of hair behind her ear. "I just didn't know when to show you."

"It's sexy," I say, toying with her. "Come here."

She walks over to me and slides onto my lap. She leans down and I meet her halfway and kiss her. She pulls back quickly and whispers, "Do you still have feelings for Rose?"

"What?" I ask, panicking as the answer is yes. "Why would you ask that, seeing how that right now I am in bed with you, not her."

"Zero," she sighs, standing up and backing up to the door. "You didn't exactly say no."

"All right, I agree!" I shout, standing up as my temperature boils over. "I am still in love with Rose, and you are just my puppet on a string that I keep around for fun. You will never fill her shoes and you will always be a stupid little whore who I will pick up when I'm in the mood for a booty call!"

Tears stream down Shea's face as she runs out of my room and slams the door to hers. In turn, I stand and also slam my door, then fall back onto my bed. I sigh and pull my hands behind my head. What is wrong with me? All my anger and hate was fading. I still have feelings for Rose, and I need her in my life. I feel jealous every time I see her with another man. I don't know why I am feeling this way now, but I know that it won't matter as I have lost all her trust and she hates me for it.

-Rose-

We arrive home from shopping and no one is around. Aither and I place the bags on the kitchen island, then we head upstairs where I play music off my speakers. I flop onto my bed and sigh.

"Sorry about going into that shop," Aither says, sitting next to me all joking aside. "It must have been hard seeing Zero."

"It's okay," I sigh, sitting up with a shrug. "It wasn't that bad."

"So, full moon tomorrow," he says with a sigh. "And we are all planning to go to the dance, why?"

"Why not?" I ask, shrugging. "It is a fundraiser, not personal invite. I think it'll be fun, and Jace says that I will lose my humanity at midnight."

"I suppose," he sighs, lacing his hands behind his head. "Have you mastered that move yet?"

Jace has been training all of us for the past three weeks to battle Vampires. H's taught us all of their weaknesses and how to attack and move to defend ourselves. I have been okay with most of the moves, but the one I have not yet mastered is the kill move. It is a combination where the attacker must use all of their power to strike the opponent several times, then use the remaining energy to either strike the enemy with a stake or to break their neck.

"No," I sigh, standing up. "I can't seem to get it."

Aither stands up as well and stands across from me. "Strike," he says, tensing his body into defending position. "Attack me. You need the practice."

I move into attacking position take a deep breath. I take my first strike; a sharp punch to the stomach, or at least it would have been if Aither didn't defend so well. I recover and strike again, and in turn he defends. Then I have an idea. I fake a right hook, then go for a left hit to the ribs. Aither recoils a little, but then quickly changes into attack. I move into a defensive position and block all of the attacks. Aither moves quickly and I am barely able to keep up with him, but I did, until he sweeps me off my feet and we collide to the floor where he pretends to push a stake through my heart.

"Killed," he puffs as my head hits the floor. "I win."

"I told you I couldn't get it," I say as sweat drips down my head. Then I come to the realization that he hasn't moved off of me and is holding me down. Sweet air flows around me and wraps me into a blanket of sweet cinnamon, chocolate, and roses. His eyes lock with mine and they seem to search me like he doesn't believe in what's happening. He blinks and his face sobers as he stands and helps me off the floor. I remember how to breathe and let out the breath that I was holding and follow him down stairs.

Later that evening, Aither, Jace, Samantha, Sam, and I all go into the woods for our nightly training. Jace marks a circle into the ground with a dagger and two of us would fight within it. Jace told Samantha and I that we should be prepared to fight in our human form, and that we should not lean towards the wolf side. Tonight, Jace has decided to make Sam and I fight first.

Sam hits with speed and power, while I dodge and work my way into his blind spot and fight back. At one stage, Sam picks up a fallen branch and scraps my upper arm. The pain shoots up my arm and through my neck, shocking my whole body and my first instinct is to turn, so I do. I turn and bark at him. His eyes widen and he steps back. Blood drips down my arm, and I turn back to a human and walk out of the circle and to where my jumper was hanging. I grab a piece of its fabric in my hand and use it to wipe the blood. When I turn back to the group, they are all staring at me.

"What?" I ask, as they look from one person to another.

"You are scrawny," Aither says, stepping forward, I look down at myself and see that I am perfectly healthy.

"I don't see it," I say, looking back to the group.

"No, not as you, you as a wolf," Jace says. "How long has it been since you have been a wolf?"

"Three weeks, I think, but I have been eating," I say, shaking my head in disbelief.

"Yes, we know, but the wolf needs to eat, and you are a feather compared to the other you, so it needs to eat more than you do,"

Samantha says, stepping forward.

"Go hunt tonight," Jace says. "We will finish up here."

I roll my eyes and turn wolf. I look back at my body and see that, as a wolf, I am skinny and underweight. I can see my spine standing out of my back. I turn away from the others and bound into the night.

I slow down and begin to sniff around. The smell of deer prickles my nose. I turn in the direction and follow the scent into an opening where a small herd of deer are grazing on the grass. I turn human and use my powers to kill two large stags. The rest of the herd gets scared and runs off, so I turn back into a wolf and fully understand what the term 'wolfing down' means, as in half an hour, I am full and all that remains of my meal are bones and the blood that covers my fur. I walk to the lake and swim to wash the blood from my fur, then turn and make my way home, I come across Tyler. He is at the clearing where I first met him. I step into view without thinking and he immediately sees me. My heart freezes and I mentally curse myself. Tyler tilts his head to the left a touch and his eyes recognize me.

"Rose?" he asks, and I turn human.

"Yeah," I say. The moon brightly lights up Tyler's features.

"What are you doing out here?" he asks, kicking his feet in the dirt.

"Well, I was hunting," I say, rubbing the back of my neck. "What about you?"

"Checking out the woods before they become a battle field," he sighs, looking around and not directly at me.

"Ah, yes," I say, recalling last year's battle. "I remember last year's battle. They barricaded the woods off and no one could go into it for a whole six months. I had no idea what was going on."

"Yeah," he sighs, turning around and walking the other way. "I have to go... prepare, so, yeah."

I roll my eyes and continue to walk away. I decide to turn wolf and head back home. I get inside and find a note saying that Sam and Jace went out to feed, Aither had a power meeting, and Samantha was hanging at the arcade. So, I was alone.

I look around and decide to test some of my spells. I remember one of my favourite movie scenes where a wizard cleans his house with a spell. I search my brain and find one. I command the broom and mops to work the floor while the dishes clean themselves. I smile at my progress, and in no time the floors and dishes are clean. I command the brooms and mops to go back and command the dish clothes to continue to clean the walls. I'm so caught up in cleaning that I don't realize the door opens until I feel the cold draft on my neck. I spin quickly and turn wolf, growling at the intruder and realize it's Cleo. She stands frozen as the cleaning objects all fall to the floor. I turn back to a human as she shuts the door.

"Hi," I say, awkwardly.

"Remember what happened last time," Cleo says, walking past me and placing her keys on the kitchen counter. "You shouldn't be using all this power. You fainted last time."

"Don't worry about me," I grumble. "I can look after myself."

"Anyway," she sighs, pulling something out of her handbag. "I brought this, as a sorry for not seeing you these past weeks. I just needed some time to think." She holds up a bottle of champaign. I smile at her and take the bottle from her.

"Thanks," I say, opening it and making two glasses fly onto the counter. I pour us each a glass as we take a seat in the lounge room. "I thought you would have brought your boyfriend around."

"He dumped me," she says, taking a seat and sipping from her glass. "But I don't really want to talk about that. I just want to hang."

"I can do that. We haven't hung out in a while. I missed you," I say, standing up. "Now that this house is mine, let's explore where we weren't allowed to go as kids."

"Sounds good," she smiles as she also stands and places her glass down. We make our way down into the hunting room and start to take books off the shelf. When we were little my father would get angry at us if we touched them. I notice there is one book left on the shelf called, *Open Sesame.* I pull it off, but it catches and the sound of pressured air being released fills the room as the bookcase moves out and turns, revealing a secret room. Cleo and I look at each other but don't say a word. We head down the stairs and into the darkness. The sound of beeping machines welcome us as we step off the last step. All around us are different types of machines. I look around as my eyes adjust. I gasp and turn wolf as I see another werewolf in the corner, I growl at the animal, and notice that it doesn't attack. I walk closer and continue to growl, and then I realize that the animal is encased in a glass tank filled with a purple liquid. The wolf is white and has a stripe like mine but it's split in half: half blue and half black. I look next to the wolf and see a human girl with black hair. I turn human and press a hand to the glass this one is filled with green liquid. The woman inside opens her eyes to reveal sapphire eyes. Next to her, the wolf also stirs and opens his eyes to reveal yellow eyes. They stare at me and I feel that I can't move. Cleo comes up next to me and looks at the base of each tank.

On the wolf's plaque it says:
Name: Marcus Bane
Species: Lycanthrope/Versipellis/Loup-garo (A.K.A-Werewolf)
Resin: Dissolved Wolfsbane
Cleo read it to me, and then the witch's plaque:
Name: Amelia Bane
Species: Beldam Enchantress (A.K.A-Witch)
Resin: Dissolved Spotted Alder Roots

"They were married," Cleo says, standing and looking at the two beings before me. "Or they were siblings."

I snap my attention back and release my hand from the witch's glass. Her eyes close, as does the werewolf's, and I step back and my attention focuses along the line of paranormals encased in glass tanks filled with resin. On the base of each tank is a plaque similar to the witch's and wolf's: the name of the being, the name of the species, and finally the resin they are encased in. After the glass cases of the paranormal species there is a large map of the city with the school circled. Next to that map is one of the inside of the school with a circle around a room that I have never seen before. There is a desk next to the maps on the wall. On the desk are stacks and stacks of books on modern and ancient folk lore and myths. There are scribbled notes in my father's handwriting. He had written all the species down with lines linked from name to name. Most are scribbled out, but the only one that's full and connected is the one linking the wolf and the witch. Confusion boils over and I run back to the witch's and wolf's case and place one hand on each. Their eyes snap open and stare at me.

"Who are you?" I ask in a whisper. All of the paranormals' thoughts flood into my mind and scrape on the edge of my scalp. "One at a time!" I scream and the paranormals turn quite.

"*My name is Amelia Bane,*" the witch says into my mind after a moment. "*And this is my husband, Marcus Bane.*"

"Why are you here?" I ask her.

"*A human abducted us all and placed us in this resin. Only our minds can speak. Our eyes will open when paranormal skin touches the glass, and, if the power is enough, we can move.*"

"How come my father has you, then? He is a werewolf," I say with confusion and I hear the woman sigh into my mind.

"*The one that holds us here is of human blood and flesh. He uses me to give him powers of a wolf and his wife one of a witch,"* the werewolf says, and I turn my head to him.

"Why does he want you?" I ask, frowning. "What does he want with you?"

"For centuries, he has been trying to create a paranormal child of two bloods and then double its power with a sacrifice and a double bite. At this stage, he and his wife have only been able to create one child, a werewitch. You," she says, and my heart locks up as the hard truth sets in. *"You are Marcus's and my child."*

"No," I gasp, going to step back but I remember I need my hand on their tanks. "I am a Salamander, and my parents are Dixie and Jeremy Salamander."

"You were carried in Dixie's womb," Marcus says. *"Her husband took our power by force. He turned himself into a pure blood wolf, and then turned his wife into a witch. They fabricated lies after lies."*

"This cannot be true," I gape. "They couldn't have lied to me for all these years."

"Make no mistake, you are our child," Amelia says, her eyes staring right at me.

"Is there a way to get you out?" I ask, as anger fills me. "I cannot leave you in there."

"No, we have been in here too long," Amelia says as a blue tear streams into the green resin.

"If we were to get out we would simply die," her husband finishes for her. Tears continue to flow. *"Dear one, do not cry over us as we are a lost cause, but I can tell you that I am proud to call you my daughter. I can see and hear everything you do. I am so proud."*

Their voices hush as their eyes close, and I slump to the ground and cry. Cleo leans down next to me and puts an arm around me.

"What did they say?" she asks in a low whisper.

"They are my parents," I sob, looking up at tanks. My mother's one single tear remains floating in her tank. The horror sinks in and my emotions rage over. "They are my parents."

I turn wolf and Cleo jumps back and runs up the stairs, closing the book case behind her. I let out a low tuned howl of sadness, and then I lay in the gap between Marcus and Amelia. Their eyes open as my fur touches the tanks, and they both sink to the bottom and watch me with careful eyes. Before I fall asleep, I hear Amelia say, *"My sweet, sweet, Rose. How we need you."* I slip into a silent slumber and dream before I could respond.

I am awakened with a violent shake of the head as someone shouts my name.

"Rose!" the voice calls, "Rose! Wake up!"

Cold water flows over my head and my eyes snap open as a cold rush of water hits me. I growl at the intruder.

"Rose, it's just me," Aither says as my focus comes back. I shake my head then look up at my parents, whom have resumed at their original positions. I let out a small whimper and nuzzle each tank before rising and stepping out of my hiding spot.

"Cleo told me everything," Aither says as I walk past him, turning human as I go. "Do you want to talk about it?"

"Nope," I say coldly, shaking my head and taking a seat at my 'fathers'' desk.

"You should talk to someone," he says.

"Get out," I sigh, rubbing the sleep out of my eyes.

"What?" Aither gasps like I had just grown an extra head.

"Get. The. Fuck. Out!" I scream, my lips pulling back in a snarl. "Get out, Aither, or I swear I will tear you apart."

I hear his boots slowly reel back. I don't want him or anyone else in this room. The tapping of his boots echo off the walls as he leaves. I sigh again and turn to a leather bounded book titled *Witch Hunt*. It goes on about how to successfully catch and kill witches. Bile rises in my throat. I swallow it and continue to flick through the book. As I reach the middle, a title catches my eyes, *The Other Half*. The page goes on about the witch's aspect or 'other half'. It talks about how to kill it and what its weaknesses are.

"What is this talking about?" I murmur, scanning the page again.

"*It's your Aspect; to find it you need to find yourself,*" my mother says. I turn to her and raise an eyebrow.

"How?" I ask.

"*Close your eyes,*" she says and reluctantly I do. "*Concentrate, and find yourself.*"

A number of animal sounds fill my head and I wince in surprise. My mother's voice echoes through my head and it is replaced by the flapping of strong wings and a screech of an owl. I open my eyes and there, sitting on my mother's tank is a large barn owl. It flies over to me and lands on the arm of the chair. It looks into my eyes and tilts its head like it was asking me a question. I look over to my mother's tank and in front of it is a small black cat licking its paws, but my mother's eyes are now closed. I sigh and look at the clock on the wall. It is late and I decide to head upstairs. I hold out my arm and the owl leaps onto it. I stroke its soft chest feathers and walk up the steps. Everyone is waiting for me upstairs, and as soon as I step into the room everyone starts to ask questions. The owl beats its wings and screeches. The room goes quiet and everyone looks at me like I was naked.

"I am going to bed," I say, heading out of the room. I pause at the door and look over my shoulder. "Anyone who disturbs me will suffer."

I walk alone to my room and silently shut the door behind me. My owl flies off my arm and finds itself a perch on one of the posts at the end of the bed. I change into pyjamas and settle into a deep sleep as soon as my head hits the pillow.

-Zero-

The last light flickers out in Roses room as I stand in the loft across from her window. I sigh and lay down, changing into my wolf form. I have noticed that there is a red strike forming in my wolf form, starting at my right eye and flicking up to my ear. I huff as a rubber band snaps in my head. I have been betraying Rose because some stupid vampire told me to. As the thought runs through my head a gasp sounds behind me. I am up in a flash growling at the intruder, the vampire. My growl drops an octave and she hisses jumps out of the loft and into the woods. I follow in hot pursuit, playing the game of cat and mouse, or, in this case, wolf and vampire. I let out a high-pitched howl as I leap and pin the vamp to the ground. She screeches and screams as she tries to scratch me with her claws. I have had enough of her games and decide to finish this. I put all my weight into my front legs and push down into her chest, but I know she can heal from it so I let out a bloodcurdling howl and mutilate her body with my fangs and claws, her black blood oozes into my fur. I turn back into a human and look at what's left: a pile of flesh and bone. I produce a lighter from my back pocket— I knew what I was going to do tonight— I light it and throw it onto her now mutilated body. Her body catches easily and the smell of burning flesh fills the woods. I heave a sigh and something fills my body, bursting and wanting to escape. I collapse to the ground and scream Rose's name. It echoes through the woods and I can't help but feel that she is in danger. Something is wrong; I can feel it in my gut. But it soothes as the pain does. I forget what I was thinking. I should have worried, but instead I just went home to bed.

I am awoken with a jolt and a cold splash to the face the next morning. I growl and blink rapidly. Shea is kneeling over me wearing her sexy lingerie.

"What the-" I am cut off when she presses her lips to mine. I push her off and growl.

"What are you doing?" I demand, wiping my mouth.

"Booty call," she scoffs, leaning in again. I push her off and half leap half fall of the bed.

"I don't want you!" I bark, revealing teeth.

"It's because that bitch is still alive," Shea growls. "She has put you under her spell. She is not one of us."

I bark again and change into a wolf. Shea copies and my room turns into a cage for dog fights. But Shea is nowhere near my fighting capability and soon I have her cornered with her tail between her legs.

"I am going to tell you this once and once only," I growl into her mind. *"If you ever touch a single hair on Rose's head, I swear to the gods that I will rip you apart and feed you to the buzzards."*

I bark again and Shea goes into the submissive position showing that she understands she knows I am top dog. I snap at her and she yelps, turning human and runs from my room. I turn human again and sigh, then head downstairs for breakfast.

-Rose-

I step onto my veranda and sigh. After I had finished talking and explaining what happened last night, everyone seemed like they had some where to be. Aither's excuse was the only one that sounded reasonable: he has to report to the council. My owl takes off into the woods and I leap off the veranda in hot pursuit. After a while I turn wolf and let out an excited howl. The wind feels good as it rushes through my fur. The owl banks a sharp left and I almost miss it. I follow the owl for a half an hour until it lands on a high fence, where it looks into the yard and screeches and then ruffles its feathers. I wonder what has it so unsettled. I leap the fence, and when I land, I look around wish I hadn't. All around me are giant traps and stuffed wolves. Except one isn't; it is laying down. She is barely breathing. I take a step forward and lower my head. There is a chain tied around her back ankle. I take another step forward and the wolf looks up, her eyes widen and then she whistles through her nose.

"No," she whines, standing and taking several steps back, *"the hunters will come."*

I walk over to her chains and sniff them. My eyes widen and I jerk my head back; the chain is coated with silver. I snarl as I look closer at her leg. Half of her fur is missing and her skin is blistered. I contemplate my choices, but I'm interrupted when I hear a car pull up out front. I think fast and pick the chain up in my mouth, pain races up my jaws as I begin to bite and try to break at least one link. I hear a yell followed by a click. I don't turn to find out what it was. Instead, I finally break half a link, then jerk my head and the chain scatters in a million directions. The she-wolf and I run for the fence, but not before the hunter empties a clip into my flank. I yelp and stumble before I could leap. The she-wolf however manages to make it over. She looks back at me and I growl for her to run, and she does, reluctantly. I feel the silver bullets reacting with my flesh as it expels them with a painful push. They fall down to the ground and I leap up, but a chain wraps around my left leg. I let out a painful howl and it is joined with a screaming cry of my owl that flies past me and into the face of the attacker, I wish it away so it doesn't get hurt. It obeys my command and it flies up to the tree.

I look behind me and find the hunter securing my chain to a thick metal post. I pull my hind leg and feel razor sharp needles pierce my skin and connect to the other side. I howl but it's cut off as the hunter decides to empty another clip into my side, missing my vital organs by mere millimetres. I collapse to the ground and cry as my body works on expelling the bullets. The hunter walks over to me and places his boot onto my neck. I let out a strangled yelp and hear the hunter reload. My heart races as I close my eyes and wait for death. I hear someone shout 'no', and my eyes fly open and widen as I see Tyler struggling with his father. The weight is lifted off my neck and my heart rate slows down. I try to stand but my leg is in too much pain, a solid thud makes my head snap back to the struggle. Tyler's father has dropped the gun and has hit Tyler's jaw.

"What you doing, kid?" Tyler's father says with a snarl. "You wanna end up like your mother and sister?"

Tyler glares at his father. "She is not one of them," Tyler says, glancing at me. "She won't hurt us."

"Who told you such nonsense?" his father says, laughing. "Tinker Bell, the magical fairy? You can't trust these demons!"

"She is not one of them!" Tyler yells, balling his fist. His father hits him again and the red mark swells under his left eye. I pull back my top lip and snarl as his dad grabs him by the hair and drags him inside after scowling at me. After an uncomfortable silence my body continues to pop bullets from my pelt. I hear a twig snap and my head snaps up to see a girl come out of the cover of a low lying tree, I growl deep in my throat and she laughs.

"Stupid wolf," she mumbles. "Why the hell would you come here?" My growl drops an octave and there's a ruffle in the leaves above. "I won't let you hurt him." she says, picking up the dropped gun and walks inside where I can hear Tyler's father yelling and the girl's calm voice followed by another woman's voice. I sigh, whistling through my nose and rest my head between my paws.

I am awoken with a loud bang, the back door slams open and I can see Tyler and his father walking into the woods, Tyler turns and steals a quick glance at me before following his father; in his hand is his silver stake. I look up and see the moon is almost directly overhead. My body starts to shake and I turn human. My body reacts to the full moon by stretching and digging at the ground. My back arches, and as the clock strikes midnight I throw my head back and scream. My scream is chorused by the thousands of others. Our screams turn into blood curdling howls as we change into wolves. My body bulks up and with a sharp tug I break free of my bonds and run for the fence, I jump it easily and follow on the path that Tyler has taken. I need to free him of his father's hold. Thunder booms overhead as rain falls from the clouds. With my senses awake my bright yellow eyes scan the area. My nose and ears try to pick up a trace of my victim. I stop sharply and sniff the ground before the rain washes the scent away.

I figure out that the group has split up, I turn left and start to sprint, following my victim's scent. My blood pumps quickly and I let an excited howl and I see Tyler come into view. I slow to a trot before he can see me. I crouch down and crawl closer. He is leaning over a set of tracks. As I crawl closer, I ready myself for the pounce, but as I push off the ground a voice shouts over the thunder. Tyler turns quickly and ducks and I miss him by inches. I land and slide to a stop. I turn and pull my lips back into a full snarl as Jace and Zero step into view. I bark at them and they both seem to growl back, Tyler is now standing in the middle of three snarling paranormals.

"Leave him alone," I bark into Zeros head. "He is mine!"

I run towards Tyler, but Jace zooms over to him and knocks me sideways. I shake my head and snarl again, but Zero turns wolf and Jace pushes Tyler onto his back. Within seconds they are gone in a blur. I roar in frustration. Zero, must have turned someone already, otherwise he wouldn't have his humanity. I set off after them and soon I can see Tyler on the back of Zero and Jace running beside them. I let out a howl and chase them into a river, where they swim over to the waterfall. I stay on the bank barking and growling because I know that if I enter the water they will have the upper hand. I howl a cry for help and it is replied by boom to the east.

My head snaps in that direction and I can see there has been an explosion; red fire burns through the rain. My focus goes back to the trio in the water to find that they are being lifted out and onto the top of the waterfall by the witch. I snarl and scratch my claws in the dirt before deciding to look elsewhere for my full moon victim. Another boom catches my attention and I turn and run towards the sound of gun fire and howling. I stop on the edge of the woods where it splits and turns into a clearing, and I am horrified by the sight. Werewolves and humans are fighting for their lives. I see the ground is littered with bodies— both of human and wolf.

I crouch under a bush and watch the fights. I want to jump in, but I feel glued to the spot with my tail tucked between my legs. The scene is brightly lit by fires and burning bodies. I hear a sharp gasp and look over my shoulders to see Tyler standing alone. My eyes flare and the urge takes me. I slowly stand and growl, urging him to run before I completely lose all control. But he doesn't move. He is like a statue frozen in time and the rain falls harder as another flash of lightning steaks across the sky. I realize that he and I are staring at each other and as another flash fills the sky I see his face, his strong cheekbones, his soaking dark hair, and his green eyes that are filled with fear. I can take his fear away. Time slows as I take a step towards him then I run quickly.

I leap with a powerful push and watch him close his eyes in approval. The lightning flashes and I knock him to the ground, landing on top of him. I whimper. I don't want to take his life. I don't want him to go down like I did. I try to stop myself, to pull back. I fight for control.

"It's okay," he whispers, closing his eyes. "I don't mind."

"But I do," I say, realizing that I have turned human and that I'm crying. "I do."

He remains silent for a while before he says. "Do it."

All of my humanity is lost now as I throw my head back and scream, morphing into the wolf. I howl and clench my jaws around his shoulder. He screams in pain and I throw my head back again and match his scream with my own howl of pain. I know I have to finish what I started, so I lower my head once more and lick his wound.

I hear a gunshot and pain shoots through my upper shoulder. I bark and turn to see Tyler's father holding a gun in one hand and a silver stake in the other. My wolf form fades and I face him, mortified at what

I have done to his son. I spread my arms out as if to embrace him and Tyler's father screams and runs at me, plunging the stake deep inside my chest and into my heart. I let out a final scream and collapse to the ground. The last thing I see is the moon being taken over by a crimson red colour.

8. Bleeding Rose

-Zero-

When I heard Rose's first and second howl I didn't worry. I knew it was a howl of sadness, not pain, but when her third one erupts through the woods my eyes widen. Jace and I sprint towards Rose. On the way I hear Samantha's howl— it's calling for me to hurry. Jace and I reach the clearing and I see Sam and Samantha fighting four hunters while Tyler and Rose lie unconscious, next to each other. My heart stops as I see a large silver stake sticking out of Rose's chest and anger boils in my chest. I shift to my human state and attack the closest hunter.

"Get Rose and Tyler out of here!" I yell at Jace and the others as I start to fight. "I'm calling for back up!"

Sam and Jace exchange a look and nod. Sam picks up Tyler while Jace's eyes fill with blood tears as he picks up Rose's body. Her head rolls backwards and my stomach launches. I break my opponents neck.

"Samantha!" I bark. "I said go, they will need backup."

She nods her head and bounds after them. I sigh a sigh of relief and turn wolf, continuing my attack.

"Now, would be a good time to appear, Aither!" I think as my jaw closes around my victim's neck. An explosion of bright colours spread through the woods: blue, white, red, and green. The fighting stops as the colours seem to dance around then explode, causing all the hunters to drop like leaves; not dead, but unconscious. The wolves turn around and run to the cover of the woods, but I run alone, running towards Rose's house. When I get there I turn human and burst inside. Water drops to the floor as I shake out my hair and as I approach the living room I see the circle as well as Tyler, Samantha, Sam, and Cleo weeping silent tears. Sam and Jace's cheeks are stained red with blood, and my heart clenches.

"Where is she?" I ask, my voice quavering

"We took her to her room," Jace says in a soft voice, burying his face in his hands. A tear leeks down my face and I decide to take my final look at her. When I open the door I expect to see Rose sitting on her bed with her sketchpad on her lap drawing, but as I step inside, my heart drops as I see her pale, lifeless body just lying there. My knees buckle underneath me and I collapse at the side of her bed.

"I'm sorry," I whisper, taking her fragile hand in mine. "I am so sorry."

I hear a cat meow and I look up to see a little black cat sitting at her feet; on the post of her bed is a barn owl. They both look at me with curious eyes. I sigh and shake my head. Lightning cracks and I stand and make my way out of the room, but not before the cat meows again. I silently shut the door and head back downstairs to rejoin the others in the living room.

The silence is suffocating. Rose has left a hole in everyone's lives. Even Jace continues to weep his bloody tears. My mind fills with memories of Rose's life, her laugh, her smile, and her lips against mine. Everyone seems to be doing the same thing: remembering Rose and her life with us. We all seem to be looking at something yet nothing at all. Lightning cracks and it seems even the sky weeps for our loss. There's a knock on the door and Lilly walks in.

"Hey guys," she says as Caleb trails in behind her. Everyone looks at Lilly and a silence fills the room. "Where's Rosie girl?"

"You don't need me here for your loss," Tyler says standing, still holding his bloody shoulder he heads to the back door. "I will leave your life alone."

"What's happened?" Lilly asks, looking around at our faces. Her face softens as she realizes. "No," she whispers, "No, it's not true!" she screams, collapsing to the floor.

Caleb's face stays hard and unemotional while Samantha and Cleo stand and sit Lilly down on the sofa. Caleb leaves and the room returns to an awkward silence. We sit here for what seems like forever, but the rain eventually stops and the moon is replaced by the sun; yet we still stay glued to our spots, either on the floor or on a chair.

The sun left and the moon came again. I decide to stand and walk into the kitchen, which is directly below Rose's bed. I stand, not really thinking, not really seeing, but then I hear the sound of boots hitting hard wood. I thought it was just my imagination, but when I hear a scream and a solid thud of a heavy object hitting the floor I was sure it wasn't my imagination because everyone else piles into the kitchen and looks at me. In a split second, we race up the stairs and pile into Rose's room. I was astonished at what we saw. Aither stands shirtless and his tattoos are aflame, but what shocks me most is that Rose is curled up on her bed, breathing. The stake was on the floor rolls on the floor.

"What did you do?" Jace asks quietly.

"Did you know that the hunter is a vampire?" he asks, looking at me. His eyes glowing white. Rose groans and curls up on herself.

"What's happening?" Jace snarls as Aither sits on the side of the bed and places a hand on Rose's back. She sighs in pain and turns over to the source of heat.

"She is in shock and needs heat," Aither says, glaring at the rest of us. "And seeing how she doesn't know the Guardians very well, I volunteered. Plus, I am the cleanest here. Now, if you don't mind— get out."

Aither is right and we all know it, so we silently file out and shut the door. We walk into the living room and organize a plan. One by one we all go for a showers, then I order Chinese food,.We finish eating and arranged sleeping patterns. We fit everyone into the two bedrooms and the lounge room easily and soon everyone is asleep. But I cannot sleep, so I silently make my way out of the house and into the barn. Indi snorts as I enter and greet her with a pat before making my way up to the loft. I cross the plank and step onto her balcony. I peer into the room and see that Rose is awake on the side of the bed.

Her eyes are bright yellow. They glow and darken as she blinks. There's another pair of eyes sitting in the dark— Aither's white ones. As my eyes adjust, I see that he has his arms wrapped around her waist and he's murmuring in her ears.

I sigh and leap from the balcony, landing as a wolf. I should leave, but I decide against it. Instead, I go back inside and fall asleep by the door. The next morning everyone pitches in to clean up Rose's home. she still has not come down from her room. However, Aither has come down a few times to get water and food for her. The morning passes quickly and soon it is lunch time. I head into the kitchen and open the fridge to find it almost empty.

"You guys might want to think about restocking the fridge," I say, going back into the lounge.

"Sure," Sam says, grabbing Rose's keys from a decorated fruit bowl. He glances at Samantha and they both walk to the door.

"You might want to think about going home," Sam says in a rough tone. "She doesn't need you here."

I nod and he closes the door behind him. I sigh when I hear the jeep pull out the driveway and I head for the back door, but I am stopped when the little black cat jumps in my way. She hisses and swipes at me with her claws.

"What the hell," I gape, jumping back. The owl screeches and grabs at me with its talons. I batter it away but it comes back and grabs the collar of my shirt with its beak, trying to pull me away from the door. I bat it away and take another little jump back, but, again, the cat is there continuing to swipe at my legs. With one final try, I leap backwards and fall, having tripped on the bottom stair. Lying on my back, I look up to Rose's room and see the door ajar.

"If anyone is down there," Aither says with a grunt and there is a snap in the background. "I could use some help."

The cat and owl dart upstairs and I follow. Inside, Rose is in wolf form and she has Aither pinned with her face close to his. She notices my presence and lifts her head and snarls.

"What's happening?" I ask, taking in the scenery.

"A piece of the silver stake broke off. It's still in her chest," Aither says, giving Rose a forceful push. She barks and nips at his hand, and I jump for her. Turning wolf, I tackle her to the side. She fights back, but I eventually pin her, Aither is next to her in a matter of seconds searching for her weak spot. Rose barks and snaps her jaws down hard; yellow lightning erupts and runs down her jaw line. Aither's face hardens as he can't find the weak point, and Rose takes this opportunity and clamps down on my leg. I yelp as the electricity runs up my leg. In shock, I leap back and wait for Rose to continue, but she doesn't come. I open my eyes and see that Aither was able to find the weak spot in the nick of time. I change into my human form and cradle my arm.

"What do we do now?" I sigh, standing over Rose. Aither looks around the room and holds up a hand. His tattoos flame and a flick knife leaps out of one of Rose's dresser draws; Aither catches it with ease and looks painfully down at Rose's face.

"No," I say with a gasp and take a step forward. "You can't just kill her."

"Relax, dog boy," Aither says, grabbing the hem of Rose's shirt and lifting it over her head. "I am going to remove the rest of the stake."

"But... it's in her heart," I protest as my arm begins to heal.

"No, it's not," he says, placing the knife under her bra. With a flick of his wrist, the bra comes undone and I don't know where to look. "As her body tried to expel the silver, she was able to get it out of her heart and closer to the centre."

Aither repositions the knife and gently plunges it in. Rose's eyes snap open and she tries to squirm, but Aither holds her down as a sweet smell of honey dew and chocolate fills the air. He drags the knife down her chest. Rose opens her mouth in a silent scream and her nails dig into the floor as her eyes turn yellow.

"Zero," Aither says, drawing my attention to him. "I require some assistance."

"What?" I ask, kneeling down on Rose's other side. He reaches into his back pocket and pulls out two silver coins. My eyes widen as he hands them to me.

"Her body will heal around my hand otherwise," he says as I lay the coins flat in the wound. The wound begins to close, but stops when it hits the coins, leaving a big enough hole for Aither to get his hand in. And that's exactly what he does. Slowly, he slides his hand into the wound and digs around. Rose lets out a small squeak as her yellow eyes brighten and the squeak turns to a deep growl as her teeth sharpen right before my eyes. Rose's arms wrap around Aither's body and she digs her nails in his back, tearing through his skin as she drags them across and blood flows out.

"Zero, I'm going to need you to hold her down," Aither says as his face hardens. I don't protest as I remove her arms off his back. She grabs onto my wrists and digs into my flesh. I curse under my breath and feel my eyes turn deep blue. Rose's eyes turn to mine and she stops fighting, but her nails are still in my wrists. She whispers something low and a deep energy runs up my arms, flowing inside of me.

I hear her voice whisper in my head so soft I don't know what she's saying. Goose flesh covers my skin and my eyes glow brighter as I feel her nails leave my skin and a cool metal replaces them, starting at my wrists and ending under my elbow. Her whispers become louder in my head and I can make out the sound, *"Black Knight"*. A cool metal spreads over my body until I am covered in black armour. It's surprisingly light.

Aither's eyes widen as he pulls his hand out. He opens his hand and he's holding the tip of the stake, but it has added technological bits and pieces. Aither closes his fist again and I can hear the tip shatter. He then drops the remains on the ground and turns back to Rose and removes the two coins, but she doesn't heal.

"Why isn't she healing," I ask, my eyes glowing with worry.

"Because she has used most of her energy on you," Aither says, scooping her up in his arms and taking her to the bed. "Go and grab the first aid box from under the sink."

I run and realize that the armour is gone. *Was it ever real?* I grab the first aid box and run back to Aither and hand it to him. He takes it and pulls out a needle and thread and begins to stitch her up, but before he could pull the tread through, Rose grabs his wrist and he freezes as she trails her hands up and stops above his bare chest where his heart beats below the skin. They seem to have a conversation with just their eyes.

After a long, uncomfortable silence, he nods his head. Rose lays her hand flat and yellow lines flow from her hand and around his body. The needle slips from his grasp and falls to the floor. The yellow lines fork and fork again and again until almost all of Aither's body, and the room, is lit with a beautiful light, filling every nook and cranny of the room. As fast as it came, it leaves, recoiling back into Rose's hand. Aither's eyes roll back and he slumps onto Rose's chest. She wraps her arms around him and strokes his hair.

"You can leave, my black knight," Rose says, her eyes glowing but not looking at mine. "Go home to your pack."

I don't argue. I don't question. I just walk out leaving Rose and her house behind.

-Rose-

I lay there with Aither resting on my bare chest, stoking his hair as the rest of the yellow fades from my eyes. With great gentleness, I push him off and leave him resting as I make my way over to my closet. I pick out a tank top, underwear, and a pair of jeans and head into the shower. I can see the scar where the stake went in thanks to the mirror. It's just a smidge to the left.

I strip off the rest of my clothing and turn the shower on. Water hits my skin and I close my eyes as I'm taken me back to last night; the smell of the dirt and soil, and the feel of rain hitting my skin. My eyes snap open with the sudden realization. I bit Tyler. The water doesn't feel comforting anymore; it feels harsh and mocking. So I step out and dry myself before changing into my clothes. When I step into my room, Aither is still sleeping, so I sneak out and head down to the basement. I almost fall down the stairs when a cat darts past me. As I enter the basement, my mum's feelings smother me. I step into sight and see her eyes already open. I smile at her and she smiles at me.

"Hi," I say, smiling and walking over to her tanks.

"Honey, we were worried sick," mum says, placing her hand against the glass. I place mine over hers and smile.

"Thanks, for looking after me," I say, walking over to dad's tank. His eyes remain closed even when I touch the tank. "What's wrong with him?"

"He has used too much energy trying to get out of here," she says, turning her head and her face softens. I take my hand away from the tank and walk over to the desk and flip through numerous pages of notes that Jeremy Salamander wrote. I find a page on all of the experiments he has conducted and all of the ways to reverse them. I come across the tanks and their usage.

"Who told you about not being able to get out of the tanks?" I ask, flipping through the pages. The cat leaps up onto the desk and sits above the book.

"Jeremy," my mother says as the cat seems to read.

"Well, it says here that two werewitches could bring you out," I say, flipping backwards and forwards frantically. "Is there any way that Lilly might be a werewitch?"

"No, she was born human. You took her power. Normally, when twins are born, one has the mother's power and the other has the father's," mum says. *"We have no connection to your sister."*

My owl lands on the arm of the chair and tilts its head to the side as if asking me a question. I hum to myself as I gently stroke my owl's feathers. I realize that it doesn't have a name and try to think of one. I run through a list of names, but the owl doesn't pay attention.

"Lilac," I whisper in a final attempt, and finally the owl looks at me. I smile and stroke its head, then glance at the clock on the wall and sigh. I stand and hold my arm out for Lilac; she jumps onto it and we walk upstairs. Aither is up and sitting in the lounge with Sam and Samantha.

"Hi, guys," I say. Samantha jumps up and grabs me in her arms. Lilac flies before she is squished and lands on the sofa.

"You are such a stupid head," Samantha says as tears fall. "Why did you have to go and get yourself killed for?"

I smile and look over at Sam as Samantha lets me go. I walk over to him as he stands, and he wraps me in a tight hug and whispers, "Don't ever scare us like that again." I smile and look up at him.

"I promise," I say, laughing. I look over to Aither. He looks in pain, "Are you okay?"

He nods, but his face says otherwise. I walk over to him and touch his forehead. It seems fine.

"What?" I ask him. He looks away from me and I sigh. "If you won't answer me that, then answer me this: is there another werewitch?"

His eyes snap back to me and widen. He nods just once and he stands up.

"He is still alive," Aither says, pacing. "We banished him onto an island of some sort."

"I have to see him," I say, almost yelling, "He can help me free my mother."

"No!" Aither shouts, turning to me. "He is dangerous. He's killed many other werewitches."

"Aither, I have to try. My mother and father can't stay in those tanks forever," I say, my eyes threatening tears. "I have to try."

"No," he says as his tattoos flare. "I won't let you." Aither vanishes, so I call Jace and tell him to bring the Guardians over. They arrive within the hour and we sit in the lounge room and talk.

"I know there is another werewitch," I say as soon as we sit. "I need to find him. He holds the key to releasing my mother."

"Rose, that's suicide," Jace says, almost laughing. "I know all about him. He is almost three hundred years old. That's more power than you."

"I don't care!" I shout, jumping from my chair and my eyes flash yellow. "I have to find him."

"I can send some of my demons to find traces of him," the warlock, Paul, says, shrugging.

"And I can try a locater spell," the witch, Tamika, says.

"I can ask the plants," Emily says. "And the animals."

"The spirit world might know something," Peter says. I look from one paranormal to the next and smile. I nod my head and they set to work, summoning their powers and helping me find the other werewitch.

"It might take a couple of days for us to get the information back," Tamika says to me before she starts. "Our powers have to scour the globe, you know."

"Take your time," I say, walking outside. Lilac flies out and lands in a tree, before quickly swooping down and catching an unsuspecting mouse that was crawling around in the under growth. I walk over to the barn and Indi greets me with a whinny. I smile and walk into her stall. I gather her reins from the hook on the inside, ride out bareback, and head into the thick woods at a full speed gallop.

I slow down and stop when I reach my destination: the apple tree where I first met Zero. I tie Indi up and she begins to happily munch on fallen apples. I turn wolf and begin to wander around, sniffing the ground to see if I can pick up any trace of the one I am searching for. I am suddenly hit and knocked sideways. I slide to a stop and look around; my ears flatten against my head and I pull my lips back in a deep growl. My growl is matched by another as a wolf steps into view. It is black and has a white tip on its tail. My ears flatten further and I growl deeply.

He charges, leaping from the ground with a thunderous bark. I dodge the attack and counter by pouncing onto his side and pinning him down. He brings his back legs up and kicks me off. I bark in frustration and circle him. He snaps at me and I go back to when Zero and I first sparred. Using some techniques that I picked up off the others, I attack again and again; each time repositioning myself so he misses me. I am agile and quick on my feet, moving with such precision and speed that I would have seemed like a white blur to the other wolf. As I circle the wolf again, I see his eyes have two different colours: one green the other yellow. The wolf lunges for me and I dodge again, turning back on myself and biting my opponents shoulder. He yelps and I take my chance and let out a loud bark that could be mistaken for a roar. The wolf yelps and goes into submissive position. I snap at him.

"Change," I growl and the wolf whimpers again. He changes and I am shocked. Lying on the ground in front of me is Tyler. He looks into my eyes and I can see that even in his human form his eyes are both different: one yellow one green. I turn human and gasp.

"Tyler," I say, kneeling down to his eye level. "Oh my God."

"Hey, Rose," he smiles, coughing. "Good to see you."

"What happened to your eyes?" I ask as we stand up.

"I don't know," he says, dusting himself off. "They've been like this since I first changed."

"Listen," I say as we begin to walk. "I'm sorry about that night-"

"No," he says, turning and taking my arms so quickly that my eyes flash yellow. "I wanted this. Jace and Zero warned me what would happen. I agreed because I wanted to get out of my human life. You changed me, Rose. Before you changed my appearance, I felt different ever since I meet you," he says, taking my hands in his. "I couldn't put the stake through your heart that night because I saw something in your eyes. I saw someone confused and strong, scared and beautiful. Like a warrior that had her cracks. I saw me."

My heart races as I look into his eyes. Images flash through my mind. Happy ones. Every time I saw him I felt something. I never knew what it was before, but now I do. He lets one of my hands go and tilts my chin upwards and brings his lips down to mine in a soft, passionate kiss. I melt into him as he pulls me closer by wrapping me in his arms. For the first time ever, I feel safe and secure. I go up on tip-toes and wrap my arms around his neck. He pulls away and blushes.

"Sorry," he says and I am surprised. "I just thought that you should know how I felt."

My heart is stunned as he begins to walk away.

"Wait," I say, my voice shaky from the kiss. "Tyler, wait."

He stops and turns around to face me.

"Where are you going?" I ask as my voice smooths out.

"I don't know," he says, shrugging. "I don't really have anywhere to go."

"Come back to my place," I suggest. "You can stay there until you get back on your feet. Or longer, if you want."

"Sure," he says. His face and eyes brighten. We walk in silence until we reach the apple tree. Indi stomps her feet and whinnies upon my approach. I smile, then take a running leap. I kick off the tree and land gracefully on Indi's back and hold my hand out for Tyler. He shoots me a crooked smile as he grips my hand. I pull him up and he puts his arms around me, sitting closer than he has to, but I don't mind. His skin feels cool against mine.

After we arrive home and put Indi away, we head inside to see the progress made on finding the other werewitch. Tyler tails behind me, his muscles tense like he is expecting someone to attack him. I slip him an easy smile and he smiles back. I take his hand and lead him through the maze that has grown in my living room. Voices all talk over each other. Candles, plants, demons, and misty ghosts scatter everywhere, and, as I step over a small sapling in a glass jar, a strong force pushes Tyler backwards, knocking his hand out of mine and pushing him to the ground. He lands on a sapling in a glass jar. The jar shatters and pieces stick into his skin as Aither appears, his face pulled into a scowl.

All the voices stop as Tyler leaps up and changes. He growls and Aither sends another six glass jars into Tyler's pelt. The Guardians moves to the edge of the room, glancing at each other with worried looks. Tyler's growl deepens as more jars are lifted.

"Stop!" I shout as the jars fly. They immediately stop just inches from Tyler's skin, and I use my powers to return the jars back to their original places. I then turn and glare at Aither.

"Get out," I say, almost in a whisper. Aither doesn't move, doesn't even look at me. "Aither, get out!" I shout and power rocks through my body. I unknowingly push him backwards. His eyes glance at me and I shout again with more power. He cringes like I had punched him in the stomach before leaving the house with a solid slam of the door. No one moves or speaks for a while.

"Continue," I say, looking back to the Guardians. They move slowly as I take the scruff of Tyler's neck and lead him into the hunting room. His claws scrape on the wooden floor boards as I open the door and guide him inside.

"Don't change," I say, closing the door. "It will be easier if you stay a wolf."

He sits in the middle of the room as I grab the emergency first aid kit. Aither had made sure to get every shard of glass into Tyler's skin, so I need the tweezers. Tyler watches my every move as I grab the tweezers and an authentic glass bowl from the cupboard and make my way back to him. All is silent as I place the bowl down next to him.

"Stay still," I say softly as I kneel next to his large body. Taking a deep breath, I start to remove the glass pieces. Tyler whimpers when I take the first piece and pull it out, but after the third time he calms down.

"I know what you are," he whispers in my head. My head shoots up as I drop the glass into the bowl, his eyes are staring right at me.

"What do you mean?" I ask, playing dumb and looking away, 'concentrating' on getting the glass out.

"A werewitch," he says, lying down. *"I saw your memories."*

I sit stunned. I never saw memories when I was turned, I didn't even feel a connection.

"Can you show me?" he asks, looking back at me. *"Please?"*

I stand quickly and pace the room. Is this a good idea? I don't think for long because my powers were pulling at me and, before I knew it, I was pulling each single shard of glass out of Tyler's body and into the bowl, my arms moving on their own, guiding and directing the glass to the bowl. Once the last shard drops into the bowl, my arms drop and I fall to the floor in exhaustion.

"Rose!" Tyler shouts, rushing to my side. He nudges my cheek with his nose and whines.

"I'm fine," I say, my voice rasping. I place my hand on his head and he helps me up.

"It's glowing," Tyler gasps, turning human and taking Aither's ring in his hands. I gape as the blue swirls turn green and curl around a golden light. The light blackens as the curls tighten and eventually crush it, and then fade back to blue. I yank the chain from my neck and drop it on the floor. I realize that the necklace would have sat in between my breasts, over the core of my power.

"Aither!" I call, anger boils inside me as I scrape the necklace off the floor and hold it by the chain. "Make yourself known to me!"

He appears in the corner of the room.

"What the hell is this?" I shout, using all my strength not to attack him.

"It is a ring," he says, acting dumb. I growl in my chest and use a spell to shatter the bowl filled with glass.

"What is this?" I demand. The floorboards' creek as I throw the necklace to him. He catches it effortlessly and my anger turns into rage. He thinks he is so cool acting dumb. From behind me I hear Tyler take a step back.

"It is my father's ring infused with the power of air to create the swirls," he says again. His lies scrape in my head and mock me.

"Lies!" I scream, digging my nails into the floor. My anger and rage boils over as I shout something that I couldn't register. From the corner of my eye, I see Tyler change back to a wolf and growl at Aither, whose eyes are wide with fear. I bare my own teeth and scream a painful cry. Tears steam down my face as I command the floorboards to lift and wrap around Aither's body. They spring forward and pin him to the wall, or at least they try. Aither is quick to react and disappears. I freeze and so do the boards as I look around, trying to find any trace of him. When I am certain that he is gone, I make the floorboards go back into place before collapsing to the floor crying. Tyler cautiously approaches and noses my cheek with his nose.

"I trusted him," I sob as Tyler lays down next to me. His fur feels soft against my skin, so I half sit up and lay my head on his back. I can hear his heart beat as electricity runs through me. In a flash, I dig my nails in to his back. He yelps, but stays still. I don't have control over my body as a fat tear rolls down my face and lands on Tyler's back. The tear spreads and covers his back, and then it washes away, leaving behind white armour covering his back, front and back, legs, his chest, and his head. I regain control and pull back, gasping. Tyler stands and turns human, the armour is still there, but this time it looks like Zero's.

"What is this?" Tyler asks, touching his arm guards.

"I guess," I say, standing and taking a big step back. "I guess I have dubbed you my white knight."

"What?" he asks, looking into my eyes and I feel powerless and stupid.

"I don't know," I stammer. As tears begin to fall, I cover my face with my hands. "I wasn't in control. I am sorry."

"No," he says, wrapping his arms around me. "It's okay. I'm fine with it, honestly."

I know he's scared. I can hear his heartbeat, and he is faking not being scared and strong for my sake. He hushes me and strokes my hair as I weep on his armoured chest. But as my rage cools, the armour disappears and Tyler pulls me closer. My name is called from the lounge room and we pull apart. I wipe my tears and walk out of the hunting room with Tyler in my shadow. As I step into the lounge, I see that the Guardians have pushed every bit of furniture against the wall.

"We can't find any trace of the werewitch," Tamika says, walking over to me. "Normally, it would take a couple of days for us to find anything, but I have reason to believe the werewitch has a blocked all methods of tracking."

"Well, then we will have to settle for the next best thing," I say, stepping around a plant. "Find a relative or a friend of the werewitch. This man is almost three hundred years old. Someone must know something of him."

Tamika nods and goes back to the circle of candles.

"All right, people," Tamika says, sitting in her circle. "Let's get to it."

As the words leave her mouth the room falls deathly silent. The candles light and Tamika begins to chant in Latin. Emily's circle of plants jump alive and take her hands as she also begins to chant. Paul goes deathly white as he falls into spirit mode; the ice glows and the room chills. As I look over to the warlock the chanting increases. the warlock's circle springs alive as demons sprout from the body parts and run out the back door and into the woods. I shake my head and walk into the kitchen and see Jace biting down on a blood bag. My stomach launches and I look away and clear my throat. Jace looks up and his eyes widen.

"Sorry," he stammers, dropping the empty bag into the bin.

"It's okay," I sigh, looking back to him when I am sure that I won't lose my stomach contents.

"Is this the wolf that is going to replace Zero?" Jace asks, nodding over my shoulder to Tyler who glares at Jace.

"Yeah, I guess so," I say, grabbing a bottle of water out of the fridge.

"Are you going to call your black knight?" Jace asks, raising an eyebrow and I slowly nod.

"Black knight, be here. I am in need of your services," I say and the wind outside picks up and carries my message to Zero.

"Who is your black knight?" Tyler asks, leaning on the island in the kitchen.

"Zero," I sigh, putting the bottle back and closing the door. "I wasn't in control."

Tyler goes to speak, but the front door bursts open and Zero walks in wearing his armour. I wave a dismissive hand and Zero's armour goes away.

"Zero, I need your father's ring," I say, holding out my hand.

"What?" he gasps. "No, I am a circle member. Only the werewitch can control who is in its circle."

"Give it to me, now," I say, using the bond I created. He stiffens and takes the ring from his finger, then hands it to me. I take it in my hand and walk over to Tyler.

"Zero," I say, as I put the ring on Tyler's finger. "You have abused your right as a circle member, and therefore I revoke your place as a circle member and give the privilege to Tyler Harding."

"You can't do that," Zero says, tensing. I look over to Jace and his skin ripples. I shake my head and he calms down. "Only the werewitch can."

"Go home, I do not wish for your presence." I say, waving a dismissive hand.

He scowls, but reluctantly goes home, leaving the house with a slam. I sigh and let out a shaky breath.

"Are you okay?" Tyler asks, placing a hand on my shoulder. I look into his eyes and smile.

"I'm fine," I say, looking out the window. It's almost dark. "I'm going for a run, alone." I add as Tyler begins to follow me. I walk out through the lounge and the circle is still chanting. I take a running leap off the veranda and land as a wolf. I sprint through the woods until I find a deer grazing. I crouch down, placing my paws carefully, and making sure I don't make a sound. The deer doesn't suspect a thing until it's too late. With full force, I leap and land on a doe and the herd scatters in panic. I devour it in less than twenty minutes, then go in search of my next victim. I continue walking until I find another lone deer. I crouch and go through the whole process again, but this time when I leap, I am knocked sideways and the deer runs away. I growl and look around for the offender. I scan the shadows and the trees until my eyes rest on a body figure. My growl deepens as the figure steps into the light. Tyler's dad's fangs extend as he hisses at me. I growl deeply and he laughs.

"Hunters season isn't over yet," Tyler's father laughs as more hunters step into view. "I called a couple of friends this time. You killed my son."

The hunters run at me, and I snarl as my muscles tense. As the hunters come closer I attack, but my attacks are almost pointless; they are all vampires, they heal quickly. I growl as some manage to sink their teeth into me, and I use a spell to expel them off me. They snarl and their fangs gleam red with my blood. My confidence drops as I continue to snarl at the vampires. A more thunderous growl erupts and the vampires are flung from my pelt. I look up to see my friends joining in on the fight, among them are Caleb and Lilly, fighting side by side.

"Sorry we couldn't get here earlier," Jace says as he plunges his hand into a vampire's chest. He pulls the vampire's heart out and smiles at me.

"How did you get Lilly and Caleb to help?" I ask, jumping over Tyler.

"Jace had to compel them to rip markings off their arms," he says, ducking as a vampire launches over him and into my jaws. *"That wasn't easy. Or pretty for that matter."*

Vampires hiss and start to surrender. Tyler's father growls and leaps for his unsuspecting son. I bark and meet him mid-leap. We fall to the ground. I turn human and hold him down, knocking the large silver knife from his hand and take it for myself. I press the knife to his throat and draw blood.

"No!" Tyler shouts in his human form. I don't look at him. I keep my pressure and focus on his father. "Rose, please, no."

I sigh and stupidly look over to Tyler's scared eyes. With blinding speed, Tyler's father knocks the knife away and holds it to my own neck. As the gang goes to attack, he presses it closer to my neck and they all freeze.

"No one move," Tyler's father hisses, pushing the knife closer to my neck. My skin hisses as blood slowly runs down my neck. "You shed my blood, I shed yours."

I struggle to get away, but in a flash his fangs are tearing at my neck. I scream as burning pain races through me.

"You're so tasssty," he hisses in my ear as he nuzzles the wound again. "Letsss have ussss another bite."

I squirm and let out a little yelp as he digs back in for another bite, but before he does, he screams in pain and pushes me away. I fall to the ground and cringe as I land head first onto a rock and my vision blurs. The wolves growl and Tyler's face appears into my vision. He looks worried and I reach up and place my hand on his cheek. All I hear is white noise as Tyler lifts me off the ground and carries me away. I twist my head to see Jace and the wolves standing around a burning body. I cringe and hold on to Tyler. A water drop falls on my cheek and I look upwards. The sky is clear. I turn to Tyler again and see his cheeks are wet. I give him a wary smile as I wipe his tears away. He smiles back at me and my heart flutters as I place my head on his shoulder before falling asleep to the steady sound of his heart.

I wake up on my bed with Tyler sitting beside me. My shoulder aches and my body trembles. When Tyler finds out I'm awake, he stands and keels beside my bed.

"How are you feeling?" he asks, taking my hand. I mumble a reply and sit up and rub my neck. I gasp and pull my hand away. It is wet with blood.

"Why aren't I healing?" I whisper to myself, putting my hand back to my neck to reduce the blood flow.

"That's what I thought," Tyler says, hanging his head. "It's my entire fault, and I should have let you kill him."

"It's okay," I whisper, squeezing his hand. "So, I'm still bleeding. I will heal eventually."

"No, you won't," says Jace from the shadows. "Mr Harding, has injected you with vampire venom when he drank your blood."

"What does that mean?" I ask, looking into his eyes and worry races through me.

"It means you go crazy and then die a painful death," he says, and a small whine escapes my throat.

"Unless another vampire sucks the venom from your blood system," Sam says, making himself seen. His hair catches in the moonlight as his eyes lock with mine.

I look from Jace to Sam and my stomach flips as I nod my head once and the two vampires are at my side in an instant.

"Who do you want?" Sam asks, and I look at them both, then to Tyler, whose eyes watch me with intense pressure.

"I trust you, Sam," I whisper, removing my hand. Sam nods and gives me a sad smile as he slides in behind me and I lean into his chest.

"Leave us," Sam says to Tyler. "This is a vampire thing."

Tyler growls deep in his chest and I sigh.

"Go Ty," I whisper as my energy fades. "I don't want you to see this."

He looks into my eyes and I force a smile. "I'm going to be okay," I say and Tyler leaves. The smile fades as Sam sets himself up. I hear his jaw crack as his fangs slide down. My body tenses and my heart rate doubles. He wraps one arm over my chest and the other around my stomach. I whimper as he digs into my neck. Pain races through me as Jace's face comes around in front of me and takes my hand to hold. My body aches and shudders as Sam takes my blood and the venom. Then, all at once, Sam pulls back and lets out a hiss. Relief flows through me as the pain is lessened and my wounds quickly heal. I sigh and look into Sam's eyes. They are red with blood lust. I squirm and break out of Sam's hold, and Jace grabs Sam and they both vanish out the window.

-Zero-

Rose comes downstairs and smiles and walks towards me. I smile back at her, but I immediately feel stupid as she walks past me and to Tyler.

"I told you I'd be fine," she smiles at him and touches his cheek. He smiles back and kisses her softly on her cheek. Jealousy rages in my chest and I tear my eyes away from her. Cleo enters the room with a laptop and a big duffel bag in her hand.

"What the hell?" Rose asks as Cleo dumps the bag on the floor.

"I want to help," Cleo says. "You and I both know that I am amazing with the computers. Plus, I can move in to the basement and help with the machinery."

"What do you mean?" Rose asks, walking over to her friend.

"Well, those machines won't run themselves, and I will be able to care for the paranormals down there," Cleo says and my head snaps up.

"What paranormals?" I ask, looking at Rose. She glares at me.

"Nothing," she says. "None of your business."

I shrug and Rose turns back to Cleo.

"Sure." She nods with a smile. "I still think we have that spare bed of Lilly's."

"I will be needing that," Lilly says, piping up and moving forward from the group and I glance at her arm. Her mark is gone. I glance at all the others and they too have removed their markings.

"What the hell," I say and they all look at me. "Where are your marks?"

"We removed them," Caleb says, stuffing his hands in his pockets. "We don't want to be in that type of pack. It does things to you."

"Oh?" I ask, glaring at him. "Then what type of pack do you want to be in?"

"Rose's," Samantha says.

"What!" Rose squeaks, almost screaming as she spins quickly. "I don't have a pack."

"Do now," Lilly smiles, taking her sister by the arm. "And you are the pack leader."

Rose groans and I roll my eyes. She will never make it as an alpha.

"Well, I suppose I have to organize living arrangements?" she says. They all laugh and I sigh. Jace and Sam run into the kitchen with blinding speed. Their eyes are red with blood lust.

"Rose," Sam hisses. "Best lock up tonight."

"What, what's wrong?" Rose asks with worry in her voice.

"Vampires," Jace puffs as he locks the front door. "Best kick this dog out."

I growl and he hisses right back at me. Rose glares at me, and I glare back and then everyone is glaring, growling, or hissing at me so I leave.

-Rose-

"What's happening?" I ask as Zero leaves and Sam locks the door behind him.

"Vampires," Sam says, zooming around the room. "They are looking for you. We don't know why. They are coming by the hundreds."

I look at the pack and they look at me. I'm the alpha, after all.

"We need to lock the basement," I say, looking towards Cleo.

"Lock me down there," she says and I stare at her. "I cannot fight, Rose."

We spend the next hour locking the doors and carrying the supplies down to the basement. After that, I lock the bookcase back in place. I look towards Tamika, who just entered the room.

"Is there a type of spell that will keep the bookcase closed?" I ask and she nods. My head clicks to something. "Wait, I thought the circle was in a trance and you wouldn't come out of for days?"

"We were," she agrees, nodding. "We have found a connection already."

"Who?" I ask, leaning on the bookcase and folding my arms over my chest.

"The werewitches circle," she says. Walking over to the bookcase, she mumbles a few Italian words and then turns to me. "The case is sealed so that no paranormal can enter or exit without your permission," she says, taking my arm and leading me out of the room. "You'd best grab a bag in case we need to make a run for it."

I slam on my brakes and tilt my head at her. "Why?" I ask.

"The vampires are coming by the hundreds," she reminds me. "It's just in case."

I quickly pack a bag and leave it by the door before returning to the hunting room. Fear spreads through me as I begin to pace, and then I look at the manacle on my wrist and sigh again. I still haven't figured out how to use it. But a thought comes to mind as I see the dots transform into eyes— little ones barely noticeable, but they are there. There is a red, a green, a clear one, a purple, and an orange one all standing close to each other and I guess that it is the circle. I can see my eye a bright yellow one sitting further away from them. I smile and feel proud of myself until I notice a bright blue one behind me, Aither. I spin quickly and he takes me in his arms, I go to scream but he covers my mouth with his hand.

"Shh," he hisses. "I am not going to hurt you. I am here to tell you that I didn't know about the ring."

I scowl at him and ask a silent question. "Theresa placed Spotted Alder Roots into my necklace so whenever you used magic it would attack it. She wanted your powers to go away."

"Why?" I ask as he slowly removes his hand. "Why would she do that?

"Because you are the first female werewitch in the history of werewitches," he says, and I raise an eyebrow.

"No, I'm not. There's been about a hundred other werewitches," I say, putting my hands on my hips. "One of them had to be a female."

"No," he says, shaking his head. "None of them were. She wants you out of the picture so that another male can try."

"She is extremely sexist against her own sex," I say. I look into his eyes and it shows that he is not lying. I sigh and tear my eyes away.

"I will always be on your side," he says, taking my hand. My name is called and I look towards the hall. I see Tyler's shadow and look back to Aither.

"You need to go," I say. He nods and kisses my hand before vanishing into thin air. Tyler enters the room as I pick up my duffel bag.

"Are you ready for this?" he asks, and I nod, trying to forget about Aither.

"You might want to get your weapons," he says, nodding at me. I look down and realize that I forgot them. I go back to my room and grab my dagger and gun. I then go down to my father's hunting room and raid his safe that is full of guns and ammunition. I rush back to the others, tying my hair into a pony tail as I go. Tyler's eyes widen and he looks away and blushes. I smile at Tyler and he smiles at me as I walk over to him and hand him a gun.

"Know how to use this?" I tease and he smiles and nods. He opens his mouth to say something, but an explosion happens to the east of the house. Vampires and demons file in by the dozen, turning my house into a war zone with blood going everywhere. The warlock uses his magic to create demons, but the house is getting crowded.

I turn and run to the kitchen counter where a number of bags are piled on the floor. I grab my keys and duffel bag. A demon leaps over the counter and I shoot it in the head; blood splatters onto me as the demon and I collide. I shoot it again and push it off me, then push myself up and into a vampire's arm. I growl in anger as it hisses at me and extends its fangs. I shoot it and count my bullets.

One..... The vampire screams.
Two..... White noise fills my ears.
Three.... The screaming stops.
Four....For good luck.

I try again and this time I am able to grab my hand bag and recover my keys and duffel from the ground.

"Fall back!" I shout, turning and running. "Get to the car!"

We all run out, grabbing the bags as we go. I slide into the front seat and all the doors open. Jace slides into the front and three circle members file into the back while Sam, Samantha, Lilly, and the other circle member squishes into the boot. The door closes and I tear out of the driveway and speed until I get into town where I slam on the brakes.

"What?" Jace says, looking over to me. "Why have we stopped?"

"The rest of my pack are back there," I say, looking out of my window to see Tyler and Caleb beside the car in wolf form panting. "We can't travel like this," I say, looking into the rear view mirror to see the circle and my pack all squished into my car. I open my door and walk to the back of the car. I open it and get Lilly, Samantha, Sam, and the other circle member out.

"We will travel in two cars," I say as the other circle member, who now registers as Emily, climbs into the front. "The pack, Sam, and I will travel in a different car."

"We only have one," Jace says, climbing out of the passenger side, then instructing Emily to get in.

"I can get one," I say. Jace starts to protest but I cut him off. "We don't have time!" I shout as a vampire hunting cry erupts from behind us. Sam and I walk into a used car sale yard. I use magic to make the dealer give us a car for free. Sam drives and, within minutes, we are back on the highway. Jace pulls out in front of us and I use magic to create two walkie talkies, and then use another spell to send one to Jace's car.

"Follow us," he says immediately.

"Okay," I say as both Jace and Sam put the pedal to the metal when another vampire cry fills the air. I whisper a spell and a yellow light forms a circle around the other car. I then raise my hand and put a protector circle around my car.

"Was that you?" Jace asks through the walkie talkie.

"Yeah," I reply. "I didn't want those bitches scratching my car."

He laughs as he says, "Good to see you still have your sense of humour."

"Yeah," I say as we leave town. "Where are we going?"

"We need to leave town," Jace says. "We're going to Salem."

"What?" I gasp and Sam glances sideways. "We can't. Cleo needs our help she can't stay down there. Salem is six hours away, we can't-"

"Rose!" Jace shouts and the walkie talkie screeches. "You are going hysterical. We have to get out of town. Salem is the safest place I can think of. Everyone down there knows about paranormals."

"Plus," Tamika says in the background. "That's where we will find the werewitches' circle."

"We can't leave Cleo," I say, getting angry. I hit the dash and scream, "We can't leave her!"

"Rose," Jace sighs, his voice softening, "Mercy Lake is no longer safe for you. In Salem, you can walk the streets as a wolf without being hunted. The humans there are friendly and in two days I will be able to go back and pick Cleo up, as well as set up a long Wi-Fi connection for her to reach the lab. But Rose, we cannot go back. It is too dangerous."

"Where will we live?" I ask with a growl rising in my chest.

"I have a house supplied by my clan up there," he says, and I wonder about his clan. There is so much about Jace I don't know about. I sigh and release the button on the walkie talkie and the car goes quiet.

I sigh again and lean onto the window. If the calculations are right, we will reach Salem in six hours, so around nine o'clock tonight. I close my eyes and fall asleep to the hum of the car.

The car swerves right and another car honks its horn, jarring me awake as Sam curses under his breath. I rub the sleep out of my eyes and yawn, as jace pulls my jeep off the road. Sam stifles his yawn and I notice his fangs before tearing my eyes away.

"Do you want me to drive?" I ask as Jace steps out of the Jeep and he and one of the circle members switch places.

"Yeah," he nods opening his door. We switch places and then continue to drive down the highway. Sam immediately falls asleep. It's only six o'clock and we still have three hours to go. I groan and continue to follow my Jeep.

"What time is it?" Tyler whispers, rubbing his eyes and yawning. He leans forward.

"Six," I whisper back, looking into the rear view. He grunts before getting comfortable again and falling asleep. The hour drags on and at seven everyone stirs awake.

"I'm hungry," Samantha complains, rubbing her eyes and yawning.

I turn on the walkie talkie. "Jace, I have a bunch of hungry werewolves here," I say, pressing the button. I hear Jace scramble for his walkie talkie.

"There's a roadside diner up ahead," he replies. "We'll stop there."

"What about something for you and Sam?" I ask, glancing at Sam whose fangs are almost fully extended.

"There will be animals around," Jace says.

"Okay," I say and the speaker goes quiet. After fifteen minutes of complaining, we finally find the diner and pull into the parking lot. The pack all push out of the car and run into the diner while Sam and Jace head into the woods at high speed. I sigh and shut the engine off.

"Are you okay?" Tyler asks, placing a hand onto my shoulder.

"Fine," I mumble, opening the door and stepping out. "Just fine."

I slam the door and make my way into the diner where the pack are piled into a booth. As the circle flows in and occupies the second both, a waiter comes over with menus. I slide in with my pack as the waiter reads the specials. We order in bulk, catching up on missed meals. I feel like I could eat seven cows, which, ironically, is probably what I am going to eat. I order several burgers with extra meat, fries, and two milk shakes. The rest of my companions order and we all fork out our money and pay. Then the pack begins to leave, heading for the restrooms. As I lean back and rub my temple a teenage boy stands next to me.

"Can I help you?" I ask, glancing to the circle. Their eyes are on me, I'm safe. The boy looks around my age. He is skinny, so I know I could break him like a twig.

"Are you a werewolf?" he asks in a low whisper.

"Depends. Who's asking?" I ask, raising an eyebrow at the teen, who steps back.

"My dad and I are heading to Salem," he says, stuffing his hands in his pockets. "We hear there are wolves down there. We're seeking refuge."

I take in his scent and find out that he is a werewolf.

"Good place," I nod, turning my attention to something outside. "Though I have never been there."

He tilts his head to the side and slowly backs off as the pack bound back in time for our orders to arrive in separate brown bags with grease spots. We dig in with no hesitation and in an hour, we have downed most of our meal. I push the rest of my food away and make my way to the bathroom. I look in the mirror and sigh. I see a broken, blood-soaked girl staring back at me. My hair is a mess and there are bags under my eyes. I struggle to fight back tears as I look down into the sink. I cry silently, and watch the tears fall from my cheeks and into the sink. I look back up and, instead of seeing a heart-broken lonely teenager, I see someone strong and capable of looking after herself. She smiles at me, and I smile at her. She vanishes and I see myself looking into my reflection again. I grab several hand towels and wet them one at a time, and wipe my face and the blood from my clothes. Then I tie my hair and wash under my nails before heading back out into the diner. My boots tap on the tiled floor as I make my way back to my booth. Eyes lock onto my body and for once I don't care what they think.

"Let's get moving," I say, pressing my hands flat on the table. "Let's not waste time."

They all look at me and begin putting the rest of the food back into the bags, then file out and into the cars. I am back behind the wheel and on the highway following behind my Jeep. After three more stops we arrive in Salem, but as we drive through the town people flee the streets and lock their doors.

"I thought that Salem's population knows about us," I say into the walkie talkie as I watch a mother carry her child inside.

"They do," Jace says, his voice shaking. "I don't know what's happening."

"That's not good," I mumble as more people flee. Sam grunts in acknowledgement from the driver's side. "Stop the car," I say and Sam shoots me a look. "The pack and I will walk in front and you guys will follow. I don't want to stay here."

Sam shakes his head and I open my mouth to protest, but a force slams both cars sideways. I scream as both cars are turned on their sides then onto their roofs. Glass shatters and I look over to Sam and see that he is knocked out. I growl deep in my chest and notice a tranquilizer dart sticking out of his chest, my eyes turn deep yellow as I see the same has been done to my pack.

With a bark in anger I tear my seatbelt off and drop out of my seat. I land on my back, but that doesn't slow me down. Rage fills my chest as I break the rest of the windshield glass. I pull a tranquilizer dart out of my own arm and leap out of the windshield and on to the bitumen. My eyes adjust to the light and I make out a body lying before my feet, and as my eyes focus I notice Jace's face, I block out the white noise in my head and let their pulses take over, they are still alive. I change into a wolf as I hear boots taping on the road. I growl as two dozen people appear on the horizon. The night air is cold as the people gasp at the sight of me. A loud boom sounds behind me and I turn around to see two giant demons standing behind me, growling. I step back a fraction and growl as my eyes glow brighter. The demons stand tall, almost the size of a house. They have deep, dark grey skin and giant mouths that could possibly swallow a car. They stand on four feet like gorilla's and have pointed ears, but no eyes.

"Get it!" someone shouts and I hear multiple guns fire. Time slows as I dodge every single tranquilizer and run toward the beasts. They pound their front feet and growl at me. I bark and dodge an attempt to grab me, then run up the demon's arm and bite its shoulder. It screams in pain and swats at me with its other feet. I run towards the back of the head and stand still. The demon flicks its snake like tongue in an attempt to find me while the other demon walks over to me and growls. I can't hide from it, so when it catches my scent I quickly leap from the first demon's head to the other demon's.

I land as the second demon bites into the first where I had just been. The first screams and attacks the other demon. I leap to the ground as the demons tear each other apart, and then turn back to the humans and growl. My eyes glow and light the night. I turn to my human self.

"You will pay for what you have done!" I scream, my eyes still yellow. I grab my gun and fire at the people. They hiss in return and run towards me. I drop my gun and change back to a wolf. As I bite down hard, yellow electricity erupts from my mouth. With a loud bark, I leap forward and attack the first vampire with rage and anger. I bite down on its neck and it screams in pain. Blood gushes into my mouth as I spit the vampire out and move onto the next. They hiss and my growl deepens.

"We have been expecting you," one of the vampires hiss. I bark and rip it apart, blood soaks into my fur as I tear through another vampire.

"We won't let you meet him," another hisses as it claws at my hind leg. "You have come far enough. Turn around and we will leave you alone."

There is no going back, I think as I let out another bark and turn in on myself to attack the vampire. I need help, but with my pack and the circle unconscious I am all alone. I need to get in touch with my inner werewitch. I summon all of my strength and power. My body and skin begins to glow bright yellow. I open my hands and a light fires from them, incinerating any vampire in sight. I hear their screams, I feel their pain, but I do not care. I do not care about the vampires.

Anger surges through me as the light brightens. When the last vampire is dead, the light fades away and I am left standing in my human form. I hear a groan and I morph into my werewolf form. I walk back to Jace and nudge him with my nose. He groans and rolls over onto his stomach. In seconds, his groan is met with more.

I turn my head to the car and carefully make my way over. My nose fills with the smell of gas as I crawl back through the windshield, but alas, I am too big in my wolf form, so I change back to a human. I hear Samantha cough as the tranquilizer wears off. I tilt my head and my vision blurs, so I shake my head and proceed to move over to Sam. Taking my dagger out, I quickly rip his seat belt off. He falls into my arms and I drag him out away from the car. Again, my vision blurs but I have to keep going. I empty the car within a few minutes and move onto the Jeep. As I break the windshield on my Jeep, I curse under my breath. This is not going to be easy to fix. The jeep is harder to move around as it lies on its side. I hear a grunt and a click behind me and I spin around. Standing behind me is one of the blood-soaked demons; the other is lying dead. I freeze and prepare to attack, but it reaches behind me and picks up the car. I pull out my gun and aim, but I hold back as the demon sets the car the right way up and then turns its head towards me.

"You are helping me?" I ask and it nods its head with a grunt. I nod back and it lays down to lick its wounds. I pull the circle out of the car one at a time and lay them with my pack. I hear yelling on the horizon and I spin. Dots blur my vision, but I can see another army of vampires approaching.

I turn to the demon and watch as he uses his tongue to smell the scene in an attempt to find the attackers. And that's when I notice the scars where his eyes should be.

"They took your eyes?" I ask and he turns towards me. "That's why you are prepared to fight them."

He nods and lets out a battle scream.

"Heal him," I mumble into my closed fist and I feel a powdery resin fill my hand. I open it to find a golden dust and blow it into the direction of the demon. It covers his scars and replaces them with his eyes. He looks back at me and I nod.

"Get us out of here," I say, and he nods, scooping up my pack in one hand and places them on his back, then he does the same for the circle. He goes to get me, but a grenade flies between us.

"Go!" I command and he leaps into the night. The grenade explodes and I am thrown backwards and into the road. My head hits first and I am knocked unconscious.

I wake on a cold, hard floor covered in blood. I sit up and look around. I am in an old dungeon with chains on the walls and bones in the corner. There is a barred door and stone walls. My left foot is chained to the wall and as I rub my head I wince in pain. When I remove my hand, I feel blood trickle down my forehead. I hear a familiar screech and look over to the barred window to find my owl sitting on the ledge. The sun partially lights the room in a small square.

"Lilac," I cough, my voice rasps and scratches on my throat. I cough again and Lilac gives a soft hoot then tilts her head. I try to get up but my muscles are sore and I slip back to the floor. I groan and hold my stomach as I feel like I am going to throw up. I hear a scraping noise, and looking up, I see a small wooden cup being pushed through the wall to my right.

"Drink this," says a voice. "You are going to need it."

I drag my body across the floor to the cup. I carefully lift the cups to my lips and take a drink. As the fluid passes down my throat I fell much better.

"Who are you?" I ask and there is a collection of chuckles.

"We are a circle," a new voice says. "Formed to protect our werewitch."

"You are the oldest werewitche's circle?" I ask in disbelief. I touch the wall and press my ear to it.

"More or less," says yet another voice. "The person who is holding us here captured and took something that is very important to us, and they use it against us so that we will do anything they ask of us."

"They play with our minds," a male voice says. "They took my eyes."

I gasp and remember the demon.

"But someone gave them back," the man says again. "I only saw a glimpse of the werewitch through my demon eyes, but she was a girl."

Gasps sound next door and questions are asked.

"There has never been a female werewitch before," a new voice says and all voices stop. I look over to the door and see a female vampire standing there. I hear my neighbours' move backwards on their chains. I am stronger and I stand to my feet.

"Most people move back when they see me," she hisses, extending her fangs.

"I am not most people," I growl, not taking my eyes off her. "But you already know that."

The vampire shrugs and says, "So, werewitch, what are you doing in my town?"

"Looking for the first werewitch," I say, stepping forward.

"Ah, but I don't want you to," she says. "The werewitch haunts my town and kills my people."

I turn into a wolf quickly and bark at her and she steps back as I continue to growl.

"No one has ever been able to use magic in these cells," she gasps. "They are enforced with a magic killer."

I turn human and make a spell to break the chains in mine and my neighbour's cells.

The vampire hisses again, but it's cut short when she collapses to the ground. Now standing in her place is Aither and sticking out of the vampire's back is a large wooden stake.

"Aither?" I ask, stepping up to the door.

"Rose," he says, taking the vampires keys. "We need to get out of here, now."

Aither fiddles with the keys, testing and trying each one. I sigh and use magic to blow the two doors off their hinges.

"All you need is a little magic," I say, lifting my hand palm up. It fills with golden dust and I blow it in the direction of the werewitche's circle.

They all gasp as the dust heals them and they look at me with a quizzical look.

There is a loud bang and vampires ascend on us, shooting their guns. I raise my hands toward the back of my cell and with a great force I use magic to explode the stones backwards. But all magic comes at a price, and my arms become heavy and my knees weak. I fall backwards and Aither catches me. He carries me out into the sun light. I shake out of my daze and Aither puts me down and we run towards the outskirts of town.

"Where to?" I ask, turning to the warlock. "Where do we go?"

The warlock looks away from me, and I clench my fist as he slowly shakes his head. I go to ask him why when a screech sounds from up ahead.

"Lilac," I say, looking upwards, and sure enough she is there circling my head. "Show us the way!"

Lilac screeches again and takes off to the east. Immediately, Aither and I follow her, leaving the others. A wooden lodge comes into view after thirty minutes after leaving the outer skirts of the city. Lilac swoops and lands on the wooden railing near the stairs. I slow to a walk and notice that Aither has gone. I sigh and cautiously walk up the stairs and to the door. I look down at my bracelet and see the circles eyes are all inside. Behind me, I hear a groan that sounds similar to a purr. With lightning quick reflexes, I turn to see the demon that I saved behind me. He grunts then screams in pain. My heart rate increases as I notice golden sand pour out of his eyes and onto the ground, taking his eyes with it. The scars return and it is like I never healed him. The demon claws at himself until he lays dead in front of the lodge.

"What the hell?" someone says behind me. I spin around and see Tyler and the rest of the gang behind him.

"I don't know," I stutter and I feel blood trickle from my forehead. I sway and grip the railing, Tyler is by my side in a flash.

"What's happening?" he asks and I shake my head and sway again, but this time I let go of the railing and go to the floor. Tyler catches me and I lean into his chest. His body feels warm; like home. Tyler sweeps me off my feet and carries me inside and lays me on the couch. I sigh and wince in pain as Tyler touches around my wound. The flesh sizzles and Tyler pulls back and I clench my teeth as pain races through my head and down my back. Everyone starts to talk at once and their voices push on the inside of my skull. I yell in pain and everyone goes quiet. There is a bang at the door and the other werewitche's circle floods into the lodge using all their powers to immobilize my circle and my pack. I cry out in pain and anger as I try to fight back, but as they look at me I see that their eyes have disappeared and all that is left are scars.

The Warlock makes his way over to me. "Where are our eyes!" he shouts, pressing down on my wound. I scream in pain and he smirks, "Give them back to us."

"I don't know what happened!" I cry out as he places more pressure on my skull.

"Then we will have to punish you," The witch says, taking out my dagger from its holster. She places it under my right eye and drags down, leaving a jagged cut that bleeds. It doesn't heal and the witch laughs. "Seems like you are in an exhausted state where you won't heal from any damage done to you. Maybe we should go for the eye next."

I try to move out of their grasp but all they do is laugh. As the witch positions the dagger, there is a large explosion that knocks them backwards and away from me. A black light erupts and a body takes form. The light dims until there is a werewolf standing there with his back towards me. I gasp as it is like looking into a negative mirror. He is black with a white stripe exactly the same as mine. He barks at the circle and they all bow in front of him. I look over to Tyler and he asks a silent question, I shake my head and wince in pain. Tyler gets up and rushes to my side and grips my hand.

"Step back," the now human stranger says, leaning down next to me and Tyler backs up. The stranger's eyes are sapphire-like, like mine. I look deep into his eyes and notice mine turn yellow and his turn black. He places a hand over my wound and mumbles something. I feel something pull and fall out of the wound. I sigh in relief and feel myself heal the wounds on my face. He steps back as I gracefully stand.

"Who are you?" I ask, mesmerized by his face.

"My name is Xavier Bane." My breath catches and my heart stops for a beat as he continues. "I am a werewitch."

I am taken aback by his words and I shake my head. The room falls quiet and I can hear everyone breathing.

"You're our brother?" Lilly asks, stepping forward. Xavier turns and faces Lilly. I had briefly explained our situation to Lilly before we left the house.

"Yes," he nods and I freeze up. "I am the son of Amelia and Magnus Bane, and I am a werewitch."

He looks back to me and I move backwards moving around the couch.

"No," I whisper, placing a hand to my mouth.

"We need to talk," Xavier says, nodding to the door. "Alone."

I stiffly nod, then make my way to the door.

"Master," one of Xavier's circle members asks. "What about our eyes?"

Xavier ignores them, but he simply flicks his fingers in the direction of the circle and they all fall backwards and then sit back up. Their eyes reappear as Xavier guides me out of the house. We walk in silence for a while with him only a step behind me.

"Where do I begin?" he exhales, running a hand through his hair.

"The start would be nice," I say, turning to face him with a scowl on my face. He nods slowly, but then sighs as he ducks his head.

"What?" I ask placing my hands on my hips. "What's wrong?"

"For me to show you what has happened, I will have to hurt you," he says and my heart skips a beat. I gather all my courage and nod my head once. His eyes widen and he tilts his head to the side.

"You are brave," he whispers. Then, in a blink of an eye, he is in front of me, griping my arms. His eyes turn black and I can see his wolf fangs extend, but he is still human. He brings back his head and barks once before plunging into my neck in the same place Zero bit me to turn me. I scream in pain as my eyes turn yellow and my own fangs extend. Images fly behind my eyes and I focus on them as they slow down. I see my mother and father— my real parents— and my mother is holding an infant boy.

9. Original Werewitch

-Rose-

"He is strong," my mother laughs as the child grips her finger. "My strong Xavier."

"What is he?" my father asks, placing a hand on my mother's shoulders and my mother shrugs.

The Images fade and are replaced by another.

The family are outside in the woods. The child is now six years old, and he is going through the change. He changes into a black wolf and howls at the moon. The pup wags his tail and looks at our parents. They laugh and smiles light their faces. The wolf pup turns human and uses magic to trap a butterfly in a ball of air. My parents' eyes widen in shock as a bright light erupts and fills the woods. Xavier scurries and hides behind our mothers dress, clutching onto the skirt of the dress and stays quiet like a good boy.

"Amelia and Magnus Bane," says the power of earth. "You have created a monster."

Voices are raised and shouting erupts in the woods as the powers try to take the child and our parents fight to keep him, but there are four powers and only two parents and eventually they lose and the powers drag the child away from the crying and beaten parents. Xavier cries out, but the world goes black as he is transported to the powers' world.

When he arrives, they immediately take him into a dungeon where he screams and cries for his mother and father. Xavier is confused; he has never been here before.

The memory fades and a fat tear falls down my cheek before the next ones starts up.

Xavier is now human. The powers used a binding spell and captured his soul. Xavier is in a fighting ring battling a bunch of humans, and he is using swords and daggers to fight them off. He is now eighteen years old, and so strong, but he wasn't quick enough to see the werewolf sneak up on him and bite his shoulders. He screams out in pain and so do I. He changes immediately and his circle forms around him to reignite his witch powers. The pain is unbearable and I scream out as he does. Tears stream down my face as the powers appear.

"What side do you wish to protect?" the power of fire asks. "Dark or light."

Xavier stands his ground and growls at the powers. "You took me away from my family," he says, turning human.

"Fine then," the power of air says. "As your punishment for not seeing our way, we sentence you to the dark of limbo. You may only step foot on earth once a year or when another pulls you out."

The world goes black and all that is heard is the sound of the powers laughing. Limbo is where you can see everything in the world, but you can never touch it. Xavier would follow our parents around and once a year, he slips into the real world and tells them everything. So on goes the tradition, until one year he watches our parents get taken by the people who pretended to be my parents. When Xavier finds out their plan he is furious, but he is too late to stop them. Instead, he watches as my pretend father made Amelia Bane conceive a child and then use his own wife to be the surrogate mother. Then the day of my birth falls upon the day that he can walk on earth. He warned my parents to secure my soul, otherwise they would lose me. He leaves again and now he watches me instead of our parents. When I thought I was alone, he was right there beside me.

I snap back to the real world. I blink as my eyes adjust to the sun's light and I place a hand to where Xavier bit me and feel it has already healed. I look around and see that Xavier is slumped in the dirt a meter away.

"Brother," I whisper. He looks up and I see his cheeks are stained with tears. He smiles at me and I smile at him. He stands and crosses the distance between us and wraps me in a hug. I wrap my arms around his back.

"I have been waiting to see you, sis," he says with a choke of laughter.

I hug him tighter, but I hear my name howled on the wind. I pull back and look around. My name is howled again and I turn wolf as I try to pinpoint where it came from.

"What is it?" Xavier asks in my mind. I see that he has changed. My

name is howled again and I take off running, I run at full speed as the howling echoes in my head. I feel that I have to get there and all my focus is on where I am needed. I run and the world blurs around me and I find myself back in the woods behind my house. I look around, but Xavier is nowhere in sight, but Zero is.

-Zero-

She appeared out of nowhere; I am taken back by her appearance.

"Zero," she says, changing to a human. "Why did you call me?"

"I thought you were dead," I say, also turning human. She raises an eyebrow and places her hands on her hips.

"Why would I be dead?" she asks.

"I could not find you anywhere," I say, wanting to hold her, to take her in my arms. "I looked everywhere for you, your house was burnt down."

I hear her gasp and she tears off towards her house. I call out, then run after her.

As we reach her house, she gasps in horror. All that is left is the ashes and some of the walls. She walks into what used to be the hunting room and heads over to where a wall still stands. She clicks her fingers and a door appears. I stumble backwards and she glances at me and sighs.

"I guess it is time for the truth," she says. She then waves her hand in front of me. *"Memento Omnia."*

I gasp and everything comes back to me. She is the werewitch child, the one I was sworn to protect, and I let her down and broke my oath as a circle member. I stumble backwards as more images connect to the puzzle that I have been unable to remember until now. I look at Rose, who is studying the door. She inhales deeply, then kicks the door, once, twice, three times, before it collapses and breaks off its hinges. She hurries down the steps and I follow her into a massive basement with desks and tubes holding paranormals. I look around and spot Cleo in a bed to the side.

Rose smiles at her friend before walking over to a large, glass tube.

"Hi, mum," she says, choking on tears. Cleo ushers me out and we wait for Rose.

"So, you remember?" Cleo asks me, folding her arms over her chest. I nod and keep my eyes on the basements entrance.

"I hope you feel bad," she says, not looking at me. "For what you did to her."

"I do," I sigh. "But it wasn't me acting. I was compelled by a powerful vampire. But I killed her."

Cleo shakes her head and sighs, "You will never understand that everything you did before that hurt, too. You were green-eyed."

I turn my back towards the door frame and shrug at Cleo. There is an explosion out front and Cleo and I look at each other. I turn wolf and run to where the explosion was. I come to a stop when I see the circle and Rose's pack accompanied by a man and another round of paranormals.

"What is this?" I ask, turning human. "Who is he?" The man's eyes turn black, and I see his muscles tense, so I turn wolf again and growl. Rose appears and smiles at the stranger.

"What happened here?" the stranger asks. Rose goes to walk to him, but I cut her off and continue to growl at the stranger. Rose changes and tackles me to the ground, snapping at me as dominance radiates off her and her eyes glow bright.

"You don't have the right to even act like you care," she barks, snapping her teeth inches away from my face.

My heart skips a beat and I show submission. She growls once more, then pushes off me and turns human. She runs to Tyler and wraps her arm around him.

"Careful, wolf," the stranger says into my ear; his eyes glow and I flatten my ears. "I have seen what you have done, and I am more powerful than my sister."

I turn my head a fraction and growl, then turn human. "Noted," I say, looking back to Rose. She is whispering something in Tyler's ear and he nods ever so slightly. She looks over to her brother and he also nods.

Rose takes the stranger by the arm and leads him down into the basement.

-Rose-

Xavier and I slip into the basement where I reunite Xavier and our parents. The paranormal movement in this room is so strong that all the paranormals can move in their tanks. I notice blue tears in my mother and fathers tanks.

"Mum, Dad," he says, rushing to their tanks. They smile at him and touch the glass.

I feel awkward, like I don't belong. I walk over to the desk and open the book. "It says that we need something personal from each paranormal," I say. There is a post it note at the top of the page. It reads that there is a personal thing from each paranormal in the right hand draw of the desk. I open the draw and I see the paranormals' belongings, each with a post it note on whoever's it is. I pull out my mothers and it is a vial with hair in it. I can smell that it belongs to Xavier. I sigh and take out my father's belonging. He has a locket with a picture of Xavier as a child in it. I close the locket and then walk around, placing each treasured item at the base of each paranormal tank, and then I place a circle in the centre of the room, half the circle is made of candles, while the other is made of perfectly rounded white stones. All this time Xavier has been talking to our parents through their minds. I look over and am jealous of him. My eyes flare yellow and I quickly look away. I finish setting up and look over to Xavier.

"Are you ready?" I ask. His head snaps to me and he nods. I pick up the book and place it in the centre of the circle. "It says light to wolf, dark to witch. I guess that means I stand here," I say, going onto the stone side, and continue to read as Xavier enters the circle. "Change to dominate forms." I change to my wolf form while Xavier's clothes change. His outfit turns into a black, elegant coat outfit including black boots, a black cloak, black gloves, long sleeved black shirt, and black slacks.

For some reason, I turn back to a human and notice my own clothes are changed. I am now wearing a long white dress with a white corset. The skirt of my dress puffs out, and white gloves cover my hands. My hair has been magically restyled. My eyes turn yellow and I look at Xavier. His eyes are deep black and stare at me, causing a shiver to run down my spine. Something feels wrong.

"Together," he says, his voice deep and rough as he holds out his hands to me. When our skin touches the candles light and the stones start to spin.

"We are the werewitches," we say in Latin. *"Hear us and do as we will. Open the doors, release the victims, shatter the glass, and break the bonds, for we are the werewitches. We command you."*

As our spell finishes, glass shatters and water covers the floors. I am thrown away from Xavier, hit the wall, and fall to the ground with the wind knocked out of me.

"Xavier?" a voice says. I look up to see all the paranormals out of their tanks. My eyes rest upon my parents. My real mother and father are standing there with their arms stretched out. "Xavier, honey."

"Mum," Xavier sighs, finding his feet and running to our parents. My heart drops. I stand and look at Xavier and our parents with jealous eyes. I turn my back to the family and walk out of the basement and back up to my burnt house. I gather my skirts in my hands and run, ignoring my pack and circle calling my name. I run so fast that the tears sting my eyes and blur my vision. I turn wolf and run even faster, trying to outrun my problems, but I can't. I detour and head to the cave where Tyler and I spent the night. I go straight to the back of the cave and curl up in a ball. My whine echoes through the cave as I fall into a deep sleep.

Tyler grins at me, and I smile at him. Then in a blink of an eye, he pulls out a stake and stabs it into my chest. I scream out in pain and the dream fades. Now, I am standing in the woods alone. I look around and call out. I see Xavier and our parents up ahead.

"Xavier?" I call out. He turns to me and scowls. "What is going on?"

"Get away from us, you animal!" he shouts. I back up and realize I have changed to a wolf. He takes out a sword and starts swinging at me. I back up with my tail between my legs and duck his attempts to hurt me. I turn and run, I run past my pack, my circle, and my friends. They all throw stones at me.

"This is just a dream," someone whispers. "Wake up."

I try to run to the voice. I try to scream or howl for help, but nothing happens. I know this is a nightmare, but it is not one I can escape no matter how hard I run or try. Then through my dreams, I hear a lonesome howl before a scorching pain races up my shoulders.

I scream out and the real world welcomes me with open arms. My shoulder burns and bleeds; someone has cut me with silver. I stand to my feet and look around trying to find my assailant. I take a deep breath, but I cannot smell a human or paranormal scent. Slowly and cautiously I venture out of the cave and smell the scenery. Still nothing. My wound heals and I can't find any trace of anything being here.

I look left and inhale, then look right. Still nothing. I growl in aggravation and wonder if anyone even cares. For once, I don't feel like changing back, so I run away from the house and away from my old life. I stop at the edge of the woods and think about my decision. My name is howled on the wind and I look back, cursing myself as I step onto the road. I slowly and cautiously walk across the road and then into the woods. My name is howled again and I resist the urge to turn around. I bark in frustration and pace, weighing my options in my head. I hear a screech from up above and I look up to see Lilac.

What do I do? I think to myself. My name is howled again and I make up my mind. Using magic, I remove my manacle from my wrist and take off, running at a full sprint in the same direction I was already going. Lilac follows me, taking sharp turns as I do. I stop in Seattle. As I run, snow begins to fall and soon the grounds are blanketed in white. I avoid the streets as it is now too cold for me to be human, and scavenge in the bins behind restaurants, but it doesn't fill my stomach. Lilac screeches a warning as a human comes around the corner carrying a cardboard box. I quickly turn human as the man looks at me.

"Excuse me, ma'am?" he asks. "What are you doing here?"

"I guess I got lost," I lie, rubbing my arms.

"You should get something warmer on," he grunts, looking me over. I smile and make my way past him. He drops his box and grabs my arm. My heart races as a twisted smile creeps onto his face. The man produces a knife out of his pocket and my inner wolf growls as he presses me up against the ally's wall.

Lilac screeches and swoops down and attacks the man with her claws. He waves his knife around and curses at her. I bark in laughter and change and Lilac flies back to her perch on the nearest light pole. My thunderous growl makes the man look my way, and he gasps in fear and I leap onto him and bite down onto his throat. He screams out in pain as I end his miserable life.

I then take the man's knife and plunge it into his heart and leave his body lying there separated from his head that lies two feet from his neck. My eyes skim the busy street and I come to the conclusion that I cannot go out there. I growl in frustration and head back into the alley where I jump up onto the dumpster and then onto the roof. I stand on the roof looking over the miserable town. I spy Tyler and Jace walking together. As they walk, their eyes scan the area around them.

They both are looking at the buildings and searching the streets for me. I watch them until they are out of sight. Someone coughs behind me and I turn to face the man.

"What are you doing up here?" he asks. I take a deep breath and keep my mouth shut. "Oh, so who are you running from?"

"How do you know that I am running from someone?" I ask, staring at the man suspiciously.

"I know things," he says with a smile. "Come with me, I can hide you."

I do not trust the man, but he is only a man; he cannot hurt me. I follow him as he opens the door that leads off the roof. He leads me down to through the building.

"I'm Rose, by the way," I say as we walk down the stairs.

"Luke," he calls back, coming to a stop at a red door. He pulls out a key and inserts it into the door, then gestures for me to come in. He gives me a quick tour before heading back to the door.

"Okay," he says, putting his coat back on. "I have to go to work, so make yourself at home. I'll be back later. Oh, and don't worry about Damon. He sleeps all day."

I frown as he shuts the door. Who's Damon? I walk around the room and then into kitchen and look in the fridge. I see a large container labeled, *Damon's DON'T TOUCH!* I smile and close the fridge after grabbing an apple.

"Luke bringing home strays again?" a voice says from the hall. My head snaps up and the apple falls from my hands. I see a sleepy-eyed male standing in front of me. His hair is messy and he is shirtless. He yawns and plops down onto the sofa. Something doesn't smell right about him, but I ignore it.

"Uh, hi," I say, looking away. "I'm Rose. You must be Damon."

He grunts and nods his head while turning the TV on. "Did Luke bring you home?"

I nod and take in his appearance: dark brown hair, finely toned body, about roughly five-foot-five with brown eyes. My eyes flash yellow and I look away. There is a screech at the window and both Damon and I look over to see Lilac pecking at the glass. Damon gets up and walks over to the glass window.

"What the hell?" He mumbles, and I realize that I am seeing through Lilacs eyes. As Damon leaves the window I go back into my own body. Damon walks over to me and I freeze. He tucks a stray hair behind my ear and smiles. I blush and look away from him.

"Your cute," he smiles, walking past me and to the fridge. "But what's with the dress."

I turn my back to him, then realize that's a terrible idea as he comes behind me and places his arms around my stomach. I freeze and smell blood on his breath. He's a vampire. Why didn't I see this before? I mentally curse myself. I don't fight or move because I know that a freshly fed vampire can kill a werewolf with ease, especially a novice like me. Damon kisses my shoulder around the scar that Zero left.

"What' this?" he asks, nuzzling the scar with his nose.

"A dog attacked me when I was young," I say stiffly, my breath catching as Damon kisses it.

"Does it still hurt," he asks, gently nipping at it.

"No," I say as he begins to travel up my neck and to my ear. He nibbles on my earring while drawing small circles on my stomach. From the window, Lilac screeches and attacks the glass before flying off.

"Started without me?" Luke says from the door and Damon's head snaps up.

"You should not dangle such treats in front of me," he says, kissing my neck again. His body presses closer to me and I gasp as I smell more fresh blood in the room. Luke closes the door and crosses to us in a flash and laughs.

"Little wolf," he smiles as his eyes turn red. "Did you really think I would be so kind?"

My eyes flash yellow and I growl. Luke slaps my face and Damon hisses at him.

"Don't bruise the meat!" Damon hisses, kissing the slap mark. "She is mine, first."

Luke bows his head and steps back and I freeze Damon's fangs brush across my skin. My breath catches as my eyes brighten. Damon pulls his head back and then shoves his fangs into my neck. I scream out and try to get out of his hold, but he tightens his grip. He shakes his head and tears into my jugular. I feel myself become numb, Damon holds me up as my knees buckle. He growls and then another echoes through the building. My eyes flicker over to the door as it explodes open.

Damon is ripped away from my body and I fall to the ground as dots blur my vision. My chest heaves and I feel like the wind has been knocked out of me. I hear a scream followed by a growl and then I see Jace walk into the room; his eyes are blood red as he rips Luke's heart from his chest. Blood splatters onto me and Damon falls next to me with a gaping wound on his neck, Tyler sniffs at my face and I reach out and I pat his furry head. My heart skips a beat and my stomach twists at knowing he came for me. He lays next to me and isn't leaving me.

"How did you find me?" I whisper, looking into his eyes. They are perfect.

"*A little owl led us to you,*" he says, and I groan and roll onto my back. "*Get on,*" he says, tensing. I groan again and turn into my wolf form.

"*I'm fine,*" I sigh. I hate hurting him, but I don't want to be hurt instead, so I stand and walk out of the apartment, but I am hit side on by Jace. I pull my lips back and growl at him. "What are you doing?" I ask, turning human.

"What the hell was that?" Jace yells. "What type of stunt was that?"

"It's called going solo," I snap, my eyes glowing. "I don't need your help, and I don't want your help. I have done it before and I can do it again."

"Yeah, right," Jace scoffs, gesturing to the room. "You really showed us. Now get on the dog."

I look over to Tyler who is laying down. "No," I say, sizing him up by putting my hands on my hips.

"Rose, get on the dog, now!" Jace says, his fangs gliding down and out of their sheaths.

"Or what?" I challenge with a bark of laughter.

"Or I will make you," Xavier says, stepping into the light. I growl at him and he returns my growl with a more alpha-like growl. But then his face softens and he holds out a hand. "Rose, I am your brother. Talk to me."

"No," I say, moving back. "You can't just show up in my life and play the brother card. I have had to face all my problems alone. I have loved and lost. I don't belong in your perfect family. I am my own family, and I don't need you. I will come back with you, but not because of you."

Xavier nods and moves out of my way as I go down the stairs and outside where the rest of the circle and pack wait. I groan as we make our way to the edge of the town. There we turn and run back to Mercy Lake, but the light leaves quickly before we could get half way.

"We will camp here for the night," Xavier instructs his circle, but I keep walking. "What are you doing?"

"You can control your circle," I say, changing then spinning around and facing him. "And I will control mine. We keep going."

"You are being selfish. Think about them!" he shouts.

"Think about me!" I shout back, tears already falling. "I have been all alone for years with my mother and father kept in tanks, and when I help release them, it's like they don't care!"

I make a spell in my head, but after the vampire bite and the running I have no energy. I collapse to the ground and cry. Tyler is the first one to move. He runs to my side and holds me in his arms, so I lean into his chest and cry. Xavier moves, but Tyler growls at him.

"I know what she is going through," he says, and I look up at his face. "I have been through it, too. Just leave her alone."

"Watch your tongue, hunter," Xavier growls and I look sharply at him. "You may have fooled her, and you may have fooled them, but you have not fooled me."

Xavier grabs me and tears me away from Tyler. I scream and Tyler goes to get me, but a wolf knocks him sideways and holds him there. I look over to my pack and the circle, and see that Xavier has his circle holding them down. My eyes glow brighter as I change and wriggle out of my brothers hold, morphing into a werewolf. I growl as my eyes shine brighter, my black stripe glows as well and encases my body until I am covered in black. My growl echoes through the woods and is carried on the wind. Xavier is taken aback, but as he regains control, he also changes and growls at me.

I bark and lunge forward swiping the air with my paw. The woods grow deathly quiet with the only sounds being Xavier and I growling as we circle each other, lunging but not attacking. My eyes never leave him. Xavier looks over to the wolf holding Tyler down and he nods. The wolf looks at Tyler and it seems like it smiles as it leans down and bites his shoulder.

Tyler's blood stains the white snow as he screams in pain. I bark and lunge at Xavier, who dodges, but only by a second. He turns and runs, but I am hot on his heels. I trip him by grabbing at his back leg, he falls into the snow and I leap onto his body and pin him down. But he is almost a three hundred years old and he fights back without hesitation, kicking up at me with his hind legs. Then he pushes me off him, but I will not give up. I bite down hard and the yellow electricity erupts from my mouth. I bark loudly and lunge at him, taking a bite out of his right hind leg. He turns back and takes my shoulder. He picks me up with no effort and throws me against the tree. I hit it with a loud thud and the snow falls from the branches.

"Surrender?" he asks, laughing into my mind.

"Never!" I shout back, standing up. But when I do, I feel myself grow in size, my stripe grows, taking over my body and makes me into a pure black wolf. Xavier notices it too and he steps back. I bare my teeth and bark. The bark is enough to make my own blood turn cold. With surprising speed, I cross over to him and pick him up by the back and shake him like a rag doll, and then throw him into the nearest tree. He hesitates to get up and I walk over to him.

He looks up at me as I bark and snap my jaws inches from his throat. He fights back by taking my front leg in his mouth. I howl out in pain and throw him against another tree. He still gets up, this time he snaps his own jaws and black electricity flows from his mouth. I bark and charge at him, he does the same. We run past each other, missing by mere inches, but no less— I still manage to bite his shoulder. He turns and leaps onto my back, and I run around and shake while kicking up trying to get him off. He bites into the scruff of my neck, and I drop and roll onto the ground. He lets go, and automatically comes back for more. I manage to bite his ear, his jaw, and his hind legs. He tries to run again, but I am hot on his heels.

My stripe shrinks and I turn back into the white wolf, but my stripe still glows with rage and anger. I run alongside him and ram him into another tree. He bites my ear and I yelp in pain, but my body keeps going, attacking with all the rage and hate that has been building up. This time I lunge onto his back and bite his neck. He howls and rolls, but I am not that easy. Before letting go, I grab onto his rib cage and throw him against a tree. Blood stains both the ground and our fur, but we keep fighting.

He turns human and sits up, holding his ribs. He sends an immobilizing spell my way, but I block it with my own spell— his spells leave a black line, mine leave yellow. I also turn human and begin to throw spells but he deflects them and vice versa. We are both growing weaker by the second.

"Give up!" I shout, throwing a powerful spell that nicks the tree Xavier is hiding behind.

"Ladies first!" he calls, throwing a paralysis spell. My eyes widen and I leap out of the way and hide behind a tree. My breath is hot and fast, my hair is not so perfect and my dress is ripped in several places. I turn into a wolf and carefully and silently move away and circle around to where my brother is hiding.

"Your move, little sis!" he calls out, but I stay perfectly still and quiet. "Fine, *descendant ad in lupus.*"

I carefully move as he throws his spell, it hits the tree I was behind and a pile of snow hits the ground; it sounds like a body.

"Gotcha!" He smirks, running from his hiding place. I run out of my real hiding place and take him to the ground. I dig my claws into his skin and he cries out and changes. Another cry sounds on the horizon and my head snap up. Tyler.

"Your move, lil sis," he groans in my head. I bark and bite down on his head, he howls and I crush his skull. I know he will heal, but I need to get to Tyler. When I am sure he is 'dead', I bound off and back to where Tyler is.

"Where is Xavier?" The witch of his circle demands.

"He couldn't make it," I chuckle, raising my hands and making yellow electricity dance around my fingers. "Now, let them go."

Xavier's circle stays where they are so I shout at them. They back off of, and then scramble away from my friends. I hear Tyler collapse to the ground and I rush over to him. Tyler coughs and blood sputters out of his mouth.

"What happened to him?" I ask, turning to Jace who is behind me.

"They hurt him," Jace sighs, rolling his shoulders. I hear a crack. "They hurt all of us."

I look over to Xavier's circle who smirks at me. I raise my right hand and bring it down like a whip, yellow electricity flies at them and they are paralyzed. I walk over to them and turn wolf.

"They told us things," Tyler coughs, and every point he makes my eyes glow even brighter. "They feed us blood and put hot irons on our skin."

"Tyler got the worst of it," Sam says, putting one of Tyler's arms around him, helping to stand.

"I think it's time for my brother to find a new circle," I growl, and their eyes widen with fear.

"Rose!" Tyler coughs, I turn and look at him and his eyes also show fear. "It's not you, Rose, don't do this."

"He's right," Sam says, chiming in. "This isn't you. Don't stoop down to his level."

My eyes fade back to blue and my energy leaves me in a rush. I collapse to the ground, but Jace catches me and immediately picks me up in his arms.

"We need to move," he says and there is a thunderous bark on the wind. "Now!"

My warlock makes a demon appear and climbs on.

"Quick, give the boy to me," he says, holding out his hands. Sam hands Tyler up to Paul.

"Be careful with him," I call out, my voice barely audible. Jace shushes me and then we are off. My pack turns to their wolf forms and run alongside the other paranormals with blinding speed and soon we arrive back in Mercy Lake. I remember all that Xavier had done, and I clutch harder to Jace as if I am going to fall, but eventually everyone has to let go. I let the fabric of Jace's shirt slip through my fingers. I fall to the ground and tumble, and because they are going so fast, they probably won't notice that I am gone until they reach the centre of Mercy Lake. My head hits the ground first and snow sprays upwards. As the snow settles, I see Xavier and his circle appear.

"*Giving up so easily, lil sis?*" he growls into my mind. I turn wolf and growl, but I can't get up. My powers and energy is still too weak. He places a front paw onto my throat and growls inches from my face. I whistle through my nose and rest my head back in the snow.

"*What do you want from me?*" I whine, digging my paws in the dirt as if it is my anchor.

"*I am facing a war,*" he says barking. "*And I need your powers to help me.*"

"*For good or evil?*" I growl through the paw on my throat.

"*That is my business!*" he barks. I try move my head away and he removes his paw as he turns human. "We are not alone," he says, breathing in the air. I inhale and sense a presence I'm not familiar with. I turn human and slowly lift my hands.

"Rot in hell!" I shout, my eyes glow and a yellow ball materializes in my hand. I throw it in Xavier's direction, but he moves out of the way.

"You first," he says, and a black ball materializes in his hands. He throws it at me and I am hit side on by a werewolf. He is a grey wolf, a pure blood. He growls and stares down Xavier. Xavier gasps and staggers backwards.

"*Get on!*" The wolf shouts in my mind as it crouches. I drag my body over to him and slide up onto his back. He barks at Xavier and runs towards him. Xavier gasps and falls over backwards. The wolf leaps over him and continues to run. I hold on tight as he picks up the pace, the wind whips past my face and I feel like I am flying. I look up to the sky and see Lilac flying with a crow. The wolf slows down and stops outside the cave that Tyler and I hid in when we were being hunted. The wolf lays down and I scurry off him and to the cave's wall.

"Who are you?" I ask, my heart racing.

"The person who just saved your life," the wolf says, turning human. In front of me now stands a black haired, blue eyed male. He stands about five-foot-seven and is definitely older than me. He's wearing a white under shirt and black leather pants with black leather boots. He smiles and bows at me. "My name is David, the *original* werewitch."

10. David

-Zero-

Rose's circle and pack arrive back at burned down house as lightning cracks in the sky. I look from member to member and see Rose is not there.

"Where is she?" I ask. Everyone looks to Jace, whose face is paler then the dead, which is ironic.

"You dropped her!" Tyler shouts from up on the warlock's demon. "We have to find her." Tyler screams out in pain and rain lets loose on the earth.

"What's wrong with him?" I ask, walking over to the demon.

"Torture," Sam says, leaning on the demon. "We have to find Rose. Zero, would you be able to take care of Tyler for us?"

"I can take him back to Aamon's. They are all out in a giant pack meeting," I say, helping Tyler down.

"Why aren't you there?" Jace questions, looking at my now scarred shoulder.

"I quit," I say simply, hobbling over to the stables with Tyler's arm around my shoulders. "Now go find Rose."

That's all it took. They vanished within a second to go look for Rose. I walk into the warm stable and lean Tyler on a stool while I ready Indi for travel. She greets me with a snort and I laugh quietly. Tyler groans in pain and I look over to him as the rain worsens.

"What the hell is with this weather?" I question to myself. "First snow, now rain."

I put Indi's reins on, then walk her out of the stall. I mount her and help Tyler sit in front of me. I click Indi on and soon we are racing through the woods and arriving at Aamon's place. I slide off Indi and help Tyler off before tying her up to a low hanging branch. Tyler gives up halfway to the stairs and I have to drag him the rest of the way. Eventually, I get him to my room and onto my bed, and then I have to go back downstairs to get the first aid kit. I sigh at the effort that I am going through to save Rose's boyfriend, but it has to be done if I want to see her again. I apply an antiseptic to the burns and bites, and then an ointment to his forehead that cools his temperature and sorts out any infections.

"You are a lot of work," I sigh to myself, sitting next to the bed. Tyler falls into a deep sleep and I quietly leave the room. Just as I reach the kitchen Tyler screams out. I change courses and head back to the room. As I enter the room, Tyler calls out Rose's name; he is having a nightmare. Tyler tosses and turns while I try to calm him down, but he wakes up and turns wolf. I step back as he growls at me. Lightning cracks in the background and he tears out of the house and into the woods. I change and run after him, but he is too quick and soon I lose him.

-Rose-

"What the hell do you mean?" I ask, confused and becoming hysterical. "How are you the original werewitch?"

"Well," he starts, but I cut him off.

"I mean, how the fuck can you be a werewitch?" I say, pacing and getting aggravated. I was told that I was the only one and then Xavier shows up and now this David character. "Wouldn't the powers find out about you? Why am I the last to know these things? Where is your circle? Why?"

David cuts me off with a muting spell and I scowl at him and he sighs and rubs his temples. "Has anyone told you that you talk too much?" he asks, closing his eyes.

I stick my tongue out at him and he laughs.

"I am the original werewitch, yes," he begins, taking a seat on the cold floor as lightning cracks and rain falls down. "The powers never knew about me because no one told them about me. My father... died along with my mother in a terrible hunting season after my birth. After that, I bounced from home to home until the age of ten, when I realized I wasn't normal and that I could do extraordinary things— like lift things with my mind and change into a wolf. That's when I found out about the paranormal world and all the things I could do. I became persistent and taught myself everything. I didn't need the powers help with anything. They found out about me when I turned twenty-one and all my normal body functions shut down. I turned immortal. By then, I was too powerful for anyone to stop me, so when they found out about the second werewitch, your brother, they trained and built him up to try and stop me, but that didn't work, so, when the third one came along they tried again. I always killed the third one but left the second one. I have gone all over the world looking for some place to hide, but they always found me until now. I have been all over the world and seen all different types of dark werewitches, but never a light. Then I heard about you; how even the great powers that apparently created us all didn't know about you. how that you were the sister to the second werewitch, that you are a light, that you were female, that you caught the eyes of the power of air."

My head snaps up and I look directly into his eyes as he continues.

"I heard that you have the knowledge of three witches in your blood as well as the strength to take down the second werewitch with amazing strength and speed. When I heard all of that, I had to go and see you. So, here I am."

I suddenly liked rumours. I use a spell and take away his mute spell.

"Well, maybe that stuff is true," I say, shrugging and he looks surprised. "What?"

"No witch can undo my spells. A witch cannot undo another witches spell... you are truly great," he says and I smile. He looks me over. "But what is with your clothing? It's ruined."

"That's sort of what happens when you fight in the woods," I say, making a spell in my head to fix my dress and my appearance. As the spell finishes, I flip my hair over my shoulders and the spell takes form. A yellow cloud puffs around my body and fixes the rips and takes out the blood stains. The cloud disappears and I am left looking perfect again, except without the shoes and gloves. "But I think it is too much." I use another spell to change my clothes to regular jeans and a black tee. David smiles.

"You are amazing," he says again. There is a growl at the entrance and I turn wolf. The lightning flashes and I see Tyler standing there. He lets out a whine before turning human and collapsing to the ground.

"Tyler!" I scream, turning human and running over to him. I pull him deeper into the cave and kneel beside him.

"Tyler, open your eyes," I say, touching his face. His eyes flicker open and he grabs my hand. "Are you okay?"

He groans and clutches his stomach. Tears form in my eyes and I clutch his shirt. He reaches up and wipes away the tear and smiles at me. I feel his pulse slipping and my heart rate doubles.

"Do something," I cry, looking up to David. He leans down next to me.

"I can't," he says, placing a hand on my shoulder and my eyes flare yellow.

"What do you mean, you can't?" I say, turning to him in anger. The wind picks up and lightning cracks as the thunder rolls. David goes to talk, but I push him backwards as more tears flow and my eyes glow brighter. "Get away!" I scream, placing a hand over Tyler's stomach and words roll out of my mouth, *"Remedia in terra tolle."*

Tyler gasps as I pull a dark liquid out of his stomach. I spin it with the motions of my hands and then throw it out of the cave. The wind dies down as Tyler's pulse grows stronger. When he looks up at me and smiles, my eyes return to normal and I help him sit up.

"Unbelievable," David gasps and I shoot him a glare and stand up.

"Why didn't you do anything?" I shout and thunder booms. My eyes flash and the wind picks up. "He could have died!"

"I couldn't do anything, because I didn't know what to do!" he shouts back and I ball my fists.

"Aren't you the all-knowing werewitch?" I question, pointing a finger at him. "You are older than my brother who almost killed me, so you must be powerful!"

"I have never seen anything like this before," he says, shrugging and leaning on the cave wall. his calmness was irritating. "Your friend had an incurable spell set onto him. No witch can undo it. I am not god."

"Well, I just did!" I shout, my eyes glowing. "You know what? I don't care! Just get out of my sight."

David sighs and runs a hand through his hair before pushing off the wall and heading to the entrance.

"If you ever need me just call my name," he says before vanishing in the rain. I turn around and sit next to Tyler.

"Are you okay?" I ask, touching his arm. He looks at me and his yellow eyes shimmer as he nods. I go to speak again but he wraps his arms around me and buries his head into my shoulder.

"I was so worried for you," he whispers, and I gently put my arms around his back. "When I found out you fell, I was so worried."

I smile and a tear rolls down my face as I kiss the top of his head.

"Rose?" He asks, moving back to look in my eyes.

"Yeah?"

"What do you think about me?" he asks and my heart skips a beat. I was unsure what to say to him.

"Well," I start. "You are amazing, strong, and you have saved my life more than once. But that's not what you are asking, is it?"

"No," he says quietly.

"Well then, to be honest, every time I see you my heart does this silly little skip and my stomach ties itself in a knot and fills with butterfly's that make me smile." I smile, tucking a stray hair behind my ear and blushing. "To be honest, I can't think straight around you. I just get caught up in your eyes. Like I am now."

The cave falls silent; all that can be heard is the rain, wind, and the thunder booming outside. I look away from Tyler's eyes and sigh. I hear him sigh as well and my heart sinks as I turn wolf and lay down.

"You are the only one that understands me," Tyler whispers so quietly that I almost don't hear it. I raise my head and look back into his eyes and he holds my stare. "No one else gets me like you. I feel a connection to you that I don't yet understand. I...I think I love you. No, I know that I love you, and I know it's crazy because we don't know each other very well, but I feel something, I do. It makes me smile like a fool and it makes my eyes light up. I. Love. You."

As soon as the words leave his mouth my heart races and butterflies fill my stomach. Without hesitation or second thought, I quickly change and crush my mouth to his. He is surprised by my action, but as he realizes what's happening, he deepens my kiss and puts his arm around my back as I run my hands through his hair, then to the side of his face. He pulls me closer and I let him. His kisses make my knees weak and I am lucky that we were sitting, otherwise, I would have fallen over. He draws me so close that I don't know where I end and he starts. His lips are so soft and gentle, and his body feels like home. Even when his lips leave mine we are still so close. He smiles at me and I blush like crazy.

"I love you, too," I whisper as we bring our foreheads together and for once in my life I feel whole. He brings his lips back to mine, but I feel someone is outside so I pull back and stand up.

"What is it?" Tyler whispers, standing behind me.

I hear footsteps drawing closer. "Someone is coming," I whisper back, making my way to the entrance of the cave. I recognise the foot pattern. Jace.

"Rose!" he calls out, but the other half is muted by thunder

"I'm here!" I call, and in a heartbeat Jace is inside the cave. Water drips from his hair as he wraps me in a hug.

"I am so sorry," he says and I push back.

"It's okay," I say, motioning for Tyler to step forward and he does. Jace releases a half scream half click into the rain and another five or so are returned as well as a couple of howls.

"We will meet the others back at the barn," Jace says and Tyler and I change to wolves. We set off into the rain. I run with Tyler and Jace beside me. In a matter of minutes, we are back at the barn and Tyler and I are shaking water from our fur.

"Questions can be asked in the morning," I say, making my way up to the loft with Tyler behind. "Sleep in forms and expect the unexpected."

I change once more and lay down in the soft hay blanketing the loft. I notice the wolves come up also and sleep in a warm ball with Tyler right beside me. My eye lids begin to drop, but they snap open when the sound of Indi's hooves hitting the concrete wakes me. I stand quickly and the others do, too. I perk my ears up and hear the sound of wolf claws scraping on the floor. I go over to the ledge and send a thunderous growl down to the intruder. No one responds and the other wolves just stand there with a dazed look on their faces. My attention is turned back to the now human-wolf that walks out of Indies stable and shuts the door, then hangs up her reigns. Lightning flashes and the human is revealed. David. I leap down from the loft to the ground level and growl, and David slowly turns and shoots me a lop-sided grin. This makes me deepen my growl and ready for attack.

"I am not going to hurt you," he smiles, holding up his hands in surrender.

"What have you done to my friends?" I growl, looking at the stunned faces of the circle.

"Well, I couldn't have an army of immortal paranormals advance on me," he smiles, putting his hands down as a crow lands on his shoulder. I look back to my pack and see Tyler has his armour on in his wolf form.

"Why are you here?" I growl, sitting and looking back to him.

"I came to offer you somewhere to stay," he says, looking at Tyler. "You have tagged," he whispers and I growl in frustration.

"Look ," I sigh into his brain. "I can't go anywhere without my circle or my pack."

"I have a very large estate deep in the uninhabited part of the woods," David says, smiling. His smile sends something through me, like a spark of electricity. "You and your friends will be safe there, but you will have to get there on foot. Sleep on it and then call my name if it is a yes." Then he vanishes and the others snap out of their daze.

"What the hell!" Jace gasps. "What was that?"

I growl and leap up to the loft. *"Nothing,"* I growl, laying down, and after a few tense moments everyone else follows my lead once more. I feel Tyler's armour melt away. I try to fall asleep, but I can't. I keep thinking about my situation. I eventually stand, shaking a wolf's head off of my back. The rain has now stopped. I jump off the loft and onto ground floor, landing softly so I don't wake anyone up, then I sit at the barn door.

Everything is going downhill. Everything is changing, and I don't know how to stop it. Lilac screeches from above and flies down to my shoulder. Her claws dig into my fur and I wince in pain. I lie down and rest my head, looking out into the woods. I open myself up to everything: the sounds and the smells. I hear many people breathing and talking all the way out to the city. I smell fresh cooked items and the smell of the woods. I pick up the smell of a herd of deer not far from here and I look back to the sleeping paranormals.

They won't notice, I think as I stand. Lilac screeches in protest and flies up to the loft again. I push forward and run out into the damp, cold woods. I find the herd grazing happily on grass and bushes. I crouch and stalk my prey, but just before I could pounce a pack of real wolves break into the scene.

I stay perfectly still as I watch the wolves separate a large female from the herd and take it down. They then cut off its breathing and drag it away. I stand from my hiding spot and slowly follow them at a distance. They drag their kill into a den where hungry pups are waiting. I walk away after a couple of minutes to find myself food. I track down the herd again and take a deer out easily. Blood stains my white fur around my mouth and on my paws as I tear into my dinner. Once I have had my fill, I lick my lips and clean myself off in a nearby pond. The sun comes up over the horizon and stains the sky in a pink, orange colour. I make my way back to the barn and hear my name howled on the wind. I growl and bark a reply that I am coming and with that I zoom back to the barn where everyone is waiting with their arms crossed.

"So, I can't go out without any one worrying?" I say, changing as I step into the barn. Jace sighs and goes to speak but I cut him off as my eyes flame. "I am quite capable of looking after myself. I have done it for the past eight years! I don't need you to worry about me. I was out eating breakfast, and I have found us a place to live."

They stand there shocked as I calm down and move past them and into Indi's stall. She greets me with a happy snort and I take her saddle and reigns and tack her up.

"What are you doing?" Jace asks, standing at the door.

"Going," I say, tightening the saddle a little. "Whether you guys are coming or not."

"I'm with you all the way," Tyler says, stepping forward. I smile at him and slowly everyone else pledges their loyalty to me. I walk Indi out of her stall and see everyone ready to travel.

"David," I say into thin air. "I am ready."

There is a caw as the Crow flies into the barn and lands on a bale of hay.

"Just follow me," I sigh, mounting Indi and walking her out of the barn. The crow calls again and is joined by Lilac as they both take off. Immediately, I click Indi into a gallop and I hear my companions close behind me. David was right. The only way through was on foot, because soon the woods became thick with fallen trees and large bushes. I had to slow Indi to a walk so I could navigate without getting hurt or caught in a bush. Up ahead, the crow and Lilac lands on a large dead tree. We stop as up ahead the woods become thick and the bushes tangle together and there is no way around it. I sigh in frustration and try a spell to untangle the bushes, but all it does is worsen the situation. I remember the night that I became a werewitch and the items each paranormal placed down. I turn around and see everyone staring at me.

"Do you guys still have the items from the night I became a werewitch?" I ask, thinking of an idea. They all look at each other and then nod. I hold out my hands, gesturing for them to hand them over. I first take my father's ring from Tyler and slip it onto my left hand, then I take the clear stud from Jace and replace my right ear stud. I take the ruby necklace and slip it over my head, tie the bear claw around my waist, and then I hold the two vials in my hands. As soon as the second vile touches my hand, my body tingles and a blue glow radiates from the items. I hold my hand with the rose out and my eyes glow bright yellow as the blue around the vile does. The bushes begin to untangle and move aside. I walk forward and the woods begin to thin out, making it easier to walk through. We continue on our way with me leading the way. On our way, a heat wave strikes us at high noon. The heat strikes me hard and I begin to sweat at the pressure of using spells and magic.

"Rose?" I hear Tyler ask from behind me. "Are you okay?"

I grunt and slowly nod my head as the heat wave increases and my spell begin to fail me and the bushes become harder to untangle. I drop my hand and everything becomes still.

"I can't do it in this heat," I say, wiping sweat from my brow. I take a string from Indi's saddlebag and tie the two vials to my hip on the opposite side of the claw. I wipe my brow again, and this time my hand brushes on the earring. A cool breeze sweeps past us, but stops when I remove my hand from the earring. I inhale a deep breath and then exhale as I touch the earring again, and all around us the air becomes cooler. I touch the rose vile again and the bushes begin to untangle one more. We press forward until the woods begin to naturally thin out. I drop my hands away from the items and the cool air stops. Up ahead I see a large two-story house with a barn outside. I take Indi's reins from Tyler and walk closer to the house. The crow and Lilac land on the house's railing on the veranda. The crow caws and David opens the door and walks out with a butler behind him.

"Welcome," he says as we reach the base of the veranda. He motions something to the butler and he comes down the stairs and takes Indi's reigns from me, but I growl at him and he backs off.

"Down girl," David says, laughing, and there is a low growl next to me from Tyler. "He's going to take your horse to the barn."

The butler tries again and this time I let him.

"Please, come in," David says, motioning us inside and we follow. Once inside, he leads us into a large dining room with a very wide and very long table piled high with assortments of food and deserts enough to feed three football teams.

"Will the wolves stay here while the others come with me," David says, opening another door leading to another room. He then turns back to us and says, "Feel free to eat anything."

He nods in my direction and I nod back as he leads my circle away, closing the door behind him. At first, no one does anything and then I realize why: they are waiting for me. The alpha eats first. I take a seat and begin to fill my plate. As soon as I take the first bite, the rest of the pack take their seats and pile their plates high with food. After our stomachs are full, we all turn wolf and stuff our faces with the leftovers. Most of us put our front paws on the table so we can reach, but to get something out of reach, we leap up on the table that surprisingly held us all at one time. We finish all of the food and all that was left was plates, bones, and empty bowls, plus a room full of happy wolves. I lick the food off my mouth, then stretch and yawn. Most of my pack has already curled up and fallen asleep, but Tyler, Caleb, and I are wide awake. Caleb is chewing on a large ham bone and Tyler is licking food off his paws.

"What are you thinking?" Tyler asks, leaping off the table and sitting next to me. I look at him and my stomach flutters. I change and so does he. We stand so close and yet we are not touching. Needing to change that, I lean in an kiss him softly.

"I love you," I say, pulling back and resting my head on his chest. He laughs softly and I hear his heart rate double as he returns my hug by wrapping his arms behind my back.

"I love you, too," he sighs, kissing the top of my head. I smile and then hug him tighter. I hear the door open and I look over without letting go and I see David at the door. I turn around in Tyler's arms so I can look at David without straining my neck. David bows to me.

"I hope your meals were filling," he says, glancing at the table.

"They were, thank you," I nod as David straightens.

"Good," he smiles, looking over my shoulders to Tyler. "May I borrow Miss Bane for a while? I have things I wish to discuss with her in private."

Tyler growls and I look up to him in surprise. I pull out of his arms and then cup his face in my hands, pulling his attention back to me.

"I will be back soon," I say, kissing his cheek. He smiles and I follow David outside and into the barn, where I find Indi happily munching on oats. Next to her stall is a large black stallion and up in the rafters are Lilac and the crow.

"Is that your aspect?" I ask, nodding at the crow. David looks at me, then the crow.

"Yes," he nods and the crow flies down and lands on David's shoulder. "This is Rajima." He strokes the bird's jet black feathers. Lilac lands on my shoulder and I stroke her feathers. The birds fly back up onto the rafters again and David begins to walk. The way he walks is like a complete gentlemen with his arms behind his back and straight posture. He walks just a touch behind me. A gust of wind blows through the barn and I turn around. The wind stops and I look at David.

"What is with the strange weather?" I ask him, tucking a stray piece of hair behind my ear.

"It's your brother," he says simply as I find an old bench. "He is siding with the powers, and they are trying to find a way to kill you."

"What?" I ask, shocked. "Why would they do that?"

"Because the powers don't like change," he says, pacing in front of me. "They did this when I was still young, about your age. They don't like the change in the status quo. For instance, they don't like me because I was the first werewitch, so they tried to kill me. And they don't like you because you are the first female. However, they befriended your brother because they could get their hands on him while he was young and bind him to themselves. That is why he is a dark, which brings me to my reason of bringing you here. We need to leave this place as the powers are closing in on us, and they will do anything to kill you and me, so we must leave."

"Where to?" I ask, standing up.

"Paradise," he says, and I raise and eye brow. "Paradise, is someplace that I made a long time ago. I made it for the paranormal species so that we could hide from the powers.

"Won't you need the powers for air and water and all those other important things?" I ask, putting my hands on my hips.

"No," he says, eyeing the items on my body. "I have a set of relics like that, left to me by my mother before she died. I set them up around my Paradise so that the important things are at my will."

"Well," I say, caught by surprise. "I will go get the pack and the circle and we will leave."

"No," he says and I turn to him.

"What?" I ask frowning and putting my hands on my hips. It's becoming a habit that I do when I am unhappy or displeased with something.

"You don't need your circle," he says, pointing at my relics. "By taking them you automatically void your circle. I have already sent them off."

"That's why you don't have one," I say, and he nods.

"They are a waste," he says matter-of-factly. "And your pack will only cause a distraction to you and your training."

"What training?" I ask, getting impatient.

"I am going to train you so that you will be able to take on your brother and the powers with ease."

That catches my attention. I look back to the house and sigh. "My pack needs me. I am their alpha."

"They will live without you. They will be safer, too," David says, and a growl emits from my chest as I clench my fists.

"I need them," I say as my fangs and nails lengthen.

"You want *him*!" David growls back. "If the pack comes you might as well throw out any training we try. Do you want them to die?"

My growl is replaced with a soft whimper as David continues in a softer voice, "With the training I am going to give you it will make you stronger, it will able you to be stronger, and with the powers seeing you away from the pack they will assume that you have left them, therefore, making them useless to them and ensuring their safety."

I look back to the house and sigh. "Can I at least say goodbye?"

David nods once and I walk back into the house where my pack is waiting. As I step inside the door they rush to my side, but only Tyler sees my sad face.

"What's wrong?" he asks, stepping forward. I look at him and tears well up in my eyes. He takes me into his arms and the tears spill over and I cry into his chest. He takes me into another room and sits me down on a soft plush couch. I look him in the eyes and notice that the yellow one glows a little.

I tell him everything, and that I have to go and that he can't come with me. He sits there and nods his head like he understands.

"I understand," he says, rising off the couch and walking to the door. I quickly stand and ,with super human speed, I beat him to the door and block him off.

"I am sorry," I say as tears continue to flow. "But this isn't goodbye, I promise. I will come back."

He doesn't say anything, but he looks away.

"Please don't make this harder than it already is," I say. He looks at me and his eyes reflect hurt.

"Please move," he says. I flinch like he had just thrown a knife into my heart. "I'll go tell the pack."

"No," I say strongly. "Please don't be mad. Please understand, I have to go, for your safety. I promise this isn't goodbye."

"Goodbye, Rose," Tyler says, looking away from my face. I flinch like he had just slapped me and then I numbly move out of the way and he opens the door.

"I'm sorry," I whisper, collapsing to the ground. I hear him pause for a moment, but then he just keeps walking. I sit up and wipe my eyes before going back out to the barn where David is waiting with sad eyes. I wipe my eyes again and Lilac flies down onto my shoulder as Rajima does on David's. David holds out his hand and I take it. As soon as I touch it, my stomach launches as we are sucked into a wormhole.

-Zero-

There is an army at Aamon's door, I think as I go down stairs and open the door. I find Tyler standing there with a look of hurt and pain on his face.

"Tyler," I say, moving aside. "Come in."

He grunts and nods as he moves inside and takes a seat at the kitchen table. I look around to see if anyone was with him, but no one else was there.

"What's up?" I ask, sitting across from him after shutting the door.

"She is gone," he says, and I automatically guess who he is talking about. "She left me." He launches into a story of how Rose left him to go to some place called Paradise and how it will help her become a better werewitch. He tells me that the pack is broken up and he needs a place to stay, I offer and he accepts. Then he stands and I do, too. He tells me everything she did and said.

"I hate her," he says with such anger. "I said I loved her and she just left me. I hate her."

I punch him in the face and he looks at me with shock.

"Pull yourself together!" I shout, "She does love you. From everything you just said, I can gather that she does love you and it pains her to leave you. I have seen the way she looks at you, I have seen the way she smiles and talks about you, and she has never done that with anyone else. She. Loves. YOU! No one else. By the things you just said, I know she didn't want to leave you, but she had no choice."

He looks at me and I ready myself for attack.

"I'm tired," he says, and I show him up to the metal room that Rose was in and he goes to the bed.

"It smells like her," he says with a sad tone to his voice as he clenches his jaw.

"This was her room," I say, touching a claw mark on the back of the door. "She was the only one strong enough to dint the metal. We could never break her spirit. I admire her for that." Tyler takes off his shirt and I see scars all over his back.

"What's that?" I ask and he turns around.

"Werewolf," he says, pulling back the covers and lays down. I back out of the door and close it. Then I go back downstairs.

The night approaches quickly and the pack piles into the door lead by Aamon. They have been spending the days at the alpha pack and the nights here. They don't give me a second glance as they make their way up to their rooms. After a few minutes, Tyler wanders down. He looks fresh out of the shower with his hair dripping and a towel around his hips.

"I have clothes for you," I say, going to my room and grabbing a pair of shorts and a shirt. I go back to him and hand him the clothes and he goes back upstairs to change. He comes back down wearing the shorts, but the shirt is in his hands.

"Too small," he says, throwing it back. I catch it and glare at his muscles before gesturing to the seat across from me. He sinks into it, folding his arms across his chest. I notice Rose's bite mark on his shoulder and glance at my own covered shoulder.

"Why don't they go away?" Tyler asks, looking at his palms. "The scars."

"The one on your back were made before you were bitten, so they stay. The bite mark becomes a scar because it's an origin mark that can help identify the wolf that bit you."

"How were you turned?" Tyler asks, moving to get comfortable.

"I was turned four moons before Rose," I start as I remember the night I wish I could forget. "I was at a full moon party that I wasn't supposed to be at. I was out at a party in the woods and a fight broke out between me and another guy. We were both drunk, and he grabbed a broken glass bottle and began to swipe at me. He hit me a couple of times with the bottle," I say, showing him my palm and my stomach where the scars are. "And I got him a few times with my fists. Then midnight came and a blood curdling howl rose into the air. He ran off, but not before stabbing me near the heart," I say showing him the scar.

"I fell hard. The party cleared out quickly and I was left there, bleeding out. That's when I saw Aamon as a wolf. My heart raced. I was looking at a wolf almost four-feet-tall. I tried to crawl away, but Aamon put his paw on my chest and howled. It drowned out my scream before biting down on my shoulder." I also show him that scar. "Then licking the wound. I was scared out of my mind, and I was injured. I lost consciousness. I awoke the next day, still in the woods where the party was, and I was freaking out. I should have died. I stayed there for the rest of the day, trying to piece what happened together, but when night came I changed for the first time, and then I ran. I didn't know where I was going. I reached this place and busted down the door and attacked Aamon, but he was stronger and faster. He knocked me down and dragged me into a basement with a girl, Shea. She was crying. I changed back and began to talk to her, asking what was going on. She was as clueless as me.

"The next day, Aamon came down and explained what was happening and what we were. When I went back to my father, he was so ashamed. He was a pure blood, and I, however, had inherited the human trait from my mother. He followed me back here and attacked Aamon, hoping to kill him. The fight lasted almost all day, but Aamon killed my father, then he adopted me into his pack as his son."

"Why are Rose's scars so big?" Tyler asks and I am stunned by the question. "Who turned her?"

"I did," I say softly, opening my hands and gazing at them. "I don't know why I did it, but when I bit her, I felt like I had to make sure that she was a wolf. I almost killed her. The overload of power made her have a seizures. I look at her scars that cover her neck and shoulder and they punish me. I never meant to hurt her."

I look up at Tyler who is sitting there stunned. I sigh and stand.

"Want to come hunting with me?" I ask, opening the door. Tyler stands and he follows me into the woods where we turn and hunt.

-Rose-

It is dark by the time David and I exit the worm hole. I look around, amazed at seeing Paradise. There are all types of flowers blooming, wild animals roaming the open fields, large villages to the north, east and west of us, and a very large waterfall to the south. Everything is just so...

"Beautiful," I finish out loud, and David looks at me and smiles.

"I suppose," he says, moving to the northern village. I follow.

"This is the village of the wolf and the witch," he says, then points to the east. "That is the village of the Vampire and the Fey." He then points to the west. "And that is the village of the warlock and the ghost."

He walks me right through the village and into the woods on the other side. As I am distracted by the beauty, David knocks me sideways and gently taps the back of my neck. I turn wolf and he fastens something around my neck. I shake him off and growl. I try to turn human but there is a force stopping me.

"What the hell!" I bark into his brain as I try to take the collar off.

"Calm down," he says, opening his hands and showing his palms. "I enhanced a collar so that no matter what you won't be able to turn back to a human. You need the training as a wolf. In these woods are suicidal wolves— they want to die— and they will do anything to get it. I have charmed them to attack you." I keep trying to get the collar off, but it won't budge. "You need the fighting practice and you need to kill them. You need to learn how to survive as a wolf for a year."

"A YEAR!" I shout, finally able to break through. *"I have to be down*

here for a YEAR!"

"Actually, it's two years," he says and I growl at him. "First, your wolf form for half a year, then you're human for the rest. And then the witch form for the next year."

There is the sound of something heavy crashing through the woods and David ducks as a large, black pureblood wolf tackles me to the ground. He is also wearing a metal collar. I throw his body off me and take up a threatening stance by standing tall, pushing my chest out and pulling my lips all the way back. I'm already pissed off and he's not making it any better.

My opponent also takes up a threatening stance and we are in a growl off. I launch forward and tackle him, but he brings up his hind legs and pushes me off. I get straight back up and go again, jumping onto his back and digging my claws and teeth into his flesh. He shakes me off. I bark in anger and he attacks, going for my neck. I move and he hits my shoulder instead. I bark and growl in pain as he tears a chunk out and blood pours. I attack again, this time I rear up and attack from above. I bring my weight down on his back, and hear him yelp as I bring my teeth down into his back. Using a lot of my strength, I pick him up and throw him into a tree. He yelps and crumples into lump on impact.

I slowly walk over to him and sniff his body. I pick up no pulse so I turn and walk away, but he's not dead. With super speed, he bites my back leg. I don't yelp, but instead, turn around and bite his neck. He yelps and I pull backwards, taking his throat with me. His body goes completely limp and I drop his throat on the ground. I begin to walk into the woods, but I yelp as I place my hind leg down. I look at my shoulder and see it's still bleeding.

"What, no healing powers either!" I call out, but there's no answer. I growl and limp into the cover of the woods. As I limp, my body starts to slowly heal. When I am fully healed, I begin marking territory by rubbing and scratching on trees. I'm not going to actually sent mark; that's just *EW*. I find a herd of deer and slowly begin to stalk them, and when the time is right, I take one down and devour it. I hear a laugh in my mind; a werewolf is behind me.

I spin around and growl at the intruder. The wolf is male. He is black with a dark red tipped tail and has no collar, but he is interested in me.

"You are in my territory," he growls, walking over to a tree and actually scenting on it. I grow at him and flatten my ears against my head. This jackass isn't helping my mood, so I stand still and growl

deeply. The wolf's tail goes up in a playful manner, but I am so not in the mood. I have been hurt and annoyed, forced to leave Tyler just when things were going good, and now this wolf wanted his way with me. I don't think so. A strong territorial growl erupts from my throat and I open my mouth wide to release it.

The wolf must be young as it still jumps around trying to play. I lunge at the wolf and it whimpers as if I had bitten it, but in no time at all it was back up and bouncing around. I attack the young one and it whimpers and retaliates with a high pitched bark. I don't want to kill this wolf, so I bite it just hard enough to pull fur out and cause a little bleeding. It whimpers and whines as I open my mouth wider, issuing a warning. The wolf tilts his head and presses his stomach to the dirt with his ears flattened. My hackles rise and the wolf rolls onto its back, surrendering. I try to remember a lesson in biology about how wolves show dominance. I raise my tail, not too high, perk my ears, and stand tall.

"Get out of my sight," I growl into the wolf's mind. In a split second, it is up and running off into the trees. My main goal now is to hold this dominance and survive the following year.

-Zero-

Tyler's depressed. I can tell by his listless eyes. I tried everything to cheer him up. I took him out hunting, then I took him to the gym where he beat the crap out of me, but he never smiled once. He is hurting over Rose. One night, while he was sleeping, I called over Tamika. Tyler came down and asked what she was doing here. I asked her to locate Rose. She tried, but she couldn't find anything. Tamika said that Rose is either dead or in a magic protected globe. This only made Tyler worse. He wouldn't eat, and I don't think he slept much, either. One morning he comes downstairs looking terrible and tired.

"Morning," I say, and he grunts an acknowledgement as he takes a glass and fills it with water. I hear another person come downstairs and see Shea.

"I thought that the pack had to go to the ditch," I say, as she also gets water.

"Not today," she says, staring at Tyler. "Hello, handsome."

Tyler glances at Shea and nods. Shea runs her hands up Tyler's arm and squeezes.

"You are so strong," she says in a soothing voice. Tyler scowls at her and pulls his arm away.

"Not interested," he grunts, moving away, but Shea does not give up and follows him into the lounge and sits across from him. I follow them and sit next to Shea.

"So," she says, folding he legs. "Do you have a girlfriend?"

"Yes," Tyler says gruffly.

"Well, I could get rid of her," Shea says with a twisted smile. She starts twisting her hair around a finger. "What's her name?"

"Oh, no you don't," I say, taking Shea by the arm and dragging her out of the room and into the kitchen. "You will not mess with Tyler's relationship with Rose."

"Rose?" Shea says, scrunching up her face and pulling her arm out of my hand.

"Yes, Rose," I say, shaking her as I take her arm and resist the urge to rip her throat out. "And you will not touch her or meddle with Tyler. Or else I will hunt you down and kill you."

Shea growls and I growl back. She knows that she can't beat me.

"Understood," she scowls, shaking my hand off and walking up stairs. Tyler comes into the kitchen.

"Tyler, you need to eat," I say as he heads for the door. He looks back at me, then continues on his way, slamming the door behind him. I sigh and rub my temples; I need to think, I need some place to go. I head out the door and change, and take off in a full sprint until I reach the place where I was turned. I dig my paws into the soil and feel the earth. I close my eyes and let my ears take over. I hear the solid whomp of a helicopter and I open my eyes and look up. There is a news reporter helicopter flying right over me. I hear a siren wailing off in the distance and I race towards it. I stop in shock of what I find. There are police everywhere as well as ambulances and reporters all standing at the entrance of a cave. A twig snaps behind me and I turn to see Tyler in his wolf form standing next to me.

"What the hell is happening?" I ask as I see a paramedic pull a dead body from the cave.

"Someone found bodies in the cave," he growls, crouching down.

"It looks like the killer of Mercy Lake has struck again, but this time we have a name," a reporter says and Tyler and I listen on. "We have just confirmed that the killer is female and goes by the name Rose Bane."

Tyler and I look at each other and then back at the reporter who now has a witness, A.K.A. Rose's Brother, Xavier.

"I never thought my sister could do this," Xavier says to the camera, faking tears. "But I guess I underestimated her, like these poor, innocent people did."

"It was rumoured that each person had a rose in their hand," the reporter says. "Can this be confirmed?"

"Yes," Xavier said, faking sadness in his voice. "My sister forced these innocent people to hold a rose while she pulled the trigger."

"How traumatic," the reporter gasps and I roll my eyes. "But every rose has its thorns. The police have pulled out at least two bodies with more to come. All have the killer's prints on them."

I hear Tyler growl and the reporter looks over, but her attention is pulled back when a gun is fired. An officer comes back dragging a body. It's Lilly's and she's still breathing.

"Is this her?" The officer asks Xavier and he squints before nodding.

"Yes," Xavier says, smirking. "That's her."

Then in a flash, Lilly turns wolf and kills the police officer who dragged her body. The reporter screams as Lilly kills another. Then, from out of the woods a gun is fired and wolf hunters emerge carrying silver stakes. I watch as the hunters subdue Lilly as a female advances forward and plunges a stake into Lilly's chest. Lilly howls out in pain and the hunter puts another three stakes into her heart. Lilly falls limp and the hunter gives a signal. A vampire appears and begins to erase people memories of what just happened. I scan the area for Xavier but he has fled the scene.

"Scan the area," the huntress says to another hunter. "There might be more."

Tyler and I immediately leave. We run at full speed until we get home.

"What the hell was that?" I say in a harsh whisper as we turn human and walk upstairs and into the metal room.

"Rose is being framed," Tyler whispers back, closing the door. I notice his hands are shaking. He slams his hand on the door. "Lilly is dead."

"Rose is going to be furious," I sigh, running a hand through my hair, picturing Rose raging through Mercy Lake. She will kill all the hunters just to avenge her sister.

"What are we going to do?" Tyler asks, his eyes full of fear.

"I guess you've never been on the other side of a hunter attack," I snarl. "Lilly was innocent and they slaughtered her for being different."

"She was hardly innocent," Tyler laughs. "She killed two people."

"They shot at her for looking like Rose," I argue. "Before that, she never hurt a single person. She never even created another werewolf."

Tyler sighs and then looks to the floor.

"What are we going to do?" Tyler asks. "The hunters are going to try and kill every wolf in Mercy Lake."

"We are going to lay low," I sigh. "Every move we make must be strategic, until Rose comes back. She's only hope."

"How is she our *only* hope?" Tyler asks.

"Because she is a werewitch," I say, looking at Tyler. "She is the only paranormal powerful enough to take down the hunters."

11. Death in the Family

-Rose-

The days roll by and I fall into a pattern of hunt, eat, and sleep. Everything revolves around those three activities.

But one day things change. As I am hunting, I am knocked sideways by a wolf with a metal collar. I automatically jump into the fight. I run at a nearby tree and jump on it, push back, and land behind the wolf. He growls, then charges at me. We leap into the air and I am able to bite his side. He lands and stares me down. I bark and leap for him, but he moves back before trying the same move. I back up as he bites down; his jaws snap together. I launch at him and bite down on his hind leg. This one is stronger than the last, and he turns in on himself and bites my back. I let go and he throws me into a tree. I see a cliff up a head and push him towards it. I bite his chest and shake him. When I let him go, he falls over the cliff, but he bites down on my neck and pulls me with him. I hit hard and I hear something break.

I yelp as my body slowly repairs. The wolf growls at me and then takes off into the woods. I chase him, but I am too slow; my back is still healing and it slows me down, and I lose sight of him. I stop to catch my breath, but I cannot rest for long as the wolf returns and I am hit sideways. He bites down on my shoulder and I yelp out in pain. My eyes glow as rage fills me. I turn in on myself and bite the wolf's neck. He moves back before I could tear it out, and he attacks again. I dodge and again go for his neck, but I miss and hit his eye. I tear it out of its socket and the wolf howls in pain before barking and blindly hitting my chest with his head. I am flung backwards and my back hits a tree, reversing most of my healing.

I bark at him. Ignoring my pain, I run towards him. I hit him on his side and he stumbles and slides through the dirt. I stumble, but gain my balance as I cautiously walk over to the wolf. I hear him growl then he moves like lightning and goes for my neck. I leap over him and onto his back and bite down on the scruff of the neck. He tries to shake me off, but I have too good of a hold. Blood soaks his fur, making it harder to hold on. I fall off but I know I cannot stay down. I get back up to pin the wolf on his back. He yelps and tries to push me off with his hind legs, but it doesn't work. I bite down on his neck. Blood splashes up my face and front legs as I rip out his throat and then drop it by his side. I huff and walk away from the dead wolf; my chest heaving as pain works its way through my body. I have a feeling that I am still bleeding, but I cannot be sure as my fur is stained with blood— both mine and his.

I walk to the lake and lap at the water before laying down in the shallows to cool my body and clean my wounds. The water begins to move towards me. I stand up and leap out of the water and onto sand as the woods and the water begin to change all around me. The grass and trees turn to sand and the water became salty. Rocks of all sizes appeared to the left of me. Then it all stops and instead of standing at the edge of a pond, I now stand on a beach with the salty waves hitting the tips of my front paws. I turn around and see that the beach doesn't end as where the beach normally turns to grass, it instead just keeps going as far as the eye can see. I decide to look around and see what I can find.

I go left and head towards the rocks. Most of the rocks have small groves in them and the ones that don't are close enough that I can jump from one to another. I manage to climb to the top of the highest rock and look out. Everything is sand. I leap down from the rocks and begin to run right. I run until I can't run anymore. I pant and lay in the sand, and look up to the sky and see the night sky looking back at me. My mind runs back to Tyler and I sit up and my heart sinks into my chest. I won't be able to see him for another two years. I should not have left. A howl rises in my throat and I pull my head back and release it on to the wind. I feel a presence beside me, so I stop howling and prepare to fight, but it is just David. He is in his wolf form.

"*I have news from Mercy Lake,*" he pauses and I become concerned. "*Bad news.*"

"*What is it?*" I ask as he hangs his head.

"*Your sister has been murdered.*"

I'm stunned by his words. Lilly is dead.

"*No,*" I say, taking a step back. David steps forward and I lunge to attack, but he ducks just in time and I leap over him.

"This is your fault!" I growl, looking back at him as he collects himself. I run towards the rocks, leaping from one to another until I reach the highest rock. Lightning cracks and rain falls. I close my eyes and feel the rain fall on my fur as sadness fills my chest and it makes its way up to my throat. I lift my head and release it in the form of a howl. Lightning cracks and I stop and I open my eyes. Another howl is released on the wind, one I do not recognize. Then another howl erupts and another and another as Paradise is filled with howls with a sad tune. I lift my head once more and howl. This time when I stop, so do the rest of the wolves. I look out over the ocean that rages and smashes against the rocks. I lay down on the rock and drift into a slumber. I dream of something evil and heart breaking.

I'm awoken with a jolt. I'm falling. My eyes widen as I see the rock I was sleeping on moving further away. I turn my body so that my feet are under me, but I am too late. I hit the rocks and I hear bones break. I growl and the bones pop back into place and fix themselves. I stand and look up to the rock. At the top is a tan wolf looking down at me. Like all the others, this one has a metal collar, but unlike the others this one was accompanied by a white wolf, also wearing a metal collar.

I pull my lips back and deepen my growl and they both jump down and land on their feet. They stand about three metres apart, growling and reading themselves for attack. I back up a fraction, but keep my eyes on both of them. This is a standoff. I assess my situation, but the wolves grow tired of waiting and attack. The tan one leaps over me and the white one follows. I duck both attempts and sprint back to the rocks. I leap from rock to rock, trying to gain an advantage. The tan wolf is on my heels and catches up on a flat rock. He attacks and we fall. It isn't from a great height, but it gives me enough time to flip him around so that he lands on his back.

His back hits first on a sharp rock and he yelps in pain. I take the advantage and go for the neck, but his buddy is back and knocks me sideways. We circle each other. I lunge and go for the neck, but he moves out of the way. I bark in frustration as he bites my shoulder. The tan wolf jumps on my back, but I run towards a rock, causing the white wolf to back off. I slam the tan wolf against the rock again and again until it lets go. I then pin it to the ground and again try to go for the neck, but again, I am thrown off by the white wolf as it picks me up and throws me into the rock I slammed the tan wolf into. Blood splatters onto the rock.

My anger turns to range and my eyes glow as I charge at the white wolf. It leaps over me too soon and I am able to stretch my head back and latch onto the underside of the wolf. I throw it into the sand and then go for the neck, but the tan wolf is back and it hits me in the ribs. I stumble, but regain my balance. I run at the tan wolf but I am picked up and thrown by the white before I reach it. Blood sputters out of my shoulder and back as I hit the sand, and pain vibrates up my shoulder and through my back as my rage turns to fury. I stand and the wolves look at me. My eyes glow brighter and I feel raw power rockets through me. I bark and bolt towards them. I leap over the white wolf, who was trying to catch me. The tan wolf leaps up onto the rocks, trying to get away. I frown and turn on the white wolf that is running towards me.

I bark and charge at him. We collide. I have the most strength and pin the wolf to the ground and bite under its front leg. Blood stains both mine and the wolf's fur as I pull back and release a chunk of fur and skin from my mouth, the wolf reaches up and bites under my front left leg and I bark as I take it by the neck and throw it into a rock. The wolf whimpers and tries to stand. I walk over to the struggling wolf and place a paw onto its bleeding throat, it cries out as I end its miserable life with a painful bite.

There is a bark of anger overhead, and I look up to see the tan wolf looking down from a rock. I run to the nearest rock and begin to pursue the tan wolf, but the wolf leaps down and lands behind me. I spin quickly and growl with the white wolf's blood dripping from my teeth. The tan wolf begins to charge, but stops as I open my mouth and release a blood curdling growl. The wolf turns and runs in the other direction. I smirk at its attempt and crouch down, I give it a head start of five seconds before leaping from my rock and tearing down the beach in hot pursuit. For suicide wolves they really want to live. Waves crash onto the sand and my paws flick up water as I run after the wolf. I catch up to the wolf and am only inches away from hitting it. With a final push, I close the gap and grab the wolf's tail, pulling it backwards and throwing it into the water. The wolf yelps and stands.

"You killed him!" She yells into my mind. I snarl at the wolf and she steps back.

"Yes," I coo, stepping closer. *"And now I am going to kill you."*

I attack and she dodges me and runs back down the beach. She almost reaches the rocks before I leap into the air and land on her back. I bite down hard and rip her head off. I leap off her back as her body collapses into the water.

Blood and sand cover most of my body, and I'm totally and utterly exhausted and in despite need of fresh water. However, there are no fresh bodies of water in sight. I suck it up and take a mouthful of sea water, but I immediately spit it out from the sour taste. I decide to head back to the rocks to see if I could find any small insects. Along the way, I find small groves in the rocks and they are filled with fresh water. I lap at the water, realising they must have filled up when the rain came. It puts a pounce in my step as I go off in search for more. Once my thirst is quenched, I continue to look for food and I am able to find, kill, and eat a lizard, but it doesn't satisfy my hunger so I go in search for more.

-Zero-

The days begin falling into a pattern. They start with a run and a morning hunt, then Tyler and I would hit the gym. We then head home for lunch and a shower, and after that, we go our separate ways for the rest of the day. But one day while Tyler and I were having lunch Shea comes downstairs whistling a happy tune.

"What's got you so happy?" I ask as she butters some bread.

"There was a pack meeting last night," she says as Tyler and I share a look. It has almost been a month since Lilly was killed and nothing has happened.

"And?" Tyler asks, tensing.

"Rose is wanted," she smirks, placing ham onto the buttered bread. "Dead or alive."

"What the hell?" Tyler and I shout, standing and knocking over our chairs. "Why?"

"For killing innocents," Shea shrugs and Tyler growls. "They have offered a reward to the first wolf who sinks his or her fangs into that bitch's throat."

"Son of a-" Tyler growls, leaping for Shea, who takes a bite of her sandwich.

"Easy," I say, taking his arm and stopping him dead in his tracks. "I know she deserves it, but you can't harm a member of the alpha pack. They will hunt you down and rip you apart."

"And wouldn't that be a shame," Shea laughs. Tyler growls and pulls his arm away from me and walks out the door. Shea giggles and waves as I follow him, slamming the door on the way.

"Tyler," I call out as soon as I am far away from the house. I hear a shout and I run towards it, ready for a fight. But all I see is Tyler beating his knuckles on a tree.

"Tyler?" I say, moving slowly towards him. He doesn't acknowledge me. He stops after about ten minutes. He's covered in sweat and is breathing heavy.

"The full moon is tonight," he says, sitting on a fallen log. "Are we locking ourselves in the basement?"

I nod. Tyler and I have been locking ourselves in the basement while the rest of the pack go and attempt to turn humans. Little have they succeeded as the hunters are still in town and they lie in wait for the wolves. We have already lost Dante, but we have also grown by four.

Tyler stands and we make our way back to the house. Once there, we head down to the basement and test the chains. We pull on them and bite them in our wolf forms. When we deem them worthy, we head back upstairs and go our separate ways.

Tyler and I meet back at the basement at ten o'clock to do some final testing and then chain ourselves up. We use manacles to chain our front and back feet together and to the wall. After that, we put iron collars around our necks.

"Eleven-fifty seven," I say, bracing myself.

"I hate this part," he says, going down onto his knees.

"What are you doing," I ask as the clock strikes eleven- fifty nine.

"I shattered my knees last time," he says, then he doubles over. I collapse to my knees and double over. It feels like a freight train hits me as every bone in my body pops out of place and realigns. I throw my head back and let out a yell as Tyler does the same. My hands turn into paws, my body grows fur, my tail bone lengthens as my body and head becomes sleeker. My teeth sharpen and I throw my head back again. As my jaw finishes lengthening, I release a blood curdling howl. I can hear howls being released in the woods. As they cut off I hear one I recognize, a howl of pain: Shea's.

As Tyler and I lose the rest of our humanity we begin to pull on the chains and try to get loose, but it is no use. Tyler and I designed the chains to be strong so that we can't get out, but we still try until the sun comes up and hands us back our humanity. As Tyler and I slip back into our human selves, there is a yell and a crash from upstairs. Tyler and I glance at each other and quickly unchain ourselves and run upstairs.

In the kitchen are the deceased bodies of Shea, James, and three of the newest wolves. My heart shatters as I can't tear my eyes away from James' dead body. He was my mentor and the only reason I was able to stay with the pack after I deserted the alpha pack.

Aamon is in full rage and is throwing things.

"Son of a bitch," he shouts, throwing a glass vase at the door. I look up to Aamon as the remaining young wolf steps forward and tells Aamon to calm down, which is a poor decision on his part. Aamon punches him in the jaw and grabs him by the collar of his shirt.

"Heads up," I say to Tyler. We both step aside as Aamon throws the guy in our direction.

"Those fucking hunters have cost me six of my best wolves! Don't tell me to calm down!" he shouts, picking up the toaster, "They are going to pay in blood."

Aamon throws the toaster towards Tyler, who simply turns sideways and dodges it. It flies right past him and shatters into the wall.

"Who's this son of a bitch?" he shouts, looking at me with blood shot eyes. Aamon hasn't paid much attention to Tyler or me since I have drifted from the greater pack.

"Made five months ago," I say, dodging a spoon he throws at me.

"By who?" Aamon shouts, swearing in Latin. Tyler glances at me and I shake my head "By fucking who?" Aamon shouts again, this time throwing a glass cup at Tyler, who catches it before it hits the wall.

"Me," I say. If Aamon knew who made him, Tyler would be killed on spot.

"Get the fuck out," Aamon groans. "All of you."

Tyler places the cup down and follows me and the other wolf out the door.

"Sorry you had to see that," I say as the newest wolf breaks off and heads into town.

"Is he always like that?" Tyler asks, stuffing his hands in his pockets.

"Only when a hunt goes bad," I say, shrugging. "So, pretty much only when the hunters are in town."

"They aren't leaving," Tyler sighs, stepping over a dead wolf body. "Normally, we would have left town by now."

"They are looking for something," I say, stunned how he says we.

"Or someone," he whispers and I glance at him. He moves behind a tree and points to something. I see hunters up ahead and I also move behind a tree.

"You said that the girl would be there!" a huntress says.

"How was I to know she has a twin?" another huntress says. "I have been locked in a jar since she was born!"

I then realize the second hunter is not a hunter at all, she is Rose's mother. The huntress lets out a sigh of frustration.

"Trust me," Rose's mother says. "I will deliver you my daughter's blood, and in return you will guarantee my son's, my husband's, and my safety."

"Why would a mother want her daughter dead?" the huntress asks, folding her arms over her chest.

"She is not my daughter," Rose's mother hisses. "She is a demon. A demon that chose the light."

"She changed my brother," the huntress sighs and I look across to Tyler who is leaning on the tree. "I know why I want her blood, but why do you?"

"Ah yes," Rose's mother laughs. "You believe that the blood of a werewitch will reverse the curse that she so humbly bestowed upon your dear brother. What was his name? Tyler?"

"Do we have a deal or not?" The huntress grumbles and they shake hands. Rose's mother gives a little curtsy and then vanishes in a blue cloud of dust.

"I hate that bitch," the huntress mumbles, walking off. I look back to Tyler who is looking off into the distance.

"You sister seems desperate to get you back," I say and he glares at me. I shrug and walk off.

"Do you think she will come back?" Tyler asks. I stop dead in my tracks and turn around.

"Your sister?" I ask, then shrug. "Sure I guess."

"No," he sighs, and I raise an eyebrow. "Rose."

I shrug my shoulders and turn my back to him.

"I want her back," I hear Tyler sigh. "My life feels empty. I need her back. Is that selfish?"

"She will come back," I say, before walking away from Tyler.

-Rose-

I catch a seagull. It's the largest thing that I have eaten since I have been on this god forsaken beach. But it doesn't fill me, and I feel myself slip into exhaustion mode. Days have blurred together and most of the time is spent saving my energy. I haven't found any food or water as it hasn't rained for days, or has it been months? I am not sure anymore, but it can't be months as I haven't fallen victim of the full moon's curse. As I lay down on a rock, I get a feeling, and it's not a good one. I feel like I'm being pulled downwards by a hook that is buried in my stomach. I pull my lips back and growl as voices fill my head and the scenery changes again.

Grass begins to rise from the sand, trees appear on the horizon,

and the sea changes size and shape. I look up and bark and run as I am almost flattened by an elephant's foot. I don't stop running until I reach the safety of a large tree that is unknown to me. I pant and sit at the base of the tree and take in my surroundings. it seems that I am in Africa. I can hear roaring lions, laughing hyenas, and a mixture of other sounds. I set out to find water, but as I near the water hole I am knocked sideways with such a force that I fall and tumble in the grass several times. I look around and growl at a black wolf with a straight, tan line running down its back with a—of course— metal collar.

I try to stand, but I yelp and fall back down. I look at my back and see that the wolf took a bite out of it and it is now bleeding. I whine because I know that I am in exhaustion mode. The wolf seems to smile and my heart beats fast as the wolf slowly closes the gap between us. The wolf places a paw on my back and I deepen my growl. I lean upwards and take a bite out of the wolf's chest. It laughs inside my head and shakes me off, then proceeds to grab me by the scruff of my neck. I yelp as he fully picks my body off the ground, shakes me several times, and throws me away like a rag doll. My blood stains the grass as I hit a tree and then the wolf pounces on me, like a cat would to a mouse or a lion to an antelope. Its claws dig into my flesh and it sinks its teeth into my hide. I cry out in pain and close my eyes as the wolf repeatedly bites and scratches at my exhausted body. Then I hear a blood curdling howl and a blood-thirsty bark.

The wolf is thrown off me and I open my eyes to see David sizing up the wolf. David has his lips pulled back and is showing his set of dangerous fangs dripping blood. I look at the wolf to see he is bleeding from a gaping wound on his shoulder. It closes quickly and the wolf and David begin to converse in a language I don't recognize. The wolf growls something that I believe is a swear word and David lunges forward with a blood-thirsty bark that even makes me want to step back. The wolf yelps even though David hasn't touch him and flattens its ears and submits to David, who is standing tall and holding his ground. David says something else and the wolf stands and runs away. David turns and walks back towards me. He turns human and leans down next to me. His deep blue eyes look at me with concern and I pull my lips back and growl.

"Easy, little bird," he laughs. "I am going to help you."

He changes form and howls something onto the wind, then from out of nowhere a bunch of native women come out of the grass carrying baskets. They sit down next to me and begin to stitch me up. I wriggle and protest by yelping and barking at the women, but they ignore me and continue to work.

"I am not your little bird," I growl into David's mind as the stitching comes to an end. *"Why do I need stitches anyway? I will heal."*

"Yes, but you will be left with scars," David says back as I stand and sit across from him. "If we didn't stitch you, would have bigger scars than you are going to have. The stitches will fall out themselves. I have taken care of the wolf for now. Go and eat while you can because he will be back."

David and the women then vanish in a cloud of dust and I take his advice and go hunting, but first I head to the watering hole and take a long drink. As I lap at the water, I keep my eyes up and make sure that I know what is where. I see a large herd of water buffalo and decide that they will be my target. I finish my drink then head around to where the buffalo are. I crouch down in the long grass and begin to stalk the prey. I pick an easy target— a wounded male with a broken horn. But my cover is blown by my fur— the white stands out too much and soon the herd are running away. However, what I lack in camouflage I make up in speed and I catch up to the buffalo in a second. I run alongside the herd for a while before plunging in and taking a hold of a large male's front leg. It trips and I pounce and latch onto its throat. As soon as it's dead, I don't wait another second and tear off a large piece of it and start eating.

About five minutes later, a pack of hyenas come and try to take away my meal. I lift my head and growl at them. They flinch but they keep coming back. I swipe my paws and deepen my growl and then, finally, they back off. They stay about five meters away from me and my meal and they wait for me to finish. I leave a naked carcass for the scavengers to peck at the bones and the marrow and I go hunting again. By the end of the day, my belly is bulging, my wounds are healing, and I am halfway happy. As night closes in on the plains of Africa, I find a tree and lie beneath it, settling in for the night as the plains explode in the music of the animals. I feel so out of place as I lay my head down and close my eyes and fall asleep.

There are people all around me. I'm in the middle of the city in Mercy Lake on a really busy day. I hear many sounds, but one sticks out from the rest: a laugh. I follow the sound, pushing though the busy crowds. The crowd thins as I come nearer to the sound. My heart squeezes and I become paralyzed as the crowd disappears and in front of me is Tyler with his hands wrapped around a girl who is not me.

"Do you have a girlfriend?" the girl asks, running a hand up and under his shirt.

"No way, babe," he scoffs with a sly smile. Tears line my eyes as he leans down and kisses her; and then he really kisses her, with a type of kiss that would get you expelled from school and grounded for life. My heart feels like it's in someone's hands that are squeezing too hard.

"Tyler!" I call out, but my voice seems distant and faded. A man steps in front of Tyler and the girl and looks at me. I can't seem to put his features together as he is in a full length hooded cloak. He drifts closer and closer. I scream and hold up my hands to shield my face. Then I wake up, but I am not in Africa. I am in my room, the room that burned down in the fire.

There is a body behind me and I turn my head to find Tyler sleeping with his arms around me. I raise my hand and gently stroke his face. His eyes snap open and instead of his green and yellow eyes, I find two sets of angry red eyes looking into mine. I become paralysed and Tyler raises something over my chest: a silver stake.

"You left me," he whispers before burying the stake deep in my heart. I scream.

I wake up and see that I am still in Africa in my wolf form with no stake in my heart. The sun is just peaking over the horizon as I raise my head and stand up. I silently make a vow to Tyler that I will fight harder and win this game so that I can come home. I head off to find breakfast. I take down a zebra, then head to the watering hole to wash it down with murky water. No pancakes and orange juice for me. I fall into a pattern over the next few days, eat, drink, and sleep. Most of my dreams are haunted by nightmares. Then one day the wolf with the tan stripe reappears and challenges me.

With Tyler on my mind, I bite own hard and lightning explodes from my mouth as my eyes glow brighter. I bark at the wolf and charge it and the wolf runs at me. We leap at the same time and collide in the air, then fall to the ground. Getting back up, I charge again and hit the wolf on its chest, sending it tumbling in the grass. I run after it and leap onto its back and bite down hard. It yelp at the sheer power of the lightning and shakes me off. I let go and land on my feet.

I pull my lips back and growl. I can feel the wolf's blood drip from my teeth as I open my mouth wider and let out a bark of fury. The wolf runs towards me and leaps into the air, knocking me down and landing on top of me. It snarls and I bring my back legs up and push it off before it can bite me. And so it goes on, both the wolf and I switch from offence to defense, but things change as the wolf calls in another wolf just as I am about to kill it.

The new wolf knocks me sideways and growls at me. I growl back and see that this one also has a metal collar. I growl at this wolf and it tucks its tail between its legs and flattens its ears on its head. I stand tall and bark. I must have looked savage with blood staining my mouth and the lightning lining it. I charge and tackle the wolf to the ground. It yelps as I bite its neck and rip its throat out. I turn to face the other wolf, but he has ran away. I growl in frustration as I look around for any sign of him. There is blood everywhere— both mine and his— but there is no sight of him, so I decide to go and hunt. After downing a gazelle, I find a place to sleep. On my way I stumble into lion territory. A pride of lions follow me at a distance until they decide that I am not a threat, then they turn around and head back to the shade of a large tree as the African heat settles in. I find a tree for myself and I lay down under it. As soon as I close my eyes I am sucked into another dream.

I am in the woods and Tyler is standing five feet away from me. He looks sad. The thing about this dream is that it feels so real. Tyler is leaning on a tree with his hands in his pockets. Something catches my attention; a grave stone. I walk over and kneel down next to it, but as I read the name I stumble backwards. It's my name.

The stone reads:
Rose Jasmine Bane
Loving daughter and best friend
Will be missed.
Under the writing is a howling wolf and above the writing is a rose. I turn to look at Tyler and see that he is crying.

"Tyler," I say, standing, but my voice sounds far away. "It's not real."

He walks over to my grave and places a silver stake at the base of the stone.

"I swear to God that I will find your killer," he whispers, then stands and runs into the woods, morphing into a wolf as he goes. I scream his name but he can't hear me. I take a step forward, intending to follow him, but my foot hits something. I look down and see wolf bodies all around me; they weren't there before. I look around and see so many dead wolves. I notice some of them, like the white one and the tan one, but there are so many that I don't recognize. Their blood stains my hands. I try to rub it off, and nothing happens. I cry, but even my tears are blood stained. Thunder booms and lightning strikes as I scream out

as loud as I can.

Then I wake up. It is now night time in Africa. I stand and shake the dirt from my fur and go hunting. I need to get my mind off the dream, but my mind always comes back to it. I growl and curse myself as I head to the watering hole. As I lap at the water, a force picks me up and throws me into the watering hole. I come up for air and see five wolves on the bank; only one wears a collar: the black and tan wolf. I swim to the bank and set my paws onto the dry land.

"That was fun," I growl into the pack's mind. *"Who should I kill first?"*

"You should give up," the black and tan wolf says as I shake the water from my fur. *"There is five of us and only one, lonely you. I have thought about it and I really don't want to die yet, so I am going to kill you first."*

"Five of you against me?" I snicker into their minds. *"I really don't like the odds. Can I call a friend?"*

"I hope you said good-bye to Tyler," the collared wolf laughs and I freeze. *"David told me all about you, Miss Bane. You are never going to see your boyfriend again."*

All joking is gone as I deepen my growl and pull my lips back. I bark at the collared wolf, but I am knocked sideways by one of his pack members. I back up, flatten my ears, and growl. My eyes glow brighter than they ever have and lightning bursts from my mouth. Some of the wolves back up a step, however, the main wolf steps forward and begins to talk to me. Most of the words get lost and I don't register them. I close my eyes and realize that if I just charge I won't get anywhere. Everything slows down as my heartbeat becomes louder and steadier. I inhale and exhale slowly, then open my eyes.

The collared wolf is still taunting me and he doesn't see me move; none of them do. I run at him and leap in the air. I collide with him and bite down hard on his shoulder. He lets out a painful yelp as the lightning hits his shoulder hard. He shakes me off and we circle each other. He thinks he can out smart me. Another wolf charges from behind me. It is predictable. I turn fast, and as the wolf fails and leaps over me, I grab it by the chest and throw it into another wolf who is also charging. Our barks, growls, and howls fill the night and my eyes and lightning lights it. Another wolf attacks me, this one aims low, going for my chest. I dodge its attack and take it from the scruff of the neck. I shake and throw it sideways; it tumbles and lands in the water, but it gets back up quickly. This time all the wolves attack at once. I bark and attack with the force of two wolves, but it is not enough and I know I won't win, silently I ask for help.

-Zero-

I go down on my knees and am turned into a wolf. I get a feeling that I am falling and that my body is being stretched. As quickly as it happens it stops, but I am no longer in the house. Instead, I stand alongside Tyler. We are both wearing armour— mine black and his white. I look around. We are not in Mercy Lake anymore. It seems we are in Africa.

"What the hell?" I ask Tyler, who is looking just as confused as me. Then we hear a noise, a bark. We look over at a watering hole to see more wolves. There are five of them attacking one, Rose. Tyler and I don't hesitate; we take off running. The armour is surprisingly light and we reach the fight and Tyler and I attack— we take a wolf each. We hit them at a run so we have the upper hand. I bite into my opponent's shoulder and throw it into the water. There is a howl and the fighting stops as four more wolves come out of the tall grass. They are hard to make out as the night sky is full of dark clouds, but the wolves form a circle around Rose, Tyler, and I.

"Loving the odds," I say to Rose.

"Join the club," she growls back into my mind. *"How the hell did you guys get here?"*

"We were hoping to ask you that," Tyler says, barking at a wolf who steps too close. *"Wow, nine against three. This shouldn't be too hard. Three wolves for the each of us."*

"Easier said than done, brother," I say, keeping my eyes focused on the wolves in my line of vision. *"Do we have a plan?"*

"Kill them all, leave no survivors," Rose snarls, her hackles raise and she snarls at a black and tan wolf with a metal collar around his neck.

The night turns into barks of rage and fury as the battle explodes before our eyes. I run to the left and Tyler goes right while Rose goes straight for the black and tan wolf. Three wolves come towards me slowly, like they are stalking prey. They split up and circle around me, but I keep my eyes on them and when they charge. I leap right over them and they collide with each other. They get back up and charge all at once; aiming for the chest, shoulders, and neck. The armour is tough, it protects me. I fight back, biting one of the wolves' shoulder. I constantly have to keep moving so that the wolves can't corner me. One of the wolves manages to find an exposed area under my front legs and it slides under me and bites the tender area. My growl deepens and I tackle it and tear its throat out. It slumps to the ground and I turn on the others, blood drips from my mouth as I pull my lips back and growl. They bark and attack at the same time. I brace myself and when they hit me I retaliate and push back. A black pure-blood attacks and bites under the armour. Blood drips for a second and then heals.

"That almost tickled," I laugh, taking the wolf by the back and throwing it into the grass. The other wolf attacks and I'm caught by surprise as it tackles me and bites at the armour. I push it off and tear its throat out. The black wolf leaps out of the grass with a booming bark. We collide and it digs its claws into my armour and bites my exposed ears. I howl out in pain, but get up. We both go up on hind legs and claw at each other's stomachs and bite at the other's body. I go down on all fours first and latch onto the wolf's hind leg. It yelps and goes down. As it does I leap up and grab onto its neck. I pull backwards and tear its throat out. By now, blood stains cover my armour and my body. I look over to Tyler just as he finishes his last wolf. I run over to him and we look around, but we can't see Rose anywhere. Then there is a bark and we run towards it into the grass where we see blood. We follow it until we find Rose fighting the collared wolf; she is bloodied and is wearing out. Tyler and I run into the fight.

"I have to kill him," Rose barks into our mind. Tyler and I nod and work to pin him down so that Rose can get to the neck. When we have him in that position Rose doesn't hesitate, ending his life with a sharp, painful bite to the throat. As Rose drops the wolf's throat on the ground, Tyler and I go down as a high-pitched sound fills our heads. I drag my head along the ground as a feeling fills my stomach, like I am being lifted up. Rose says something into our minds, but I don't register it as the high-pitched noise gets louder and louder. I close my eyes tightly, and when I open them I'm back where I came from and in my human form. I'm on the couch in the lounge room at the house. There is a ringing noise in my ears, and as it fades I hear the kitchen door slam as Tyler races in.

"What the hell just happened?" he asks, wide-eyed. He and I are both shaken up.

"I don't know, but it was real," I say, lifting my shirt to find fading scars.

"How was that even possible?" he asks as he begins to pace.

"Are you seriously asking that?" I ask, raising an eyebrow. Tyler stops and looks me in the eyes, "My guess is that it has something to do with the armour. What exactly happened when Rose gave you the armour?"

"She dug her nails into my back and a voice whispered in my head," Tyler says as he begins to pace again.

"What did it say?" I ask, leaning forward on the couch. "Exactly."

"It whispered, 'White Knight'," he says. "What happened to you?"

"Same thing," I shrug. "She dug her nails into my wrist and whispered, 'Black Knight'."

"What does this all mean?" Tyler asks, growing angry.

"I don't know," I say, then an idea hits me and I stand up quickly. "But I might know a few places where we might find out."

I walk outside and the midday sun greets me. My eyes adjust to the light as I stalk through the woods.

"Where are we going?" Tyler calls out, jogging to catch up to me.

"There is a library," I say quietly to him as we continue to walk. "It was built for the paranormal years ago. It's where we can go and find information."

"Where is it?" he asks quietly as I round the corner.

"Under a library of course," I whisper as we stop at the town's library. We walk up the stairs and into the building. I motion for Tyler to keep quiet and let me do the talking. We walk up to the counter where a brunette librarian is working. She looks up at me and our eyes lock.

"What can I do for you?" she asks, glancing at Tyler.

"We need access to the room," I whisper, leaning on the counter. She smiles and nods.

"You know where it is?" she asks and I nod. I push off the counter and Tyler and I walk off to the back of the library where a large antique wardrobe is. I open the door and motion Tyler inside. He scowls at me, but gets in. I follow behind him and shut the door behind me.

"You're not going to molest me, are you?" Tyler asks. I roll my eyes and put my hand into a secret, hidden compartment where I find a lever. I pull it and an eye scanner appears on the opposite wall. I press my eye close to it and, when it scans me, there is a click and the floor opens up to stairs. Tyler follows me down and once we're out of the wardrobe the floor closes. We reach the library where paranormals of all kinds are buzzing around.

"What the hell," Tyler gasps as we move to the front counter. A pissed off librarian looks at me with a scowl.

"What do you want," she says, chewing loudly on gum. "I don't have all day."

"Where is the werewitch section?" I ask.

"Go straight down there," she says, pointing. "First left, second right."

I nod and we are on our way. The closer we get, the fewer paranormals there are. A sign signals that we've reached the place.

"Split up, we will cover more area," I sigh, taking a book from the shelf and carrying it back to the table where I flip it open and begin reading. The book covers what the werewitches are and how they are created, but they always refer to male werewitches and there are no females on record. I flick through the contents page and see nothing that I don't already know. I leave it on the table and then go for another book. I flick through the contents pages and find nothing. I go for another and then another. On my fourth or fifth book, Tyler calls my name. I go over to his table and see that he has a very large leather bound book opened to a page called *Werewitch Tagging*.

"It says that when a werewitch finds a person worthy they will be tagged," Tyler says, reading the text. "'The paranormal will be taken over by armour and will be dragged to the werewitch when the werewitch is in a high danger risk. The werewitch must have a strong connection to the paranormal.'"

I notice some pictures on the opposite page and I point to them.

"'The process of tagging'," Tyler continues reading. "'When a werewitch tags, he will cause the paranormal to bleed with his fingernails. An energy will flow into the paranormal blood system, causing the magical armour to appear. The armour will disappear after the process and will only reappear when the werewitch needs it. The tag allows the werewitch to have a connection to the tagged paranormal. It allows the werewitch to take energy from the tagged paranormal and will allow the werewitch to call on his tags when in despite need of help.'"

Tyler flips over to the next page. At the top is the heading, *Paradise*. Tyler gets up and walks away, so I take his place and read all about Paradise. It tells me how it was created and where to find the entrance. I jot the address down then continue to read. It tells me how the original werewitch can control it with relics, and it shows images of David and pictures of Paradise. I close the book and place it back on its shelf along with the rest of my books. I walk over to Tyler, who is reading a book on the werewitch species. In particular, the page that shows how to kill a werewitch.

"What are you doing?" I ask and he doesn't look at me.

"Did you know that a silver stake won't kill a werewitch," he says, pulling a silver stake out of his jacket. The stake has leather around the hilt so he can handle it. "The stake needs to be either dipped in pure Spotted Alder Roots, or combined with bronze."

I make a fist around the paper that holds the address of the entrance to Paradise.

"Let's get out of here," I say, walking towards the exit. He stands and tucks the stake in his pocket. He stops at the counter where he leans on the counter.

"Where can I find Spotted Alder Roots ?" he asks, and I stop in my tracks and turn around.

"In the woods, obviously," she replies, taking out a piece of paper with the picture on it. I growl and head for the stairs, pulling the release leaver as I go. Tyler follows me out of the library, then we split up. I go home and he goes deeper into the city.

-Rose-

They appeared out of nowhere and then vanished once the fighting was over. I walk around with my nose to the ground. I can smell their scents, proving they were here, but I can't tell where they went. They just spun out, like something was in their heads, but I didn't feel anything. I trust that they're alright and that they are back on earth. I at least got to see Tyler again. My head snaps up as something catches my eye: the sun rising over the horizon. The fight took all night and I am utterly drained, so I go to find a place to let my wounds heal. I take down and eat a zebra as I go, and then I find a large boab tree and lay down under it. I am sucked into another dream.

Tyler is in the woods, he is looking for something. He is holding a flash light and looking upwards. When he finds what he needs, he goes down onto his knees and begins to dig at the base of a tree. He pulls out a root and smiles as he pulls more and more out. He cuts the root from the tree using a large knife. Once he has filled a bag hanging from his shoulder he walks away. I follow him back to Aamon's house where he goes down to the basement. There is a long plastic table where he dumps the contents of the bag and in the light I can see what tree the roots belong to, Spotted Alder. I stumble backwards and gasp. What the hell he is doing? I almost scream when he pulls out a silver stake and lays it on the table. He takes the mortar and pestle and begins grinding the roots. When they are finely ground, he puts them in a pot and places it over a small burner using a tripod. He boils the Spotted Alder until it liquifies, then he dips the stake into the liquid. When he pulls it out, it hardens and moulds over the stake like wax. I close my eyes hard...

And wake up. I look around and see that is midday in Africa. I stand and stretch out. These dreams are getting too weird. The heat begins to intensify and my fur is not made for this place. I go to the water hole and lay in the shallows panting. Then a pulling feeling starts again. I become queasy and I know I am changing locations. I feel the water hole get shallower and dry up until I am standing on dry land. I look around as the grass shrinks and all around me is dry, flat lands filled with dirt. The change then bursts into action again and bamboo explodes along with other Chinese plants like cherry blossoms. Once the change finishes and I lose the queasiness, I stand and go to look around. I weave in and out of bamboo and duck the low hanging branches of the cherry blossoms.

The scene is beautiful, and I only wish that Tyler were here to see it. A strong wind picks up and rustles my fur and plucks leaves from the trees and blows them around. The smell is incredible and I inhale deeply before searching for my water source. After an hour of searching, I find a lake surrounded by lush vegetation and rocks of all sizes and weeping elms with their branches hanging in the water. I crouch at the edge and lap at the water. It's cool as it goes easily down my throat, quenching my thirst and making me feel cool and content. But as soon as I finish drinking, everything becomes quiet. Not even the whisper of the wind is heard. I feel so lonely and it is suffocating.

The silence gives me time to remember the things I was putting out of my mind. My mind travels back in time, back to the cave where Tyler and I kissed. I remember what it felt like, his soft lips against mine. How it felt when I ran my hands through his hair. I close my eyes and draw in a deep breath. I can even smell the scents from that night: the smell of the rain and of Tyler's body. I wish he was with me right at this moment, but he isn't. I have a feel of needing inside of me. He is the only thing keeping me alive. I sigh and lay down at the water's edge and see my reflection. I gaze at myself for a while until a dark spot catches my eye. I look up and see a black werewolf walking on the opposite side of the lake. It stops suddenly and looks at me. I see its collar and my fur stands on end. I stand up and stare at it for a while. It sits and looks at me also, and we stay like that for a while, but then the wolf stands up and moves into the water. The wolf starts to swim across to me. I turn and run away, zigzagging back through the trees and the bamboo, but somehow the wolf catches up and tackles me to the ground.

"*Nothing personal,*" the wolf says as I bring my hind legs up and push him off me. He charges and I bark and charge as well. The wolf leaps into the air and I duck, turning quickly and leaping on the wolfs back as it lands. I bite down hard and the wolf yelps out in pain and turns on me. He manages to shake me off and I collide with the trunk of a cherry blossom. I get back up and deepen my growl. The wolf laughs.

"*Now, it's personal,*" he says before charging head first. He collides with my chest and pushes me sideways. I try to strengthen my stance by digging my claws into the soil, but the soil is too soft and the wolf is too strong. I try to bite it, but it holds me where I can't reach. My body collides with the cherry blossom and I hear the bark crack. The wolf reels back and slams into my body. I yelp as spots cloud my vision. The wolf repeats the process again and again. The tree snaps and falls away from my body, and I growl and stand back up. The wolf backs up and it seems like he is smiling with a wide grin. I bark and charge while the wolf stands strong and laughs.

"*I'll give you something to laugh at,*" I think and I bite down hard on his throat. The wolf yelps and begs for mercy, but it goes in one ear and out the other as I pull back and rip out its throat. Blood splutters on the ground and there is a boom in the sky. I look up as dark, heavy clouds form and spill their contents onto the earth, soaking into my fur and weighing me down. I shake in an attempt to rid most of the water, but it's immediately restocked. I need to find a place to shelter so I head off in search of a cave. After going into several occupied caves, I finally find one that is empty, I walk to the back of the cave and curl up to sleep. Thunder and lightning fills the cave with sound and light and the soft pitted patter of the rain lulls me into a deep sleep.

I am back in the basement. I look around and see Tyler in the corner. This dream doesn't feel as real as the others, the edges seem blurred.

"*I have been waiting for you to return,*" *Tyler says, looking over my shoulder. I turn around and see myself standing at the top of the stairs.*

"*Tyler,*" *I breathe, walking down the stairs.* "*I have missed you so much.*"

I watch my other body walk to Tyler and wrap around him in a hug. Tyler doesn't react like I thought he would. I hear my other self gasp and she pulls back.

"*Do you have silver on you?*" *I ask with a worried face, and Tyler shrugs and pulls the silver stake out of his jackets pocket. Both me and the other me gasp and step back.*

"What are you doing?" the other me asks, backing up as Tyler steps forward.

"You left me," he whispers and I watch as Tyler holds the other me down and positions the stake over her heart. I don't scream, I don't yell for help. Then there is a bang and the basement door flies open and another Tyler runs in. He heads for his own body and crash tackles it and the second body absorbs the first.

"Rose," he calls out. "If you are in here, then you need to do what I just did."

My heart rate doubles as I run at my other body. As we collide, I absorb my second body. My vision clears and everything seems real. I look at Tyler and he stares at me.

"Tyler?" I question, stepping forward. "Is it really you?"

"Rose," he breathes. He runs to me and wraps me in a hug. "I would never hurt you."

"It's you," I whisper, falling deeper into his arms and choking back tears. "How are you here?" I ask, pulling back.

"It's called a dream jump," he explains. "Witches can place a subject into someone else's dream. I got the witch from the circle to put me under. We have been trying for the past few days, and finally I'm here."

"Why are you here?" I ask, raising an eyebrow.

"It is hell on earth without you," he says and I step forward. "Every day I wait and hope that you will come back, and when you didn't I needed to see you. So I searched for a way." Tyler wraps his arms tighter around me and I feel home again. I look up and see that Tyler is also crying. I go on tiptoe and kiss him. He returns the kiss passionately and I wrap my arms around his neck. Then suddenly the scenery changes and we are upstairs in the metal room.

"What the hell?" I say, pulling back.

"You can control things with your mind here," Tyler says before pushing me backwards onto the bed. I laugh as he puts a leg either side of me and kisses me again and again, then he moves to the side of my face and then down my neck to my collar bone. His hands come up and unbutton two buttons on the shirt I am wearing. It's like cold water to the face. I push him off me and I stand up.

"No," I say, realizing I am out of breath.

"Don't you want to?" Tyler asks, getting up and walking to me.

"Believe me, I want to," I sigh, stepping back half a step. "But not here."

"Why not?" he asks, raising an eyebrow.

"Because I want it to mean something," I sigh, hoping that I am not making him mad. "Not just something that happens in a dream."

"I understand," Tyler says, stepping closer and smiling. He kisses my forehead and everything becomes blurred.

"What's happening?" I ask, stepping back and he smiles a sad smile at me.

"You are wakening up," he says, fading to nothing. I call his name but that only wakes me up faster.

-Zero-

Tyler snaps out of his sleeping state with a loud gasp of air.

"Are you okay?" the witch from the circle asks and Tyler smiles.

"I'm fine," he smiles, nodding his head and sliding off the bed. "Thank you so much."

"Oh, it was nothing," the witch blushes and I roll my eyes.

"So, how is she?" I ask, folding my arms across my chest and leaning on the door frame.

"She's okay," he says, making his way outside, but I block the door way and growl.

"Did you even ask?" I growl, getting frustrated. "Do you even care?"

"Of course, I care!" he shouts back, his yellow eye glows a bit. "I'm not some heartless monster that will betray his girlfriend in a blink of an eye. I didn't need to ask her if she was okay, because I could tell that she was."

I growl and move out of the way and he walks downstairs. The witch follows him and then I follow her. Once downstairs, I see Tyler opening the door for the witch. She smiles and leaves.

The house falls quiet and the only thing I can hear is the wind outside. Aamon and the newest wolf left to become part of another pack as staying here was getting too dangerous. He told me to house sit for him until he returns. Tyler would go off during the day to do something while I would go work at the local supermarket.

Tyler looks at me and sighs before heading back upstairs. I go to the fridge take a mouth full of milk from the bottle. I have been having trouble sleeping since Rose called us down to Paradise. I needed to know that she is okay, so I take the address of the entrance to Paradise off its magnetic clip and grab my jacket. The wind was going wild as I pull out the piece of paper and begin to walk. I need to head Northwest of where I'm standing. I turn wolf and take off running, letting my senses lead the way.

The woods start to become thick and I have to squeeze past bushes with thorns. The thorns catch on my fur, but I ignore the pain and push through. The woods start to thin out as the sun comes over the horizon, and I push out of the final bush and let myself heal before changing and heading to a house. I knock three times and wait. I hear footsteps on the other side of the door and brace myself. The door opens and a butler steps out.

"Can I help you?" he asks, closing the door behind him.

"I am looking for David," I say and the butler nods and walks over towards a barn. He opens the door and there are five horses inside, one of which is Indi. I see the butler pull a piece of rope and then he turns to me.

"Master David will be with you in a moment," he says, then leaves me alone in the stable. Indi pokes her head out of the stall and I walk over to her; she nudges my chest and I laugh.

"So, this is where you got off to," I mumble, patting her neck. "Why aren't you with Rose?"

"Because Rose is a very busy person at the moment," a voice says from behind me. I turn around to see a man standing there with his arms crossed over his chest.

"Are you David?" I ask, becoming nervous and jittery.

"Yes," he says. "Who are you?"

"My name is Zero," I say, holding my ground. "I know that Rose is with you and I want to see her right now."

"Not happening," he laughs, walking over to a post and leaning onto it. "Rose is very busy and needs to concentrate on the task at hand. She has done well so far and if I pull her out I am afraid that she will slowly stumble backwards and we cannot have that. I already know that Tyler is planning something and I know he is contacting her through sleep jumping, and I am on top of it. Now I bid you farewell as there is business to attend to down in Paradise. Goodbye." And with that he left. I sigh in frustration and leave. I look at the thick woods filled with thorny bushes, and inhale sharply before I take off running, changing as I go.

-Rose-

There is a light fog outside the cave and it blankets the woods of

China. I look around, trying to pick up the scent of an animal I can eat. Finally, I find a deer's scent and I stretch to prepare for the hunt. I follow the scent to the water where I see a tiger eating my pray. I growl in frustration and there is a laugh from behind me. I turn to see an old Chinese woman with a cane, laughing. I tilt my head and she turns and walks away. After a few steps she stops, turns, and motions for me to follow. I tilt my head but reluctantly follow the old woman. She leads me to a gazebo that faces the water, and as we near the gazebo the sky opens up in a downpour. The lady sits down on the floor and motions for me to sit as well. As I sit she gives me a big smile.

"You have been through much," she says as I lay down. "Much sadness, much pain."

I let out a small whine and she moves closer to me and strokes my head.

"I see more on the road ahead," she continues, losing her smile. "Pleasure, shadowed by pain; happiness shadowed by sadness, but you must endure. You are the one who will bring peace on earth."

I bring my head up and tilting it, I look at her.

"My name is Hua Li Kuo. I see much in you. Much strength, much power. You are stronger than the one werewitch, but you are blinded by love." Hua says and I put my head down again. I'm interested in this woman. "I see your love for a man, a strong man, a handsome man. But you have to let him go, leave him behind if you want to win the war ahead, if you want to save the world from its self and return the balance. I see that you love him and he you, but the world needs you. They just don't know it yet."

I let out a whine. I don't want this. I don't want to let Tyler go, but as Hua says, the world needs me. I to trust her.

"*I am afraid,*" I say into her head, not sure if she can hear me.

"Of what?" she asks, and I am surprised that she can hear me.

"*I don't know if I can do it. I am afraid I might fail,*" I admit to the old woman.

"A man can move a mountain," Hua says, looking down at me.

"*How?*" I ask, tilting my head and looking back up at her.

"By moving one stone at a time," she says, smiling.

"*But I don't want to give him up,*" I grumble, looking away from her and I hear her laugh.

"You don't have to," she says, stroking my back. The sound of the rain hitting the gazebo roof calms me. "He and you are inseparable; you just need to loosen your hold on him so that you can focus on your training."

I don't say anything this time. I just lay there and let the noises of the forest take me over. I lay on my side and Hua continues to stroke my soft fur. I soon fall asleep.

12. The End of a Year

-Zero-

There is a slam down stairs and it shakes me from my sleep. I'm out of bed and out the door in a matter of seconds. I run down the stairs and into the kitchen where the noise came from. As I round the corner and enter the kitchen, a glass cup is thrown at me. With lightning reflexes I dodge the glass and my eyes adjust. Tyler is in the kitchen having a fit; slamming doors and breaking things. His eyes are red and tear stained.

"Tyler!" I shout over his yelling. He stops and looks at me. "What the hell?"

"I can't contact her," Tyler says, collapsing. "It has been about a two or more months and I can't contact her. The witch says that it might be because she has blocked me or she is dead."

"Or she might just be busy," I say, crossing my arms over my bare chest. I look up at the wall clock and yawn. It's midnight. "Can you just go back to bed? I have work tomorrow and so do you."

Tyler grumbles and moves past me, hitting me with his shoulder on his way. I sigh and when I hear his door close I go upstairs to bed and fall asleep immediately. I am not worried. I know that Rose is okay. Then I realize that it has been a year since Rose has been turned.

-Rose-

The wolf falls dead; its blood stains the snow around me. I have moved location twice now, from the Chinese bamboo forest to the bush lands of Australia, and now I am somewhere high up in the snowy mountains. I have fought many battles and won all of them. There were times where I wanted to give up, and each wolf I faced grew stronger than the last one. My mind was always clear and focused on the matter at hand.

I stretch out and shake snow out of my fur. The sun comes up over the horizon and kisses my fur good morning. After hunting down a mountain goat and having my fill, I find a cave in the mountainside and fall asleep on the cold, hard floor. Tyler hasn't contacted me in a while. I assume he has been too busy, but as I fall asleep a small part of me wishes that he will contact me.

An intense pain causes me to wake up howling. The pain is like something is dragging me down by my stomach. I am not changing location; it isn't the same feeling. I change and scream, rolling over onto my stomach and the pain intensifies. I hear my name being shouted and David appears as my body goes into shock and I begin to have fits. My scream echoes throughout the cave. Then I pass out and everything goes black. I wake up screaming. I have changed locations and am now in a bedroom on a king sized bed. My skin itches and I begin to claw at it, screaming as the pain rakes over me. I hear my back crack and I roll over onto my side and tuck my knees to my chest.

David calls my name, but I can't answer because I'm in too much pain. I straighten out as I hear another crack. I scream and my body goes into shock again. I hear voices that I don't recognise— I don't care who they are— and I scream out and claw at my body again. The last word I hear before I black out is Zero.

-Zero-

There is a knock at the door. I open the door and to my surprise David is standing there.

"It's Rose," he pants and my heart drops. "She is having fits. You must come with me."

I nod and he holds out his hand. I take it and am pulled foreword as a black cloud forms around us.

When David and I exit the cloud everything is blurry and my ears are filled with white noise, then, as everything clears, I hear a painful scream. I look around and see a door ahead and it sounds like the screaming is coming from that room. I look at David and he nods sadly. My heart sinks and I run for the room. When I open the door my heart stoops beating. There, on a king sized bed, is Rose. She is wearing a torn and bloodied white dress. It is just like the day after she was turned. I rush to Rose's side and take her hand. Her hand tenses in mine as she lets out a scream of pain and begins to flop like a fish.

"Rose, snap out if it!" I shout over her screams; she stops moving, stops screaming. The only way I know she is alive is by the small rise and fall of her chest.

"Zero?" she squeaks, looking at me.

"It's okay, Rose," I reassure her. "I am here."

"It hurts," she moans, rolling over still and facing me. "God, it hurts worse than the last time."

"I know," I whisper, squeezing her hand.

"Where's Tyler?" she asks looking around. "Is he here?"

I don't know what to say, so I look over to David and sigh. "No, he isn't here, Rose."

She groans as she lets go of my hand and rolls over as another fit takes over.

"You have to do something," I growl at David. "You are supposed to be the all-powerful werewitch!"

"I have tried," he says, looking down at the ground. "I don't know what to do. I'm not God."

"Tyler!" Rose screams out before coughing up blood.

"What did you do last time?" David asks looking at me.

"We called an ambulance," I say, looking at Rose. "But it took all day for her to calm down."

Rose screams Tyler's name again and I look at David and shrug.

"It is worth a shot to get Tyler," I say as Rose begins to tear at her own skin. David shrugs and vanishes. When he comes back he has a wide-eyed Tyler with him just as Rose's fit gets more violent. Tyler rushes onto the bed and takes Rose into his arms. She coughs again and blood goes all over his shirt, but he doesn't flinch. Tyler talks to Rose in a hushed voice and she begins to calm down.

"Tyler?" she says, her voice rasping.

"It's okay," he hushes. "I'm here, I'm here."

Rose lets out a painful sigh and falls deeper into Tyler's chest and begins to sob.

Tyler kisses Rose on top of her head and wraps around her tighter as he also begins to cry.

Rose's body seizes again and she screams out. She begins to thrash out and at one point she ends up scratching Tyler's chest. Tyler lets Rose go and kneels next to her. He tries to calm her down again by talking, but she screams louder and begins to claw at her own dress, tearing it, and something catches my eye. On her chest is the scar that the stake made when Tyler's father staked her. Around it are other scars. Rose's dress tears again and I notice more scars. Some bigger than others, but they are scars none the less.

"What happened?" I growl at David, who looks down.

"She was caught in a really bad battle while in exhaust mode," he says softly. I growl but turn my attention back to Rose, whose face is covered in tears. My heart breaks as she screams out.

"It hurts, it hurts!" she screams, tearing at her chest. Tyler looks at me with worried eyes and I sigh.

The sun goes down and Rose begins to calm down a little. As her fit ends I feel her forehead.

"She is burning up," I state, removing my hand as Tyler sits behind Rose and holds her hand. David vanishes and returns with wet towels and a bucket with ice water in it. Tyler and I take a towel each and press it to Rose's forehead and face as well as her neck. She sighs in relief, closes her eyes, and falls asleep on Tyler's chest. A thick silence fills the room; David breaks it by asking me to come outside with him.

"How often do these fits happen?" he asks, shutting the door.

"It first happened the day after she was bitten," I say, rubbing the back of my neck.

"What did the doctors do?" he asks and I think back to that day.

"They say she lost a lot of energy," I recall. "She was held there for a day or two. She needed her sugar levels replaced."

David nods his head.

"I am going to need you two to stay here until she is fully healed," he says. "I have errands to do and I won't be able to watch her. There is a fridge in the room fully stocked with whatever you need."

He vanishes and I sigh and head back into the room where Tyler is humming to sleeping Rose.

"What did he say," Tyler asks when I close the door. I tell him what David said and he nods.

"My two handsome nurses," Rose mumbles, opening her eyes. "I don't need a nurse."

She tries to get up but gasps in pain and grabs her ribs. Tyler moves behind her and eases her back down.

"You sure fooled me," he jokes, softly kissing her on the head.

"Shut up," she grumbles, but then she smiles softly and leans into Tyler's chest. I go to the fridge and grab out a block of chocolate and walk back over to Rose's side. I open the block and break off a piece and hand it to Rose.

"You need it," I say as she takes the block and takes a mouse-sized bite. I hand the block to Rose who lays it on her stomach. She begins to cough and Tyler and I move into action, rolling her into recovery position. She coughs up blood, then her cough turns to a groan and that groan turns to a growl. We hear an unearthly crack as her jaw realigns. She is changing, turning into the wolf.

Her back arches and fur starts to cover her body as her nails turn to claws and she rips the bed. More bones crack and she screams. The change is slower than usual, like it was a full moon. She scrambles under the covers where she finishes the change and Tyler and I scramble to the door. We hear Rose growl turn into a blood curdling howl as her wolf form stands up and the covers fall off her back. She focuses her yellow eyes on Tyler and I and growls.

"Rose, it's us," I say, raising a hand. She responds by flattening her ears and pulling her lips back. I step back and she tucks her tail between her legs before jumping off the bed and running at the window across the room. Glass shatters as she jumps through the window and takes off running towards the woods. I groan, change, and run after her. Tyler follows, but the sky opens up and we lose her scent as she enters the woods.

"*Split up,*" I say to Tyler as we enter the woods and we immediately split off from each other.

-Rose-

I have to get away; I have to run. Images flash through my mind. Tainted red, I see nothing but death. I feel death's cold fingers scraping against my fur. My mind becomes quiet as I run. I focus on my breathing and listen to my own heart beating in my chest.

My chest begins to ache and I slow down to a stop.

I find somewhere to rest until I catch my breath. My body changes and I am naked. I don't even care. I sit with my back to the tree and my knees to my chest. I sit there all alone, my body aching and my heart pounding. The sound of the woods calms me; the sound of the birds and the animals, the smell of wet leaves. I hear a twig snap and Tyler steps into the clearing. I look up and change into a wolf. He steps back a fraction, and once he is sure that I won't charge, his face softens and he sits next to me. I lay my head in the dirt and whine. He sighs and pats my head with slow strokes.

"What happened?" he asks and I whistle through my nose. "I've missed you, Rose."

I put my head in his lap and he smiles.

"*I have missed you, too,*" I whine into his head. He strokes my fur

205

for a while before standing up. I look up at him and he smiles.

"Come on," he laughs. "Let's get you back to where you need to be."

I reluctantly stand and follow him back to the house I was in. As we approach, I see David yelling at Zero. I run and jump, landing in between the two with my back towards Zero. I bark at David, who steps backwards and puts his hands in the air.

"Quick to defend your pack," David says to me and I pull my lips back and flatten my ears. "Instincts over rationality."

"Why doesn't she turn to her human state?" Zero asks Tyler.

"She's ... Uh... A little *bare* at the moment," he smiles and Zero raises an eyebrow before suddenly realizing.

"Oh," he says as David gets it, too.

David leads me inside where he tells a butler to bring clothes to 'my room'. David then leads me to what I presume is my room. I jump up onto the bed and manage to get under the covers. I change form and poke my head out the top of the sheets, while holding the sheets to my body as a butler comes in with clothes. David and the others leave the room and I get changed. The butler has brought in a black tank top, a pair of jeans, and some underwear. They all fit perfectly. I look around the room and see that it is similar to the room I was previously in. It has a king-sized bed, a walk-in wardrobe, an ensuite, a mirrored dressing table, and a balcony.

"Are you going to be okay?" Tyler asks. "You know, when we go?"

"Of course, I'm going to be okay." I smile, then register his face. "Why?"

"David will have to wipe our memory," Zero says and Tyler looks down.

"Why?" I say, looking at David with a tight scowl.

"Because you need to train and I know that these two will want to find a way to get you back," David says. "Listen, I wish I didn't have to do this, but I do. Otherwise, your training might as well go out the window."

I look at Tyler who looks at me with sad eyes. I walk over to him and place a hand on the side of his face. He puts a hand over mine and closes his eyes, almost like he is in pain.

"I love you," I say, taking his hand. "Please, don't forget that."

"How can I?" he says, opening his eyes with a sad smile before kissing me on the forehead. "I love you, too."

"Ready to go?" David interrupts, and I scowl at him again as Tyler lets go of my hands.

"I love you," he says before vanishing with David in a cloud of smoke. I sigh and go out to the balcony where there are several hanging pots above me tied to the bottom of the balcony above mine, and there are three longer pots connected to the railing of my balcony. One of the hanging pots is empty, but the rest are filled with herbs and other plants. I smell them each and am able to point out catnip, Wolfsbane, Vervain, Belladonna, and Hellebore. I go to the empty pot and sniff and immediately pull back as there is Spotted Alder Roots in the pot. I go back into the room just as David reappears.

"Let's go," he says, sighing and exiting the room. I follow him.

"Where to?" I ask, jogging to reach him.

"To your training arena," he says, opening a double door. On the other side is a school like gym with wooden floor boards and padded mats leaning against a wall and some light gym equipment. What really catches my eye is a very large cabinet mounted on the wall. I run over and open it. Inside it is all kinds of weapons from daggers to axes and crossbows to swords. I smile and take a sword down. I swing it a few times. It feels light in my hands, but I know this can do maximum damage. David catches my attention by clearing his throat. I look over and he is scowling, so I drop my head and put the sword back in the cabinet before closing it.

"Let's start you off on getting your muscles right," he says, stepping aside to reveal a pink boxing bag. My face drops but I do what he says. David waves his hands and my clothes change to sweat pants and a white tank top. For the rest of the day, David has me run laps, use the boxing bag, sit ups, push ups, and other painful workout methods. By the end of the day, I'm laying on the floor drowning in my own sweat; my body is aching.

"Are we done yet?" I ask after finishing cool-down stretches. David nods.

"It was an okay workout for your first day," he says and I sigh. "But you are going to have to do better than that if you hope to please me tomorrow. Now, go shower. You stink."

I growl, but do what he says, I use the gym's shower before using magic to change back into the tank top and jeans. I go back out into the gym to see that David is nowhere to be seen, so I go to my room and lay down. After a while, there is a knock at my door. I tell the person to come in and a woman enters. She's roughly around mid to late twenties and caring a tray.

"Hello, ma'am," she says, closing to door. "Master David said to bring you this. I am Ellen and I am your maid."

"I don't need a maid," I argue as she sets the tray down.

The maid stands back as I remove the lid from the tray. Underneath is a lovely piece of chicken parmesan with salad and chips. My stomach grumbles as I pick up the knife and fork and dig in. The chicken melts in my mouth and the salad is dressed with a lovely Italian dressing.

"Thank you," I sigh, melting into the pleasure of food. The woman keeps her eyes trained on the floor. After I finish my meal, she takes the tray back out, closing the door behind her. I go over to the walk-in wardrobe and open the door. I am astounded of what's inside: all types of clothes, dresses, jeans, shirts, and skirts. It's all in here and after a close inspection I find they are all my size. I change into pyjamas and climb into bed. The bed is so soft and there are a billion pillows. I hear a screech and jump out of bed and race to the door that leads to the porch. I see Lilac sitting on the railing and when I open the doors, she flies in and lands on the back board of the bed. I smile, close the doors and the curtains before climbing into bed and getting comfortable. Before long I fall asleep.

I am awoken by the loud buzzer of the alarm clock. I groan and shut it off. I look at the time and almost scream. It's three o'clock!

"Wake up," David says loudly as he comes into the room. "Time to train." I groan and drag myself out of bed and change into my gym clothes before heading down to the gym. David has pulled out some of the gym's equipment and he tells me to rotate, so I warm up with a lap of the gym and then start to rotate on the machines. If I thought my muscles hurt before, I was so wrong. By the end of the day, my muscles are aching and my heart's pounding. I look at David and he shrugs before leaving. Again I shower, change, and head to my room where I fall asleep. David wakes me up rudely and the process starts over again. He had me boxing and working my leg muscles and again, I finish and go to bed, to be woken again rudely. This goes on and on until the end of the month where David gives me weapons to practice with.

I train hard, swinging swords, firing arrows, and throwing knives. At the end of the month, I am good at almost all the weapons, then in the third month, I start hand to hand combat, and I completely fail. He mops the floor with me in less than three seconds, but I get up again, only to get a busted nose and thrown to the ground. Again and again I try, but I just get humiliated each time. After two hours of practice, he dismisses me and leaves the gym. I punch the floor and scream out. I am terrible compared to him, and he hasn't even broken a sweat yet. I go to the change room and take care of my nose, but instead of leaving the gym, I keep practicing on the boxing bag until the end of the day. The next morning, I wake up at two and head to the gym. I do laps and other work out exercises until David arrives and we fight hand to hand again. I manage to hit him once, but he still busts my nose and wipes the floor with me. After two hours, he dismisses me and I leave. Instead of going to my room, I head outside where Lilac greets me and I walk into town, which is surprisingly busy. People bow as I pass by. It's like I am royalty. I enter a humble little baker shop and the smell of freshly cooked breads and pastries welcome me.

"Good morning," the baker says and I look around. I am the only one in the shop and the baker is talking to me. "Can I help you with anything?" he asks. He's a short, fat man wearing white chef clothes and an apron, which is covered in flour. I shake my head and the baker bows before continuing to bake. I leave the shop and continue to look around before heading home, but the vampire and the fey village catches my eye. I turn towards it and make my way to the woods that separates the villages. Then, from out of nowhere, David appears, grabs my wrist, and shakes his head.

"You are not ready," he says with a stern look on his face. I take a step back and he lets me go. His eyes change to a bright jade-green colour. I turn and run to the house. I run into the maid and she looks up and I gasp. Her eyes are so familiar; they are dark green. I step back.

"Can I help you, ma'am?" she asks and I shake my head, too stunned to speak. I run down the hall and into my room. I shut the door and slide down it. Something is defiantly wrong here. The maid's eyes looked so familiar, but I just can't put my finger on it, and for the first time in months my mind travels to Tyler. Is he doing okay? I miss him. I want to be in his arms.

-Zero-

"Faster!" I shout into Tyler's mind. He and I are running for our lives, theoretically. We are training, running, jumping, and fighting. Tyler and I go running every afternoon after work. But it isn't just Tyler and I who are running. We managed to turn two new wolves last full moon and they were great. Both female and both fast learners. The one I turned, Edith, is fantastic. She and I bonded closely and have developed a relationship. We reach back to the house and turn human. Tyler and his turned go inside while Edith and I stay in the fresh air.

"That was exhilarating," she puffs, leaning on the house. I smile and plant a kiss on her lips. There's the sound of a glass breaking inside and Edith and I run in where Tyler is backed into the corner of the kitchen and he is in wolf form, ears flattened, and lips pulled back. Edith goes to Avery and I face Tyler.

"What happened?" I ask as he turns human.

"She made a move towards me," he growls, glaring at her. Then to me, "With her lips."

I sigh and tell the girls to go upstairs.

"Rose is coming back," he growls before I could say anything.

"I believe you," I say, nodding. "But when?"

Tyler glares at me and his yellow eye shimmers. I shrug and leave him be, and go up into my room where the girls are. I hear the kitchen door open and close as Tyler leaves again.

"I'm sorry about that," Avery says. "I didn't mean to cause trouble."

"It's okay," I sigh, leaning on the door. "He is still hooked on the last girl. Technically, they never broke up."

Avery looks at the ground and sighs.

"I just wish I could find someone," she sighs as tears flow. Edith reassures her and I take my cue to leave.

-Rose-

Knocked to the ground again, bleeding nose again, sore muscles again, quickly healing eye again. I am getting tired of fighting, and this is only the first round.

"Get up," David says, but I stay down. "Get up!"

"No," I groan and David pulls me up by my arm.

"You need to keep fighting!" he shouts, and I ball my fists.

"What's the point?" I shout back, ripping free of his hold. "What's the point of fighting if I just get knocked down again and again? I can't do this anymore, David. I don't want to do this anymore!"

"You have to!" he shouts as I walk past him to the door. "Do not exit this room, Rose!"

"Watch me!" I shout, taking the handle and pulling down, but it won't budge. David has put a spell on it. I scream and use an unlocking spell, but David just locks it again. I turn and fire yellow lightning at him blindly. I unlock the door again and leave without a hassle this time. I hear David run to the door, but I put a spell on it so it won't unlock until I am in my room.

When I get there, I slam the door and use a spell on it as well, then

I flop onto the bed and cry. I want to go home. I want to be with Tyler and, most of all, I just want to get out of here. Something snaps me out of crying. A noise. It's coming from under the bed. I stick my head over the side of the bed and peer under. There, under the bed, is a cat; a small, sooty grey cat.

"Here kitty, kitty, kitty," I say, holding out my hand, but it hisses and backs up. It swipes its paw and I pull back. Then an idea pops into my head. I go outside and get a handful of cat nip, then go back inside and jump on the bed. I turn upside down and hold my hand out and smack my lips together. The cat meows and takes a step forward. When it smells the cat nip, it pounces and I pull back. It then jumps up onto the bed. I make the cat nip vanish and the cat calms down. I hold my hand out again and it moves forward and rubs it's head on my hand. It curls up in my lap and begins to purr. I stroke its fur and notice that the cat has wisps of black in it. I gently put it aside and head for the shower. While I am in there, I realize the cat's method of attack: it backed up before finding a chance and lunging. After a shower I go into the room again, where I find the cat curled up on the bed fast asleep. I notice that the cat is wearing a collar with a tag on it.

"Let's see who you belong to," I say, gently sitting on the bed and removing the cat's collar. He meows at me, but I ignore him. The tag only reads six numbers and I try to think what that might mean. A soft knock at the door disturbs my thoughts.

"Who is it?" I call, putting the collar down and moving towards the door.

"It's me, Ellen," she says from the other side of the door. "I'm checking in to see if you want anything to eat."

I undo the spell on the door and open it just so I could look through.

"Can I get a hamburger with fries?" I ask, then thinking about the cat say, "Oh, and some tuna, a glass of milk, a bowl, and a milkshake."

"You're hungry today," she sighs, shaking her head.

"Well, I have to keep eating if I train every day," I laugh as she leaves down the hall. I sigh, shut the door, and replace the spell. The cat pops it's head up and looks at me with cautious eyes. His eyes are deep yellow, unlike my brighter wolf eyes, and they follow me as I cross the room and back onto the bed and cross my legs. I pick up the collar again and notice there is no name on it either.

"Who are you?" I ask as the cat rubs its head on my knee. I smile down as he looks up to me. There's a knock at the door again. I answer it and find the maid holding out a tray. I take it and thank her before closing the door. This time, I only lock it and I don't use a spell. When I open the tray the cat perks its head up. I put down the plate of tuna and fill the bowl with the glass of milk before putting it on the floor as well. The cat leaps off the bed and begins to eat. I smile at him again and sit on my own bed to eat as well.

"Well, if you are going to stay here," I say to the cat, "I am going to need to call you something." I think for a moment and then notice how the cat's fur looks like smoke. "Smokey," I say and the cat turns. "That's your new name, Smokey."

Smokey huffs and turns back to eating as do I. I pick up Smokey's old collar and with a small spell I change it. Instead of 000006, it now reads Smokey. I finish my burger and turn to my fries, but a screech at the window startles me; Lilac is attacking it. She flies to the balcony and taps at the glass. I get up to let her in, but Smokey steps in my way and begins to meow.

"Lilac is a friend," I say, stepping over him. As I open the door, she swoops past me and straight to Smokey, who hisses and swipes his claws. I take the scene in and take control of Lilac. She calms down and roosts on the bed again, but she never takes her eyes off Smokey; her feathers are ruffled. He quickly finishes his meal and drink before scampering under the bed.

I lay down on the bed, stretch out, and then fall asleep. I wake up that afternoon to find Lilac gone and Smokey on the bed. He stirs and wakes up with a stretch, front paws forwards hind quarters up, and he slowly moves over to me. I scratch behind his ears and he purrs happily. I stand and make my way to the door and Smokey stays put. I leave the room and head into the gym. David appears as I shut the door.

"Ready for another go?" he says and I nod. He lunges forward and I move back. He stumbles forward and I strike, using a sidekick and hit his ribs. He recovers and goes again. This time I pivot, and then manage a punch to the side of his stomach. I then grab the back of his shirt and throw him backwards, but he manages to also grab my shirt and pulls me with him.

We both regain our balance quickly and are back at it. I even manage to give him a bleeding nose. He throws me into the wall and I see spots. David goes to punch and I move quickly. He ends up hitting the wall and I hear a crack as he winces, but he keeps fighting. I take my chance and use a swift kick and knock David to the floor. We both are now drenched in sweat. I expect David to get up and he does. He grabs my leg and I end up on the floor. He then fakes to put a stake in my chest.

"I win," he puffs with a half-smile. I groan and he helps me up. "That was better," he says, snapping his fingers and a butler comes in with water and a towel.

"Thanks," I say, heading for the showers. He and his butler leave and he starts discussing an issue.

After a shower, I head up to my room where Smokey is waiting. He meows and starts to become frantic.

"What's wrong, boy?" I ask, shutting the door and then sitting on the ground. He hisses at me and I see his canines are longer, almost vampire like. He jumps at me and I stumble, but he wasn't aiming for me— he pounces on a small mouse. The mouse makes a small squeak before he ends its life and carries it out to the balcony where he devours it. My heart calms down and I stand up any go to the bed where a letter is sitting on the pillow. I pick it up and slice it open. Inside is a note that reads:

Dear Rose,
When are you coming home? I need you in my arms again. Everything feels so empty and unreal. You make my life seem worthy and happy. Living with Zero is a real pain in the neck, but it is the only place I got. I hope everything is going okay where you are. I love you with all my heart and nothing in the world will change that. I am having nightmares about nothing, really, but all I see is black eyes and dead bodies. I saw your body once and I had to write to you to see if you were okay. In another dream, I saw you with another man. I pray this isn't true, but if it is, I hope he treats you right and I hope he loves you. I love you, Rose, and I can't wait for you to come home. Love, Tyler.

A fat tear rolls down my cheek and I go over to the desk and get out a piece of paper and write:

Dearest Tyler,
I can't begin to explain how happy I am to be writing to you. I'm fine. I can't wait to get home either— it shouldn't be too long now, and I miss you, too. I am alive and well. I too used to have bad dreams. I wish I could be there with you to fight those dreams away. My heart feels empty without you here. I have so much that I want to tell you, but I

can't in case this letter gets lost. Noting could change my love for you, Tyler, and when I get back I am going to prove it. No other man will do for me, you are the only one. I MEAN IT! Never will I kiss another's lips or gaze into his eyes. Never shall I hold another's hand because only yours fits into mine. I love you so much. My love for you is like an undying flame, and with every day it burns brighter and higher. I miss you and I wish you were here with me so I could hold you. All my love and a little bit more,
Rose xoxo

I spray the paper with a light smelling perfume before sealing it in an envelope. I use red lipstick and kiss the back before running out and into the maid.

"So, you got his letter," she smiles and I nod.

"I need to mail this," I say, holding up my letter. She smiles and takes the letter from my hand.

"Don't worry," she smiles, walking away. "I'll make sure my son gets it."

I come to a halt and turn to look at her. She looks at me and I remember what those eyes remind me of: Tyler's.

"You are Tyler's mother?" I ask, astounded.

"We'll talk when I return," she says, walking off. I stand there with my mouth in an O shape. Later, Ellen enters my room and closes the door with a soft click. Smokey runs under the bed before he could be seen. She sits on the bed and looks at me with those soft eyes.

"Are you Tyler's mother?" I ask and she nods. "But, he said you were dead."

"When we were attacked it was a full moon. Wolves attacked me but never made the change," she says, and I notice how alike she is to Tyler— same eyes, similar shade of hair— she looked about twenty five. "David found me and changed me. I dedicated my life to him after I finished mourning the loss of my daughter and family. David moved me to Paradise and I helped him keep it intact. When I found out about you and how you changed my son, I was mad at first, but then I found out that he stopped hunting and I envied you. I never wanted a werewolf life for him, but I also didn't want him to continue hunting."

Ellen smiles at me.

"And when I saw that Tyler wrote to you, I knew that David wouldn't let you read it, so I placed it in your room," she says as a tear rolls down my cheek. She stands and bows to me. "I have duties to do, but I will see you later."

She never came back.

The next morning I fought harder and faster, but David still knocked me down. Hard.

"You think that I will let you go home if you fight like that!" David shouts and the wolf side of me growls.

"I am trying my hardest!" I shout, feeling my jaw crack.

"You are the worst werewitch I have ever faced! You are never going to see him again if this is your hardest!" he shouts and I look away from him. "I have hit a chord there haven't I?" he asks, but I don't answer. "Oh, my God, you're in love with your little hunter boy, aren't you? You know he has probably found another hopeless little girl," he taunts and a growl erupts from my throat and he laughs. "He is probably doing things to her that he never was able to do to you."

I snap and kick David's leg out from under him. He lands with a solid thud and my eyes turn yellow and a noise escapes me— it doesn't sound human at all. He gets back up, and I lunge forward and hit him square in the jaw, he didn't see the move coming. I lunge again, but he catches my fist. I use my other hand and he catches it, too. I growl and pull my lips away from my teeth. I notice his stance and my lip twitches upwards. I jerk my left knee upwards and hit him square in his groin. He groans lets my fists go. I bring my right leg up and kick him in the side and send him flying into the wall. He hits the wall and I hear something crack. I smile as I run at him and take a fistful of his hair. I let out a half choked scream and, using my super strength, I fling him forward. He face plants on the floor and groans as he gets up again. I have my stance and fists ready as he attacks, running towards me. Just when he is going to collide with me, I strike with my fist, hitting him square in the nose. I hear a loud crack and he falls to the floor.

"Don't ever talk about Tyler like that!" I shout at him. When he doesn't reply, I step back. When he doesn't move, I exit the room and go up to my room. There, I have a shower and find a duffel bag. I shove random necessary clothes into it before zipping it up. I grab a piece of paper out of the dresser draw and scribble on it:

I QUIT!

I storm out of the room and hear a jingling behind me. Smokey's following me, looking at me with wide eyes. I run outside and go south of the mansion, to the rolling green meadows.

Once there, I try to find out how to open the portal.

"This isn't something you can quit, Rose," I hear David say as he walks up to me. He has a soft face, looking guilty.

"Watch me!" I shout as I keep looking for the portal. Tears sting as they spill over. "Where the fuck is it?" I scream, trying to find it. I hear Lilac screech as she lands on my shoulder. She nudges my cheek with her head and I shake her off. I collapse to the ground and lie on my back.

"Rose," David says quietly as he lowers himself to my level. "I didn't mean anything I said back in the gym. I was trying to find a way for you to fight harder. This fight is bigger than all of us, and now you've figured your trigger: Tyler. You fight hardest when you think of him."

"But, what if it's true?" I shout, sitting up. "What if Tyler has found someone else? What if he has forgotten about me?" I hear David sigh and I look him in the eyes.

"When I saw him with you before he had to go, I knew. I knew that there was something strong between you two," he says with a soft smile and I wipe my tears. "I can tell that he definitely loves you and he wouldn't replace you, because he loves you."

I sigh as my muscles relax and I lay on the grass and look up to the sky. Out of the corner of my eye, I see David lunge forward, but he calms as he realize I haven't fainted.

"You know you almost killed me back there," he says quietly, and I look sideways to him. "In the gym, you hit me with a force that it shattered my nose and sent pieces into my brain. If it weren't for my healing abilities, I could have died from brain damage."

I sigh and a meow catches both mine and David's attention.

"Who is this?" he asks as Smokey sits down next to me.

"Smokey," I say, stroking the cat's fur. "Found him under my bed."

David sighs, turning his back to me.

"You know your way back?" he asks and I nod. He sighs and takes one glance at me before walking away.

-Zero-

I open the letter box and cart the mail inside. There is the electricity bill, a piece of junk mail, and a letter sealed with a kiss. I turn it over and see that it is registered for Tyler.

"Tyler!" I call as I enter the house. "Mail!"

I hear the door open and then quick footing down the steps. I almost run into him as he rounds the kitchen corner.

"Whoa there," I say, handing him the letter with a teasing smile. "Who's it from? Secret admirer?"

He doesn't reply, instead he sits down at the kitchen table where he opens the letter and reads it. As he gets deeper into the letter, his mouth pulls back into a smile. When he finishes the letter, his smile looks too big for his face. He runs upstairs taking the note with him and shuts the door and I can hear shuffling around.

"What was that all about?" Edith asks, entering the room.

"Beats me," I shrug, kissing her cheek.

13. Witches Pentagram

-Rose-

It has been a few weeks since the incident where I nearly killed David. I've managed to control my temper and only use it when necessary, but I have beaten David five times now, and, overall, that is an achievement. After training one day, I open my door to see a letter from Tyler on my pillow. I immediately jump on the bed and rip the envelope open. The letter reads:

My lovely, sweet Rose
I can't get you off my mind. I keep thinking about how much I love talking to you and how sweet and angelic your voice sounds; how good you look when you smile and how much I love the sound of your laugh. I daydream about you constantly, replaying the best moments of our life, like when we first met. I wonder what will happen next time we're together & even though you are like a world away, I know I love you. I know we haven't spent a lot of time together, but every moment you are away I feel our connection grow stronger. I am dreaming of your return. The nightmares have moved to a minimal ever since I got your letter,
Thank you
All my heart and Soul, Tyler

I wipe a happy tear from my face as I set the letter down, and then I notice something: the envelope has a bulge in it. I pick up the envelope and hold it upside down and a necklace falls out. The necklace has a beautiful yin side of a yin and yang pendant on it. On the pendent there is white wolf sitting under the black dot. I clasp the necklace around my neck and read a letter that was attached to it.
Happy Birthday, from last year and this year.

I run to the calendar on the wall and see that today is my birthday! I go over to the desk and write back:

Dearest Tyler,
You stole my heart, but you know what? You can keep it. I am counting down the days until I can see you again. I too am dreaming of what it is going to be like. Sometimes it scares me that when I see you again that you will have another woman on your arm. I am so glad to hear that the nightmares have stopped. My training with David has intensified and it is getting harder, but I think of you and your smile and pull through. No words in the world can express how much I love you, so I just want you to know that you are the world to me. You are my gravity, holding me to this place. I find this love strange; I sometimes ask myself why we feel this way to each other. Is it fate? Destiny? Then I realize I don't care. All I know is that I love you and that nothing will change that.
Lots of Love,
Rose xo

I sealed this letter the same way I sealed the other: with a kiss. I go out into the hall and look for Ellen. I consider telling Tyler about her, but I couldn't find evidence to prove it. When I find Ellen, I ask, "Hi, can you send this to Tyler again?" Her eyes light up as she nods and takes the letter and walks off.

Over the next few days I get better and faster, striking with precision. David makes me work on balance and foot work. I manage to surpass him once or twice, but he is always better and able to regain control. One morning, I walk into the gym to find no equipment or weapons out; just David standing there with a tin of black ink.

"Uh, what are we doing?" I ask and he smiles.

"I am not doing anything," he says, putting the tin down. "You are going to create your pentagram. Welcome to your first day of your witch lessons."

I smile as I feel my magic bubble at my core, and my gym clothes vanish and are replaced with my long white corset dress, high-heeled white boots, and my hair is restyled again. All at once, my magic takes over and yellow lightning shoots from my fingers. My eyes glow as the lightning dances around the room, and then a jade green colour catches my eyes. I look over and see that David is also creating a pentagram, but without lightning. Instead, he is using vines.

My lightning makes a crack and etches deep into the floor as it makes contact. The creation all comes together and I see that I have created a circle, and inside that circle is a star. In the spaces in between each point is the elemental symbols for fire, water, earth, and air, then, in the last space, there is the symbol for spirit. The lightning dies down, but before it does it zaps the ink tin and the ink oozes into the markings until the etching in the floor is filled with black ink. I feel a power surge through me and I inhale deeply. David looks at me with a raised eyebrow. I look away and touch my necklace.

"May I look at that?" David asks and I nod. I unclasp the necklace and hand it to him. He smiles and flips it in his hands before placing it at his feet. "You need to make this your talisman."

"What is a talisman?" I ask and he smiles.

"A talisman is a witch's source. It anchors them to their designed power," he says, gesturing to the elements of my pentagram. Then he gestures to a black and white ring on his finger before stepping out of my pentagram. "Without a talisman, a witch's power can become deadly and uncontrollable. Just concentrate and it will come to you."

I take a deep breath in and then let it out. I place my hands in front of me with my elbows out and the necklace begins to float and I close my eyes. The necklace floats in between my hands and I open my eyes. The necklace then clasps back around my neck. I let out a shaky breath and drop my arms.

"All right," David says, breaking the silence. He is now holding a cage with two little mice in it; one black one white. "I will teach you how to channel your powers from your circle here, but practice small spells on these two when you have spare time."

I nod my head and he dismisses me. I take the caged mice and head up to my room where Smokey pops his head up as I enter.

"These are not food," I say to Smokey and Lilac, who flies in. I go and change out of my dress and, with a sigh, I take the black mouse out. It scampers around my hand and I smile. I think of something to do. I put a small spell on it so it will change into anything I say.

"Grow," I whisper and it does. It grows and grows. "Stop." It does. It is now the size of a large dog. I tell it to shrink to its natural size and it does. I smile as I put it back in its cage and shut it. My hand goes up to my necklace and my mind travels back to the moment I met Tyler. The thing I first noticed was his eyes.

"No," I mumble. I shouldn't be thinking about him; it will make me depressed. I sigh as I flop down on the bed and look at the ceiling, Smokey comes over and rubs his head on my hand. I smile at him and he meows before biting my hand. I gasp and jump back and off the bed. Lilac appears and swoops towards him, but he meows and runs under the bed. I look at my already healed hand and sigh. Lilac is still trying to get to Smokey as he hisses and swipes his paws.

"Lilac, enough. He didn't mean it," I say and she flies out the window. There is a knock on the door and Ellen comes in. My face brightens and she shakes her head.

"Master David wanted me to bring this up to you," she says, handing me a very old looking book. "It has everything you need to know about the paranormal species."

"Thank you," I say, and she heads back out the door. I sit down on the bed and open the book. On the first page it says, *"For a werewitch's eyes only."* I sigh and turn place it on the night stand. I then curl up and go to sleep for a few hours. When I wake up, I decide to give reading another shot.

I sigh and go over the page a few times. This is important and I shouldn't take it lightly, but I already know some of this information. Using a spell, I create a book stand and place the book on it. I take the white mouse out of the cage and place the same spell on it that I did to the other one. I make it change into several different animals before I get bored and turn back to the book and sigh and sit on the bed. Smokey now jumps up onto the bed and looks at me with sad eyes.

"I forgive you," I say, scratching him behind his ears. He purrs and I slide off the bed. "Come on, maybe all you need is to go outside."

He jumps off the bed and takes off running. I sigh and shut the door. I walk around the garden, which was filled with all kinds of flowers and other plants. I hear a meow and turn around to see Smokey trot past me. I smile but keep my eyes on the mansion. I have only seen the first floor and I don't know what is on the other floors— and I don't think I want to. Who knows what types of skeletons David has in his closets, and with two other stories that is a lot of closets.

"Rose," I hear an unfamiliar voice say. I turn quickly and see a man. He has black hair, stands just taller than me, andis wearing a jeans, a black shirt, and a black jacket.

"Do I know you?" I ask and he nods. I raise an eyebrow and he sighs.

"My name is Christian," he says and I scowl. I have never met a Christian before. "But you know me as 'Smokey'."

My heart skips a beat as I gasp and take a step back.

"Wait," he says, moving forward and grabbing my hand. "Please, listen."

I inhale deeply and smell death. "Vampire," I gasp and he nods. I jerk my hand back and he lets go. I go to run but think otherwise. "I'm listening," I say and his eyes widen, but he relaxes as he stuffs his hands in his jacket.

"Yes, I am a vampire, but I am not like the others," he says and I raise my eyebrows. "When I was turned, instead of staying a vampire, I turned into the cat. I don't know why or how, but I did, and after I bit you, I felt like I could change at any time. You saved my life, and I wish I could have told you earlier, but I don't think you speak cat."

I laugh and he smiles. I look back to the mansion and sigh.

"Does David know what you are?" I ask and he shakes his head. "I will keep your secret and you can still stay with me."

"Thank you, Rose," he says and I shrug.

"Want to go back to the room and read a book about the paranormal species?" I ask, and he nods as he shifts back into the cat. Back inside, I take the book off the stand and I sit on the bed and read the next page. The heading is Vampires. Next to the heading is a picture of the vampire's fangs.

-Things to know about the Vampire race-

In the early years of the 1100's in Mercy Lake, when it was still being developed and Native Americans roamed the woods, animal testing was being used on a bat. The experiment being conducted was to increase the age, increase the health, increase the speed and stamina, and decrease the vulnerability of the normal human being. The test was performed by Viking healers who were set to the task of preserving their village. The bat was freed months later, after several experiments were concluded a failure. Little did they know that they created the start of vampirism.

The bat bit a man in the village, named Jason Tylorn. The man started to feel a hunger for blood and his lateral incisors and his canines grew to a point. He became incredibly ill and couldn't move from his bed. One night while his wife was pressing a cold towel to his forehead, he leapt up and sank his fangs into her neck and drank her dry. After the first tasting of blood, he attacked again. He killed his daughter and drank her dry as well. Then he let loose on the village, they retaliated, and he healed at super-fast speed. And with super speed, he ran at the attacker and drank, but he never killed him. The Canine fangs held the venom to create more like him. Jason poisoned his victim, which then created the second vampire.

Vampire fangs reside in the Lateral Incisors and the Canines. When a vampire is not feeding, both the Lateral Incisors and the Canine Fangs are hidden inside the gums and the normal looking tooth is shown, but when the vampire is hungry or feeding, only the Lateral Incisors are shown. This is done by the tooth reshaping and forming to a point. If a vampire is hunting and its purpose is to create a new vampire, the Canines form into a fang. The only time both fangs appear is when the vampire has been deprived of blood for three days or more. The skin of a vampire appears normal, however, when a vampire is created, the poison turns the skin to small scales. They are hard to detect, and this makes the vampires skin harder to be penetrated by objects; it acts as body armour. Vampires have a unique skin movement called la ondulación *or the ripple. This occurs when the vampire is angry or upset. The scales will wave by lifting, then dropping. No one knows why or how the ripple came to be, but some believe the ripple has an effect in why vampires don't cast a shadow or a reflection.*

I put the book down as the words sink in. The first vampire's name was *Jason Tylorn.* Jace is a vampire who was in my circle and his last name is also Tylorn. Could he be the same one? *La ondulación,* the ripple. I have noticed Jace and Sam display the rippling effect. I continue reading onto the second heading.

-Changes-

A vampire can change its form like a Werewolf can. They will change into the form that created them all: a bat, and this change can happen at any time. After a vampire has bitten its victim and injected the venom, the victim changes its physical appearance. Its appearance changes so that the vampire is more sexually attractive so that it can lure in its prey easier. One of the major changes that happen to a Vampire is the replacement of water in their body. Every drop of water in their body becomes blood, so when a vampire cries they cry blood tears. Vampires can be discovered with a strong nose— they smell like death— but only the most concentrated nose can find this out.

I look over to Smokey who is leaning on the back board of the bed with his ankles crossed and his hands behind his head.

"So, if you cry, your tears are blood?" I ask as I place the book on the stand again.

"I don't know," he shrugs. "As soon as I was turned, I turned into a cat, and cats don't cry as far as I know."

"Do you think there is any way to test it?" I ask, facing him and raising an eyebrow. He shrugs with a concerned look in his face and I laugh.

He smiles and there is a shout sounded in the distance. I run out onto the balcony and look around. It sounded like it came from town.

"Want to go for a leg stretch?" I ask, walking back inside. "Into town?"

He nods, stands, and changes into his cat form and we walk out the front door. Once outside, Smokey changes into his Christian form and we walk into town. I try to locate where the shout came from, but I am distracted by every girl we walk past. They giggle, smile, and wave at Christian, but he ignores them.

"You know, I bet they would faint if you smiled at them," I tease as an easy smile appears on his face. "I think you could find a nice girl here to settle down with, instead of living under my bed."

"They are not my type," he says as the smile disappears.

"Right," I sigh. "You probably prefer the type that don't turn every full moon."

"Don't assume," he says with a small half smile. "You will make an ass out of you and me."

"Okay then," I smile as we walk past two girls who fix their dresses to make their large breasts almost fall out. "So, what is your type?"

"Not them," he says, cringing as I smile. We walk for a while longer until Christian steers me into a grocer and he asks for an assembled picnic basket.

"I can't pay for this," I say and he smiles at me. He then takes his right boot off and tips it upside down. A sack of money fall out and he catches it in his hands and looks at me.

"I got it covered," he smiles as he puts his boot back on and pays the grocer. He then steers me out of the shop and we head into the woods. We pass several women, all of whitch try to get his attention. After walking deep into the woods, he sits at the base of a large tree and pats the space next to him, and I sit down.

"Okay, what is all this for?" I ask and he smiles.

"For releasing me of my curse," he says, handing me a chicken sandwich. "I have been in my cat form for fifty years."

"So, how old does that make you?" I ask, taking a bite.

"Seventy one," he says, speaking with food in his mouth.

"Wouldn't you be more stiffed limbed after being in a cat form for fifty years?" I ask and he shrugs.

"I stretched my legs after you fell asleep," he says. "I didn't know what was going on, so I went outside and tried to figure it out. I have a question for you, now," he says and I nod. "Why are you being so nice and acting like we are BFFs?" he asks and I think for a while.

"I don't know," I shrug finishing my sandwich and pulling out an apple. "I just figured that I don't have a single friend down here. You told me everything as soon as you could, and you told the truth. I figured that I could trust you."

He shrugs and my stomach rumbles.

"How are you still hungry?" he asks with a light laugh and I shake my head.

"I'm not," I say, putting the apple back into the basket and standing up. "But the wolf is."

"Ahhh," he says, nodding. "Well, don't let me hold you back."

"I will be back soon," I say before running off and changing into my wolf form. I hunt and feed on two deer before heading back to Christian. He is leaning on the tree with his eyes closed. It makes me ache for my sketch pad. I emerge into the clearing and he still doesn't stir. I decide to emit a deep growl from my chest, and he snaps awake and his eyes widen. I laugh as I change human.

"Calm down, sleeping beauty, it's just me," I say. He smiles at me and then sits down and I sit next to him.

"So, what about the girls? I saw one leaning against the butchers shop. She looked okay," I say and he sighs as he rolls his eyes. "So, what is your type?"

He sighs and starts to fiddle with his hands. As he shrugs, I wait for a moment, but he remains silent.

"All right then," I sigh, standing up. "We have to get back to the mansion."

He nods and we pack up the leftovers. As we walk back to the mansion, I am suddenly jerked sideways and slammed into the side of a building. As I focus, I see a tall man with his arms on either side of me. He has a twisted lop-sided grin. A growl erupts from my chest and it is matched with another, but this one is a growl that indicates pleasure, kind of like a purr.

"So you are the new werewitch on the block," he says, widening his sickening grin. "Kind of cute, but can she hold her own weight when I do this."

He holds my hand on the wall and places his feet on mine. This means that he is now pressed up against me. I growl and struggle to get out, and this only makes him laugh. And so I bite his neck.

"Oh, I like it that way, baby," he laughs and I struggle again. This man smells strongly of alcohol. I hear a hiss and then I see a grey blur and the man is tackled. I refocus to see Christian and the man sizing each other up.

"Oh, this is precious," the guy says as he glares at Christian. "The all-powerful werewitch needs a vampire protector." Christian hisses and extends his fangs. "Protector or lover?" the man asks, glancing at me as Christian hisses again and his skin ripples. The man changes into his wolf form and growls at Christian, who hisses again and attacks. I watch as the two spar.

Eventually, the wolf pins Christian down and holds his growling muzzle close to Christian's face. At this point, I react and jump into action. I run towards the wolf, changing as I go, and hit the wolf's side. It shakes me off and I growl a deep, intense, animalistic type growl as I flatten my ears against my head. The wolf returns my growl and a circle of people surrounds us. It's big enough so we can spar as wolves. The wolf makes the first move as he runs at me. I charge and we collide. I manage to get him down, but he brings his back feet up and pushes me at the gut. I stumble backwards and it leaps forward and tries for my neck, but it gets the base of my left ear. I yelp out and he lets go.

I growl and he growls again, there is a moment of silence before he slowly begins to circle me. I contradict his method and circle him, too. Then, in a sudden blur he moves. I react quickly and jump as he goes in for a tackle. I leap over him easily and land behind him. I lunge forward and grab the wolf by the back leg. The wolf yelps as I shake its leg in my mouth before throwing it backwards.

I here a loud pop and know that the back leg is defiantly out of place. However, it doesn't take long for the leg to pop back in and the wolf is up again and fighting harder. I bark and bite down on its shoulder and throw him again. Blood splatters on the pavement and the wolf growls and gets back up again. He bites my ribs, but I turn in on him and bite down on its back. It lets go of me but latches onto the base of my neck. I fall to the ground and I am turned into a human. There is a gasp from the crowed and the wolf too turns human.

"Let us see how good you are at hand to hand combat," he says with a twisted grin. I get up quickly and touch the base of my neck where it is still bleeding; the man sees this as a distraction and goes to punch my nose. I catch his fist in my hand and he punches again with his other hand and I catch that, too, with my bloodied hand. I turn his hands back at the wrist and I hear two loud cracks. I smile as he shouts out in pain and goes down on his knees. I send an electric current from my hands into his and he screams out.

"Let us see how good you are at witch craft," I say with a twisted smile as I push his wrists back further and apply more shock. He groans and grinds his teeth together as I go down to his level and grab his heart through his chest. "Oh wait," I say with a small laugh. "You can't do witch craft."

"Papa!" a child's voice screams as I go to pull the man's heart out. I see a young girl about six or seven years old. I look back at the man's face and he is crying. "Please mam, please don't kill my papa. I know that he's not a good man, but he is the only family I have left."

The girl's eyes are shinning with tears. I look at her, and then to her father. "Go home," I say as I remove my hand from his heart. He slumps forward and I stand up. Using a spell for persuasion, I say, "Go home and take care of your daughter. You are all she has left. Stop drinking and take care of her."

I turn my back on the man as his daughter runs up to him and takes him into her arms,

"Thank you," she says, and I stop mid step and turn around. "Thank you for not killing him." I nod once and turn again and walk away, ignoring the feeling of blood on my hand and neck. I walk over to Christian who is standing as part of the circle.

"Let's get out of here," I mumble as I walk past him. He follows behind me, ignoring the picnic basket I dropped. We walk back to the mansion in silence with Christian a few steps behind me. When we get to my room, I make a test tube rack and test tubes appear. I take one of the test tubes and fill it with the werewolf blood that is still dripping off my hand.

"Uh, what are you doing?" Christian asks with a nervous laugh and I shrug.

"Never know when you might need werewolf blood for a spell," I say, placing the cap on the tube and putting it back in the rack.

"I'm a homosexual," Christian says out of the blue and I turn to face him. "That's why none of the girls are 'my type'."

"Okay then," I say, going into the bathroom and washing my hands.

"That's it?" he asks as I come out wiping my hand on a towel.

"I guess," I say, shrugging. "Unless you want me to say something else or react differently, I can do a very good scared or horrified impression."

"I'm just saying that others would have reacted differently," he says, sitting down on my bed. "I mean a gay vampire is rarely heard of."

"Well, I read a book once," I say with a cocky smile. "Why are they rarely heard of?"

"It is a stereotype," he sighs. "Vampires are supposed to be all sexy like and trying to get with the opposite sex— like werewolves are supposed to be all wild and buff, and warlocks are all supposed to be male, and witches-"

"Are supposed to be female," I finish with a laugh. "Wonder how you're going to tell David?"

I look out of the window and see the sun sinking in the sky. "Wow, the days here are sure different," I say, yawning and crawling into bed. Christian gets up and stands as I climb under the covers. Christian goes into his cat form and curls up at the end of the bed. I whisper a goodnight to him and close my eyes.

"All right," David says, snapping me out of my daze. Today I am starting on witch training. David came into my room earlier this morning and woke me up from my peaceful dream, and now I stand in the middle of my pentagram with David on the outside.

"Witch training is the easiest training of them all," he continues as he circles me. "All we have to do is unlock each of your elemental sides," he says, pointing to each of the symbols etched into the floor. "Starting with water and ending with spirit, each element will take at least a month to unlock. So, that takes five of the six months we have together. The last month we will practice fighting with it, so today we will start with water. Please stand in the water section."
I walk out of the middle and to the left, and stand in the water section.

"Now meditate. Clear your mind and let the element touch you with its grace," he says and I roll my eyes, but I do what he says. I sit with my legs crossed and my eyes closed. "Water is the element of calmness and is filled by peace of mind," I hear David say.

I sigh and raise my hand as I open my eyes. "Yes?"

"How long do I have to do this for?" I ask and he sighs.

"Once you enter the section you cannot exit until the element is unlocked." I look at him with wide eyes and he nods his head. "You need not worry about food. Your pentagram will keep you energized and healthy for as long as you are in its circle. Now concentrate, breathe."

"Gee, thanks for the tip," I say, rolling my eyes. "Breathe. Wow, I wouldn't have thought of that."

He groans and I close my eyes, and on his command inhale deeply and then exhale. On the exhale, the symbol lights up blue and water leaps out of the etching and flows around me, touching me ever so gently with its cool droplets. I inhale and exhale again, and the water explodes, going in every direction away from me. I hear David gasp and I open my eyes to see a perfectly dry room, but by the look on David's face the water was defiantly here.

"Was that good?" I ask, standing up.

"How did you do that?" he asked. "You just unlocked water. It took me a month to unlock water."

"I guess women are better," I say, standing and flicking my hair while David's face is full of shock.

"So ... Can I go?" I ask, stepping out of the circle. Mortified, David shakes his head and I raise an eyebrow as he gestures to the second space in the circle. I sigh and take a seat on the ground and close my eyes.

"Now," David says, still reeling from shock. "Fire is the element of power and is fuelled by anger."

I sigh and roll my eyes behind my closed eyelids. I inhale deeply and hold it for a few seconds before releasing it, expecting fire to explode all around me. But it doesn't. I carefully open one eye and then the other when nothing happens. David makes a huh noise.

"Well," he says with a shrug as he walks to the door. "I guess water was just your element. See you tomorrow."

"Wait... What?" I call, but he is already out the door and locking it. I let out am exaggerated sigh and stand up, walking to the edge of the section, but just as I was about to step out I hit an invisible wall. I press my hand on the invisible wall and try to push through, but it's no use. I am stuck in here. I sigh and sit back down. I so can not take a month of this. I lie down and brace my feet on the invisible wall and close my eyes again. This time I'm flooded with memories of me and Tyler. I remember the first time I saw him in history class when he made a brief eye contact, but looked away soon after. I remember how a little piece of me immediately didn't like him. I guess it was that little piece of active werewolf that was in me, but now that he has changed, it doesn't nag me anymore.

I open my eyes, sigh, and stretch out. The section of the pentagram I'm stuck in was two meters in diameter and I'm able to lay straight, but it's uncomfortable. I close my eyes again, not intending to go to sleep, but eventually I do.

I wake up to the sound of a bang. I gasp and sit up. Looking around,

I don't see anyone, but outside of the section there's a plate of warm cookies and milk. I know they are warm because I can smell them and I see heat coming off them. Next to the plate is *The Book of Paranormal*. My stomach growls and my attention turns towards the cookies. I go to grab one, but someone with a twisted sense of humour has placed the cookies just outside the invisible wall. I growl because this isn't just a plate of cookies. This is a mixture of cookies includingplain, triple chocolate,re peanut butter, raspberry, jam jellybeans, smarties, and even gooey chocolate, and they are on a plate as big as my head and piled at least thirty centimetres high. I punch the invisible wall and then I scratch at it. I missed breakfast this morning and, God dammit, I'm hungry. I stop scratching at the wall like an animal and think.

I close my eyes and feel my magic under my skin. I use my power to pull the plate and book towards me. My magic is shaky and it falters a few times, but eventually I get my hands on the plate of cookies. I sit in the middle of the circle and smile at my achievement. I slide the book onto my lap and then open it as I take a bite of one of the cookies. I almost moan in pleasure as the flavour hits my tongue. Once the pleasure of the cookie passes, I turn my eyes towards the pages of the book.

Allies and Enemies-
The vampires ally themselves with the fey (commonly known as fairies) and the warlocks, and they are natural enemies to the werewolves.
-Common Myths-
Myth: Vampires are allergic to the sun.
Fact: Vampires are not allergic to the sun; they are able to walk in it with ease and in fact it is rumoured that they like it.
Myth: Vampire can be slain by silver.
Fact: Vampires are allergic to wood not silver. They are often mixed up.

I sigh as I take another cookie off the plate and bite into it. Melted chocolate oozes into my mouth and there is an explosion of flavour. I know almost all of this information, but it is good to refresh the knowledge.

-Weaknesses-

Vampires are weakened by vervain. Vervain is a potent herb   . If a vampire touches vervain, the skin is burned and then blistered. Vampires are killed by real holy water, wooden stakes, crosses, and the bite of a werewolf. Wood is a natural substance, and vampires are allergic to this because they are the least natural paranormal. The religious items such as water blessed by a real priest (holy water) and wooden crosses are fatal to a vampire because, like warlocks, they are rumoured to be the spawn of Satan, and some say this is true to a point. If a vampire is bitten by a werewolf on the full moon, the wolf can inject the venom found in their saliva. This will cause the vampire to die a slow, painful

death. Vampires turn to dust once killed.

I turn the page and see it is the start of the werewolf section. Next to the heading is a picture of a marking, probably Native American. Then I realize that I know this marking; it's on the shoulder of the head werewolf that resided in the giant ditch in Mercy Lake. So I read on:

-Things to know about the werewolf race-

During the 1200s when the vampire population flourished in Mercy Lake, the gods needed a way to minimize the population, so they mixed the blood of a human and the blood of a wolf into a golden chalice. They then gave the chalice to a Native American man called Kiyiya (now known as Tamurl). As Kiyiya drank the blood, his body began to reshape and realign; his hands reshapes to form paws, his nails turned to claws. The werewolf looked nothing like a wolf. It had a sleek head and stood about four feet tall. The werewolf was black and had an unusual white marking on its right shoulder. It looks like a howling wolf as shown above. The werewolf was able to shift in between its human form and its werewolf form.

On the first full moon after Kiyiya was turned, the werewolf side of him took over and he turned three of the people in his tribe. They became werewolves like him, all with different and unique fur colours. The werewolves were sent out to destroy the vampires that were not in control of their hunger. With Kiyiya as their leader, they managed the population of the vampires. Once that was finished, the gods granted Kiyiya one wish; he wished that a deep ditch would be created so the whole werewolf species had some place to hide, and he asked if this ditch would not allow humans in. The gods granted this wish and then left the species alone in hope that they will kill each other off, but they did not think that the werewolves would get along as they were supposed to be savage beasts.

The venom of the werewolf is found in the saliva, and to administer the venom the wolf has to break the skin of the victim. This has to be done at the base of the neck at the top of the shoulder. The werewolf then has to lick the wound to administer the werewolf gene.

So Kiyiya must be the leader of the large pack. I pick up another cookie. I take a deep breath, bite into the cookie, and continue to read.

Changes-

After the victim undergoes his or her first change, their body's immune system strengthens and they never age again. Any old scars or injuries made before the change (Including the bite mark on the shoulder) will still remain on the werewolf's human body. One way a werewolf can get hurt and not heal like a werewolf should is when the werewolf is in exhaustion state. This is when a werewolf has fought hard or has not been fed for three days or more.

-Allies and Enemies-

Werewolves will ally themselves with the witches and the ghosts. They are natural enemies with the vampires.

-Common Myths-

Myth: Werewolves only appear in their wolf form under the full moon.

Fact: Werewolves can change to their wolf form at any time, not just under the full moon.

Myth: Werewolves only change at night.

Fact: Werewolves can stay in their wolf form until it dies if it wishes.

Myth: You can become a werewolf by performing a magic ritual.

Fact: The only way to become a werewolf is if the werewolf venom is injected into your system by the process of change.

Myth: If you are unarmed and attacked by a werewolf, your only chance for survival is to climb an ash tree or run into a field of rye.

Fact: Werewolves are poor tree-climbers, but they have great patience. They are not bothered by rye.

Myth: Werewolves turn to dust once killed.

Fact: Only vampires, warlocks, and fey turn to dust when killed. If a werewolf is killed, its body will decompose like a normal body would.

I close the book as the new information runs around my head. I put the book down and sigh again. I sit in the middle of the circle and meditate again, then, all of a sudden, images rush into my brain again. They're the same images I saw when Tyler and I were out riding, except they are slowed down. I can make out a fight or a war, but I can't make out who's fighting whom. I see someone go down in my peripheral vision. As I turn to see who it is, the scene changes to a graveyard where a coffin is being lowered into the ground. The vision changes again and I see a small infant being passed from one hand to the other. My eyes fly open and I inhale deeply. I have no idea what happened but it has drained me.

-Zero-

"Tyler," I call out, and before I could finish my sentence he is downstairs and by my side.

"Mail?" he asks and I shake my head. After his second piece of mysterious mail, he has been getting happier.

"No, all I was going to say is that we need to get ready for the full moon." I say and his smile falls as he walks into the basement and we start to test the chains. Edith and Avery come downstairs with a tray of lemonade.

"Hello, lovelies," Edith says, passing me a glass and kissing me on the lips before passing Tyler a glass. She looks at the chains on the floor and scrunches her nose. The girls' first full moon was spent locked in the basement, and they made sure we knew they didn't like it.

"What's wrong?" I ask and she turns towards me.

"I want to spend the moon outside," she whines and Avery agrees.

"I want to be in the moon," she says. "I want to bask in its glow."

"You want to die?" I ask and the girls fix me with a glare. "That's what will happen if you go out on the full moon. The woods will be crawling with hunters and all your humanity will be gone. The first thing you will want to do is change the hunter, and they are prepared for this. They will shove a silver stake right into your heart. If you do manage to bite the hunter and administer the poison, you will die. They drink wolfs bane, it's in their blood system. You bite them, it'll be in yours and you will die a slow and painful death. I forbid it."

We figured out that the hunters were drinking wolfs bane when we eavesdropped on a pack meeting from the alpha pack. The wolves that had bitten hunters were dropping like flies, and when the Alpha Pack captured a hunter and tortured the information out of him, even they decided to tie themselves up with chains.

"You don't own me," Edith says. I look at her as if she just slapped me. "You may have changed me, but you don't own me. I am going out into the full moon tonight and there is nothing that you can do about it."

She and Avery exit the room I sigh. I follow her up, intending to talk to her but there is a knock at the door. Tyler is upstairs and answering it in a heartbeat. In the doorway is African-American woman about Tyler's age. She has straight, black hair and brown eyes. I hear a growl erupt from Tyler's chest.

"Down boy," The woman says and Tyler still glares. "I am not going to hurt you."

"What are you doing here, Lexi?" he asks, and I look at him. "You are not welcome."

"I left the hunter's clan, stupid," she says, and now I growl. "I came looking for you."

"Why?" he asks, and she pushes past him, but I am right there with my arms over my chest and a growl erupting from my throat.

"Because I knew you probably needed help and it is good to have a valuable asset to the team," she sighs, turning around and looking at Tyler with a smile. "So, here I am."

"I don't need help," Tyler says.

"Who the hell is this chick?" I ask, looking at Tyler.

"One of my exes I used to hunt with," he says, still glaring at her.

"Ouch," she says with a laugh. "We did more than just hunting."

"How the hell are you a valuable asset?" Tyler asks, changing the subject as she smiles.

"I know exactly what the hunters are planning," she says, ticking them off on her fingers, "When they plan to do it, and what they want."

Tyler growls and looks out the kitchen window. The sun is slowly sinking in the sky.

"Got somewhere to be?" she asks, and Tyler looks back at her.

"Not until midnight," he answers. "How about we move into the kitchen where we can talk more about how you are a 'valuable *asset*'."

We move into the kitchen and just catch the girls leaving. I look at the sun and then to the pair in the kitchen.

"I am going to go talk to them to see if they won't change their minds," I say, running a hand through my hair. "Are you going to be okay here?"

Tyler nods and I quickly go and chase after the girls.

14. Hell Hath No Fury

-Zero-

The girls didn't change their minds and around eleven o'clock I turn around and head home, praying they don't get killed.

"She sounds like a bitch," I hear Lexi say as I open the door and enter the kitchen, except they aren't in the kitchen; they were in the lounge room.

"She isn't," I hear Tyler growl and I decide to linger around the corner. "She is better than you ever were."

"So, have you slept with her yet?" Lexi asks and I hear Tyler suck in a sharp breath as Lexi laughs. "So this girl is what twenty now, and you have done nothing? Wow, you *have* changed." I hear Tyler growl and I take this as my cue to appear.

"Tyler," I say and they both look up. Lexi is sitting on the lounge and Tyler on an individual recliner. "We should probably get going."

Tyler nods and stands.

"You can wait up here or leave," he says as he walks out of the room and we make our way downstairs where we chain ourselves up and begin the painful process of changing.

The next morning, we wake up on the cold floor in our human forms. My muscles ache and protest as Tyler and I unchain ourselves and make our way upstairs. Lexi is sleeping on the couch.

"What are we going to do about her?" I whisper as we walk into the kitchen.

"I don't know," Tyler sighs as he rubs the back of his neck. "She could help us."

"Yes, I could," Lexi says, walking into the room with a yawn. Tyler fixes her with a cold hard glare and she smiles. There is a loud bang at the kitchen door and Tyler and I look at each other before he goes and answers it.

"Rose?" he asks with a gasp and I go to the door. There she is, standing there with Edith around her shoulders. Her face says, *'Are you kidding me?'* and I realise that this is not Rose.

"Lilly?" I ask and she smiles and pushes her way inside. Tyler and I are gobsmacked as she walks into the lounge and sets Edith down on the couch.

"Could only save one of them," she says and I rush to Edith's side. "Thankfully, she didn't turn a hunter, and the hunter that stabbed her was sloppy. She's going to survive."

"How the hell are you alive?" Tyler asks, gaping at Lilly. "We saw you die."

"Technically, I'm still dead," she shrugs. "I'm a ghost."

"That makes sense," I say and Tyler nods. "Why are you here?"

"The ghosts have decided to ally with the wolves every full moon to help them against the hunters," she says and we all hear Edith groan. I shush her as she stirs awake.

"What the hell is going on?" Lexi asks as she enters the room. Lilly turns into mist before she is seen.

"Nothing, Edith just had an accident on the full moon," I say and she frowns. Then all of a sudden her eyes go wide and Lilly appears with her arm in Lexi's chest. Lilly is see through and misty.

"Lilly, no!" Tyler says, lunging forward.

"Why not?" Lilly asks, looking over at Tyler who stops mid-step. "She is a hunter. She is probably here to kill you. She was there when I died. She was one of them who held me down." As Lilly gets angrier she begins to mystify more, I flash back to that day. I do remember seeing Lexi there.

"Let her be killed, Tyler," I say, standing up. "She was there at the fight. Save us the torture and let Lilly kill her now. She's no use to us."

"No use!" Tyler shouts. "She can help us find out what the hunter are up to, and we can be prepared for every move they make!"

Lilly removes her hand from Lexi's heart and chest and then places it flat over the wound. The wound heals and I look at Lilly with raised eyebrows

"If she can truly help you three against the hunters, then I say she is your best shot," Lilly says, glaring at Lexi. "But I swear to the angels that if you turn on them, I will rip your heart out and shove it down your oesophagus."

Lilly then mystifies and leaves the room. This is going to be hell:

three werewolves living with a werewolf hunter.

"All right then," I say, turning to Tyler. "Since you gave her the leniency to live, you will look after her. You will not leave her side. If she goes to the bathroom, you wait outside. Follow her everywhere. I don't want to hear an argument. The only way you can get out of it is if you kill her."

Tyler grunts a reply and then he leads Lexi outside.

"This is a terrible idea," I mumble to myself as I check on Edith again— still sleeping. I go upstairs and run a shower, but as I step in I am immediately burned. I quickly jump out and growl.

"What the hell?" I mumble as I wrap a towel around my waist, and test the sink in the bathroom. Again I am burned. I pull my hand back then check the kitchen, and again I am burned. I check the basements tap and yet again I am burned. I go upstairs and call out Tyler's name from the kitchen. He comes inside with Lexi with her silver stake out. I look at her with a scowl.

"Nice towel," she giggles, putting her stake away. I growl deep in my chest.

"Why don't you wash your hands Tyler?" I ask, still glaring at Lexi, Tyler shrugs and walks over to the sink where he turns the water on and puts his hand under it. It burns and blisters. He gasps and pulls back before looking at Lexi with the devil's glare.

"Oh yeah," She says acting as if she just remembered something. "The hunters put wolfsbane in the water system so that any wolf who bit a human would go through the same thing as if they bit a hunter."

Both Tyler and I growl and she shrugs. I go to say something but from the living room there is a scream of pain. I run in to see Edith screaming and scratching at her chest. Then in one fluid movement, Lexi is there and shoving her stake into Edith's chest.

"NO!" I shout as Lexi removes the stake from Edith's chest. I turn wolf and leap towards her, but I am knocked sideways as Tyler hits me. I growl and glare at him.

"*We need her,*" he says into my mind.

"Bullshit," I growl back. "*She is nothing but trouble.*"

"*She can help us stay alive!*" he says in my head. "*She is my friend. Please, Zero, she put Edith out of her misery. Edith would have suffered too much otherwise*"

I say nothing but growl at Lexi, whose eyes show nothing but fear. I deepen my growl and then walk upstairs where I turn human and change into clothes before going back downstairs.

I enter the lounge room to see Lexi and Tyler lounging together. I growl deep in my chest as I gently pick Edith up. Tears sting my eyes as I take her deep into the woods and bury her. Rose needs to come back soon or else I fear the worst.

-Rose-

The days were beginning to pass by and I had no other entertainment other than a book. I had not picked up the book since I found out about myths about the werewolves, so I flip it open to the weaknesses of the werewolves. It reads:

-Weaknesses-

Werewolves are weakened by an herb called Aconite or commonly known as Wolfsbane. The reaction of this herb to the werewolves is much like the case of vervain and vampires: burns and blisters. Werewolves are killed by a silver stake to the heart, and venom from a vampire. Werewolves are allergic to silver because silver is the earthly symbol for the moon and a part of the moon can kill a wolf and the other part can control the world. If a Vampire bites a werewolf with its canines, it will not only kill a werewolf, but it will also cause it agony in the time before it dies, resembling being slowly burned from the inside.

This book does not hold much information that I don't already know, but I flip to the witches section that has a black cat sitting next to the title. I go to read but the gym door opens and David walks in. I stand up and turn to look at him.

"What's wrong?" I ask as David turns to me with his jade green eyes blazing.

"Shut up, you spoilt brat!" he spits and I can smell the strong scent of alcohol on his breath. "I have looked through your past lives and all you have gotten is respect and power. I had to work all my lives to get what I wanted, but you just had it handed to you on a gold platter. Queen, Princess, Pharaoh, all of it! You had it all and all I got was slavery, whips, and binds," he says, throwing something onto the floor. David's fingers light up with the green glow of power. I gasp and take a step back. I have no idea what David is talking about. "You had titles like 'the great' and 'the magnificent'. I was lucky to get a scrap of bread!" David goes on and on and on about how my lives are great and wonderful whilst his were bad. I notice that the thing David threw onto the floor was a thick book. My eyes glow yellow and I feel fire crackle under my skin,

David shoots a bolt of green lightning at the side of the gym and screams, "Even now you are stronger, greater than me!" He begins to pace in front of me and the fire beneath my skin bursts through as the symbol comes alive. The fire does not dance around my skin. It's not slow or calm; it's raging and shoots straight up, putting a wall between me and David's rage. The fire is hot and angry. I stand in the middle of the symbol and watch as different warm colours streak through the fire: red, orange, yellow, and even deep blue. My yellow eyes widen as I reached out and put my hands in the middle of the fire. It does not burn. It's not even hot. The fire begins to shrink and my skin seems to absorb the flames. The fire then dies and the symbol unlocks. I look at David's face of rage as he takes my arm and tries to shove me into the next symbol.

"NO!" I shout, putting my hand flat to his chest and pushing him backwards. My eyes flame and yellow lightning cracks and dances around my knuckles. "I am not yours to boss around. I am not your pet. I don't know what you are talking about when you say past lives, but I don't care! Don't ever speak to me that way again or I will leave this place and you will lose a valuable ally."

David goes to speak but I shoot lightning across the gym.

"I have not finished!" I shout. "You are drunk. Sober up before you come to speak to me about continuing my training."

I take the books from the floor and take them back to my room where I slam the door and lock it with a spell. I then slide down the door and to the floor where I put my head in my hands and cry.

"Hey, what happened?" Christian asks, coming out from under the bed and turning human.

"I want to go home," I sob as he takes me into his arms. "I want to go back to Tyler. I don't want to be here."

Christian hushes me and I cry into his chest. I wipe my tears, then move up onto the bed where I lie on my back. Christian joins me in his cat form and I gently scratch behind his ears and he purrs. I look at the two books on the floor and then roll away from them and fall asleep.

I scream and lash out as I wake up. I'm not sure what I was dreaming about, but it was not good. I look around and see that I am still in the room. I sit up quickly, and then get out of bed and rush into the bathroom. I look at my reflection in the mirror for the first time in a while. Ever since I turned back into a human after my year as a werewolf, I have avoided my own reflection. But now our eyes meet. I can see the scars from the battle I was in as a wolf, and trace a scar that starts at the right side of my lip and down to under my chin. I remember how this one was created. While in Africa, the wolf that attacked me scaped me with one of its claws while it tried to hold down my head. I sigh and walk back into the room just as Christian comes in from the balcony.

"Bad dream?" he asks, tilting his head. I nod once. "What happened?"

A shiver runs down my back and I shake my head and Christian shrugs. There is a knock at the door. My eyes flare yellow as I jump.

"Who is it?" I ask as Christian shrinks into his cat form.

"It's David," a quiet voice says and a growl erupts from my chest.

"Are you sober?" I ask, slowly walking to the door as Christian runs under the bed.

"Slightly hung over," he says with a groan and I roll my eyes. "Rose, I am so sorry."

I sigh and undo the spell on the door and open it. David stumbles in— he must've been leaning on the door— then straightens up.

"Rose, I am so sorry," he says again and I place my hands on my hips and raise an eyebrow as if to say, 'What are you sorry for?'. "For everything. I was drinking and reading at the same time. Not a good combination."

David saunters over to the chair at my dresser table and takes a seat.

After explaining why it is important that I unlock my powers, he leaves me alone saying that it is my choice when I begin training again. I decide immediately to train, knowing that I would be able to get back to Tyler. I go down to the gym with Smoky on my heels. As I open the doors I see no-one is in here. I shut and lock the door, leaving an engraving on the outside that reads:

"Do not disturb."

"So what exactly are you doing in here?" Christian asks, changing form.

"I have to unlock my elemental powers so that I can become more powerful than I already am," I say, taking a seat in the earth side of the pentagram.

"Right, and I have to be here because?" he says as I close my eyes.

"Because, I might be stuck in here for a month and if I am I want someone to keep me company," I say, drawing in an deep breath then letting it out. This section does not feel like the others did. It feels unwelcoming. I get a sick feeling in my gut and my face scrunches up. I feel a pulling force pulling me towards the edge of the circle. I take another deep breath and then let it out. The force lessens, however it is still there, nagging and pulling at my stomach.

Over the next few days, Christian and I talk and we get to know each other more. It turns out that he was abused as a child; his father would beat him and his mother was constantly drunk. His aunt and uncle ended up taking him in and caring for him along with their other two children. He was the kid that always got picked last for everything, andwas picked on because of his sexuality, causing him to sink into depression. He would cut lines into his wrist just to watch them bleed and when his aunt found out about his sexuality he was sent to church where the priest and everyone would look at him with harsh, judging eyes that were always cold and they would always look away if he looked their way. When he was turned into a vampire/cat, no one cared that he disappeared. Somehow he made his way down to Paradise where a woman with many other cats adopted him, hence the number on his collar. I felt sorry for him. He would often leave the gym to get something to drink, but he would always come back often with food for me.

As the days turn into months, I begin to worry.

"What if I can't unlock it?" I ask Christian as I let out yet another deep breath. "I've been in here for two months now."

"I don't know anything about this 'witchy' business," Christian shrugs and I stand and begin to pace.

"I am going to lose my mind if I don't get out of here soon," I sigh, leaning on the invisible wall.

"Keep trying. You'll get it soon," David says, entering the gym and startling me and Christian. My eyes turn yellow and his fangs come out.

"Who is he?" David says, looking at me then to Christian. "A replacement for Tyler?"

"I would never replace him," I say, glaring at David who holds his hands up in surrender. "Why are you here?"

"Just checking the progress, that's all," he says, walking towards my pentagram. "You know, I don't like vampires in my mansion," he says and I see Christian ripple as David steps closer. "They belong in their own town."

I roll my eyes and David turns his eyes towards me.

"I came here for another reason, too," he says, and I raise my eyebrow. "I need that book back. The one I threw on the floor in here."

"It's in my room," I say and David nods and goes to exit the gym. "What is that book for anyway?" I ask, and David stops and turns around.

"Any Paranormal that has ever lived is in that book," he says and I raise an eyebrow. "You can see their past lives and anything they have ever been. Does that answer your question?" I shrug and David turns to leave.

"So, can Christian stay?" I ask before he leaves. He grunts in acknowledgement and I smile.

"I bet the reason that you can't unlock this one as easy as you did the others is because the Power of Earth hates you," Christian says once David left.

"Could be," I agree as I lean on the wall again. "She is a temperamental bitch."

"Well, I better go and feed," Christian says as his stomach growls and mine does too in an echo.

"Lucky you," I mumble, sitting back down to meditate.

-Zero-

"Anything for me?" Tyler asks as I come in from collecting the mail.

"Not unless you want a coupon for a mani/peddi at the spa," I say, putting the mail on the table

"Oh well," he shrugs and Lexi leans over the table and grabs the coupon, flipping it over twice before putting it in her back pocket. It has been two months since Edith's death and almost two years since Rose has left us. The days are all blurring together and things are getting more difficult to manage. The werewolf population is dwindling, either from death or they have fled town. The water supply is still contaminated with wolfsbane, so we have had filters installed that are so fine that not even the smallest speck of wolfsbane can get through. The alpha pack has moved on out of town and, as far as I know, there are only a few werewolves left in Mercy Lake including Tyler and myself. The down side is that we can't go hunting and feed ourselves, so Tyler and I put money in each week to buy a mass amount of mixed meat that we feast on so that we don't starve to death. Lilly has appeared a couple of times since her reappearance as a ghost, but she never brings good news. Apparently, the ghosts are giving up on fighting because they overhead the hunters talking about calling ghost hunters and they are retreating to safety. Everything is going downhill at a fast rate, and I fear that soon even Tyler and I will have to leave Mercy Lake. The only thing keeping us here is the hope of Rose's return.

15. Reappearance of the Werewitch

-Rose-

"COME ON!" I yell, balling my hands into fists and pressing the heel of my hand to my eyes. "Unlock, you stupid element."

It has been another month since I have entered this stupid part of the pentagram and I am getting frustrated. I lean forward on my knees and slam the side of my fists into the hard floor of the gym. David stands in the corner leaning on the wall.

"Isn't there some way to speed up this process?" I ask, looking up at him. He smiles as Christian enters the gym from his afternoon drink. A thick, rich smell fills the room and my head snaps to Christian.

"Please, tell me that is coffee," I say, standing up. He nods. "Please, tell me it's for me."

"It's for you," he smiles, making his way over to me. I get excited and just as he is about to reach me there is a loud crack and a large, thick vine shoots up in between us, making Christian drop the coffee. Another vine shoots up on the opposite side and the two vines begin to twist around, making a cocoon around me as rocks fly up and harden the cocoon. The rocks and vines begin to knot and slowdown to a halt and everything is silent, then the vines and rocks begin to unwind, vanishing back into the floor. Christian, David, and I stand there in shock. I make the first move, stepping to the edge of the section and put my foot out. Once it is outside, I quickly run out, not wanting to spend another second in that hell hole.

"I'm free!" I shout and Christian and David laugh. Without knowing it, I step into the air section and curse, "Shit!"

But I need not worry, because as I take a deep breath, the symbol glows and air rushes upwards. It's cool as it whispers around my body before disappearing back into the symbol. There is a thick, defining silence in the room as I let out the breath I was holding and step slowly out of the section.

"What just happened?" Christian asks, his fangs out of their sheaths and his skin rippling.

"I think that might be her main element," David says, looking at me as I raise a questioning eyebrow. "Witches will always have an element that they are good at and an element that they are weak at. Whatever their strong element is, that's what their power colour is."

"But mine is yellow," I state and David nods.

"When a witch is undecided, their power colour is yellow. If they are still undecided for six years their colour darkens to black," David says, which explains Xavier.

"So, your element is earth?" I ask and he nods. I walk over to the spirit section and look at the symbol. "What colour is Spirit?"

"I don't know," David says, folding his arms over his chest. "A spirit witch has never been heard of before. Spirit is a strong element and most witches don't unlock it for months, even years."

I feel a strong pull towards this element and my talisman begins to glow and pull toward it. I walk into the section and as soon as I am in a loud crack echoes through the gym before going silent. After a heart beat, there is a wispy mist that slowly begins to rise from the symbol. My eyes glow bright yellow and yellow lightning cracks at my fingertips. There is a low hum that echoes through the room and the mist begins to get thicker as a random and unnatural wind picks up and begins to gently blow through my hair. The mist gets thicker still and the wind begins to get wild.

As some light gym equipment is knocked over and the light bulbs explode. The lightning at my fingers shoots out and forks; the ends of the lightning hits the invisible wall and bounces back to me. The mist flows back into the symbol and the wind dies down. I close my eyes and take a deep breath and when I open my eyes. I'm wearing my white dress. An urge pulls me to the middle of the pentagram and I follow it. When I reach the centre, I face the spirit section and take another deep breath. Lightning shoots up from the centre of each section, blue for water, red for fire, green for earth, white for air, and yellow for spirit. My eyes focus sharply on the spirit lightning, then in a sudden flash, it flies at me. Normally, I would have run or taken a step back, but I felt cool and calm as it makes contact with my skin and I absorb its power. Its overwhelming power sends me to my knees. My heart races as the room falls silent.

"What now?" I ask, looking up to David who is standing there shell-shocked.

"What the hell is happening?" he mumbles, pressing the bridge of his nose with his thumb and forefinger. "It took me several months to unlock that."

"Like I said, sometimes women are better," I say, standing back up and feeling this new energy flow through my veins. "So, what now?"

"Now, we throw you a ball," David says walking out of the gym and I run after him.

"What do you mean, a ball?" I ask, catching up to him.

"Your coming out ball," he replies, walking into another room I've never been in before; the kitchen.

"I'm not gay," I say to him then, realising what I said, I look behind me to see Christian walking behind me looking at the floor.

"Fine then," David says, not breaking his step. "It will be your reappearance party, and everyone is invited."

My heart skips a beat as David keeps walking and exits the kitchen and into another room; a library.

"I said that you are free to go when you finish your training," he says, taking a seat at a desk. "What better way to go free then with a party with all your friends."

"Including Tyler?" I ask, raising an eyebrow and David looks at me.

"Obviously," he says, turning around again and pulling a paper out.

"Well, I kind of always liked masquerades," I say, shrugging and David laughs.

"Then a masquerade it will be," he says, taking out a pen and writing on the paper then looking up at me. "You can leave now."

I am taken back by the sudden rudeness and turn to walk away.

"Wait," he says and I turn again. David hands me a small money pouch that he produced from his pocket. "Go and buy you and him something pretty."

I take the pouch and then walk away.

-Zero-

There is a knock on the front door and when I answer it there is a man wearing a suit standing there. He has a silver tray that holds two envelopes with mine and Tyler's names on them.

"A letter for you, sir," he says, handing the letters to me. "And one for Tyler."

"Uh, thanks," I say, taking them. When I look back up, the man is gone.

"Tyler," I call, closing the door behind me and going into the kitchen where Lexi and Tyler are laughing about something. "Letter."

"Leave it on the table," he says and I look at him. "I'll read it later."

"Could be from that person you are always writing to." I say, putting the letter on the table.

"Rose," Tyler mumbles and Lexi groans as he quickly grabs the letter and opens it. I open mine at the same time and frown, there is a small invitation that has a fancy writing on it:

Zero
You are cordially invited to celebrate
the reappearance of the werewitch with a Black and Red
masquerade ball tomorrow night by the hour of six till midnight.
Meet at the house in the woods.
This invitation is a plus one.

I look up from the letter and see Tyler reading it over and over again.

"What's that?" Lilly says, appearing next to me.

"An invitation to a party," I reply, scanning over it again. "A black and red ball tomorrow night. A plus one invitation."

"A reappearance ball, for a werewitch," she says reading over my shoulder. "Does that mean Rose?"

"Could be," Tyler says, putting his invitation down on the table and turning to Lexi. "Mind being my plus one?"

"I would be delighted," she says with a flirty smile as she stands up. "Let's go shopping."

Tyler smiles and follows Lexi out the front door, grabbing his wallet as he goes.

"I'm getting bad vibes from them," Lilly says, folding her arms over her chest and I sigh and agree.

"Want to be my plus one?" I ask, grabbing my wallet and keys as she and I walk to the front door.

"Why not," she shrugs, following me out the door and into my car.

After an hour of shopping, Lilly and I go home with a casual black suit for me and a red cocktail dress with frilly skirt for her.

As open the door, I hear laughter and both Lilly and I roll our eyes as we enter the kitchen. I am praying to God that Rose is the reappearing werewitch, otherwise, as always, I fear the worst.

-Rose-

Christian and I stand in the massive ballroom on the second floor where a where a group of paranormals are setting up a speaker system and a DJ stand while other paranormals are setting up flowers and indoor plants as well as cleaning the floors.

"Nervous yet?" Christian says to me and I let out a sharp breath.

"Little bit," I say with a small smile. "I have changed so much over these two years. I wonder if Tyler still loves me?"

"Who wouldn't love you?" Christian says as we walk over to a long table where David is planning on putting food.

"You?" I say, walking along the table.

"Yeah, but I am gay," Christian shrugs. "But if I wasn't, I would probably try to go for you."

I laugh and a shout catches my attention. One of the workers has dropped the giant chandelier and it shatters into a million pieces.

"David is going to kill me," he mumbles as he starts to nervously chew his nails and I frown.

"*Praefigo*," I whisper and the chandelier assorts itself back together. "*Erexit*," I whisper again, and the chandelier lifts itself up onto ceiling where it is meant to be. I give a smile of satisfaction and continue to walk as the workers look on in astonishment.

"Rose," David says, appearing behind me and making me jump.

"Jesus Christ!" I hiss, turning around and he smiles. "What do you want?"

"I need to talk to you," he says as his smile vanishes. I raise an eyebrow and he looks over my shoulder to Christian. "In private."

I look over to Christian who shrugs, then I reluctantly follow David out of the ballroom, down the hall, and into his office.

"What is it that you want to talk about?" I ask as he sits behind his desk and I sit on the other side.

"How are your periods going?" he says abruptly and I almost fall out of the chair.

"WHAT!" I exclaim and he looks shocked.

"Your period," he says. "Some women refer to it as 'Their time of the month' where their-"

"Yeah, I know what a period is," I say, cutting him off. "I haven't had any since I was turned into a werewolf."

"As I suspected," he mumbles to himself and I look up at him with a questioning look.

"What does that mean?" I question and he sits back in his chair.

"Well, werewolves and witches are both fertile paranormal creatures," he explains, fiddling with a pen as if he is a doctor. "They both can reproduce children. However, werewitches are infertile creatures and we cannot reproduce. I thought it would have been different seeing how you are female."

I sit there speechless and frozen in place. I never even considered that I was infertile. I thought that it was a perk of being a werewolf to be able to reproduce and not have to suffer the pain of menstruation.

"Is there anything you need to know?" David asks and I look into his eyes. He looks at me with concern; his eyes stare right into my soul and I have to tear my eyes away before I completely break down.

"What was my previous life like?" I ask numbly.

"Well," he sighs, taking out the book from under his desk and opening the cover and flipping a couple of pages. "In your most recent life, you were a decedent from the ancient Native Americans. You lived on a cattle ranch with your husband, who was a werewolf but never told you. You two kids, a basic life, and always had enough money to keep the ranch running. Your husband then went to war and never returned— he stepped on a mine. You died a natural death."

I sit there numb in the chair with a small smile on my face. "Thank you," I say silently as I stand and exit the room and head back downstairs to my bedroom where I take out my dress and smile. It is a beautiful red dress, and I believe it is an over statement, but I want to make a statement. I take out my mask and smile wider. It is a red mask with black glitter spirals and black wire on it with a red silk ribbon to tie. And the shoes, the shoes are just casual small-heeled red shoes. I take a deep breath and let it out slowly. I've always thought I would have children at some point in my life. I never thought I was infertile. There is a knock on the door and Christian opens the door slowly and pops his head inside.

"Your guests have arrived," he says, sliding inside wearing his outfit for the night, a red suit with a black under shirt and trimming, a red tie, and black dress shoes. "Why aren't you dressed yet?" he asks, and I wonder how long I have been standing here.

"I guess I'm just nervous," I say, clenching my hands into fists. "Things are getting a little intense."

After a quick shower, I change into my dress. My heart races as

Christian ties my mask to my face, then offers me his arm and escorts me up to the ballroom. As I see the door draw closer, my heart drums loudly and my hands start to shake. Tyler is going to be inside; he is going to be there, waiting for me.

I wonder if I've changed.

Christian nudges my side and I stare at him with wide, scared eyes. He smiles at me reassuringly and then opens the door.

-Zero-

The door opens and all eyes look to see who enters. The room collectively holds their breath as a woman in a red dress glides in gracefully on the arm of a tall man with black hair. Instantly, I know the woman to be Rose, her blue eyes seem to shine through her mask. Mid-step she freezes. I follow her line of sight to Tyler, who stands with Lexi by his side. Her eyes glow bright yellow and the man she walks with nudges her out of her trance.

From besides me I hear Lilly's breath catch.

"She is beautiful," she smiles and takes a step forward.

"Remember," I warn, following her closely. "Some people think you're dead. Rose might be one of those people."

Lilly ignores my warning and immediately runs to Rose and embraces her.

I watch as Rose's face pales under her mask; her eyes flare yellow as she steps back and stares at her sister.

"Lilly?" Rose gapes. Lilly nods her head and smiles widely. Rose takes another step back, her hands shaking. "I was told you were dead."

"I am dead," Lilly whispers as her body mystifies. Rose's eyes widen as Lilly turns corporeal again, then she smiles and hugs her sister again, laughing.

"Zero?" Rose asks, looking over Lilly's shoulder to me and I nod my head. She looks up again at Tyler and steps out of Lilly's embrace. I turn to look. Tyler is looking right back at Rose, but he is staying with Lexi. The man in the red suit touches Rose's arm and whispers in her ear. She nods and then turns her gaze away from Tyler to talk to her other guests.

I stare at the man in the red suite and my heart skips a beat when his eyes land on me and flare red. Vampire.

Before I can open my mouth to speak, I hear Rose gasp. I turn to see Xavier hugging his sister in his arms.

"Something is wrong," Xavier whispers. Rose tenses as he steps back and holds her at arm's length. "Very wrong. Something is very, very wrong, sister."

In a sudden flash, David appears and looks to Xavier. Xavier takes a step away from Rose and her eyes look to David.

"Come with me," David says and Xavier nods his head and follows David out of the room.
Rose frowns for a moment before making her way around the room and talking to her friends with her vampire protector never far behind her.

"So, who are you to our lovely Rose?" the man in the red suite says, coming up beside me.

"My name is Zero," I start, but he cuts me off.

"*Ahh,* her turner," he says and I nod once. "My name is Christian."

"Her lover?" I ask, quizzically. The vampire laughs.

"Her friend," he says, following Rose.

I watch Rose speak with her circle, smiling and laughing. I watch Tyler approach Rose from behind and say something. Rose turns quickly and their eyes lock.

-Rose-

His eyes are on me and mine are on him. He is wearing a black suit with a black under shirt and a red tie. He also wears a black mask with three silver skulls at the top of the nose. My breath catches as he lets go of the African-American woman who's holding him. He reaches out and touches my face before embracing me in a tight hug. I release the breath I was holding and hug him back, feeling that he still loves me.

"I've missed you so much," he sighs, tightening his hold on me.

"I've missed you, too," I say, sighing in relief. The music changes and I smile and take his hand in mine. "Dance with me."

I lead Tyler to the dance floor and he smiles as he spins me in his arms before grabbing my waist and pulling me close. I look into Tyler's eyes and they shine through his mask, however, they are *both* shining green. My heart skips a beat and I reach up and place a hand on Tyler's cheek.

"Your eyes have changed," I comment as we dance slowly to the beat of the music.

"I guess they must have changed themselves," he says, looking straight into my eyes and smiling. "But yours haven't changed a bit— still that beautiful blue."

My eyes turn yellow as my heart races and a blush spread across my cheeks.

"And yellow," he laughs, spinning me under his arm then back to him again. It feels like we are the only two people in this room. I can only hear the music and our hearts beating in time with each other. Tyler spins, then dips me, and brings me back up slowly. I look into his eyes and see my yellow eyes have returned.

"There it is," I whisper, noticing my eyes are still yellow. They fade and as the music reaches the climax, I bring Tyler closer to me and pull him into a kiss; a powerful, passionate kiss. Tyler wraps both arms around my waist and pulls me even closer.

With one hand on my waist and the other in my hand again, we continue to dance, but slower. I rest my head on his shoulder and close my eyes. An unsettling feeling comes over me and I open them and look into the crowd. I see Tyler's friend watching with her arms folded over her chest and her eyes glaring at me. I frown and she looks away, then vanishes into the crowd. The unsettling feeling leaves me as I focus on Tyler; on how his hand feels in mine, how his shoulder feels under my hand, and how it feels when he touches my waist. I can hear our heats beating to the same rhythm. It's the welcoming rhythm that lets me know that I am home and this is where I am meant to be, forever in his arms. The song ends and I lead Tyler off the dance floor and out onto the large balcony looking out over the gardens and the nearby villages.

"Rose," Tyler sighs as he pulls me close. "I have been so lost without you. Every day I felt numb and alone."

"I am here now," I say, kissing his cheek. "I won't ever leave you again."

"Who was that man that walked you through the door?" he asks. I laugh as I feel the jealousy roll off of him.

"Jealous?" I smile, turning to look into his eyes.

"No," he says abruptly. "More like curious. He's a vampire, isn't he?"

"Yes, his name is Christian," I say and Tyler frowns. "And he is gay. You have nothing to worry about."

Tyler smiles and then looks out to the town with a smile on his face.

"So, who was the girl you were with?" I ask stiffly as I stand and move to the ledge and looking out onto the town. "You two seemed close."

Tyler puts his jacket around my shoulders and leans in close. "Jealous?" he laughs, kissing my cheek and when I don't reply his face softens and he wraps his arms around my waist and pulls my back to his chest. "That's Lexi. She's an old hunting partner and a crazy ex-girlfriend." I stiffen in Tyler's arms and he kisses my cheek. "You have nothing to worry about, Rose, you are mine. She's been helping Zero and I out with the crises that have been happening."

"What crises?" I ask, spinning in his arms and looking into his eyes.

"I will tell you all about it later," he says, kissing my lips. "Right now we have to get back to your party."

"If I must," I smile, handing him back his jacket. The rest of the night goes smoothly, consisting of dancing, socializing, and more dancing. Tyler never leaves my side and his hands stay in mine. When the clock strikes midnight, David reappears.

"The night has come to its end," he says as the music stops. "Would all visitors please follow me to the rooms where you will be staying?"

David opens the ballroom doors and the crowd follows him. I hold onto Tyler's arm as he begins to pull away.

"Your room is this way," I say with a smile. He lets me take his hand and lead him to my room. As I close my door, Tyler comes up behind me and kisses my neck as he wraps his arms around me.

"You're driving me crazy," I say as I lean into the kiss.

"I can stop if you want," he says in-between kisses. I shake my head and he turns me around in his arms.

Tyler continues to kiss my neck and presses my back up against the door as he locks it. All my thoughts leave me as I slide my hands under Tyler's jacket and help him out of it, and then I start on his shirt buttons. He moves his kisses up to my lips and a deep growl erupts from his chest.

"Did you just growl at me?" I gape, my eyes widen as he pulls back and smiles at me.

Tyler makes another low passionate growl and crushes his lips back to mine. He unties the ribbon on my mask and it falls to the ground. I, in turn, take his mask off and look deep into his eyes and I am secretly glad that I still see his yellow eye. As I clumsily undo his last button, he reaches to my side and unzips my dress. I slide it down past my hip where it then falls to the floor and I step out of it along with my shoes. Tyler shakes off his shirt and I push him backwards and onto the bed. Once all our clothes are scattered around the room, I let out a shaky breath.

"Are you all right?" Tyler asks, looking up from kissing my neck. I nod nervously, running a hand through my hair. "This is your first time, isn't it?" he asks, sitting up and pulling me up with him.

"I always said I would wait for the right guy," I shrug, blushing.

"And, am I the right guy?" Tyler asks, raising an eyebrow.

"Of course, you are," I say, taking his body in. "You are more than right," I say, blowing out a nervous breath. "You are... Perfect."

And with that last word, Tyler and I give in to the passion. He presses his lips against mine and lets out yet another passionate growl. He pulls my body close to his, deepening the kiss. He lays me back onto the bed and I let go of reality; he is the thing holding me to this earth, he is my sun and my moon, he is the one I love. He kisses my body and I absorb the passion and return it with a moan of ecstasy. He kisses my stomach, my chest, my neck, my jaw, and my lips. I don't know where my body ends and his starts, and, to be honest, I don't care.

Once the passion had ended and Tyler had rolled off of me, we lie on the bed, as close as we've ever been, tangled up in each other's arms and the sheets. My body aches, but in a good way. My nerves feel electric and alive; his touch is exhilarating as his fingers trace lines on my body. I fall asleep in his arms and, for once, everything seems good.

I wake up in the morning alone in the bed. The first thing I see is Tyler's shirt on the floor. I smile and stretch before getting out of bed and getting dressed. I use a simple locator spell and follow it to the kitchen where Tyler, Zero, Lexi, and Christian are looking for something. I silently run up behind Tyler and cover his eyes.

"Guess who," I laugh and feel him smile.

"That wouldn't happen to be my totally gorgeous girlfriend, would it?" he laughs as I uncover his eyes.

"Congratulations, sir," I say, jumping into his arms as he turns around. "Now claim your prize."

"Can I have the shirt?" he asks with a teasing smile.

"Maybe later, handsome," I say, kissing his lips as he sets me down. As our kiss breaks, I notice a scar starting at his lips and trailing under his chin. I look to the rest of the group as they open and close cupboards franticly. Lexi leans on the kitchen bench with a bored look on her face.

"What are you guys doing?" I ask as they stop rummaging.

"David told us to help ourselves to anything in the kitchen," Zero says, opening a cupboard. "But there is nothing here."

I smile as Christian opens the fridge, showing me that it is empty, but then I see a something they miss, a blur in the right hand corner— a tell-tale sign that a spell has been used to hide the contents of the fridge. I glide over to the fridge and grab onto the blur, and with a tough yank, the spell comes undone and everything in the kitchen becomes visible.

"Tyler should cook us something," Lexi says, perking up. I look at her, and without the mask she seems familiar.

"And why should I do that?" he asks, standing behind me and pulling me into a hug

"Because you used to cook for me all the time when *we* were dating," she shrugs and my eyes flare as anger fills my chest and a rumble vibrates through my chest.

"Are we dating now?" he scoffs. "You should know that I don't like being ordered around. That's one of the reasons I dumped your sorry arse."

Zero and Christian make an *oooh* sound and I smile as her mouth hangs open in a silent *'O'*.

"Who is going to cook then?" I ask, getting the attention off her.

"Not Zero," Tyler says with an easy laugh. "He burns water."

I sigh and walk over to the fridge and pull out a carton of eggs, bacon, bread, tomatoes, and an assortment of fruits.

"How the hell does a fridge hold that much?" Zero asks as he and the rest of the boys sit at the counter with Lexi. I'm happy to see Lexi and Tyler sitting at opposite ends.

"Zero," I sigh, putting the rest of the ingredients on the counter. "You turn into a four foot werewolf whenever you want and on full moons you can change someone into the same creature, and you wonder how a fridge can hold food?"

"Touché," he says with an approving nod of his head.

"All right, now watch this," I say, taking a deep breath and then letting it out. I clap my hands together and rub them in a circular motion. A thin, yellow sand-like dust of magic spills from my hands and onto the bench and sparks and fill the room with white light. When the light disappears, the food that I placed on the bench has been rearranged onto plates and magically cooked.

My audience claps, except for Lexi, of course. I smile as they take a plate of food each and begin to eat.

After breakfast, I use magic again to wash the dishes.

"So, what have you got planned for today?" Tyler asks as I finish my spell.

"I was thinking that I could show you the town," I smile, kissing his cheek.

"Sounds good to me," he says and I lead Tyler back to my room to find that it has been cleaned.

On my pillow lies a small white note that reads:
Have a good day. -E

"Who is 'E'?" Tyler asks. My heart jumps as I grab his hand and use a locator spell. We race down the halls and I find the one I seek.

"Ellen!" I call as she comes into sight. She turns around and Tyler freezes mid-step as he sees her face.

"Mum?" he questions, I can hear his heart racing.

"What are you doing here?" he asks, his face pales. "Are you a ghost?"

"No," she smiles, stepping forward and reaching out to touch his face. Tyler growls deeply and takes a step back. Ellen pulls her hand away and says, "I'm a werewolf."

"Why didn't you come back?" he asks and Ellen gives a sad smile. "Why did you abandon us, abandon me? You should have come back. If you'd have come back-"

"You wouldn't have met *her*," she says, inclining her head towards me. She does have a point and my heart skips a beat. He wouldn't have been a hunter, and he probably would never have met me. Tyler looks at me and I avoid his eyes.

"I cannot forgive you for this," he says, turning his back and walking away with my hand still in his, taking me with him. When we get back to my room, I head into the bathroom and take a shower. As the hot water hits my back I think of what might have happened if Tyler's mother did go back after being turned. I hardly notice Tyler step into the bathroom and then into the shower with me.

"Rose?" he asks, placing a hand on my back, pulling me out of my thoughts.

"If you could take it all back," I ask as he steps under the water with me. "Would you? Would you change your mother's turning, becoming a hunter, meeting-" the words catch in my throat. "Me, becoming a werewolf, all of it. Would you take it back if you could?"

"Where did that come from?" he asks as water drips down his face.

"Would you?" I ask again and he sighs.

"No," he says confidently and my heart races. "Not for the world. If I hadn't met you, other things would have happened. I would probably be dead."

He takes my chin and tilts it towards him. I let out a shaky breath and he tenderly kisses my lips. I run my hands through his wet hair and press myself closer to him as he wraps his arms around my waist. After our shower Tyler and I change into clothes and head into town. Whilst shopping, we run into a very nervous looking Cleo.

"Hey," I say, catching her attention and walking up to her. "How are you doing?"

"Good," she says, quickly. "Just surrounded by paranormals and questioning my sanity."

"I can take it all away," I say, looking over my shoulder to Tyler. "I can make you forget about paranormals, if you want."

"No," Cleo breathes, shaking her head. "I don't want to forget."

"How are the others?" I ask. "I didn't see them at the party."

"Sam and Samantha have skipped town," she says. "And Caleb has…. passed on. He was grabbed by the hunters."

My heart stops beating and my hands go to my mouth and tears fill my eyes.

"It's funny," she laughs harshly. "After the bastards killed him, they took his parents to the morgue and showed them his body, letting them think that everything was okay. I was there at his wake. I knew what happened but I couldn't speak out. I was afraid they would send me to the loony bin… or kill me. They dressed as police officers and even said that it was an accident when really they were the ones who… who murdered him."

Cleo looks at me with wide eyes and then steps back, her face paling as if she has seen a ghost.

"What's wrong?" I ask and she shakes her head and swallows nervously.

"Are you the thorn?" she asks, her hands shake.

"What?" I ask, confused. "What does that mean?"

"There was a mass murder in Mercy Lake and—"

"She didn't do it," Tyler says, glaring at Cleo as he stands behind me. "She was framed. Zero and I believe it might have been Xavier."

"Xavier," I gape, and remember seeing him at the party last night. He seemed so scared of something. I told myself that I would look into it today. I completely forgot. I run out of the shop and then back to the mansion. I take a deep breath and follow my nose to Xavier.

I walk into the gym where Xavier sits in the middle of a pentagram.

"What the hell?" Xavier exclaims, standing up from where he was sitting. "Rose? What are you doing?"

"What are *you* doing?" I ask, stepping forward. "Last I saw you, you were trying to kill me and last night you were hugging me. What was that all about?"

"It was our mother's doing," he says as a visible shiver runs down his spine. "She's planning something. She used magic on me to make me do things I didn't want to do. Kill... kill innocents. She is conspiring with the hunters and the powers. Rose, they took hold of me, forced me to do their bidding. When I came down here their control vanished; my mind was clear and yet also cloudy. I knew I had to find you, to warn you. But David took me down here, told me that I need to clear my head by unlocking my powers."

"He can get a little pushy," I agree. "Why does out mother want me gone?"

I sit down on the floor away from Xavier, still keeping my guard up.

"Because apparently you are evil. You chose the light," he says, looking down at his hands. "She cannot control you. Maybe it is me who is evil. I have the blood of so many innocents on my hands, and no matter how I wash, it remains there."

"I have the blood of innocents on my hands, too," I say and he looks up at me with wide eyes. "But I chose the light. You can, too. You can be good. You can *do* good. Xavier, you are not a bad person simply because our mother made you to be."

"I don't want to be bad," he sighs, looking down at his hands again. "But I chose the darkness. How can I be good if I am darkness?"

"The darkness is not always bad," I contradict. "Darkness can be good, it provides balance. The sun needs the moon, the earth needs the sky, sound needs the silence, the light needs the dark, pray needs predator, and good needs evil, otherwise there would be no balance; things would fall out of hand."

"How does the prey need the predator?" he asks, arching an eyebrow.

"If there were no predators, then the prey would flourish and destroy the earth," I explain.

"They would eat the grass to nothing. The earth would shift out of balance, everything would die."

Xavier smiles at me, but when he talks I cannot hear the words. White noise fills my head as I stand to my feet.

"I... I have to go," I say, my head spins as sweat beads on my upper lip. I try to walk out of the gym, but my knees buckle and I fall. My head hits hard and my vision blurs. My body becomes numb as I stare at Xavier. He shouts at me, but I cannot hear him.

I feel something trickle down my forehead and then red blood falls into my eyes. Pain rockets through me, forcing my numbness away. I feel my back arch and I lose control over my body.

I hear a deep growl rumble through my chest and fear rises through me. I press my forehead to the floor and pain shoots through me. I scream out and my vision blurs once more.

16. Sight of a Wolf

-Zero-

Lilly and I walk through the mansion with Lexi.

"This is boring," Lexi pouts.

"You started following us," I sigh. "We didn't say you had to come with us."

Lexi glares at me and opens her mouth to speak, but a scream cuts her off and I turn around, my werewolf senses heightening. The scream echoes through the hall and I turn to Lilly whose eyes are wide in fear.

"Lilly," I say as she begins to mystify. "Go get David. I think it's Rose."

Lilly disappears and I turn into my werewolf form and Lexi gapes and steps back as I begin navigating through the halls, trying to find Rose. My ears perk as I hear the sound of nails scratching against the floor. I whistle through my nose and then run through the halls and down the stairs. I growl deeply as I hear someone calling for help. I hear Rose scream again and my hackles rise. I break down a door and charge into the room where the noise is coming from.

"I swear, I didn't do it," Xavier says, holding his hands up.

I find Rose crouched on the ground in front of me. She's bleeding from her head and claws at her shoulder, digging into her origin scar. I flatten my ears as my tail tucks between my legs. I take a step forward and lower my head. Rose has her head down with her forehead to the floor and her back arched, her arms are crossed against her chest and she holds herself as she screams. I whine and step closer. Rose stops screaming and angles her head towards me. I cannot see her face, but by the way she shakes, I can tell she is crying.

"What's happening?" Lexi whispers, entering the room and standing by my side. I do not answer her, keeping my eyes on Rose.

David and Lilly walk in behind me and stand next to Lexi, gaping at the sight of Rose. More people rush into the room, attracted by the scent of Rose's blood. Rose becomes aware of the amount of people in the room and growls deeply from her chest. David takes a step forward and Rose pushes her head down to the floor. My armour appears on my body and Rose pulls me into her control. Against my will, I step towards Rose and stand between her and the others. David holds his hands up to me and I pull my lips back and growl. Rose echoes my growl, and it turns my blood cold. Her growl sounds so animalistic, one that a human should not be able to make.

I hear Rose's bones popping and breaking as she arches her back. I look back at her as she lifts her head and screams, covering her eyes with her hands, and then pulling her hands down her face, smearing blood over her skin. She drags her hands down and away from her eyes and blood stains her face. Xavier starts shouting at me to help Rose and I look at him and growl deeply, warning him to stop talking. I take a step back and turn to Rose. She sighs and holds the back of her hands to her eyes.

"It's too bright," she rasps, power pulses through the room and the lights explode overhead. I leap forward and protect Rose from the falling glass. When the room settles I step back and then nudge her hands with my nose. Rose stares at me with yellow eyes, then her pupils dilate and her irises expand through her sclera. She stares at me with wolf eyes. I whistle through my nose and she reaches out and touches my head.

A sickening crack echoes through the room as Rose closes her eyes again and screams loudly. Her body pulls away from mine and she transforms.

-Rose-

My eyes feel like they are burning in my skull. I cannot see a thing. I can sense Zero standing in front of me, but beyond him I feel nothing. I cannot see his face and everything becomes murky and the pain is unbearable. I growl deeply as colours burst through my vision. Blue; everything is covered in blue. I blink rapidly and scrape my head along the floor of the gym. I can hear their hearts beating loudly and I can smell their fear.

It's too bright, I think as I rub my paws over my eyes. The colours swirl around me as my vision becomes clearer. I look to Zero, and he whines and flattens his ears. He is afraid. Is he afraid of me?

I have to get out. I think as I look for a way out. My ears flatten, my hackles rise, and my tail tucks between my legs. My heart races. I feel caged, trapped with the walls closing in on me. I growl loudly. I have to get out and into the woods. The door is closed and people stand in the way. I look over to the large windows, and without a second thought, I run to them. I jump through the glass, shattering it with my body. I can hear people calling my name, I ignore them and run faster. I run through the town and into the woods. I breathe deeply as I run; my lungs ache as I push myself to go faster, to run further. I run to the thickest part of the woods. I push myself. I need to go further than that, but mid-run I morph into a human and land back first into the dirt. I gasp for air as my lungs try to catch up.

A buzzing noise fills my head, it sounds like a million bees swarm in my head. Pain races through my back as I sit up. I suck in a deep breath and look over my shoulder. A stick sticks out of my back, right below my left rib cage. I take deep, slow breaths as I reach back and pull it out. My blood stains the ground as I feel my back bleed; it's not healing as it should. I close my eyes and scream out as the pain amplifies. My body begins to spasm again, I fall forward onto my knees and bite down on my tongue the metallic taste of blood fills my mouth. I grit my teeth together and fall onto my hands as I spit the blood out of my mouth.

My whole body feels as if it is burning. I dig my hands into the dirt as the buzzing bees in my head become louder. My elbows buckle and I fall. I lie on my stomach and press my face to the cold dirt and lie as still as I can.

I perk my head up as I hear people looking for me, I hear their footsteps— one set of feet are especially close. I turn my head as a black werewolf steps into the clearing, on its tail is a white tip.

"Of course, you found me," I groan. The wolf sits and perks its ears towards me. Colour swirls around the wolf: reds and pinks and blue. So much blue.

"I will always find you," Tyler says softly. *"Let's go back."*

Tyler takes a step towards me and I cringe as a spike of pain hits me. I lay my head back in the dirt and close my eyes. Tyler crouches to the dirt and blue, so much blue, swirls around him. Tyler crawls towards me and presses his nose to my cheek.

Something rises in my stomach; a bad feeling. Something bad is approaching, and although it hurts, I turn into a wolf and growl. I could hear sticks snapping beneath heavy feet.

"Tyler!" Lexi calls and I deepen my growl, warning for her to turn back. She does not seem to hear my warning as she steps into the clearing, and more colours cloud my vision. Red, so much red. Red and black and red and black...

I snarl and open my mouth as she stares at me. I see the corner of her eye twitch and then pain rockets through me. I yelp and fall to the dirt in my human form.

"Is she okay?" Lexi asks, the red around her swirling thickly.

"Does it look like it?" I groan, rolling over and away from Tyler. Thick red blood spills from my mouth as my stomach heaves. I hold myself up on my hands and knees as my stomach heaves again and bile rises through my throat and then out of my mouth. Tyler shifts to his human form and kneels besides me, holding my hair away from my face. My stomach contents empty on the floor and I begin to dry retch. At this point in time, I probably look disgusting. My face is crusted with dried blood, my eyes probably blood shot, dirt sticks to my body, and sweat drips down my back. Tyler gently rubs my back, but I push him off and stand on wobbly legs.

"Are you sure you should be standing up?" she asks, I growl deeply at her. Her voice infuriates me. She speaks to me as if I were just a dumb child.

Using super speed I run off, retreating further off into the woods.

As I run everything moves in a blur. I don't see the tree until it's too late. I try to veer away from it, but my shoulder slams into the trunk and I hear a loud crack. I'm spun around and land on my back again. I wince in pain as my head spins. I hear the huff of a wolf and I look up to see a grey wolf walk towards me.

"David?" I ask, he looks at me as I feel my nose start to bleed.

"*I am taking you back to the mansion right now,*" he says in a forceful way as he crouches in front of me. "*Now, get on my back.*"

David is covered with a multitude of strong colours. I climb up onto David's back and he stands as Tyler and Lexi emerge together. Their colours mix together. The colours are too bright, and I look away and press my face to David's fur.

"*Go and get the others,*" David orders, growling at Tyler. "*Tell them I have Rose and am taking her back to the mansion.*"

I hear Tyler turn and bound away.

"*Hold on,*" David says, as he starts to move. I hold onto his fur and listen to his heart as he runs through the woods. We reach the mansion in a manner of minutes.

I climb off of David's back at the door of the mansion and stand on shaking legs as he changes back into a man. He catches me before I fall and then carries me to my room. He lies me down on my bed as Tyler walks in.

"Am I dying?" I ask weakly. My voice cracks as tears line my eyes and break through some of the crusted blood. Tyler rushes to the bathroom and then returns with a wet face wash.

"No," Tyler reassures me as David leans against the door frame, watching me as Tyler wipes the blood from my face.

"Ty, I don't want to die," I say as tears escape me. Tyler turns on the lamp on the night stand and I wince at its light.

"Listen to me," he says as he stops wiping. "You are not going to die. This is the first time this has happened, isn't it?"

I shake my head and place my hand on his temple. I find the block in memories that David has placed in Tyler's mind and I tear it down. Tyler's eyes go wide as all of his memories come back and the colours around him begin to change rapidly. My eyes burn and I wince at the brightness in the room. Power surges through me and it shatters the light on the table.

"Rose?" Tyler asks, snapping out of his trance. "What was that for?"

I groan and begin to shiver. Tyler ignores what just happened and continues to wipe my face.

-Zero-

Everyone approaches Roses room at the same time. David is leaning on the doorframe and when he sees us, he scowls and shakes his head.

"She needs some space," David says.

"We need to know what happened." Lilly scowls, crossing her arms over her chest. "She's my sister."

"We have a right to know," I say and David looks at me.

"You two only," Zero says, gesturing for Lilly and I to enter. Rose looks over to us for a moment before rolling away and covering her eyes.

"Rose?" Lilly asks, knelling next to Rose and gently placing her hand on Rose's back. "What's wrong?"

"It's too bright," she groans. "Too many colours."

"I don't understand," Tyler says. "I don't know what's wrong."

"You guys are idiots," Lexi says from the doorway. "Come on, Tyler, you have to remember what this is. We were in hunting one-o-one together and they covered this," she says but Tyler stares blankly at her. "Wolf's Sight."

Tyler's eyes widen and then he looks at Rose.

"She has all the tell-tale signs," Lexi shrugs and I raise an eyebrow. "Her wolf eyes are able to be seen in her human form. It takes a lot of pain and shifting for her to be able to receive this, three times maybe? She is now able to see human emotions, their auras."

"She has had seizures three times now," I comment. David took my memory block away when we went looking for Rose.

"That sounds about right," Lexi agrees. "Once a year, the body will try to unlock the sight, causing the body to have fits and seizures. On the last change, the wolf eyes will appear present. And he or she will be able to control them when they reappear, and, apparently with enough power, the werewolf can see the auras without his or her werewolf eyes. It is like when a dog or any other animal senses fear, except she can see the colour of the emotions. Paranormal hunters fear the wolf sight because a paranormal hunter is rumoured to have a black outline. It's like when animals know if something else is a threat or a danger to them and the animal would either fight or run. We're not sure what causes the sight. All we know is it's a dead giveaway to a hunter."

Rose growls and so do I. We both notice how she says 'we' a lot.

"Why the hell does she keep growling at me?" Lexi asks.

"Obviously, she doesn't like you," I say, tensing. "Neither do I."

"Settle down everyone," David says and I relax, but Rose still growls defiantly as Lexi gazes at Tyler.

"Rose, I could find you an emotion colour chart if you think that would help," David says as a cat comes in through the balcony. "But you need to rest."

"And shower" Lexi mumbles, thinking no one heard her, but I heard her. I growl as she walks past me, then walk out with Lilly behind me.

"What?" Rose screams. In a blur, she pushes past me and forces Lexi into a wall, her eyes glow bright yellow. They are her normal eyes.

"You will stay away from Tyler from now on!" she shouts as her teeth sharpen to wolf fangs. "Do you hear me? Stay away from him or I will rip your throat out and feed it to you!" I take control of the situation and peel Rose off of Lexi, who whimpers and collapses to the floor gasping for air.

"What the hell was that?" I ask, turning Rose around so she looks at me.

"She kissed Tyler," she growls her wolf fangs looking deadly and snapping in Lexi's direction. "She kissed Tyler while I was in the woods dying!"

I let Rose go and she stalks back to her room where she slams the door.

"Well, that was stupid of you," Lilly says appearing with her hands behind her head. "I have the 'cool' temper genes, Rose does not."

"Figured," Lexi says, standing and stalking away.

-Rose-

After my *friendly* encounter with Lexi, I storm back into my room and slam the door. If that bitch thinks she can get away with kissing Tyler, she is sadly mistaken. I take a long, hot shower to relax my muscles, and then change into a tank top and short pink pyjama shorts. When I go back into the room, Tyler's sitting on the edge of the bed, hanging his head and looking guilty.

"What's wrong?" I ask and he looks up.

"She kissed me," he says with disgust.

"As long as you didn't kiss her back," I shrug, wincing in pain. Tyler stands quickly, steadying me.

"I'm fine," I argue, but he still makes me sit on the bed. I pull him down with me and crush my lips to his. He crawls on top of me and I smile against his lips. I pull his shirt over his head and he grabs mine in his fist. But the mood changes as I gasp in pain and he quickly pulls back.

"Let's put this on pause," he says, his breath hot and heavy. "You need to rest. You do," he says, cutting off my protests, and gets off the bed and picks up his shirt on the way out the door.

"No, stay," I beg, sitting up. Tyler looks back at me.

"I can't," he says with a smile as he comes over and kisses my forehead. "We'll get... distracted."

"If I promise to be a good girl, will you stay?" I ask with a smile. Tyler drops his shirt on the floor and I move over as he crawls under the covers with me.

"No sex," he says sternly. "You have to-"

"Rest," I sigh and he laughs. "Yeah, yeah, I know."

I snuggle up to Tyler's warm body and rest my head on his chest as he puts an arm around me. His heart beat lulls me to sleep and I close my eyes and move in even closer.

When I wake, I'm still in Tyler's arms. I look at his face and he so peaceful. I look at the area around his body and my eyes change to the werewolf eyes that allow me to see his aura. His colours are bright and they swirl as if they are dancing. The aura fades as my eyes return to normal, I stare at Tyler as the moon shines through my balcony and highlights his face.

I move closer to Tyler and a smile spreads across his face.

"I'm not sleeping," Tyler says, opening his eyes. Blood rushes to my face as I smile. "Are you feeling better?" he asks and I nod. Tyler puts his hand my cheek and then tucks a stay piece of hair behind my ear. Tyler pulls me close and presses his lips to mine and places his hand on my lower back.

"Please restrain yourselves," David says, appearing in a puff of blue smoke. Tyler and I growl at the same time and pull away from each other.

"Ever heard of a door or knocking?" Tyler asks, sitting up.

"Xavier has requested to see you," David says, ignoring him.

"Can't it wait untill morning?" I ask, sitting up next to Tyler.

"No, it can't," David says in his serious voice. I groan in protest, but slowly climb over Tyler to get out of bed. I grab his hand and pull him with me. As I walk past David, he puts a hand on Tyler's chest and growls deeply.

"Alone," David says. I scowl and take his arm from Tyler's chest.

"I don't care what he wants," I say, forcefully. "Tyler is coming with me."

David glares at me but says nothing as I exit the room with Tyler's hand in mine.

"Remind me never to get on your bad side," Tyler laughs once we are in the hall. I laugh and we make our way to the gym. When I open the door, Xavier stands up.

"I said alone," Xavier says, and I roll my eyes.

"I don't care what you want," I say, shrugging my shoulders. "I have had a really bad day and I am not in the mood for doing what people tell me to do. Now, what do you want?"

"Something to do," Xavier suggests as Smoky comes out from behind a shelf and meows at me. "Rose, I'm bored. There is nothing in here except this cat."

"He kept me plenty of company when I was locked in my pentagram," I smile, kneeling down to scratch Smoky behind his ear and Xavier groans. "Look, unless you want to be vulnerable to mother's magic again, I suggest that you suck it up and concentrate."

"Fine," Xavier mumbles, sitting back down and closing his eyes. I smack my lips together and Tyler and I vanish in a cloud of smoke. We reappear outside in the garden where he and I walk around hand in hand.

"Would you like to have dinner with me?" Tyler asks.

"It seems a bit late for dinner," I say, frowning. Tyler sighs and bumps his shoulder against mine.

"Tomorrow night," he says, and I stop walking and stare at him with wide eyes.

"Are you asking me on a date?" I ask, and Tyler smiles and nods his head. Blood rushes to my cheeks as I fumble for words. "Wow, I can't even remember the last time I went on a date."

"Let me handle it." Tyler smiles, as we continue our walk through the   gardens.

The next morning, Tyler and I wake up to the sound of laughter and the smell of pancakes. I look at him and he looks at me, and in a flash he and I are out of bed and racing to the kitchen. Cleo, David, Jace, and Zero are watching Christian try to flip pancakes.

"Good morning," David says with a relaxed smile. "I found the charts."

David smiles at me and something stirs inside of me. His eyes shine as he smiles, and I tear my eyes away and focus on the other people around me.

"What the hell is going on in here?" Lexi asks, storming into the kitchen. "Some people are trying to sleep here."

"Well, too bad that we don't care," Jace says and I laugh.

"Easy for you to say," Lexi glowers. "You don't need sleep. You're dead."

A thick silence fills the room until it's filed with a deep and angry growl, and it wasn't from me. If looks could kill, Lexi would be vaporised in a second by Jace as his teeth sharpen to a point; his fangs gleam in the light as he flashes them at Lexi.

"Wow, tough crowd," Lexi laughs.

"Why are you even alive?" I ask, narrowing my eyes on her.

"Because Tyty fought for me to stay alive," Lexi says with a wink towards Tyler. I growl deep in my chest as a mist forms around Lexi. Lilly suddenly appears and restrains Lexi, giving me a clear shot to her heart.

"Do it, Rose," Lilly says. I take a step forward, my magic sizzling under my skin.

"Rose," Tyler whispers. I turn around and look into his eyes; they are full of fear. I look back to Lexi and she smiles smugly.

"Forget," I say in Spanish, and watch as Lexi's eyes widen. *"Return."* Lexi vanishes from Lilly's arms, back to earth and out of Paradise.

"Where did she go?" Lilly asks, looking around.

"Back to Mercy Lake," I say, turning around and walking off. Anger surges through my chest. The look in Tyler's eyes were so fearful of me. He didn't want me to kill her. He still feels for her. I go back to my room and lie down on my bed, not sure on how to feel about Tyler's reaction.

I stay in my room all day, calming myself down. As the sun sets, there is a knock on my door. I take a deep breath and open it to find Tyler standing on the other side with a wide smile, holding a bouquet of red roses.

"Time for our date," he says. My cheeks flush as he hands me the roses. I place them into a glass vase.

"I'm not even dressed yet," I blush, going into the wardrobe.

"Nothing fancy," he says and I look at him and smile. He is wearing denim jeans with a black shirt and a long leather coat. I smile and step into the walk-in-wardrobe and close the doors behind me. I look around and smile. A few minutes later, I emerge wearing black jeans, a red tank top, and a pair of red high heels.

"Wow," Tyler says as I step forward.

"I'm your red riding hood," I say, spinning around before stepping into Tyler's arms and pressing my lips to his.

"What does that make me?" Tyler asks, taking my hand.

"My wolf," I kiss him again. A cloud forms around us, and when it disappears we stand in David's barn.

"So?" I ask as he and I start walking. "Where are we going?"

"Wait and see," he answers with a smile. He takes me to the beach where a blanket, candles, and a picnic basket is set out.

"Is this for us?" I gape, putting a hand over my mouth to stop me from squealing.

"Of course, it is," Tyler smiles. I turn around and jump into Tyler's arms. He laughs as he places me down again. I take off my shoes and walk down to the picnic blanket.

"I had help from Cleo and the others," Tyler admits, smiling as I take his hands. I don't care who helped him. This is amazing. The sound of water crashing into the beach makes my skin prickle as Tyler and I take a seat on the picnic blanket and watch the sun sink in the sky and the stars start to shine. We are as close as ever; his arms around me and my body presses to his.

I lie down next to him and we stare up, looking at the stars that shine above us. Tyler looks around nervously and my heartbeat races.

"What are you doing?" I ask, and Tyler looks back to me and smiles. "Are you looking for someone?"

"No," he smiles, kissing my cheek. "I've missed you so much."

"I've missed you, too," I say, then become silent.

"What's wrong?" Tyler asks, and I let out a shaky breath as I tell him everything that has happened since I left; how many I've killed, what I have been training, what I know, and that I am infertile.

"Do you think I care about any of that?" he says, tucking a piece of hair behind my ear as he kisses my forehead. "I've killed innocents; werewolves and people alike. I don't care about what you've done. I care about you."

His words send a shiver down my spine. I stand to my feet and Tyler raises an eyebrow at me.

"Where are you going?" he asks with a laugh as I pull him up with me.

"For a walk," I shrug, holding his hand and walking along the beach. A cold gust of wind blows and I shiver. Tyler immediately pulls off his jacket and helps me into it. I kiss him passionately and then we continue to walk. I make my wolf eyes appear and sneak a look at his aura. He's lit with a clear red, meaning passion, and it's tinted with light pink, meaning compassion and affection— I read the colour chart David gave me while I was in my room all day. Just as I am about to send my eyes away, a deep, muddied red catches my attention in the distance. The colour symbolises anger. The colour is highlighted, and I remember that hunters have this highlight. I stop walking and tense.

"What's wrong?" Tyler asks and I make my eyes vanish.

"Hunters," I whisper, but as the word leaves my mouth a gun fires and Tyler goes down. I scream in surprise and something hits me. I look down and see a tranquilizer dart in my shoulder. I pull it out and smell it and the scent burns my nose; Wolfsbane, which is now coursing through my body. A spasm occurs in my arm, but that's it. I look around as my fangs lengthen and sharpen. I see hunters step into the clearing all heavily armed with guns and stakes. I step in front of Tyler's unconscious body and growl. A hunter fires his gun and a tranquiliser hits me in the shoulder.

"Can't I have a normal date with my boyfriend without getting bombarded by you guys?" I groan, pulling out the tranquiliser and throw it at the hunter's feet, the hunters fire at the same time, and I dodge their tranquilisers and attack. I grab one and pull his arms behind him;

he drops his gun. I bite into his shoulder, making blood sputter into the sand and then I break his neck and let him slump into the sand. My eyes glow bright and I snarl, showing my deadly fangs.

"Scary," a huntress says, moving forward. It's Tyler's step-sister. I growl and she pulls out a gun and fires.

"That doesn't affect me much," I growl, pulling out the dart and she fires again. It's a different dart. This one is filled with Spotted Alder Roots. I fall to my knees and my hands shake. I look down to my hands and see my veins appear closer the surface. I take a deep breath as my lungs ache before I collapse into the sand. The last thing I see is Tyler's sister walking up to me and smiling. And then there was nothing, just darkness.

17. Mercy Lake

-Zero-

Rose and Tyler have yet come back from their date. It's the morning after.

"Don't worry," Christian says, coming into the kitchen with a smile and a wink. "They are probably at a hotel or something."

I try to take in what he says, but something is buzzing between the connection that Rose and I have thanks to the tagging, I have an irritating feeling in the middle of my back between my shoulders as well as a sting in the crook of my arm. Something is definitely wrong.

-Rose-

I wake with a stinging in the middle of my back between my shoulders. Something is dripping on them. I try to sit up but I am pulled down. There is a silver collar around my neck and it's hooked to a short chain. My ankles are held down with a similar thing. My skin hisses and blisters at the touch of the silver. I cannot stand; I can't even lift my head. I groan and strain to look at where I am. It's like a small tin garden shed with a hard concrete floor. The stinging on my back is caused by a large ice block suspended above me, the ice is made of boiled wolfsbane and Spotted Alder Roots. The heat of the shed is making the ice slowly melt and drip onto my back, burning a hole through Tyler's coat. I sigh and lie my cheek on the floor, wincing at every drop that lands on my back. The shed door opens and Tyler's step-sister comes in.

"My name is Elisa," she says and I growl. "But people call me El. Then again, you aren't a person, are you?"

"Well, that's racist," I laugh, straining against my chains. "What do you want, El?"

"The cure, of course," she says and I look at her with a raised eyebrow.

"What cure?" I ask and she glares at me, all laughter gone.

"The cure for lycanthropy. It is rumoured that werewitch blood cures it, your blood," she says as she begins to pace. "However, we tried it and it didn't work."

"Guess you got played," I laugh and she pulls out her gun and shoots my body with normal bullets. I groan and glare at her as my body expels them slowly.

"Tell me the cure!" she shouts and I cough.

"Why should I?" I snarl, glaring at her. "You have killed countless of my friends and family. I am not going to help you. Not now, not ever!"

"Tell me!" El screams, emptying a mag into my body, then changing the clip. "This one is a mix of silver and bronze bullets."

"Dance around the subject chanting Merry Christmas in Latin and then feed it my blood." I sigh, lying my head on the floor.

"Why Merry Christmas?"

"Christmas is when the original werewolf was made," I lie and she leaves, slamming and locking the door. I smile, knowing that if I was to tell the hunters that if there is no cure they will kill me on the spot. I sigh as another drop of the death cube hits my back. I need time to plan an escape alive.

I hear a scream in frustration and a smile spreads over my face as the door unlocks and opens.

"You little liar!" El screams.

"You really think I'm going to tell you?" I smile, resting my cheek on the floor.

El screams again. She pulls out a knife and stabs it into my shoulder. Blood trickles down my arm as I grind my teeth against the pain. El pulls the knife out and stabs the centre of my hand. I scream and she smiles.

"Are you going to tell me the cure?" she asks as a tear escapes me.

"Why do you want it?" I ask. There must be a reason that she wants a cure.

"My mother committed suicide after you killed my step father!" she yells, kicking my face.

"You put a spell on Tyler. He would never ever want to give up hunting. If I can change him back, he will be able to hunt with me again, and I wouldn't be so alone."

"Your dear father was a psychotic vampire," I laugh as El removes the knife from my hand.

"You have no idea what you're talking about," El hisses, standing on my bleeding hand. "My father would never stoop so low."

"Well, he did have his fangs in my neck," I growl as she adds more pressure to my hand. "And he didn't kill me when he put a stake in my heart."

"Watch your tongue," El hisses, kneeling next to me. "Or I will cut it out."

"Yeah?" I smile, looking into her eyes. "I can heal from that. But the question is, how will you heal when I rip your heart out of your chest?"

El scowls and then stands to her feet before stalking out of the room. As the door slams and the locks slide into place, I watch the wound on my hand heal. I can feel my energy draining. Soon I will slip into exhaustion. I have to distract El, get her angry so that she makes a mistake. One mistake is all I need, it's all I need to escape and free Tyler. The thought of him makes my heart race. What if he'ss being treated the same way I am?

-Zero-

The day passes and still no sign of Rose or Tyler. David paces in the kitchen and I watch him, confused by his concern.

"Where is she?" David asks, growling softly as he paces.

"I don't know," I say as Christian comes into the kitchen.

"She still hasn't come back?" he asks and I shake my head. "Something is defiantly wrong. Tyler said that they would come back."

"We will raise the alarm," David says, ceasing his pacing and walking out of the kitchen. Both Christian and I follow. "I shall alert every paranormal across the globe. I'll tell them that Rose is missing. But we'll need to start somewhere. I'll send teams out to Mercy Lake."

David turns to me. "Comb through Mercy Lake, leave no stone unturned," he says. I nod my head and he assigns me a team, consisting of Jace and Cleo as well as a few others from Rose's circle.
David sends us to Mercy Lake using his magic. The first place I search is Rose's burnt down house, hoping to pick up a fresh scent.

"Why do we have a human tagging along?" Jace asks as we reach the house. "She is going to slow us down."

"She is one of Rose's best friends," I say, taking a deep breath. "She knows more about Rose than any of us. She won't slow us down, I'll watch over her."

"Fine," Jace grumbles as I morph into my werewolf form and begin

to sniff around. I cannot find a new scent, but I leave no rock unturned. I look at the basement where her mother was kept. We open the door and again there is nothing.

After her house, we go to Aamon's house in case Tyler took her there, but again nothing.

"Where did they go for their date?" I ask, coming out of Tyler's room.

"I don't know," Cleo says, her voice draped in fear. "But Tyler did mention something about a beach."

"We will look there," I say, turning wolf and laying down so Cleo can get on. Jace, Christian, and I run at full speed and reach the beach in no time. Lilly is there with her party of searchers.

"Good," Lilly says as we step onto the beach. She comes over and takes me by the scruff of the neck. "We have found the blanket where they started, but my party doesn't have a werewolf. So, take a good whiff, dog boy."

I shake out of her hold and sniff at the blanket. It's soaking wet from when the water came up and washed the beach. However, there is one corner that is not yet wet. I sniff that, taking in every smell. I find Tyler's scent and follow it down the beach.

Then I reach a point where they stopped for some reason. Tyler fell— his scent covers the sand in a larger area. I take another deep smell and soon more scents flood through my nose. Rose and Tyler were surrounded. As I walk around nervously with my nose pressed close to the sand, I stand on something sharp. I growl and lay down. Cleo gets off of my back and I change back into a human and pull what I assume to be a needle from my hand, but it isn't a needle. Upon closer inspection I realise that it's a tranquiliser dart.

I pull the cap off of the dart and hold the tube close to my nose, hoping to smell what type of tranquilizer was in the vile. I take a deep breath and immediately pull back as my nose hair tingles. Wolfsbane. Cleo finds another tranquilizer vile and I sniff it. This one was filled with Spotted Alder Roots.

"Tyler and Rose were walking," I say, laying out the scene by pointing out exactly where everyone stood. "Tyler got hit first and went down. Rose might have been hit, too, but it didn't have an effect on her. She killed someone," I say, pointing to blood higher up on the beach.

"How do you know it isn't hers?" Lilly asks, her form wavering between corporal and spiritual state.

"Because it doesn't smell like her," I say, continuing to lay out the scene. "A hunter shot her after that with Wolfsbane, and then Spotted Alder."

"Where did they go after that?" Jace asks and I shrug.

"I don't know," I say, looking around. "They just vanished. No sign of where they went."

The phone David gave to me before we left buzzes and then chimes.

"David says that a very important book has vanished from Paradise," I say, reading the text.

"What book?" Lilly asks with a raised eyebrow.

"I don't know," I say re-reading the text. "It just says that it is an important book and to keep an eye out for it."

-Rose-

The shed door opens with a loud creak and I look up to see El step in.

"You have given me too many wrong answers," she says, and I notice a book in her hand. Not just any book, but The Book. The book David gave me on paranormal.

"Where did you get that," I growl and she laughs.

"This?" she says, holding it up. "I had a spy go into Paradise and retrieve it. Maybe it has the cure in here."

She goes to open the book and I have to think quickly.

"Ignite!" I shout, using as much power as I can, the book begins to smoke in her hands. El gasps and throws the book to the floor and it bursts into flame. El calls for help, but before she can even think to put the fire out, the book turns to ash. I don't know what she would or would not have found in that book. I never had the chance to read it all. But I know that if she distributed every paranormal secret among the hunters, they would stop fearing us. Their fear is the only thing keeping the balance between us even.

Two big men step into the shed. They look to El as she stares at the ash, which vanishes into thin air.

"Tie her up!" El screams and the men advance towards me. They unchain me and stand me up. My mind races as they handcuff my hands together with silver. El watches as the men drag me backwards and hoist me up and hook me to the ceiling. I listen to my skin sizzle from the silver. I grind my teeth together as El stands in front of me, her face red with rage.

"You have ruined everything!" she yells, punching me in the

stomach. "I could have healed Tyler by now, and you ruined it!"

She pulls out a knife and thrusts it into my shoulder. I scream out in pain and she smiles as she drags the knife downwards, leaving a gaping wound on my right shoulder down to the top of my breast. Blood pours out of the wound and tears fill my eyes as she removes the knife and walks out of the shed.

"Next time I see you, you'd better tell me the cure," she says, slamming the door behind her. I groan and look at the wound she left; it isn't healing as fast as it should. I sigh and hang my head. I am slowly slipping into exhaust state, so I think fast. I think of David's training. I move my hands as best I can as my eyes begin to glow. Lightning flashes from my finger tips and to the ground, etching into the concrete. I make my pentagram and then make my own blood flow into the etching. It dries quickly and I make the lightning retract back into my fingers and watch my wounds heal faster, but as the lightning retracts, it hits one of the cuffs and it opens. I gasp as I am left hanging by my right hand. My arm stretches and it feels like I am being torn apart. I try not to scream as I use lightning to break the other lock, and my body falls to the ground. I hold in a scream, but the hunters hear my body hit the ground and, in a matter of seconds, El and her two meatheads bust through the door with stakes at the ready. I growl and pounce, needing to move fast.

I think of my training as I attack one of the hunters. I scratch his shoulder, then crawl up onto his back and tear out his throat with my teeth, blood sprays from his throat and covers the floor as he makes a choking sound and collapses. I growl and my bloody red teeth sharpen as my eyes light up so I can see their auras.

"The wolf sight," El gasps. Her aura is muddied blue with bright tints of muddied red, and, of course, is highlighted in a thick inky black. She is scared and angry. Angry people are easier to kill.

I rush towards her and watch as her eyes widen and her colours dance. Before I can reach her, something attaches itself to my back. Electricity flows through me, locking all of my muscles down. I look over to El's other guard and growl as he turns a dial and the pain is amplified. I scream and press my body to the floor as El handcuffs me and then injects me with a mixture of wolfsbane and Spotted Alder Roots.

When I wake, the first thing I feel is pain. My instincts scream at me to run, to get out. I am in a deep, free standing bathtub filled with boiling water mixed with wolfsbane and Spotted Alder Roots. I scream and thrash around, trying to escape from this burning death. El stands over me with a twisted smile on her face as I realise I am held down with my hands chained to the side of the tub. I growl and try to keep my head and face out of the water.

"Why don't you understand that I am trying to help you?" El asks. I let out a small whimper as tears run down my face, the salt burning my cheeks. "All you need to do is give me the cure and all of this will end."

"Go to hell!" I scream, continuing to thrash and struggle. El pulls out a silver stake and presses it to my throat. My heart races as I stop moving. My eyes dart around the room, looking for a way out. I take in my surroundings quickly. I'm in a white bathroom where everything is white and has a large mirror. As my eyes rest on the mirror, something moves and catches my attention. However, my attention is pulled back as El presses the stake harder to my blistering skin. I scream and try to move away, but she grabs a fistful of my hair and holds me up.

"What is the cure?" she asks. I keep my mouth closed. El sighs and then dunks my head under the water. I scream and bubbles erupt from my mouth. She hoists my blistering face up and then back under like I am a cookie. As she hoists me up once more white noise fills my ears. I try to look around, I try to see, but I can see nothing. My eyes have been burnt out. I am temporarily blind and deaf as well. Everything, including my own screams, is muffled by white noise. I wait for El to push me back under but she doesn't. Instead, there is a scorching pain on my wrists. The pain amplifies and I hear my heart beating loudly in my ears as I try to breathe through the pain.

El pushes me down once more, holding me down until everything becomes numb and I lose consciousness.

I wake up back on the cold, hard shed floor with my hands, feet, and neck tied down. My body burns and my head pounds. I squint as my eyes adjust to the darkness of the shed. I scape my ear along the concrete, but I can't even hear my chains rattling. I take deep breaths; my lungs and throat burn. Tears leak from my eyes. The salt in my tears sting the burns on my face, but the pain barely registers.

I want to go back, back before I was ever a werewolf, back to when I was just Rose. My future seemed so bright. I was going to graduate, go to college. I had plans to see the world, then settle down with a man to have children. My tears continue to fall from my eyes as my heart breaks. I know that no matter how far back I go, I will always end up the same. I was born this way, I was born a werewitch. I look to my wrist and frown, it has been branded. I look to my other wrist to find fading pink scars. I look back to the branding and stare at it, but it does not heal. Anger surges through me. El has branded me with a wolf head, a symbol I have seen on Tyler's stake.

The door to the shed opens and I growl as El steps in, smiling.

"Are you going to tell me the cure?" she asks and I glare at her. I keep my mouth shut and she sighs and snaps her fingers.

My eyes widen and my heart races as Tyler is dragged inside by two men.

"How about now?" She asks as a gun is pressed to Tyler's head and I panic. I can see the fear in Tyler's eyes. He looks like a trapped animal. My heart beats faster.

"There is no cure," I say. My fear makes my voice crack and shake. "There is no cure."

El looks at me and shakes her head in disappointment.

"That is not the answer I am looking for," she sighs.

"No," I gape, pulling against my bonds and ignoring the pain. "El, I swear to you, there is no cure."

"I don't believe you," she sighs, and looks to the man holding the gun to Tyler's head. She nods her head once and the man smiles.

"El, no!" I gape. My heart stops as my world is ripped apart. Time slows down as the man holding the gun pulls the trigger and Tyler is killed. I watch his eyes roll back in his head and they let him fall to the ground with a solid *thunk*.

I scream and thrash around desperately trying to break free so that I can rip these people apart. Before I can, a hunter puts a stake into my heart. My screams get caught in my throat and I gasp like a fish out of water. My limbs grow stiff and I watch as my skin turns grey and my veins appear closer to the surface. The movement creeps up my arm and finally to my face. The last thing I see is El with a scowl on her face. I feel my body grow cold as the last of my tears falls from my eyes.

My finger twitches, my heart begins to beat faster, kicking back to its normal speed. I open my eyes, but I can't see anything. I can hear everything, however. I can hear a van's wheels on the road and the heart beats of the people around me. I groan as I realise that I am not dead, but alive and still in the hunters possession.

"She is awake," I hear a hunter say and I stay still. "Radio the boss."

A hunter radios El telling her that I have awakened.

"*We are almost there,*" I hear her voice say through a radio. I let out a sigh as my body starts to heal the many wounds and cuts that I am not sure how I got. El and the other hunter converse again and I can't register what they are saying. My eyes begin to heal and there is movement in the van as a hunter comes forward and squirts something into my eyes. I scream out as the wolfsbane blinds me again. My teeth sharpen and I growl as I try to move, but I am chained

"Sit still," the hunter says in a rough voice. "Unless you want another dose."

I do as he says and sit quiet and still. I'm afraid of what they are going to do to me and where they are taking me.

A couple of minutes later, the car comes to a stop and a hunter takes my bounded hands and leads me out. I feel the presence of many more hunters when we step onto the grass and dirt.

"Did you know that a werewolf, or any of the paranormal species, cannot drown?" I hear El say, although it seems that she is not talking to me. "They just simply go to sleep and wake up whenever they are revived."

There is a struggle to my left as I feel El's presence in front of me. She touches my face and I flinch as she continues to talk.

"I will make you a deal," she says and I let out a shaky breath as two people begin to chain and tie weights to me. "If you can save her in twenty four hours I will let you have the two years of preparation. If not, you will only have the one year. If you fail to rescue her then I will have my witch complete the curse after two days. Deal?"

I was going to ask what she was talking about but something opens up underneath me and I fall down. Water hits my body and I am dragged under, down, down, down into the watery abyss. I scream and bubbles burst to the surface. I have weights around my waist and chains on my ankles, which leads to more weights. It's the same situation for my wrists. As I fall deeper down, pressure builds in my ears and my nose burns as water is inhaled, which cannot be good for my lungs. When I reach the bottom I am still conscious. Air begins to escape me. I long for it. My lungs burn as they try to take in oxygen, but all they get is water. I can hear my heart beating in my ears. Blood rushes to my brain and it causes my head to ache. Fear is consuming me as more of my precious air goes up in bubbles. The water is cold and that coldness is taking over my body. I hear my own heart start to slow down and I know the end isn't far. I close my eyes and let my last gasp of air escape my mouth in the form of tiny bubbles. And then I don't feel anything at all. My body is numb and my heart stops beating.

18. The Rescue

-Zero-

I search the woods, lifting my nose into the air to try to find Rose. My nose prickles and my eyes widen. I can smell Rose, and without a word to the others I take off running. My feet pound against the ground as I run against the wind.

And then her scent fades. I stop and lift my head high; my ears press against my head and I growl.

"Zero!" a wolf calls, bursting into the clearing. The wolf stares at me with wide eyes.

"Tyler?" I ask as the wolf steps closer.

"Help," he huffs. Fear rolls off of him. *"It's Rose."*

"What about her?" I ask, growling.

"Zero, what is going on?" Cleo asks, griping my fur. I ignore her as Tyler whines and takes off again. I follow him, running behind him with Jace beside me. Cleo's hands grip my fur harder as I pick up the pace.

Tyler finally stops at the edge of Mercy Lake. He stands in his human form, looking out to the middle of the lake.

"What the blazing hell is going on?" Jace asks. The vampire's skin ripples as Tyler turns around.

"You have to help her," he says, pointing to the middle of the lake. "She needs help."

"Where is she?" Jace asks. My heart races as Tyler's hands begin to shake.

"In the middle of the lake, at the bottom," Tyler replies. Jace leaps off the bank without question and swims to the middle before diving under the water. Tyler begins paces anxiously; he and I watch and wait. Jace's head appears and I watch as he swims back to the bank, huffing and heaving.

"I need blood," he says, "I can't get down deep enough, I'm too weak."

"I'll do it," Cleo says, climbing off of my back and walking towards Jace. I step forward growling.

"I haven't fed for days," Jace says as his four fangs slide out. "I could turn you."

"I don't care," she snaps, cutting off our protests and revealing her neck. "We don't have time to argue."

Jace looks to me as I flatten my ears and growl at him.

"She is right," he says before launching forward and sinking his fangs into her neck. Cleo screams out in pain. Tyler grabs me and holds me back as I try to stop Jace from feeding.

"He needs to save Rose," he growls in my ear. I morph back into a human and punch Tyler in the jaw. But as I turn around, Jace let's Cleo go and then dives back into the lake.

Cleo whimpers as she falls. I race over to her and catch her before she hits the ground.

"Cleo?" I ask, gently shaking her shoulders. I pull her further onto the bank and lay her on her back. I put my finger to her neck and find no pulse.

"This is your fault," I growl to Tyler as he watches the lake.

"What is taking so long?" he asks, after several minutes of waiting.

"I don't know," I sigh, looking out to the lake. As I look out, I don't notice Cleo's eyes open. She grabs onto my wrist and bites down hard. I shout and try to pull myself away from her gaping maw. Tyler kneels next to me and tries to remove Cleo's fangs from my arm. I shift my form, ripping my arm from her mouth, but it's too late; she has tasted my blood and has finished her transition into a vampire. I snarl at her as she bares her fangs at me. Tyler shifts his form as well and we hold our ground.

Cleo snarls once more before turning and running off, deep into the woods.

"*Do we go after her?*" Tyler asks. I shake my head as my wound heals.

"*She'll be fine,*" I say. I to look at the lake just as Jace breaks the surface with Rose. Jace calls out to us and in a flash, Tyler and I race into the water and swim out to Jace. When we reach him, he puts Rose onto my back and holds onto Tyler and we carry them back to land.

Once on the bank of the lake, Tyler changes and pulls Rose off of my back.

"Rose?" he asks, lying her on the ground. "Can you hear me? Open your eyes."

Rose is unresponsive, Tyler takes a deep breath and then begins to compress Rose's chest.

-Rose-

"Can you hear me?" I hear an unfamiliar voice say. "Open your eyes!"

Air is blown into my lungs and then a force pushes down on my chest. I gasp as water from my lungs makes its way up and out of my mouth. I lash out and latch onto something solid. I dig my nails down and feel thick liquid flow out. I open my eyes, but my vision is distorted. I can barely see the grass in front of me. I need energy and take it from the men in front of me.

After all, they are mine. I can feel a pull telling me they are my tags. I hear them shout and my eyes start to clear. I look at their faces and they are in pain.

Your killing them, a voice says in my mind. My heart races as I let them go. My vision distorts as I remove my tags. I cannot hurt them. I need to heal another way.

I fall back to the dirt.

I awaken in a strange place. There are people looking at me. My head aches and my body feels numb. One of the strangers moves closer to me. His hair is dark and his eyes are green and yellow. My eyes widen as he says my name and smiles at me, but I frown. I don't know this man. I feel the earth move below me as I lose consciousness and fall back to the ground.

-Zero-

Rose looks at Tyler as if she had never met him before, then her eyes roll back and she passes out.

"Is she okay?" Tyler asks, looking at me, then to Jace.

"I don't know," he says, shaking water from his hair. "We need to get her back to Paradise."

"I'll alert the others," I say, turning wolf. I lift my head up and howl and a vampire scream is returned. Tyler picks Rose up and we trek back to David's house.

"Where's Cleo?" Jace asks.

"She turned," I growl and Jace sucks in a deep breath and then tilts his head.

"I'll find her," he says. "Take Rose to Paradise."

I glare at Jace as he splits from the group and races off into the woods. Tyler and I walk through the woods and Tyler explains what happened.

"El was looking for a cure for me," he explains and I frown.

"Did they hurt you?" I ask and he shakes his head.

"Not until the end," Tyler says. "El ordered a bullet into my forehead. Of course that didn't kill me. They let us go."

"Why did they let you go?" I ask. The sound of our feet hitting the ground starts to annoy me.

"They want a war," he says and I stop in my tracks.

"What do you mean they want a war?" I ask as a growl rises in my chest.

"The only reason they let her and me go is because they want a war between hunters and paranormals," he says as we continue to walk. "If the hunters win, they have a witch that will put a curse on the paranormal race that will make us easier to kill; if we win, the hunters will leave us alone forever. They said that if I could rescue Rose from the lake within twenty-four hours they will give us two years to prepare for the war."

"What does Rose think of this?" I ask and he doesn't answer. "Tyler?"

"She doesn't know yet," he says, clenching his jaw. "It was the only way to save her."

We walk in silence until we get to the barn. The rest of the search parties stare at Rose with wide eyes. I push through the barn and pull on the rope hanging from the rafter. The door to Paradise opens and we step through. David is waiting on the other side, he transports Rose and Tyler and myself back to Rose's room.

"What happened?" David asks. "How did you escape."

"Tell em', Ty," I say, keeping the growl from rising. Tyler explains everything to David about how he was kept in a room while Rose was kept elsewhere. Tyler tells us that he could hear her screams, and that El wanted the cure for lycanthropy. When Rose told El there was no cure, Tyler negotiated for their release. El agreed to release them, but said that in two years the hunters will wage war against the paranormal species.

What is not clear is why they dropped Rose in the middle of the lake.

"You agreed to what?" David yells, and Tyler flinches as David's eyes turn green.

"It was the only way Rose could have been saved," Tyler defends his decision and David yells in frustration. Rose moans as she turns over in her sleep.

"We'll talk about this later," David hisses, blowing out a hot breath. "In the meantime, Rose needs to rest."

As soon as David leaves Rose awakens. Her eyes slowly crack open and she frowns.

"Rose?" I say, leaning down next to the bed. "How do you feel?"

Rose stares at me for a moment before getting out of bed and shuffles past Tyler to get to the bathroom. Tyler tries to talk to her, but she acts like he isn't even there. She begins to undress herself as she turns on the water for the shower. I turn around and avert my eyes.

After Rose has showered, she slowly staggers her way into her wardrobe, changes into a silk nightgown, and then walks over to me.

"Are you okay?" I ask, worry dripping from every word.

"I don't know," she admits. "I don't feel well."

Rose's face pales and she slumps forward into my arms. My eyes widen as I pick her up and lay her back down on her bed.

"What's wrong with her?" Tyler asks.

"She's been tortured and drowned," I say, my words dripping in hatred. "What do you think is wrong?"

Tyler glares at me for a moment before turning on his heels and storming out of the room, mumbling something under his breath. A few moments later, Christian walks into the room, his eyes filled with fear.

"Is she okay?" he asks.

"I'm not sure yet," I sigh, running a hand through my hair. Christian shrinks down to his cat form and jumps up onto the bed where he curls up at Rose's feet.

"Keep an eye on her," I say as I exit the room. Christian meows in return.

"Has Jace come back yet?" I ask David as I enter the kitchen.

"No," David sighs, leaning forward and pressing his forehead to the bench.

"What are we going to do about all of this?" I ask. He sighs and begins swirling his fingers on the bench top.

"The only thing we can do," he says— as his fingers move, green magic trails behind— "We're going to call all the original paranormals and any other paranormal willing to fight. With Jace already here and the location of Tamurl known, we should be able to decide on an action as soon as Rose heals."

"Something doesn't seem right," I say and David tilts his head towards me. "Why did the hunters drop Rose into the lake. What purpose did it serve to drown her?"

"Unless Tyler isn't telling the whole truth," David suggests.

"And that's another thing. When she opened her eyes on the bank of Mercy Lake, Tyler was right there. Literally, she was staring right at him, and yet it seemed as if she did not know him. Even when she awoke only moments ago, she ignored Tyler completely."

"Tyler did say that he was shot dead in front of her," David suggests. "Perhaps she thought she was seeing things, thinking that he was truly dead."

"But Rose did not seem sad or distraught about the thought of him *being* dead," I say. David sighs.

"I don't know what to make of this," David says, standing. "We will have to wait until Rose is fully awake to have answers."

I decide to inform Rose's brother of the situation to save him worry.

"Is she okay?" Xavier asks as I enter the gym. He is still stuck in his witch pentagram and I feel kind of bad for him.

"Not sure yet," I shrug, sitting on the cold floor. Xavier sighs and I tell him what Tyler did.

"Stupid boy," Xavier growls and I glare at him.

"Would you rather have Rose killed and the curse set upon us now?" I ask and he shuts up. According to Tyler, if he refused the war, the hunters would've killed Rose on the spot and set the curse; which everyone is unsure of what it is. It feels like Tyler did a good thing.

"I wish I could do more than sit here," Xavier says, sighing in frustration. "I feel so useless."

I shrug, then stand and leave the room not knowing what to say. I go back to Rose's room and knock lightly on the door.

"How is she doing?" I ask as I open the door. Lilly appears in front of me and sighs.

"Still sleeping," she says and Christian meows from the bed. "How's Tyler?"

"I don't know; he took off," I say and she nods.

"You might want to go and check on him," she says as Rose rolls over with a groan. "He might be hurting from this too. He might do something stupid."

I take a deep breath and follow his scent out into the gardens. He's sitting on a bench staring the rose bushes.

"Hey," I say, sitting beside him. Tyler grunts in acknowledgement. I sigh, and then ask, "What's wrong?"

"It's all my fault," he sighs and I raise an eyebrow.

"What do you mean?" I ask and he sighs. "How is this your fault? If it is anyone's fault, it's the hunters'."

"I could hear her screams," Tyler says. "I could feel her pain. They tortured her, while I was kept in a cosy room."

"You cannot blame yourself for this," I say. "You didn't get to choose what they did to you. They are the villains here. You did everything you could to save her."

My head snaps up as a scream sounds from inside the mansion. Tyler and I race into Rose's room where she's sitting on the far corner of the bed. David is kneeling at the edge of the bed, trying to calm Rose down.

"Where am I?" She asks. Tyler pushes himself foreword and the hairs on the back of my neck stand on end as I watch Rose's eyes dart around the room.

"Safe," he says, sitting on the bed and embracing her in a hug. "You are safe."

Rose pushes away from Tyler. I can hear her heart racing and smell her fear.

"Who are you?" She asks, with tears streaming down her face. Tyler freezes as he moves away from her. She looks around the room in a panic.

"Where am I?" She asks and my heart stops.

-Rose-

There are strangers all around me, staring at me as if I am some sort of freak. My heart races. The man who hugged me stands back, staring at me as if he were broken.

I awoke in this room and watched a cat turn into a man. When I screamed, a man appeared out of nowhere. He told me to take deep breaths and to calm down. And then two more men came into the room.

I know one of them, he is in some of my classes, but I don't know where I am. The other one, the one who hugged me, seems familiar, like I've seen him before. But it's only a feeling.

"Rose, do you know who I am?" the man with sandy-blond hair asks as he kneels by the bed. "My name is Zero."

"I know you," I stammer, he smiles at me warmly.

"Do you know who you are?" he asks. I nod. "Tell me who you are."

"My name is Rose Salamander," I say and Zero tenses. "Daughter to Dixie and recently deceased Jeremy Salamander"

"How old are you?" He asks, his warm smile slowly fading.

"Eighteen in July," I say after a brief pause.

"Shit," he curses. I frown as he stares at Rose with wide eyes. "You have been in an accident and have forgotten the past three years of your life," he says and my heart stops.

"No, I haven't," I argue, looking to everyone else. They all stare back at me. My eyes rest on the stranger who hugged me and he has a fat tear rolling down his cheek. I do not know his face.

The boy looks away quickly before turning to the rest of the people in the room.

"She needs her space," he says, breaking the silence as he walks out. The cat who turned into a man walks out of the room behind him, leaving me with Zero and the man who appeared out of nowhere.

"David," Zero says to the man. "Is there a spell to fix this?"

"Not that I am aware of," he says, rubbing the bridge of his nose. "I can't find the book that I gave Rose. The book has a number of spells in it that could help her."

"What do we do, then?" he asks, standing and David looks at me. Shivers run down my back and he motions for Zero to step into the hall with him. Once they leave the room I immediately jump out of bed and go to the window, which turns out to be a small veranda with hanging pot plants on it. I open the door/window and step out onto the veranda. I glance back to the other door before jumping the railing and landing on the grass. I take off running. There is a town and I avoid it, going straight for the woods. I need to find my way home; I need to go home. I run through the woods, but nothing seems familiar. It's nothing like the woods behind my house. I stop running and catch my breath. My heart races as I look around the woods, trying to find something familiar.

"Rose?" a voice says from behind me, I turn quickly and see the male who hugged me. "What are you doing out here?"

"I..." I take a step back and trip on an exposed root; in a bat of an eye he catches me.

"I can hear your heart beating," he whispers. He is standing behind me with his arms around me. I let out a shaky breath. "Calm down, I'm not going to hurt you."

"Please," I sob, fighting against his hold. "You must have me mistaken for someone else. I don't know you."

"You do know me," he whispers in my ear. I break out of his hold. "Listen to your heart, Rose."

"It's telling me to run," I say and he looks at me with sad eyes, then something grabs his attention. He opens his palm and stares down at a piece of paper.

"I have to go," he says, and walks towards me. My heart rate doubles as he reaches out and touches the side of my face. "I'm going to make you remember."

I take in his scent and, as he walks past me, a small part of me whispers to turn around and follow him. However, a larger part of me is screaming at me to run like hell and don't look back. I stay there, glued to the spot, lost in this big world where everyone is crazy. I am Rose, and they all claim to know me. They're all mad.

"Rose, what are you doing?" the man called David asks, appearing out of nowhere. I look into his unnaturally bright green eyes and take a step back in fear. "It's okay. I'm not going to hurt you. You can trust me."

"I don't even know you," I say. The sky above us begins to darken as tears fall from my eyes. "You need help. I am not the Rose you are looking for. You're crazy."

"You do," he says, looking nervously up to the sky. "Look deep into your heart. You do know me."

His soothing voice begins to irritate me and thunder booms up above us as the wind picks up speed, whipping my long hair in front of my face. I feel like I should trust him, but the voices in my head all scream at me to run. This man is clearly dangerous. He appeared out of nowhere as if it were magic.

"Just leave me alone!" I scream. Lightning cracks, the sky opens up, and rain begins falling.

David takes a step back. I turn on my heels and run away as fast as I can. The wind blows in my face and the tears sting my eyes. I run faster and harder than I have ever run before; it almost feels like I am flying. The storm rages, lightning cracks, and thunder booms to the beat of my heart. My eyes become fogged and everything goes blurry. I slow down and come to a stop. I am deep in the woods where the trees block out the sky. I sit at the base of a large tree and press my back against its trunk and look up to the canopy as I wrap my arms around my body. My nightgown is soaking wet; the rain hits my skin like small needles. A twig snaps and I watch as a giant wolf steps into view. My eyes widen as the wolf stares at me. He is almost four and a half feet tall! The wolf crouches on the ground and slowly crawls towards me, whining through its nose.

The wolf is dark grey with wisps of light grey in its fur. It continues to whistle as it comes closer and closer, stopping only when he is at my feet. It licks my toes and I flinch. I'm not scared. Some part of me tells me this is natural. I shake my head as a shiver runs through me and the wolf looks up at me with its dark eyes and whines. I slowly reach out to the wolf and touch its head. It closes its eyes ad leans into my hand. A howl echoes through the woods and the wolf in front of me stands and turns its back on me. He walks away from me and my heart skips a beat.

"Wait!" I call desperately, not wanting to be left alone. The wolf stops and looks back at me. Another howl is sounded on the wind and my wolf's ear twitches. It walks back to me and nudges me with its head. I stand and he nudges me forward. It then stands next to me and howls softly. The howl that is returned sounds angry and the wolf growls deep in its chest. It walks away and I reach out and grab the scruff of its neck and walk alongside it. It looks back at me as we walk and it seems like it is smiling at me and my nerves calm. As we walk, the wind dies down until it's nothing but a small whisper. I look down to the wolf that walks beside me and loosen my grip on its fur. This isn't my wolf. I don't know what I am thinking, but I know that this wolf is not mine. I let go of its fur and cup my hands around my mouth and then howl.

The dark grey wolf stops walking and looks at me with questioning eyes. I ignore him and howl again, wanting to hear my wolf's howl.

I have no idea what I am doing, but the part of me I have been ignoring has torn through the layers of ignorance and is calling out for my wolf. I howl again and again, wanting to hear his howl, needing to feel his fur. A tear falls from my eye as I howl louder. This time, a howl cuts me off. It's my wolf, and he is calling back.

I need him with me. I open my mouth and howl again, trying to convey that I need him. The dark grey wolf nudges me with his head, wanting me to keep moving. I shove his head away and sit in the dirt. I am not going to move until he is with me. The wolf growls in protest and I bare my teeth at him. I have no idea why I am being so brave; this wolf could squish me with one paw. The grey wolf throws his head back and howls with me. His howl is mixed with a deep growl.

A wolf howls back. He's closer, but before I can even think about howling again, the wolf steps into the clearing.

His green and yellow eyes stare at me. I stand as he looks at me.

Tears sting my eyes as I move without thought. I launch myself towards the wolf. He takes a step forward and I wrap my arms around his neck. He stiffens from the surprise and looks over my shoulder to the dark grey wolf before sitting and hugging me back by resting his head over my shoulder. I press my face deep into his fur and cry. His fur is soft against my skin. I'm so afraid of the world around me and part of me wants to run away from it all, but there is that stronger part of me that wants to stay here next to my wolf. There is a howl on the wind and my wolf looks up, breaking out of my hold. His ears perk and a growl erupts from his chest. I stand and look back to the dark grey wolf that looks at my wolf with angry eyes.

The dark grey wolf nudges me with his head, and I step forward. My wolf looks at the dark grey wolf and bares his deadly looking fangs. The dark grey growls and my wolf stands in front of me, his hackles raise and his growl drops deeper. I take a step back as he presses against me and begins to herd me away from the grey wolf. I take the fur on the back of his neck in my hand and we walk alongside each other until we reach the end of the woods where David stands. My wolf growls before turning around and vanishing back into the woods.

"Rose," the man says, drawing my attention away. "I won't hurt you."

David holds out his hand towards me, and, reluctantly, I take it. He and the dark grey wolf walk me back to the mansion. They walk me around the side, into the garden.

"Listen to me," David says, stopping in front of a raised garden bed. "Things have changed, you are not human. You have lost three years of your life. Do you understand what I am saying?"

"How can I be 'not human'," I argue, folding my arms across my chest. My eyes are dragged to the dark grey wolf that sits and looks at me with curious eyes. "What else could I be if I'm 'not human'?"

-Zero-

I sit, looking at Rose. Her arms are folded over her chest and her eyes are filled with confusion.

"What else could I be if I'm 'not human'?" she asks, looking away from me and to David.

"You are a werewitch," he says, simply. "Like me. Part werewolf, part witch. You were captured by hunters. You were tortured." He says, gesturing to her left wrist. I look and notice the branding for the first time. It's the symbol of a Native American wolf, burned into her skin. "We suspect that they placed a curse or spell on you to forget who you are."

"That is ridiculous," she says as I lay down at her feet. "You're insane." Her voice quavers and I can tell that deep down she knows that what David is saying is true.

"Please, try to understand," he says, sighing. "Keep your mind open."

"You're mad," she says, taking a step back. "There is no-." She looks over David's shoulder and her eyes go wide. I look up to see Tyler running forward with a bronze tipped silver stake in his hands. With quick thinking she pushes David out of the way and steps forward— straight into the stakes path. The stake goes straight into her stomach and Tyler stands there mortified. My heart sinks. It all happened so fast, David, Tyler, and I stand there, frozen to the spot.

"You were going to kill me?" David snarls. I watch as Tyler's eyes widen as he reaches for the stake that protrudes of Rose's abdomen. I feel David's anger before he attacks. He morphs into his wolf form and clamps his jaws down on Tyler's shoulder, pulling him away from Rose. Tyler shifts his form and defends himself from David. I charge forward and try to diffuse the situation, knowing that Rose would never forgive me if I let him die.

19. Remembrance

-Rose-

My eyes widen as the stake is thrust into my stomach. I stagger back and gasp. The man's eyes went wide and in a flash he and David collided and turned into two big wolves. The dark grey wolf rushed to help and I all I could hear was barking and growling. I look down at the man's stake. *Tyler,* a voice in my head says. *He is Tyler, you are Rose Bane.*

Memories fly through my mind, memories of the last three years of my life: becoming a werewolf, a werewitch, meeting Tyler and falling in love. I grip the stake's leather handle and with a hard yank, pull it out and pain shoots through my body. My body heals instantly and the pain I felt becomes nothing but a dull feeling. I turn into a werewolf and take in my surroundings. I look to the three werewolves fighting in front of me. David attacks Tyler and Tyler fights back, with the help of Zero. The sharp smell of blood hits my nose, I see Tyler's shoulder bleeding, anger boils through me. I launch into the fight, shifting my form as I go. I land on David's back and bite down on the back of his neck, blood splatters on my face as I pull him away from Tyler. David growls deeply and turns to me. When his eyes land on me everything falls silent. Tyler whimpers, then steps back. Zero crawls back with his ears flattened and belly to the dirt. David stares at me, not moving.

"*I'm sorry,*" Tyler whimpers, into my mind. "*I was going to help you remember.*"

"*Don't ever do something that stupid again,*" I growl, looking at him. "*You could have died.*"

"*Rose?*" Zero says, stepping forward, his tail between his legs.

"*I remember,*" I say broadcasting my voice to David and Zero.

"*He tried to kill me,*" David growls, his fangs dripping with blood. I flatten my ears and pull my lips back and growl as I stand tall.

"I was trying to help her," Tyler says, turning human and standing up with his hands raised, palms open. I look back at him and tilt my head. "My sister said that she put a curse on you and the only way to get rid of it was to give her the head of the original werewitch."

"He should be punished," David growls. I turn and growl deeply at him.

"You will not touch him!" I shout, my hackles rising and my mouth opening. David and I size each other up. David lunges forward and I bite down hard, yellow lightning erupts from my mouth. My body bulks up and my black stripe spreads and takes over my body. David's growl drops an octave and I stand tall, not moving. We growl at each other for what seems an age, finally David sighs and shifts back to his human form.

"I won't harm him," he says. I shrink down back to my normal werewolf form. "I give you my word."

David vanishes in a green cloud of dust. I roll my shoulders and shift form. I turn and face Tyler. He stares at me in his human form. My heart races as I run into his arms. He holds onto me and kisses my forehead. I look over Tyler's shoulder and stare into his eyes.

Thank you, I mouth. He nods his head before turning on his heels and walking away. After a minute of being captured in Tyler's tight embrace, he loosens his gip and goes in to kiss me. I move my head and he kisses my cheek.

"What's wrong?" he asks, pulling away, oblivious to the blood surrounding my mouth.

"I have blood all around and in my mouth," I say with a small laugh. Tyler doesn't respond, and he looks at my lips. In a heartbeat, he crushes his lips to mine and circles his arms around me. Suddenly a raw, animalistic hunger awakens in me. I move closer to Tyler and bunch the back of his shirt into my fist. Fire and passion burns through me and a growl rumbles in my chest as I press closer to Tyler. Tyler runs a hand up my back and into my hair. He tugs it back and leans in closer. He begins to trail kisses down my jaw line and to my exposed neck where he roughly kisses my scar. What brings me back to reality is when Tyler growls deeply and bites the base of my neck. I gasp as my eyes flies open as I push Tyler back and clutch my bleeding neck; the wound is small but it stings.

"Rose," Tyler gapes, as he comes to terms with the situation. "Oh, my God." He collapses to his knees and looks at me with shining eyes.

"Something came over me," he utters, putting a hand over his mouth. I inhale deeply and sigh as I feel the wound heal.

"It's okay," I say, taking my hand away from my neck. "I'm fine." Tyler stands and crosses the distance in between us. My back hits the wall of the mansion as he places his hands on the wall, above my shoulders.

"There's something about you," he says, inhaling my scent. "You drive me crazy, I was losing my mind locked up by the hunters."

I let out a shaky breath as he tucks a stray piece of hair behind my ear.

"I want to tear them to bits," he says, his yellow eye shines bright.

"What happened to you?" I ask quietly. Tyler unbuttons his white shirt and lets it fall off of his shoulders.

"Bite me and find out," he says, tapping his origin scar. I move forward as my eyes turn yellow.

"Why can't you just tell me?" I ask, my heart races.

"You need to see for yourself," Tyler says. My teeth sharpen as I move forward and then gently rub them against his skin before sinking them into his shoulder.

"Open your eyes" Tyler murmurs as he presses me back to the wall, running his hand through my hair.

I open my eyes as he requested and images flash across my mind.

"Where are you taking her?" Tyler asks. I'm seeing through his eyes. He is in a van with his hands bound tight.

"To Mercy Lake," El says to him as she taps Tyler's shoulder. "When you recover, tell her to bite here."

"What do you want from us?" Tyler asks as El moves to sit across from him. Tyler picks at the dried blood on his forehead.

"The cure of course," she scoffs and Tyler rolls his eyes. "But since that it apparently non-existent. I want a war."

"A war?" Tyler echoes numbly. His sister nods. "What type of war?"

"One that will go down in history," she says, proudly. "Paranormal hunters against Paranormals."

"What do we get out of this?" he asks, scoffing.

"I wasn't finished," she says, scowling at him. "When the hunters win, the remaining paranormals will have a cursed placed on them. It will make them easier to identify and kill. If the paranormals manage to win, which is highly unlikely, the hunters will agree to leave the paranormal species alone, in peace."

"How long do we have to prepare for the war?" Tyler asks as the

van slows down to a stop.

"All in good time, brother," she says, grabbing a syringe that I know is filled with wolfs bane. El forces Tyler's mouth open and pours the wolfs bane down his throat. It burns me as well as him. She holds his mouth closed until he swallows, rendering himself mute. She opens the back door and grabs Tyler's bounded hands. She helps him out and his eyes adjust to the brightness of Mercy Lake. He looks to his left and sees me. He mouths my name and tries to scream past his blocked throat.

"Did you know that a werewolf or any of the paranormal species cannot drown?" El says, walking over to me. "They just simply go to sleep and wake up whenever they are revived." Tyler struggles against his captors as El reaches out and touches my face. I flinch and she walks away.

"I will make you a deal," she says, and Tyler struggles as men begin to tie weights to my body. "If you can save her in twenty-four hours I will let you have two years of preparation. If not, you will only have the one year. If you fail to rescue her at all, then I will have my witch complete the curse right after two days. Deal?"

Tyler nods slightly and a portal opens up underneath my body. Tyler watches in horror as I am dropped over to the middle of Mercy Lake. He tries to run after me but El holds him back.

"When dear Rose is recovered," she says, pointing to Tyler's shoulder. "Make sure she bites your shoulder and uses her wolf abilities to see this. I want her to know what she has done."

I remove my mouth from Tyler's shoulder, too scared to see what happened next. My wolf fangs slide back into their sheaths and my eyes turn back to their sapphire colour.

There is a thick silence that covers Tyler and me in a blanket, and I watch his wounds heal.

"A war," I whisper softly, once his wound is healed.

"Yes," he says, stepping forward and wiping the blood from my face. I take in what he is wearing and mentally gasp. He looks heavenly, like an angel.

Silly wolf, a voice laughs in my head and I look around. *You have no idea what an angel looks like.*

I look around, frantically trying to find where the voice came from.

"Are you okay?" Tyler says, taking my hands in his. I look into his eyes and smile.

"Yes, I'm fine," I stammer, shaking my head. "I think I should get cleaned up. I don't feel well."

"Oh," Tyler says. He takes my hand and leads me into the mansion, then into my room. He takes me into my bathroom and kisses me softly before closing the door between us.

As I step into the shower, the screen moves as the heat fogs it.

Welcome back, it says and I gasp. As soon as I read it, it vanishes. *It's El.*

What do you want? I ask, writing back into the fog.

A war.

Why?

You know why, she writes back. *However, I would like to meet you and talk to you. Alone!*

Where and Why? I write in shock.

To discuss my terms and yours as well. In the clearing of the woods. There is a party tonight, very open.

Fine. I write, but I am not coming alone.

There isn't a reply after that, so I continue my shower.

Once I finish my shower, I step out wrap myself in a white towel. I expect to see Tyler sitting on my bed, but instead it was Zero.

"Oh, my God," I sigh, clutching the towel closer to my body.

"Sorry," he mumbles, looking away. "Tyler told me to keep an eye on you."

I purse my lips together and make my way into the walk-in-closet and change into a black corset top and black jeans. I then throw on a black leather duster and knee high boots. I tie my hair into a tight bun and locate my secret weapon draw and arm myself. I strap a holster to my thigh and then slide a Beretta 92FS into it. I then slide a dagger into my boot and then take a deep breath and open my wardrobe doors. Zero almost has a heart attack.

"Rose, what the... why are you dressed like that?" he asks.

I ignore his question and head for the kitchen where Tyler and David are talking in hushed voices. When I enter they stop talking and stare.

"We have a date tonight," I say, sitting on the kitchen island as I begin to fill David, Tyler and, Zero on what happened in the bathroom.

"It is a suicide mission!" Tyler exclaims after I have finished. "You can't go."

"I have to," I contradict.

"Why?" he asks. "It's too dangerous; she could kill you."

"If she wanted me dead she would have killed me while I was in her control. She wants to discuss our agreements."

"Let me go instead," he says and I gasp out in pain as something cuts into my hand. I open it and find a message, carved into my flesh.

NO! Rose must come!

I gasp as I watch the blood trickle out of the wound that doesn't close.

"It's not healing," Tyler says, taking my hand in his and looking at David with concerned eyes.

"She has a witch using a blocking spell," David says, taking my hand from Tyler and whispering a spell. I scream out and he jumps. The wound is cut deeper and blood begins to flow.

"How the hell was that supposed to help!" I shout, yanking my hand away and David stands there confused.

"You need to go and see El," David says. "But you are not going alone. Zero, Tyler, and myself will accompany you."

"Me, too," Lilly says, appearing next to me.

"Don't forget about me," Xavier says, leaning the door frame of the kitchen.

"No, not you," I say, roughly. "You still have to open your pentagram."

"I have," he says, walking towards me. "I did it while you were missing. I finished this morning."

"What's your specialty?" I ask. Xavier smiles at me and opens his hand, holding it in front of him. A clear water droplet pools in the middle of his palm and then dances around his hand.

"Water, is my element," he chuckles as the water begins to dance.

"When are we leaving?" Tyler asks with a growl in his voice. I turn to face him. As I do, there is another painful sting in my other hand. I hold the bloody message up for everyone to see. *Meet me at the party in two hours.*

I then make a bandage appear and wrap my hands.

Tyler looks at me with scared eyes before turning on his heels and walking to our room. I chase after him and catch up to him in our room and close the door behind me.

"What's wrong?" I ask as the door shuts. Tyler moves suddenly and presses me up against the door. His shirt is already off and his eyes flare with anger.

"How can you ask me that right now?" he says and I gasp. His hands are on either side of my shoulders and his hair falls into his eyes.

"I feel like I just got you back," he whispers before turning up the volume. "I have just gotten you back and already you want to go running off into danger!"

"Tyler, El said–"

"I don't care what she said!" he shouts as he slams his palm on the door, causing the wood to crack. "I can't risk losing you, not again."

"You won't lose me," I say as my heart calms down. I put a hand to the side of his face. "You will be there to protect me."

"But I couldn't last time," he says softly as he brings his head closer to me. "I couldn't protect you last time."

"David, Xavier and the others will be there, too," I say as he rests his head on my neck. He pushes his body to mine and presses me harder against the door.

"I never want to let you go," he says as I trace a scar line on his back.

"Do you know that we have the same scars?" he asks, moving away from me and looking me dead in the eyes. "I've seen your scars, they match my own. Do you want to know why?"

I trace the scar on his chin as he dose mine.

"Why?" I whisper, looking at his lips.

He takes my hands in his and presses them to his bare chest. "Because we were destined to meet each other, a destiny written before we were born. The same werewolf attacked me that attacked you. It was meant to be, you and I."

My breath catches as he kisses my lips ever so softly. I sigh and melt into his kiss. He wraps his strong, muscular arms around my waist and draws me closer. I relax my body and lace my hands together behind his neck. I gasp against his mouth as pain pinches my back; my muscles spasm and I push Tyler back.

"I'm sorry, Rose," he says with tears running down his face. I look down into his hand and see a needle, my muscles tighten and then relax. I stand up straight and glare at Tyler.

"Not effective as you thought?" I say, and Tyler's eyes go wide.

"But, it was filled with straight wolfsbane," he gasps, dropping the empty needle. His hands are burnt from just holding the needle.

I look at my hands and clench them before turning them over and looking at the picture of the upside down wolf that is burned into my skin.

"My body must have built up a tolerance to the plant," I sigh.

"Yeah, your body did it all by itself," a man's voice in my head says and I look around the room, trying to find its source.

"Shush, Raum," another male voice says.

"Rose, are you okay?" Tyler says, and I look back to him.

"Fine," I mumble. Taking the door knob in my hand, I open the door and look in the hallway for the voices.

"Balthazar, what is she doing?" the voice asks. I growl as its laugh fills my head.

"Balthazar, she is a loony."

"Shush!" the other voice says and all goes quiet.

"Rose, what are you doing?" Tyler asks and I sigh.

"Nothing," I say, walking out of the room. "Get ready, we're leaving in an hour."

I hear no protest from Tyler as I leave and enter the gym where Xavier and David are gearing up.

"Ah, Rose," David says, approaching me. "Just the girl I wanted to see. I have a gift for you."

"What is it?" I ask as David pulls out what looks like a white handle from a whip.

"Wow," I say bluntly. "Have any other incomplete weapons I can use?"

I hear Xavier chuckle and in his hands is a similar handle, but it's a black one. He smiles and water runs from the handle. Xavier whips it around his head before cracking it in front of me and water sprays my nose.

"You can bend you main power through this," David says, handing me the handle and I take. A sudden connection is made and I gasp. It feels alive and warm to the touch. My eyes flare yellow as long yellow lightning appears from the handle. I crack it and instead of the normal whip sound that Xavier's made, mine makes a thunderous crack and leaves a long crack in the gym floor.

"Hmm," I say as the lightning moves back to the base and disappears. "I like it."

"I thought you might," David says, handing me a thigh holder for it. I strap it on my thigh and then slide the handle into place.

"How do I look?" I ask, and David smiles.

"Like a death angel," he smiles and the echoing laugh is back.

"Balthazar she looks nothing like death or an angel," it laughs and I groan.

"Raum!" the other voice hisses. *"Leave her be."*

"David," I ask, ignoring the voices. "May I ask you a question?"

"Of course," he says. "I know many things."

"Do you know of any paranormal by the name of Balthazar or

Raum?" I ask and David shakes his head and Xavier shrugs his shoulders.

"We should get going." David says.

"Just a moment," I say, making wolfsbane appear and float in front of me. David and Xavier gape at me as if I've lost my mind.

"Can you touch this?" I ask, and David looks at me with concerned eyes. I reach out and grab it with my hand and there isn't any burning or blistering. The skin doesn't even tingle at the touch. David looks at the plant, then to me, and then to Xavier.

"It's real," Xavier says, taking in a deep breath. "The smell burns my nose."

"How long could you do that?" David asks, touching a single purple petal of the flower. The petal burns his finger and he pulls it back instantly.

"I don't know," I say, touching the delicate flower. My arm begins to burn and I pull back my coat sleeve to see a new 'note' inscribed in my flesh.

Hurry up!

"I think we should go," I mumble, making a wrap for this new wound. David agrees.

-Zero-

Rose comes out of the gym with Xavier and David behind her; all are dressed in black. I too am dressed in black clothing. Tyler and Lilly join us at the front door of the mansion.

"Ready?" Tyler asks, looking at Rose with cautious eyes.

"Depends if you try to stop me again," she replies and Tyler nervously looks at the floor as Rose casts a worrying glance around the room.

David snaps his fingers and a green cloud rises up from the floor, consuming the whole group. A series of sharp pinch covers me; it feels like a dozen tiny needles piercing my skin. I close my eyes tight and hold my breath. Somewhere in the fog my hand grasps another, and when it doesn't move away immediately, I hold it tight. When I open my eyes, we are standing on the soft ground of Mercy Lake. I look down to my hand and trail the other one up to see Rose's face. She smiles softly at me before giving my hand a squeeze and letting it go. I catch Tyler glaring at me and I immediately look away.

"Ready to go?" Rose says, looking up at the night stars. We're unable to find the moon behind the clouds.

David and Xavier walks up to Rose and they walk side by side until we reach the clearing where the party is. It isn't hard to spot as there's a giant bonfire lit in the middle of it and I smell the stench of alcohol and illegal drugs from a mile away. My heart clenches. This is where I was turned.

A light catches my attention and I turn to see Rose's wolf eyes shining yellow. She proceeds to point out several hunters. Then El appears and Rose growls softly. She lays out the game plan and we set it into motion. We are all to pick a hunter to tail, and, if anything threatening happens, hold them at bay. Tyler, Lilly, and I take the three furthest away from El while Xavier and David take the two next to her. Rose walks up to El and the guy I'm tailing clips his gun holster. I make my move and put my hand at the back of his neck. For anyone who cares to look, it would seem like a friendly gesture, but I can crush this hunter's neck in an instant if he makes the wrong move.

"You might not want to move, mate," I warn, softly growling in the hunter's ear so that he knows what I am.

-Rose-

"You were looking for me?" I ask, appearing in front of El. She jumps and the two men next to her reach for their guns. In an instant, Xavier and David appear and hold onto the hunters' arms.

"I wouldn't move if I were you," I explain as they glare at me. "Meet David, the original, and Xavier, my brother. You move and they will send enough electricity through you to power three homes."

The men scowl but put their hands up in surrender.

"Impressive," El comments with a chuckle. "But do you think that they are the only men I have?"

"Look around, princess," I say, and she looks to Zero, who has his hands on the back of a man's neck; to Lilly who has a hand on a woman's arm, and around her hand is frost; and finally she looks to Tyler, who's holding a knife to a man's ribs.

"Did you seriously think I came ill prepared?" I say, shaking my head. "Tsk, tsk. Should have known better."

"I can still kill you," she says and I growl. "Do you seriously think I care about these people?"

I was about to reply when Christian appears out of nowhere and holds a hand to the back of her neck.

"Looked like you needed help," he says. I smile at him as El scowls at me.

"Shall we walk, then?" El asks and I purse my lips together before nodding once. Christian and I walk away from the party with El despite everyone's glares.

"So, werewitch," El starts as Christian keeps a hand on her neck. "Do you have any questions or conditions before I go ahead?"

I nod and begin to list the conditions. "I know we have two years to prepare. My conditions are that one, Tyler will not be killed before or during the war, and two, I choose the place we fight."

"Easy enough," El shrugs, glancing slightly upwards. "Where is it you'd like to fight?"

"You'll find out on the eve of our fight," I growl and she scowls. "Just have one of your witches make this spell," I say, handing her a piece of paper that has a spell written on it. "On the night of our fight I'll take you to our war zone."

"How do I know it isn't a trap?" she asks, raising an eyebrow.

"Because the spell will pull both sides," I explain. "If I was to send you into a pit of lava, then I'll go there, too."

El grunts before starting her conditions. "You will not kill a single hunter until the war. No matter what they do," she says and I wrinkle my nose. "And if you lose, then I get my witch and my warlock to place a curse on the whole paranormal species. *If* you win, which I think is unlikely." Christian tightens his grip and she cringes. After glaring at him, she continues, "The hunters will leave the paranormal species alone forever."

"Is that it?" I ask and she nods. "Good, because I have a question for you; followed by a request." El nods again and I continue, "What is with the branding?"

With a quick movement, she pulls out her silver stake and activates it. I step back quickly and growl while Christian tightens his grip so that his fingers sit at least a centimetre beneath the flesh. El cries out and Christian hisses, baring all four fangs.

"The brand is an upside down wolf, commonly used as a symbol of the werewolf's end," she says, squirming to get away from Christian's grip. El deactivates her stake and puts it back in its holster at her side. "What is your request?"

"My first one is to end the spell that is cast upon me that allows you to communicate with me," I growl and she laughs.

"It has already ended," she says and I unwrap my hand to see it healed.

"My second request is that we make an unbreakable vow," I say and she raises an eyebrow. "It's a spell that, if broken, will turn the person who breaks it to ash."

El considers the proposal for a minute before nodding once. I hold out my hand and she holds out hers. I take it in mine and a golden line circles our hands locking them together.

"I vow to never break Elisa Harding's conditions. If I do, may my body return to the dirt from which it came," I say, and half of the circle turns red.

"I vow to never break Rose Bane's conditions or I shall turn into ash and dust," she says and the rest of the circle turns red and my eyes brighten to their yellow forms.

We stay locked for a minute before the circle returns to golden and releases us.

"I would have thought you would make a request for you not to be killed," El says, rubbing her wrist. "But instead you only said Tyler."

"I already know there is a high chance that I will die," I say, glaring at El as she rubs her hands together. "I want to make sure Tyler doesn't join me. He deserves to live."

"Trust me, Rose, my step-brother does not deserve a thing," she smirks. "Especially, not from you. Oh, and one more thing, the moon."

20. The Seers

-Rose-

Both Christian and I look up to the moon now sitting almost directly over our heads. My eyes widen in terror as I see its full glow looking down on me. I growl and Christian hisses.

"We have to get back to the others," I say as I feel the full moon curse creep through my blood. I gasp and go down to my knees. I hear a shout and guess the rest of my party have gone down as well. El gets out of Christian's grasp and runs back to her men.

"Leave her!" I growl as he starts to go after her. The pain starts in my stomach and I dig my nails in the dirt. "Get out of here!" I shout at Christian. He looks at me with wide eyes. "Christian I will turn soon and I won't be able to stop myself from attacking you. You're a vampire, a werewolf's immortal enemy. For God's sake, get out of here!"

He turns and, in a blur, he disappears. I hear my bones crack and realign as my teeth sharpen.

The process of becoming a werewolf on the full moon is the most painful thing I have ever experienced. It's like my own body is pulling me apart from the inside. My mind feels like it is slipping, giving into the monster's instinct. The beast roars as the cage springs open; it latches onto my body and we become one. My eyes see the swirl of colours, the emotions of the people ahead of me. Even though I cannot not see their bodies, I can see their auras. My body launches forward, moving me towards my prey. I howl to see who is out here with me in the hunt. There is no reply. Once these woods used to explode into sound, but tonight they remain quiet. My mind reels. *I have to get away,* I think. I change direction and move away from the people at the party, my heart hammering in my chest. Did I just *think*? I don't *think* when the moon takes over. I just *do*. I should not have humanity on such a night. My eyes scan the woods and I see a different colour, one that peaks my interest. I move towards the light, however, it isn't just one colour; it shifts and changes. I walk silently towards the colour and as I push through the final bush, a werewolf appears attached to the colour. The wolf looks at me with wide yellow eyes. He tilts his head and his colours change.

"Do you have the sight?" he asks. I tilt my head slightly. *"You see my colours?"*

"Yes," I say, sitting in the dirt. The wolf indicates to follow him and I do. He leads me to the old wolf ditch now deserted and empty, except for the swarm of colour similar to the wolf's— ever shifting and ever changing. I flatten my ears and tuck my tail between my legs as he and I begin our slow decent down into the ditch. I whine as I put one paw after the other.

The male wolf stands next to me, nudging me to go further. I stare at this strange wolf. He is indeed a pure blood— born of werewolf parents. I see his chest inhale and then, as he exhales, he throws his head back and lets out a thick howl. The colours below us begin to shift and move, then one moves closer towards me and him. Then, from out of the colour comes a white pure-blood she-wolf. She glares at me.

"Mother," the wolf besides me greets the she-wolf.

"Why have you brought a marked wolf here?" She growls at her son, though her eyes never leave me.

"Mother, she has the sight," he says.

"No marked wolf has ever possessed the sight," she snarls, flattening her ears. *"They are too ignorant."*

I am getting fed up of her attitude and the full moon is pulling at the beast sitting beneath my skin. A deep, dangerous growl erupts from my chest. The she-wolf glares at me and her green eyes glow bright and my yellow eyes match her brightness, making her shifting colours brighter.

"Stevenson," she says, finally looking to her son. *"It seems you are right. She indeed has the sight. Go and show her how we spend our full moon."*

The male wolf bows his head and then turns me around and pushes me out of the pit.

"What happened to Tamurl?" I growl as he leads me back to where the party was.

"He and his pack left Mercy Lake out of fear of the humans," he says, moving closer to me.

"Are you afraid of the humans, Stevenson?" I ask, shifting away uncomfortably.

"My friends call me Steve," he says with a chuckle as we come to a stop at the edge of the party. *"But no, we are not afraid of humans. So, tell me which ones are poisonous?"*

The beast within me wants to jump on the first human, but as I take a closer look I find that I can use my sight to see which humans are infected with wolfsbane. Their colours are tainted with a pale purple and dark green colour, the colour of the wolfsbane plant. I scan the crowd and many of them are drenched in the fowl plant my body hates. But then I find two people who aren't infected. The hackles along the back of my neck rise as I crouch down in the dirt.

"Don't hold back," Steve says into my mind, gently persuading the monster out of the cage.

"Yes, hold back, Rose," another voice on my head says, and my ears flatten.

"Let her go, Balthazar," another says. *"She has to learn what this gift costs."*

Something snaps in my head and the beast tears out of its cage with a powerful pounce. I growl and leap into the clearing. Humans scream and run off in all directions. I follow the two I want. A couple: male and female. Steve runs besides me and we both let out a hunting howl of fun. We catch up to the couple and as I pounce on the male, Steve pounces on the female. We bite into their flesh and lick their wounds, but that wasn't enough for my beast. I turn into a human as the blood hands back my humanity, but the beast does not retreat. I lay against the pleading male and lick his wound again. I growl and bite into his neck, letting the blood stain my mouth and run down my throat. It feels cool and refreshing. I want more. I drink from him until he is almost dead and then I pull his heart from his chest and throw it to the ground. I look over to Steve who stands over the woman he tackled. She squirms and tries to move away from him. Steve smiles at me before turning to the woman on the ground and decapitating her with one bite. He then moves back and stands as a human.

Steve has short black hair, thick muscles, and toned abs. He's almost naked except for the loin cloth around his waist. He looks at me with golden-brown eyes as he leans on a thick tree with a smile on his face.

"Good job," he says as his eyes brighten. My yellow witch eyes appear as a smile crosses my face. He then takes my hand and we run through the woods, as wolf and humans, killing deer and any other game we can find. By the end of the night, my clothes are stained in blood, yet the monster will not vanish. After killing a deer, Steve and I come together. He gently slides the duster from my shoulders and then begins to undress me. There's a nagging feeling at the back of my head that I ignore as he loosens my corset and lays me in the dirt. He removes my assortment of weapons carefully before sliding off my boots and jeans. He grinds his hips against mine and growls low in his throat as he kisses my neck.

In a swift motion, I push him into the dirt and hover above him in my underwear. Suddenly, the sun hits my back and forces my humanity back into my hands and the monster back into its cage. My eyes widen and my stomach launches as I see Steve smiling up at me.

"Oh, my God!" I scream, pushing away from him. "You're disgusting."

"You didn't object," he says with a twisted smile. He's right, I didn't object. Why didn't I object?

He tries to advance on me again, but this time I punch him in the jaw and he staggers back. I reach for my clothes and put them on quickly and place my weapons back on my body.

Feeling a lot safer, I turn back to Steve and growl.

"What did you do to me?" I question as I wipe blood from my mouth.

"Nothing," he says, wiping his jaw with a smile. "The full moon pushed us together. We are obviously destined to be together as mated alphas."

"I would never do that," I argue with a dangerous growl. "Take me back to your pack."

Steve doesn't argue. He gets up in a swift movement and leads back to the ditch taken over by his pack. This time, I don't see the colours and walk right in with no fear.

"How was your first night?" the white wolf says, turning human in front of us.

"Terrible," I say, before Steve could say anything. "But that's not why I came back. I came back because Paradise calls you."

Steve and his mother stiffen on the spot and growl at me.

"You brought a parasitic pup into this pack!" she shouts at her son, who steps back.

"I didn't know," he says, growling at me. I growl back. The other fifteen wolves in the pack growl and pose to fight. In a quick movement,

I grab my whip handle and power yellow spirit though it. I crack it and everyone freezes.

"My name is Rose Bane," I say loudly so everyone can hear me. "The first ever female werewitch. Every paranormal hunter in the world is threatening every paranormal species with a war in two years. We need you in Paradise to help fight this war."

"A werewitch you say?" The mother, and, I guess, the leader of the pack, says and I nod. "Fine, we will accompany you to Paradise. A war this big calls for action. We will follow you there."

I nod once and put my whip away.

"Take my hand and make a chain," I say and the first to grab my hand is Steve. He smiles at me and I scowl and focus on the spell.

"*Trasnsportus' tricarius*," I say, clutching my talisman with my free hand. A yellow cloud forms around me and the pack. It closes around us until we can't see anything, then when it clears, we are outside David's barn. I open its large doors and step inside and pull the rope and wait for David. He is accompanied by Tyler and my heart sinks. Tyler's eyes light up when they see me and he runs to me and wraps me into a hug. From behind me I hear Steve snort. I burry my head into Tyler's neck, trying to forget what happened.

"Who are these people?" David asks me, and before I can answer the white she-wolf steps forward.

"We are the Seers," she says, and I turn around in Tyler's arms so he holds my waist. "Werewolves with the sight."

"What are you doing here?" he asks.

This time, I step forward. "I brought them here," I say, moving next to David. "They will fight with us in the war."

"Who are you?" the white wolf asks David.

"I'm the original werewitch," he says, growling at them. "I do not tolerate rudeness."

The doorway to Paradise opens and he welcomes them in. Tyler and I go in first and I immediately portal to our bedroom.

"What happened?" Tyler says, looking at my blood soaked figure. "Did you have to fight them?"

"No," I sigh with a shaky breath. I glance at his worrying gaze before averting my eyes.

"What happened?" he asks again and I sigh before telling him about last night, starting with what happened with his sister. He has a right to know. His face begins to fall as I tell him about Steve and me. Once I finish, he and I stand in thick, unbreakable silence. Tyler doesn't look at me and his jaw is clench. He doesn't say anything, and turns on his heels and storms out, slamming the door behind him. Hot tears burst from my eyes as I break down. I fall to the floor and cry.

"Now, look what you did," the voice that told me to hold back says. *"Raum, look."*

"I don't care," he says. *"She could have held back."*

"Shut up!" I growl, my teeth sharpen and my nails lengthen.

"She hears us, Balthazar," Raum says.

"Leave me alone!" I scream and Raum laughs.

"Rose?" A voice asks on the other side of the door. "It's Zero. Is everything okay?"

"Leave me alone!" I shout digging into the carpet. I feel him stay by the door for a second before leaving. I curl up into a ball as Raum continues to taunt me despite Balthazar's warnings. I hold my hands to my ears and shake uncontrollably.

-Zero-

Something is definitely wrong. Tyler stormed out of Rose's room and then she started screaming. I try to tell David, but he's talking to Jace, who had come back last night with Cleo. As I enter the kitchen Jace looks at me.

"Cleo is going through a tough time," he says to me. "She's in the room down the hall to the right. Go and comfort her."

"But-"

"Go," David says, and I do as I'm told. As I enter Cleo's room, Tyler's mother comes out clutching her wrist.

"David told me to feed her," she explains, walking away. I enter the room and Cleo looks at me with wide eyes and blood running from her mouth.

"How's Rose?" she asks as she shakes. "Did she make it? No one will tell me."

"She's fine," I lie, because the truth might set her over the edge.

"I can tell you are lying," she says, standing in a swift motion. Her body has changed since her transition. She is taller with a slimmer body and longer hair

"I don't know what's wrong with her," I admit, ducking my head.

"Show me to her room," Cleo demands and I do; not from compulsion, but because I am worried for her. As we reach her room, Cleo enters without knocking. Rose is lying on the floor in a tight ball with her hands around her head. She groans in pain and is covered in

309

blood. Cleo isn't discouraged.

"Rose," Cleo says. Rose looks up with shining yellow eyes. Rose is standing in an instant.

"Cleo?" She asks with tears running down her face. "Where have you been?"

"Got turned into a vampire," she says and more tears stream down Rose's face. Cleo shakes her head. "Don't, it was my choice to save you. Jace did it. It was painless."

"I'm sorry I haven't been around," Rose says, wiping her tears.

"There is no need to apologise," Cleo says and Rose becomes quiet. "Let's get you cleaned up."

Rose nods and lets her friend lead her into the bathroom. There is a muffled conversation from behind closed doors as I sit on the bed. Christian strolls in in his cat form and leaps up onto the bed.

"Thanks for following us," I say to him and he meows. "Rose could have died had it not been for you."

"She says she is hearing voices," Cleo says coming out of the bathroom. "She says their names are Balthazar and Raum. They mean anything to you?"

"Nothing to me," Christian says, morphing into a human.

"Me neither," I say, shaking my head and Cleo sighs. She didn't need to, vampires don't breath.

"Is there anything we can do?" Christian asks.

"Yes, one of you go and get her a cup of hot chocolate," she orders. "And the other should go and find Tyler."

"You go find Tyler," Christian says to me. "You know him better than I do."

I nod in agreement and we split up and I begin my search.

It took me an hour, but I finally found him in the gym destroying a boxing bag.

"Hey, tough shot," I call. He glares at me from the corner of his eye. "Rose needs you."

"Go and find Steve," he growls and I raise an eyebrow.

"Who the hell is Steve?" I ask as Tyler continues to beat the bag. "And why would she want him?"

Tyler then tells me what she told him. When he finishes the story, the boxing bag breaks and falls to the floor.

"She said the full moon pushed them together," I say and he grunts. "Has she ever been one to lie? Remember when she lost her memory and she began to howl in the woods even though she was human?" I ask and Tyler grunts again, and then moves on to the weights. "Well, the howl she was emitting I've only heard once before— when a female wolf is calling for her partner. When the two of them have been separated, her heart begins to pull at her to howl for him. That is exactly what she did. She called for you. You are her mate and wolves mate for life. She doesn't give a fuck about that other werewolf. The full moon can make wolves do stupid things— I should know— but there is one thing I know for certain: she loves you. I can see it when she smiles. That it is you she is thinking of. Her eyes sparkle when she is around you. You light up her world. How is it that you are the only one that doesn't see that?"

"Where is she?" Tyler asks. I smile and lead him out of the gym and to her room.

"She won't eat or drink," Cleo says as we enter. I look at the bed and see her curled up in a ball wearing a red silk nightgown. There is no spark in her eyes.

Tyler pushes past me and kneels at the bed. When she sees him tears spring to her eyes.

"Tyler," she sobs. "I'm so sorry."

"Shhh," he says, wiping the tears from her eyes. She chokes back a sob and reaches for him.

"I'm all sweaty," he says quietly, but she ignores him and touches his face. "Watch her," he says, pulling away and heading into the shower. Rose rolls over and moves closer to the wall. After a minute, Tyler emerges from the shower wearing only jeans.

"Leave us," he says and we all do. I shut the door quietly behind me and walk off in triumph.

-Rose-

I feel his body make a ditch in the bed and I freeze. I feel Tyler's hands on my waist and he pulls me to him, and I struggle to get away. He should hate me. Why doesn't he hate me? I hate me.

"No," I argue as Tyler pulls me towards him.

"Don't fight me," he says as his grip tightens. I cannot fight out of his hold. Tyler pulls me into his lap. I try to fight him by blindly hitting his chest; my eyes fog with tears as I continue to hit his chest. However, my hits seem to have no effect on him as he silently wraps his arms around my back and presses me to his chest. I give in and cry, burying my head into his shoulder.

"Why don't you hate me?" I ask with a sob.

311

"I could never," he says. From his voice I can tell he is also crying. "I could never, ever hate you, Rose."

"I'm so sorry," I say, moving closer and wrapping my arms and legs around him. He tightens his hold and buries his head in my neck.

"I love you, Rose," he murmurs, kissing my neck. "I love you like no other."

I kiss the side of Tyler's head and then trace the scars on his back.

I move back and trace the scar near his lip. His yellow eye shimmers as he stares at the scar on my lip.

"How did you get your scars?" I ask. "Tell me your story."

"A black wolf with a tan line down his back," Tyler says. "The same one you killed. He attacked me during a hunt and knocked me onto my back. He would have killed me if it wasn't for... for my father. He was able to knock the wolf back and it fled before he could kill it."

"Our scars are almost identical," I point out. "It is very peculiar."

Tyler presses his lips onto mine, cutting off any further questions. I move closer to his body and wrap around him. His kisses roughen and he growls in his throat— a growl of possession, of passion. I match his growl and arch my neck as I lean over him. The passion takes me over as I push him down to the bed. He smiles against my lips and rolls me onto my back.

"Why do you do this to me?" he asks, putting his hands on either side of my head. "You make me crazy, Rose."

I smile up at him and my yellow eyes appear. There is a knock at the door and I curse as Tyler jumps.

"What!" I call, angry from the interruption. I open the door and a man stares at me with wide eyes.

"Who are you and what do you want?" I growl and he averts his eyes.

"I am Ezekiel, brother to Stevenson," he says and my eyes flick around his body. He has the same brown eyes and the same black hair. However, he is fully dressed and has smaller muscles.

"What do you want?" I growl again and he lets out a small squeak.

"My mother wants to see you," he says. Instantly, Tyler is behind me widening the door. "Alone," he adds quickly. "She says she want me to take you there right now."

There is a deep growl from behind me and I turn to see Tyler glaring.

"Well, go tell you mother that I have no reason to see her and I don't want to see her," I say, facing Ezekiel again. He bows his head and then walks off. I shut the door behind him and in an instant Tyler wraps me in his arms.

"Was that the man?" Tyler asks with a growl and I shake my head.

"His brother," I explain. "His mother wants to see me."

"You're not going, angel," he says and I pull back.

"Angel?" I ask and he shrugs.

"Trying out pet names. You don't like it?" he asks and I laugh.

"Try all you want, babe," I say kissing his lips.

"Don't like that one," he says in between kisses and I laugh. There is another knock on the door and I growl deep in my chest.

"What?" I call, opening the door to David who raises an eyebrow. "I mean, yes?"

"The leader of the Seer pack wishes to have an audience with you. Alone," he says and I growl, because I know I can't refuse. I turn apologetically to Tyler.

"Go," he says angrily, his yellow eye brightening. "I'll wait here for you, angel."

I smile and slip out of the door and come face to face with Ezekiel. I glare at him and he growls back, with a new found courage in his chest. David leaves us and Ezekiel takes me to the edge of the werewolf village where his mother and Steve are waiting. I growl and his mother laughs.

"You have fire," she says.

"What do you want?" I ask rudely and she smiles.

"I want to know who you are cheating on my son with," her question is a slap in the face and I take a step back. "Never the matter," she says, waving a dismissive hand. "What I called you out here for is for a date," she says and I put my hands on my hips.

"A date?" I echo and she nods. "For what?"

"For the wedding of course," her words stun me and I freeze on spot. Then from out of nowhere there is movement from behind me. Arms wrap around me. I look up to see Steve with his arms around my waist.

"Let me go!" I say struggling, but he only laughs. "I will never marry you!"

"Yes you will," his mother growls as he tightens his grip and moves a hand upwards to my breast. I growl and claw at Steve's arms.

"Don't you dare!" Steve's mother says, pressing something to my stomach. I look down and see a bronze tipped silver stake pressed against me. I growl and she pushes the stake deeper. I gasp as the stinging pain sets in.

"You will marry my son," she growls and Steve smiles as he begins to roughly kiss my neck. There is a deep growl from behind us. Steve's mother gasps and I see a hand at the bottom of her jaw.

"Let my sister go, or I'll turn your brain to mush," Xavier says and I smile, but it vanishes as Ezekiel comes out of nowhere and presses a gun to his throat.

"I don't think so, pal," Ezekiel says, his face twisting into a smile and I growl.

"Inferior parasite," Xavier growls as Steve smiles and ignores the scene in front of us and continues to grope me. There is a thick growl from behind us and I crane my neck to see Tyler behind us in his werewolf form.

"Let. Her. Go!" he shouts into our minds. His lips pull back and a bloodcurdling growl is emitted from his throat. The stake's pressure is increased and I grind my teeth.

"So, you are the parasite stealing my girl," Steve says over his shoulder and Tyler barks loudly as he opens his mouth and bares his fangs.

"Let her go and I will kill you quickly," Tyler says. I see his hackles rise. Steve turns both him and I around to face Tyler, which is a mistake because the stake is no longer pressed against me. I immediately morph into a werewolf and bring my jaws down on Steve's shoulder. I throw him towards Tyler and in a heartbeat Steve changes and he and Tyler square off. I then turn to Steve's mother and she glares at me. I'm hit side on by Ezekiel in his werewolf form. I go up on hind legs and come down on him. He moves quickly and, just as I'm about to attack, I freeze. Unable to move, David steps out of the shadows and my heart leaps into my throat at the sight of him. He looks at me for a moment before releasing me from the spell, then turns to the others.

"Tsk, tsk, tsk," David says, shaking his head in disappointment. "I'm a very hospitable man, but I do not encourage childish squabbles."

I look to Tyler. He stands frozen in his wolf form, snarling at Steven; his mouth open wide, ready to kill the wolf in front of him. I remove the spell from Tyler and he looks to me, his eyes wide.

"Aren't we more mature than this?" David continues as I release Xavier. Tyler stands next to me as I shift into my human form and listen to David chastise the werewolves.

"Rose will marry whomever she pleases," David says. "It is neither your or my decision in the matter. If you continue down this path, you will find that I can become quite unwelcoming. I will kill you and throw you out of my Paradise if you chose to continue on this path."

I smile at David and he winks at me as Tyler and I walk back to the mansion. Xavier stays and lectures the frozen family.

My nerves and temper run high. I don't even notice Tyler shift back to his human form. I keep walking with my hands clenched at my sides. The voices are back. One was telling me to keep calm and keep walking, however the louder one, Raum, was telling me to turn around and rip the family to pieces. I was half considering Raum's proposal when Tyler takes my hand in his and smiles at me.

"Come with me," he says as we enter the mansion. I let him steer me into the gym. The first thing I see are the three pentagrams, Xavier's, David's, and mine. He leads me to a boxing bag and hands me a pair of boxing gloves.

"You can hit this one," he says as I take the gloves.

"How did you know?" I ask, slipping one glove on.

"Because I know the look you get when you want to kill someone," he says, standing behind the bag. I smile and slip the other glove on. I take a punch. It's weak.

"Is that all you got, angel?" he asks and I stare at his chest.

"I'm not really dressed for this," I argue, taking off the gloves and gesturing to my night gown.

"And what are you dressed for?" he asks raising an eyebrow.

"Wouldn't you like to know," I say. He smiles as I wink at him before walking into the gym's locker room and changing into a pair of sweat pants and a tank top. I emerge and Tyler stares at me.

"Should I change, too?" he asks. I shake my head and gaze lustfully at Tyler's bare chest.

"You are perfect as you are," I say, looking him up and down as I slip on the gloves again.

Tyler sets himself behind the bag again and I take a swing. I hit the bag and then glance at Tyler.

"Is that it?" he asks, and I raise an eyebrow before pushing my whole body into the next hit. Tyler makes an 'ooff' sound as the shock hits him. Something wakes inside me and I begin to attack the bag with more forceful hits and kicks.

"How about we stop now," Tyler says after a couple of minutes. He seems out of breath and worn out as he rolls his shoulders.

"Sorry," I say, blushing and removing the gloves. "Guess you never really get used to the strength."

"It's okay," he smiles as I wipe sweat from my brow.

"Tyler," I sigh, and he raises an eyebrow. "I'm scared."

"Of what?" he asks bringing me into a hug.

"What if I can't win this war?" I say quietly. "What if I can't do what everyone is expecting me to do?"

"No one is expecting you to do this all on your own," he says, kissing the top of my head.

"This is only the beginning, isn't it?" I whisper, looking up into his eyes and his grip tightens.

"I don't know," he admits.

After a solid hour of mixed workouts, Tyler and I call it quits and heads back to my room hand him hand and shoulder to shoulder. When we get back, we shower and then head into the kitchen to eat.

"Good, you're making dinner," David says, coming in behind us. "I'm starving."

I roll my eyes and use my multiplying spell to make dinner. When I come into the dining room with only a single plate of food everyone looks at me. Whilst me, myself, and I was making dinner, the rest of the gang joins us.

"Why am I the only one cooking for all of you?" I sigh. "Can't you all find your own dinner?"

"I could always drink your blood," Jace says with a shrug.

"Not if you want to keep your head," Tyler growls and that's when things became tense. Jace argues that he is an original and he cannot be killed by a weak wolf. I sigh and make another spell to multiply the food so that everyone has a plate. The room goes silent as I take a seat and begin to eat. Everyone looks at me for a minute before digging in and making small talk across the table. It was mostly Tyler and Xavier talking about our family history, which Xavier seems happy to share with everyone. Even David seems happy to talk about our family history as he's apparently been tracking my family for some quite some time. According to him, at one point there were Bane hunters. I ignore the rest.

Jace fills Cleo in on what it means to be a vampire and what her strengths and limitations are. It all seems content until Tyler's mother enters. Tyler becomes quiet and interested in eating his food. I sigh and roll my eyes.

"Madam Bane," she says and I stand. She gestures for me to come with her and I excuse myself and follow her. Tyler watches me leave with confused eyes.

"A letter has come for you," she says in a quiet voice. "It says it's only for your eyes."

She takes me into the study and hands me the letter. *Only For the Dearest Female Werewitch is* written in red. I frown and carefully open the envelope.

"Should I get Master David?" Ellen asks and I shake my head. I carefully pull the letter out and it is also written in red, but the texture is different. It's written in blood. I swallow a growl rising in my throat and read.

To Rose, the Bane of my existence.

You thought you could take away my memory? Well, I got them back. I have heard about the war and I AM going to fight with the hunters. You will lose. You should ask Tyler about our past, it is quite a story. He is still a hunter, look at his colour. Once a hunter, always a hunter. That is how it goes. He still loves me! You will pay for all you have done. This is only the beginning... The beginning of the end.

Love and Hate,
Alexus A.K.A. Lexi.
Let the fight begin.

My hands begin to tremble as I use a spell to test whose blood she used to write this letter. It's my blood. My heart races as my hands begin to shake. I feel anger boil through my stomach and rise in my chest. Lightning dances on my knuckles and I scream in anger.

The lightning on my fist strikes out as I stare at my blood on the paper and a single thought fills my mind.

What happened between Lexi and Tyler?

-Epilogue-

There is a scream from the study and Tyler is out of his chair and the dining room in a heartbeat. He rips the study doors open to see Rose standing with her back towards the door and her hands flat on a large mahogany desk.

"Rose?" Tyler asks, taking a cautious step forward. "Is everything okay?"

"Yes," she says, still not turning around. "Everything is fine."

Ellen steps out of the shadows and Tyler goes still.

"What's happened?" Tyler growls and Ellen gestures for him to follow her.

"Nothing for you to be concerned about," Ellen says in a soft voice. Tyler glances back to Rose, who still hasn't turned around. He growls at his mother, who taps him over the head. He follows her and as she closes the study doors he sees Rose reach up and wipe a tear from her face. The doors shut with a thud and Tyler wonders what could be wrong. His mother leads him silently out of the mansion and into the garden.

"What is Rose to you?" his mother says, stopping in front of a rose bed in full bloom.

"Why is it your business?" Tyler asks with a growl and Ellen laughs.

"I have seen your trail of broken hearts," Ellen says, glaring at her son. "I have only seen one so close to you, which is Alexus. I do not want to see this one hurt as the rest were. You need to tell Rose about what *really* happened between you and Alexus."

"She doesn't need to know!" Tyler shouts as his yellow eye fades. The immaculate colours of the roses fades as the delicate petals begin to drop. Ellen's eyes lower as the flowers begin to flex downwards.

Tyler looks at the slowly dying roses around him. His eyes widen and the pressure becomes too much. He runs, morphing into a werewolf as he goes. His heart pounds in his chest and words become strong in his head.

Who is she to you?

Do you love her, boy?

Should she love you?

"No!" he barks as his vision turns red and he comes to a halt. *"No more!"*

"I love her!" he screams at the non-existent voices. He turns human and digs his hands into the dirt. "I love her," he whispers as thunder booms ahead.

What about Lexi?

"What about her?" Tyler asks, grinding his teeth to stop him from yelling.

You love her, too. After all, you were forced apart. It never truly ended.

Tyler's eyes roll as the memory of Lexi flashes through his mind— a memory long forgotten with the use of magic.

It was six years ago when Lexi and Tyler broke up. Tyler was moving on with his family.

"I'll come up with a plan," Lexi promised him. *"A plan so that we can be together again. To cure our curses."*

"It isn't something we can cure," Tyler argued. *"I would rather die than become... a monster."*

"I've heard a rumour," Lexi whispered, moving closer to Tyler. *"That a werewitch can cure a werewolf."*

"But I'm not destined to be a wolf," Tyler said. *"I'm destined to be worse."*

"But if you were to be bitten by a wolf before your curse takes place, then you will be a wolf and not the monster," Lexi said. *"There are rumours that there is a girl, like us, destined to be a new werewitch. She is in Mercy Lake.* Your hometown. *Go to her, woo her, make her fall in love with you, but remember that none of it is real. If she falls in love with you, she will be willing to do anything for you. Including curing you of being a wolf. Make her do that, then come back to me."*

"But, to become a wolf, she will have to turn me," Tyler said. *"I would bond to her, I would* be *hers. Everything would change. I wouldn't love you anymore."*

"But I will love you," Lexi said, kissing Tyler's lips. *"I will find you, make you remember me. I'll make sure that the werewitch does not put her hooks too deep into you. I'll use your sister, if I must."*

"Step-sister," Tyler corrected, making Lexi laugh.

"You have to forget this," Lexi said, placing a finger on his temple. *"Forget me and move on. It will be easier that way."*

Lexi erased Tyler's mind. She used magic. Tyler remembers how his heart raced. They began to fight. Tyler screamed at Lexi and she screamed back. They broke up and went their separate ways.

Tyler was never truly honest with Rose. While she was being

tortured by his sister, he was being treated with kindness. He and Lexi stayed together.

Lexi reminded Tyler of what it felt like to be with her. She also told him everything— what he needed to do to fool Rose and everyone else in Paradise.

Tyler never stopped being a hunter. He wants the paranormal species dead. They are the reason why Tyler's life had gone bad.

The *werewolves* killed his mother.

The *vampires* turned the man he called father.

And just like his father, Tyler vows to fight the paranormal species until he is the last paranormal left.

"I love Lexi," Tyler smiles, looking back towards the mansion. "I have to go back to her."

...

ABOUT THE AUTHOR

L.Q. Hebb is a young author and has been writing since 2010. She was born and raised in Townsville. When she wasn't in school she was glued to the computer typing feverishly. Hebb completed her first novel early 2013, completed her second novel early 2014 and graduated grade twelve later that year. L.Q. Hebb still lives in Townsville writing every chance she gets.